THESE VALIANT STARS

MUSKETEER SPACE
BOOK 1

TANSY RAYNER ROBERTS

You are not mine
    But in your eyes I see a constellation,
    Each star a gleaming promise
    Braver than you or I

These valiant stars draw us deeper
    Into a love-madness
    That would burn the steel walls
    of the world

"FRAGMENT ON PHOTO-SILK,"
*COLLECTED POEMS OF THE
MUSKETEER ARAMIS,* © SOLAR
IMPERIAL 39822.PARIS

CONTENTS

CHAPTER 1
REASONS TO HATE MOTHS

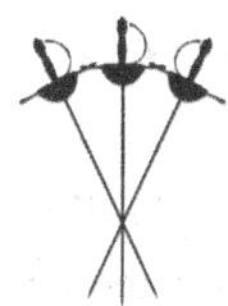

Dana D'Artagnan nosed her musket-class dart into the mechanic's bay on Meung Station, in orbit around the planet of Valour. She hadn't even glanced at the planet on her approach – planets held little interest for her. This station was the last (and cheapest) recharging stop before she reached her destination.

Not for the first time, Dana wished that her Papa had chosen a colour other than bright yellow when he retooled Maman's creaky old ship for her journey. Dana had a fat enough credit stud that she could pay to have the dart resprayed, but only if she didn't worry too much about paying the rent for her first month in Paris.

Paris was more important.

Of course, the ship she landed next to in the bay had to be a brand-new Moth fighter, so sleek and silver that everything around him looked extra shitty. But Dana wasn't going to let that bother her.

She jumped down from the hatch and slid under the belly of her dart, releasing the power spheres one by one. All six of them needed recharging. As she carted the large spheres two by two to the charging console at the back of the bay, she heard boots ringing against the metal floor, and then laughter.

"Oh, what is that thing?" said a woman. "Do spaceships even come in that colour? Would anyone seriously walk into a shipyard and say sure, I'll have the canary yellow one."

A male voice spoke lower, in a similarly mocking tone. Dana couldn't catch the words. Cheeks hot with embarrassment, she stalked back to her ship and climbed under to get the next two spheres.

The bootsteps came closer. "A daffodil," said the woman. "No… better. He's a buttercup!"

Dana counted silently to ten, then scooped up the power spheres and marched to the charging console again. The hatch of the Moth fighter closed as she passed, which meant at least that she didn't have to face the owner of that mocking voice.

As she returned for the final spheres, the hatch reopened, and a woman leaned out of the Moth. She was at least a decade older than Dana, with long black hair that swung over her shoulder.

Not a pilot, not with hair like that. She had to be a passenger. A wealthy, entitled, sarcastic passenger.

"Nice ship," said the woman. Almost immediately, her mouth twisted up into a smirk. It was then that Dana noticed her scar: a long, jagged line that started a little above the corner of her eye and slashed down her jawline. "What do you call that colour?"

"Buttercup," Dana said, and continued with her work.

As the spheres hummed away in the charging console,

the station report on Dana's dart came through. The last leg of her journey hadn't done too much damage to the hull, despite the meteor storm they had weathered near the Daughters of Peace, but it was going to take six hours for new software to upload into the navigation system, and for the spheres to fully charge.

Time enough to have a drink or three, and maybe rent a room for a sleeping shift.

Dana took a quick sonic shower, buzzed her black hair even shorter against her scalp, and changed into a fresh flight suit. She hesitated about the jacket. It looked smart, especially with the three platinum studs at the collar. But while it was the fashion to wear identity and credit studs publicly, she wasn't sure if she should be so cavalier about the third, which contained her formal application to the Royal Space Fleet on Paris Satellite.

Would it be any safer if she left it here on the ship?

She straightened her jacket. It was blue with gold trim, and made her flight suit look more official, like she was already a Musketeer.

After a moment's thought, she popped the three studs off the collar of the jacket and pressed them one by one against the side of her neck. They burrowed in with a tingling sensation, glittering brighter against her brown skin than they had been against the jacket. Old fashioned to wear them this way, but if she lost the jacket, she would still have everything important to her. Her credit, her identity, and her future.

She had a photo silk tucked into one of her pockets, an extravagant gift that Maman had pressed on her – it displayed images of Maman and her old pilot friends from the golden days, including a certain Treville who was now Amiral of the Musketeers.

"That will put her in a good mood if nothing else," Maman promised, before kissing Dana quickly and all but shoving her into the flight deck of the 'Buttercup'. "She's a hard nut, Treville, and I don't imagine she's softened with age. This might blur the edges a little."

Dana looked at the photo silk now, with its rotation of vintage images. Musketeers smiling, laughing, playing pranks on each other. A life so very different from the dull monotony of Gascon Station. It was everything she had always wanted.

She kissed the edge of the silk and shoved it back in the pocket of her jacket, for safekeeping.

The bar was crowded and noisy. Dana was glad she had her studs securely on her neck where it was harder for people to brush against them, and rather less glad for the formal jacket. She wouldn't be able to stay in this stuffy bar for long, not without losing some layers.

The beer helped. It was cold and fresh and real, unlike anything her ship's food printer could make. The first one went down fast, and she ordered another.

All the software in her head was jangling up a storm, not happy about the separation between pilot and ship. Dana wanted, *needed* to be flying again. Alcohol dulled those senses for a while, gave her half a chance of relaxing away from her metal shell. But it didn't help with her general desire to kick and punch things.

A couple of Mendaki pilots introduced her to a game of

Pharaoh, and while their trailing tendrils meant they could spin the cards suspiciously fast, they were also generous about buying rounds of moonshine shots. Dana was basically wasted by the time the Milord walked into the bar.

She would have known he was a New Aristocrat even without a closer look at his identity stud. Every inch of him was gene-modified and glowing with artificial health. White skin, silver hair and piercing eyes. It almost hurt to look at him.

He did not belong in a grotty place like this, with the grease-stained engineers, gambling aliens and the handful of pilots lured in by the cheap price of moonshine.

Which might explain why the Milord did not purchase a drink, but instead allowed himself to be guided into a back room.

Dana lost her stake, and then another. Her fellow punters snickered at her, if that was what the shivery, mocking sound they made with their mouth-tubes meant. The dealer shuffled and dealt again. More drinks miraculously appeared on the table. The room became hotter.

A false breath of cool air flooded the bar as a new pair of rogues swaggered in. One was the woman from the Moth, her shining sweep of hair pinned back with decorative combs, to show off the scar that cut through half her face. She had a lad in locs at her side, wearing coveralls. He must be an engineer – no self-respecting pilot would venture out in such scruffy gear even in a crap-hole like this. The engie stayed at the bar and ordered himself a beer while the woman headed past the Pharaoh table to the back of the bar.

Dana pulled her gaze away, but not fast enough. The

woman saw her and raised a hand in a mocking salute. "Ho there, Buttercup."

Rage blistered behind Dana's eyes. She turned back to the game, just in time to hear the dealer sing "Bank!" Every player leaned in to have their credit stud scanned, to update the wins and the losses.

She had lost too much. With her debt settled, she pushed away from the table. Time to piss, and get back to the ship to sleep off the drink. No comfortable room for her now.

Paris. Think about Paris.

The bar blurred around her as she took a few steps. Damn it. At this rate, she'd have to take a dose of Sobriety from the vending slot at the door, and that only meant she had wasted more money on this stupid night.

Dana staggered out the back of the bar and made her way along a small grey corridor until she reached the convenience stalls. Someone had charmingly painted the words 'Sea of Tranquility' over the door. Safe in a stall, she leaned her head against the cool surface of the wall and peed every drop of liquid out of her body. It took some time.

Doors banged, nearby.

"This is classy, sweetness," said a mocking voice. Male. Fancy accent. The Milord, perhaps? Or another like him.

"Last place anyone would expect to find you," said a voice, female. Sarcastic enough to be the woman from the Moth, but Dana would not be prepared to testify to that. For all she knew, the voices came from inside her own skull.

"Break the news to me gently," said the Milord with something like a laugh. "I'm so close to Valour, I could kiss it, so it's too much to hope that's where you're sending me. Some other planet – the dregs of Freedom? God, don't make it be Freedom, I haven't a thing to wear for the arse end of the solar system."

"Truth."

"I hate getting my feet wet."

"With the amount the Cardinal is paying you, I think you can buy new boots. It won't be for long, gumdrop. You're to integrate yourself into the minister's staff, and make sure you're with her when she leaves for Valour – that will put you in a perfect position to plant a suggestion where it can do the most good —" A soft sound, which could have been a kiss, or an information stud burrowing into skin. "Think you can handle that?"

"I live to serve, Ro, my darling."

"You'd better. Don't fret, you can go back to your Valour project as soon as this wraps up. Wouldn't want to keep you from that respectable family of yours."

Doors banged again as more noisy drunken customers came in. The voices of the conspirators were drowned out.

Dana stood. Still drunk, but able to walk. She tidied herself, washed her hands in the sonic spray, and finally headed out to the bar.

Her Mendaki pals waved their tendrils at her as she passed, but she gave a rueful smile and shook her head. No more of that.

At the door, she hesitated by the vending slot. Sobriety felt like giving up, and besides, she was nearer pleasantly drunk than she had been. Surely she could make it back to her ship in one piece without deleting tonight's consumption. On the other hand, a capsule of Hydrate would not be a bad idea.

Someone shoved her from behind, and she banged her forehead on the vending slot.

"Sorry, sailor," said a cheerful voice, and when Dana turned, she saw the woman from the Moth, far from apologetic. "All a bit much for you, is it?" she smirked, with a nod to the vending slot. "No shame in that, Buttercup."

Dana breathed faster. She felt her hands tightening into fists.

The woman noticed, and her smile widened. "Oh, please," she said. "Try."

Dana hit her. That was her first mistake. The woman from the Moth leaned away from the blow so fast it barely tapped her jaw, and then with one thudding motion had Dana on the floor, an elbow jabbed hard into the soft skin of her bared throat.

The floor hurt. Everything hurt. Dana stared up at the woman and wondered if it counted as cheating if you threw up on someone during a fight. At this angle, she was more likely to throw up on herself. Best keep it down.

"Now then, citizens, take this outside, shall we?" declared a burly bartender, marching over to them. "Or upstairs, if you'd prefer, no questions asked," he added in a lower voice, where it could only be heard by Dana, her opponent, and the engie in locs who was there now too, tugging at his boss's arm.

"Ro, don't," he said in a pleading voice. "That's enough."

"Well, Buttercup?" the woman from the Moth asked, still smiling as she pressed her elbow more forcefully against Dana's collarbone. "Fancy a duel? I don't make this offer to just anyone."

The engie swore quietly, and walked away, washing his hands of her.

Dana blinked up into the face of her enemy. "Yes," she said. "Yeah. Bring it on."

Before Dana D'Artagnan left home, her Papa had some advice for her. As he ran Maman's old ship through that last coat of (ugh) colour and polish for the journey, he said: "Fight as much as you can, lovey, it sharpens your reflexes. The best pilots are demons with their fists. Just look at your mother. She was a menace in every bar fight, and there was no one faster than her at the helm of a dart. Everyone knew it."

"That was why I crashed so many," laughed her Maman. "Fight if you must, Dana. Pilots are all half crazy, thanks to all that shit they wire into our heads. If you want them to take you seriously, you have to embrace the crazy. Let go a little. Kick some heads in on your day off. But for fuck's sake, don't duel."

Here she was, in a room above a seedy bar, with the metallic taste of the psychic drug still sharp in her mouth.

Drug-duels were illegal, which was why the bartender had kept his offer quiet. Still, they had gathered quite an audience. The Mendaki card-sharks were exchanging bets, and pilots and engies alike were happy to scan their credit studs again in such a splendid cause.

Dana sat on a straight-backed chair, with the woman from the Moth opposite her. Between them glowed the static of the game.

Her enemy looked older in this light. Ro. No last name.

She had to have more than a decade on Dana, though she held herself like a younger woman. Like she knew how hot she was. And oh, the bitch would not stop smiling.

"Red," said Ro. "Have you duelled before, Buttercup?"

My name is D'Artagnan, Dana wanted to shout, but the last thing she should do was give this crowd her name. "Blue," she said. *Anything but yellow.*

She didn't care what history her parents had with that bloody buttercup-coloured ship, she was selling it the second she got to Paris Satellite. The fleet would provide her with a new dart when she was accepted into their ranks. Musket-class, all the way, state of the art. She would never have to hear the word 'buttercup' ever again.

The static dissipated, leaving a holographic starscape hanging in the air between the two players. Two tiny spaceships sparked into life: a blue sabre-class dart, and a red Moth fighter.

The bartender, who had set them up for this and taken a fee from each of the players because the bribe-hungry officials here on Meung Station would demand a cut of tonight's illicit proceeds, now darkened the room so all that could be seen were the two ships and the faces of their players.

Dana had taken pilot drugs before. They were a necessary part of training, placing you inside the navigational computer of your ship, helping you to build the necessary reflexes to fly as fast and as sharp as you needed to. Blending the synapses of your actual brain with new software programmed into your head through a series of implants. When you flew, your hands and head were both directly plugged into the helm.

Eventually, you learned to fly with the implants but no

drugs to connect you. Dana preferred that, the streamlined flight. As soon as she was able, she had stopped using pilot drugs altogether. Sure, they were supposed to make you a more 'perfect' pilot, but there was something creepy and mechanical about the process. She loved the helm at her hands, and the stars inside her head. She hated the sensation of not being able to tell where one began and the other ended.

It had been a surprise to no one when the tools of the pilot trade were turned into illegal gambling drugs. In Maman and Papa's day it hadn't even been illegal, not until the first back-alley deaths rolled in and Something Had To Be Done.

"You might as well stick each other with metal blades," her Maman had muttered, when she first told Dana about friends she had served with in her youth, Musketeers who spent too much down-time on Duel until there was nothing left of their brains but mush. The warning was clear. Only idiots let pride and honour get in the way of actual brain function.

Dana inhaled now, and the blue dart in the scape quivered. There it was. Almost like a real ship, she could feel its controls and its computer, blossoming inside her thoughts. She could direct it, up and down, back and forth.

If that ship was damaged or destroyed, it was going to hurt like hell.

"Game on," said the bartender.

Thirty seconds into the duel, it became evident that Dana had been very, very wrong about the woman from the Moth. Long hair be damned; she was a pilot. An exceptional one.

It was fun at first, like any other game. Dana and the

Moth dodged and swooped around each other, shooting laser cannons through the false starscape, hiding and refuelling behind asteroids and occasionally (quite by accident) blowing up whole planets.

The first time that the Moth caught a glancing strike across Dana's bow, she felt a flashburn in the back of her skull, and almost couldn't see for a few precious seconds. That part was true, then.

The reason that pilot drugs were used in training and long-haul interstellar voyages but never in combat was because any damage to the ship rebounded to the pilot. It wasn't always fatal, but it was no lover's kiss.

The Moth closed in, chasing Dana's dart from asteroid to asteroid. Ro was good, and she was practiced, and more than that, she knew exactly how to shoot Dana's avatar so as to hurt her, to send just enough flashburn or sharp electric shocks through her brain. Enough to sting, to shock, but never quite enough to finish the game.

She was toying with Dana, and that made Dana angry. She was good at being angry. Nine times out of ten, being angry made her better at whatever she was doing.

She saw how to do it now, and next time the Moth flitted between two safe spots, Dana slipped in from an unexpected side. This time it was her laser cannon blasting hard across the Moth's wing.

Ro rocked back, gritting her teeth against the pain. Dana did exactly what the Moth had not been doing, closed in for the kill.

But no, the Moth was fast, too damned fast, and his pilot knew the layout of this game far better than Dana. They spiralled together out of the asteroid belt and into blank, empty space. Dana whirled her dart around to fire, but the Moth was there first, facing her dead on, and the laser cannons flashed bright.

Her vision was red, all red, and she could not feel the dart in her brain any more. Dana coughed and choked on her own spit, not knowing why until someone turned her roughly over and she realised, *floor, I'm lying on the floor again, fuck, I never even made it to Paris.*

Everything hurt, and she could not see.

Then it stopped hurting.

CHAPTER 2
PARIS, AT LAST

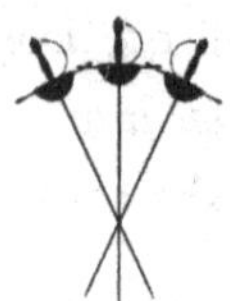

Dana awoke, and wished she had not. Every stubbled hair on her scalp felt like a needle pressing directly into her skull.

She coughed, and tasted blood, then vomit, and finally an odd metallic tang. *Duel.*

If her mother was right, and all pilots were crazy, Dana had just proved… something. She was not sure what, except that next time she saw that woman from the Moth, she was going to break her nose.

She could tell even without opening her eyes that she was lying in her old bunk on the musket-class dart that her parents had been so proud of providing for her to make her way in the world. There was a comfortable hum in her head that she only felt when she and the ship were this close to each other.

Buttercup.

"He's a good ship," Maman had told her. "A lucky ship. Not as new as some, but he served me well and he will serve my daughter well."

"The only one she never crashed," Papa laughed in reply.

"Name him yourself," Maman said firmly. "When you've flown together a little way. Never mind what he was called before – he's your ship now."

For one horrible, weak moment, Dana wanted to be back with them, to have never tried to leave Gascon Station.

It could be worse. At least the bastards who had set her up for that duel had been civic-minded enough to dump her back on her ship in safety. Dana struggled off the bunk and into the sonic shower, peeling off her clothes as she went. The jacket, at least, was undamaged. She'd need that in Paris.

The sonic wave stung her neck, and she shut it off quickly, leaning in to check herself in the mirror.

Three small, red holes marked the place on her neck where her credit stud, identity stud and finally her application to the Space Agency had all been ripped off her skin. All three had been stolen while she was unconscious.

Anger poured through her, and she swore every foul name she could think of about that bitch, the arsehole from the perfect brand-new Moth. Alone in the shower, Dana punched and kicked the walls until her knuckles hurt worse than her head. She couldn't swear anymore, couldn't even think the words she wanted or needed.

There were backups, of course there were backups. That was how the galaxy worked: everything was data, and everything could be printed anew. The information on her credit studs was backed up here in the ship she would always now think of as the *Buttercup*. Her money, her identity files and pilot records, even her application, they were all backed up.

Except, of course, that someone had brought her home.

Slowly, Dana stepped out of the sonic shower and made her way along the narrow ship to the flight deck. She sat naked at the computer, ignoring the voice in her head as the helm tried to coax her into flight.

Let's go, space space, come and fly, come and fly.

Sometimes, having a spaceship in your head was a lot like having a large, nagging pet who couldn't think beyond the next walkie.

Dana called up her information quickly. She wasn't angry anymore, had no rage left in her veins. But oh, her credit account had been hacked, of course it had. No number left but zeroes.

An odd numbness spread across the back of her skull. Hopefully this was shock rather than actual Duel-induced brain damage. Dana printed new studs for herself, one for her ID and another for her Paris application. A third for her empty credit account. A fourth, to clone and back up every iota of personal information in the ship's archives.

She could go to the station's militia and report this theft. As long as she didn't mind sharing the story of the illegal Duel racket they had going on here on Meung.

Or she could cut her losses and find out what price the *Buttercup* (damn it) would make at one of the vendors here. She could get a seat on a commercial venturer or the solarcrawler and still make it to Paris. That was the sensible thing to do. Maman and Papa might not even learn she'd done it, not until later when she had a job and a new ship to crow about.

There were many benefits to this plan, up to and

including never again having to wince with embarrassment when someone made up a cute pet name for her bright yellow spaceship. At least now she wouldn't have to brazen it out when everyone assumed the paint job was her idea.

Still, when Dana entered the commands to detach her consciousness from the *Buttercup*'s controls, she felt like a traitor. Right up until the end, she heard a tiny litany inside her head: *Don't leave, let's go flying, space space space, let's see the stars!*

Ro, that was the pilot's name. Dana memorised it along with her dark eyes, her scarred cheek and her long sweep of hair. She would recognise her again, if she saw her, and she would get her revenge.

It wasn't until Dana was in her seat on the venturer *Sun Wukong* bound for Honour, Luna Palais and Paris Satellite, that she realised she had lost something else. The photo silk of her mother's youthful adventures was no longer tucked safely inside her jacket pocket.

Had her thief taken that too, or had she somehow left it behind on the *Buttercup*? Dana did not know, but it was enough to make her angry at the Moth pilot all over again.

So much for softening Amiral Treville's hard edges with a spot of family nostalgia.

Paris Satellite was the biggest space station that Dana had ever seen. There was none of the grimy elbows-in mentality she knew from Gascon Station, where she had grown up. Even the orbiting cities around Truth, the furthest she had previously travelled across the solar system, had a tendency towards economy of materials and space.

Paris was all gleaming steel, plexi-glass, and wide-open spaces. As Dana disembarked from the venturer with the rest of the passengers, shaking off the headache she got every time she flew as a passenger, she spotted genuine trees growing up out of paving stones in the main avenue, for all the sky as if this was a dirtside city.

This was where her parents had lived, worked, fallen in love. Paris, the satellite of dreams, in orbit around Luna Palais, Honour's only moon.

You could practically smell the red dirt of Honour on the boots of the locals. Not that Dana had any interest in planets, or moons for that matter. She only had eyes for the pilots who hurried this way and that, their flight suits a rainbow of colours that told you exactly who they flew for. Pigeon grey for the satellite's general service pilots, red and gold for the Cardinal's Sabres, and blue and white for the Musketeers. The occasional black flight suit marked out a Raven, members of the independent Courier Corps.

Button pushers, as Maman always referred to them with a sneer. In a galaxy where most communications were instant, and anyone (with enough credit points) could send the data for an item of choice to be printed on any planet they chose, the Ravens represented an antique profession.

It had been Dana's private dread that they would be the only ones who offered her employment. Boring ships, boring trade routes, boring co-workers. Everything that the Musketeers were not.

Dana fingered her collar studs nervously. Plain black plastic, instead of the platinum she had set out with.

Nothing to strut about. Perhaps she was an idiot for thinking such things mattered. But oh, she could do with an injection of confidence right now.

The important thing was that the commander of the Musketeers had been born on Gascon Station too, and knew what it was like to try to forge a career from the provinces. Surely the name D'Artagnan coupled with Dana's excellent training record would be enough to impress Amiral Treville.

The photo silk niggled at her, though. It would have been a nice touch: something to make this meeting personal, and to show that Dana was more than just another recruit.

Possibly it would have also been helpful to make an appointment.

Amiral Treville was a mountainous figure, with dark slab-like arms and a barrel body, enveloped in the bright blue and white uniform of the Musketeers. Her black hair was buzzed pilot-short. She showed no sign of having anything but hard edges, and every inch of her presence made it clear she still thought of herself as a pilot first, an administrator second.

This did not in any way prevent her from giving the pilots under her command one hell of a hard time.

As the morning dragged on, Dana waited in a plexi-glass walled corridor, above the maze of docks and airlocks that housed the ships of the Royal Space Fleet. She sat there, invisible in the crowd. Behind and around her, pilots sprawled across tables in their cafeteria, sharing food and conversation. There were more women than men, which matched the numbers she remembered from training – the Royal Fleet was at about 75% women which was lower than her mother's day when it had been closer to 90% thanks to the previous Regence's belief that women made the best pilots.

Dana's belated attempt at an appointment had been met with rolled eyes from the assistant at the front desk, but she was given a number in today's queue, with no guarantee that Treville would find time for her.

The number was 78.

So, Dana waited. There were view screens all around, running curated feeds – plenty of gossip, expensive shopping options and occasional injections of local politics, along with hourly five-minute episodes of *Love and Asteroids*, the latest hit soap.

Without fail after every episode of *Love and Asteroids* (which was packed with scandalous tales of adultery, swordfights, military coups and bar brawls), some sort of morality vid would play, to balance things out. As one shift ended and another began, Dana saw the Regence's famous inauguration speech about the sanctity of marriage contracts three times, and the Cardinal's equally famous 'all gods followed us to the stars' sound byte eight times, if you didn't count the parody version which was used to sell cola shots.

On the whole, the interior of Amiral Treville's office was far more interesting than anything the holo-channels had to offer.

From where she sat, Dana's eyes kept being drawn back to Treville as she strode back and forth in her office, usually barking at the comm channels or tapping at a panel on her standing work station. Every pilot that docked their ship had to cross this corridor to reach the rest of Paris Satellite including their sleeping quarters.

The Amiral missed nothing.

Several times, Treville lunged forward to fill her doorway, bellowing out into the corridor, usually at a pilot who was attempting to sneak past her without reporting in. The unfortunate in question would be dragged into her office and berated behind the soundproof plexi-glass.

No wonder this was a popular cafeteria for all the pilots, not just those wearing the blue and white of the Musketeers. The food printers were standard enough, but they came with the entertainment option of watching your peers being publicly roasted.

Amiral Treville, Dana decided, was terrifying.

When Dana's number was finally called, her mother's former colleague managed something like a welcoming smile. It looked more like a tired grimace, but Dana appreciated the effort.

They sat opposite each other at a low desk on the far side of the office, perhaps the first time Dana had seen the Amiral off her feet all day.

"Dana D'Artagnan," said Treville, rolling the name thoughtfully around in her mouth. "Your father was one of the best engies in Paris back in the day. And your mother…" For a moment, the smile did not seem forced. "No one flew like Alix D'Artagnan."

"She's still the best," Dana admitted.

Treville shrugged. "Can't imagine there's much skilled work flying to be done out on Gascon Station these days. I grew up there myself, you know. Apart from the Mendaki invasion three generations ago, nothing has ever happened there."

It was true. In the most recent intergalactic war, which had ended eight years ago, the shape-changing aliens known as the Sun-kissed had famously invaded every planet in the solar system except Freedom. Even if Dana hadn't always known that her station orbited a world at the arse-end of the solar system, every chancer who ever blew through Gascon Station made sure to let her know just how far from 'civilisation' they were.

Amiral Treville tapped the plastic application stud that Dana placed on her desk between them. A screen flickered up, displaying Dana's training transcript. "We don't get many applicants from remote training, but you've acquitted yourself well here. With these kinds of marks and hours logged, I'm surprised you didn't take this stud two levels up, directly to the Cardinal's Own. Most new-qualified pilots try there first. The salary is almost twice what we have to offer."

"I don't want to be a Sabre," Dana said indignantly. "I want to be a Musketeer!" The thought of what her mother would say if she came home in red and gold livery made her want to throw up.

Twice the salary. She knew that the Sabres were still coasting on the glory that came from saving the solar system at the end of the War of the Sun-kissed, but Dana had never guessed that it would have such ramifications.

Amiral Treville almost laughed, but stopped herself in time. "You're sweet, kid. I wish half of my gals had that attitude. But being a Musketeer… it doesn't mean what it used to. If not for the Regence's nostalgia for the world before the war, we would have disappeared into the Cardinal's filing cabinet years ago. A historical footnote, rather than an item in the Royal Budget spreadsheet that gets smaller every year."

Dana knew which way this conversation was going, and she was desperate to say something, anything to change that look of mild pity on Amiral Treville's face. As she racked her brain, though, she saw the amiral's eyes flick away, already distracted by something more important in that plexi-glass corridor of hers. "Excuse me, Dana. Some business that can't wait."

Treville leaped to her feet and marched to the door, flinging it open. In an enormous voice using every inch of her impressive lungs, she bellowed: "ATHOS, PORTHOS, ARAMIS! Get in here, you bastards!"

CHAPTER 3
SHOUTING AT MUSKETEERS

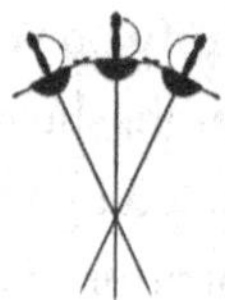

Dana had hoped for so much of this meeting with Amiral Treville. Had she been an idiot to think that her skills would be instantly recognised, that Treville would be interested in meeting the daughter of an old colleague?

Instead, Treville's attention was drawn to two pilots who entered the office with guilty expressions. Two, when she had called for three.

These pilots in bright blue and white jackets over well-worn flight suits; they had what Dana wanted. They were Musketeers. They didn't look especially happy about it, though. From their stance, it was not the first time these two had been called in to experience the rough end of Treville's managerial style.

Ignored at the desk, Dana observed them both.

One was tall and elegant, with dark hair scraped up into a tight topknot – the second most common hairstyle for pilots after the buzz cut. She was casually beautiful in that femme manner that Dana could never manage – all legs and cheekbones and effortless grace. A pearl pin fastened her hair in place – it looked genuine vintage rather than something printed to fit in with retro fashions. An elaborate henna tattoo ran down her neck and collarbone, then emerged again at the wrist of her left hand, flowering in lacework all the way to her light brown fingertips.

The shorter Musketeer was round in all dimensions, including a bosom that must surely get in the way of her helm controls. She had a cheeky, pleasant face beneath a head shaved almost as closely as Treville's. She also wore a version of the Musketeer uniform that Dana had never seen before – a long blue-and-white coat cut to flatter her size, in expensive cloth rather than the more common artificial blends. She wore the coat with a wide, bedazzled belt that glittered with a small fortune in pearl studs.

As if all that wasn't enough swish and vanity, this shorter Musketeer had the blue and white fleur-de-lis mark of the service painted in exquisite miniature upon each of her manicured fingernails.

"I can count, you know," said Amiral Treville dryly, scanning the corridor once again. "Where's your third partner in crime?"

"Athos? Oh… sick," said the elegant one, which would have been more convincing if the short one hadn't come in with "Still on patrol," during her friend's hesitation.

Treville loomed at them both, looking thunderous. "Sick?" she repeated. "Are you sure you don't mean drunk?"

Dana had a momentary impulse to hide beneath the desk.

"Space pox," said the round one, with some authority.

"He can hardly walk. You know what Athos is like, Amiral, he catches everything going."

"So, he sent you ahead," said Treville, her voice eerily calm. "To explain why three of the Royal Space Fleet, the Regence's Own Musketeers, were arrested for duelling?"

"That's a lie!" said the elegant one, convincingly outraged. "We weren't duelling, Amiral. Just fighting. My body is a *temple*."

"Six of the Cardinal's Sabres were there too," put in the other. "That's mitigating circumstances. They might have drawn weapons first."

"They did draw weapons first," hissed her elegant friend.

"That is exactly what I said, Aramis. I'm glad you agree. They drew weapons first. Which is why we didn't duel with them." The round Musketeer hesitated, and then smiled in a friendly way as if she hadn't at all lost track of their version of events. "Clearly, a misunderstanding. For which I am sure the Sabres are every bit as sorry as we are."

Treville slowly breathed out, her whole massive body trembling. "I don't care about the Cardinal's Sabres, Captain Porthos. I'm not responsible for their antics. As it happens, I know the Sabres were there, because they're the ones who arrested you! I've spent an hour this morning trying to convince the Regence not to hand the entire Royal Fleet over to the Cardinal and take early retirement. Is that what you want for me? Gardening leave on the third Daughter of Peace? Anyone got a straw hat I can borrow?"

Dana drew her gaze away, not wanting to witness this

humiliating scene. For this reason, she was the first to see the man hovering at the glass door.

He wore a blue-and-white jacket over a flight suit like the others, but he could not possibly be a pilot. His hair was too ridiculous.

You thought that about the Moth pilot at Meung Station, she reminded herself sternly, remembering the scarred pilot's rebellious sweep of black hair that had caused Dana to underestimate her.

This Musketeer, if such he was, had taken rebellious fashion to extremes. He had fair skin, and gratuitous ginger-gold hair that fell straight to his shoulders – a safety hazard if ever Dana had seen one. He also had a beard and drooping moustache that was like nothing she had ever seen before.

Perhaps it was some kind of practical joke.

The man was pale and sweaty beneath his gratuitous facial hair, looking distinctly unwell. If this was the missing Athos, perhaps he had the space pox after all.

For a moment, he caught Dana's eye, and grinned at the disapproval he saw on her face. Then he rapped hard on the plexi-glass door, interrupting Treville in the middle of her tirade about how her best and brightest were turning her into a galactic laughing stock.

"And here he is," Treville drawled with great sarcasm as Athos let himself into the office. "Finally ready to grace us with your presence, Milord? Enjoyed your cup of tea and cucumber sandwiches before you sauntered over to pay your respects, did you?"

"You know I only live to serve you, boss," said Athos in a deep, respectful voice. As he spoke, Dana realised why Treville had mocked him with that word 'milord' (which she had heard recently on Meung Station, applied to an entirely different gentleman). Athos had the cut-glass accent of a New Aristocrat, and the exaggerated manners of one too. What on earth was such a fashionable fool doing in the Royal Space Fleet?

"You live to make trouble," Treville grumbled. "Your fellow Musketeers here assure me there was no Duel consumed during your run in with the Sabres. Is that true?"

"Not a drop, dear Amiral," Athos confirmed. "We simply engaged in an old-fashioned brawl. You know the sort of thing. Fisticuffs." He mimicked a gentle boxing match, as if to convince her of his innocence. "It was very noble and historically authentic."

Treville rolled her eyes. "How quaint."

Dana could not help noticing that Athos had a calming effect on Treville. There was something about his presence that apparently made street fighting and the Regence's displeasure a little more forgivable.

"I have led my friends astray," said Athos, with a formal bow. "And I take the entire blame for it – oh, bollocks." His face drained of what little colour it had, and he lost his balance.

Both Aramis and Porthos dove for him, but Treville was there first, helping the man to lie back on the floor, pale and shaking as he was. "Athos," she demanded, unbuttoning his jacket. "Are you actually bleeding on my floor right now, you fucking liability?"

"Bandage seals must have broken," he gasped, playing up the wound for all it was worth. "Don't mind me, I'll just lie here for a moment and then I'll be fine."

"Why did you not get him to a medibay?" Treville barked at Aramis and Porthos.

"Well," said Porthos with an apologetic smile. "To be fair, Amiral, we were on our way to fetch medical assistance when, uh, you called us in here."

"We thought we'd better hop back here to get him patched up," said Aramis helpfully. She patted Athos on the head as if he were a beloved pet, and smiled a sweet, charming smile.

There was a red stain, a small one, on Athos' chest. Dana stared at it from a distance as Treville called for medics. They arrived in short order and began patching him up rather more effectively than he and his colleagues had managed.

Only when Athos had been taken away on a stretcher did Treville, the last of her anger worn away, stare down his two partners in crime. "Blades, then," she said in a heavy voice. "You've been fighting with actual blades, you utter…" but her words trailed away before she could locate a harsh enough noun.

"But not with Duel," said Aramis gravely. "For you have expressly forbidden…"

"Get out of here," Treville growled. "Keep an eye on that boy of yours. I want him back in the sky in three days."

The two Musketeers slid out, not bothering to hide how relieved they were to escape with their skins intact. Treville slammed the door behind them.

"As you can see, Dana," she said without ceremony, sitting back behind her desk. "None of the useless pricks I currently have serving under me have gotten themselves killed lately. You might think it would be worth betting on

Athos, but he has the luck of the devil and can even turn being stabbed into some kind of poetic statement. The Musketeers are in the shit with the Regence, our funding is at an all-time low, and there are no new ships on our horizon. I'm probably going to have to lay off a dozen gals this year. There's no position for a newcomer to step into, no matter her family history."

Dana felt the ceiling slowly press down around her. This was it, then. She was being dismissed. "Would it have made a difference if I brought my own ship?" she asked, hating herself for saying it, but she would always wonder if she had lost her chance because of that Duel back on Meung Station, and the sale of the *Buttercup*.

"I'm afraid not," said Treville, handing back the application stud with a sympathetic pat of her hand over Dana's. "They still let me print ships, thank God, it's all the other budget lines that have disappeared. I've nothing to offer you, kid. My pilots are even providing their own uniforms these days, which is how Porthos gets away with that gaudy belt of hers. If it makes you feel better – very few applicants get into the Fleet on their first application. Try again in a year or two, if we're still here. In the meantime, you've got more than enough flight hours to put in for the Pigeons or the Ravens. They're always hiring, and it's good basic experience to flesh out your CV."

Pigeon or Raven. A grunt, or a courier. Neither of them was the job that Dana wanted. "Thanks anyway," she said, trying to keep her chin up.

"I'm sorry," said Treville, meeting her gaze. "We're not what you imagined, are we?"

"No," said Dana, more sharply than politeness allowed. "You're really not."

Dana left Amiral Treville's office with two copies of a letter of introduction added to her application chip – one for the Pigeons and one for the Ravens. She had not yet decided which to try for.

The thought of being a courier made her want to pack up and go home. She was here to be a Musketeer like her mother before her, to defend the Regence's peace and protect the innocent, not to ferry messages back and forth.

As a Pigeon she would at least be guarding the safety of Royal Space, even if she might spend half her time on her feet instead of in a flight deck. Palace duty did not pay so well as the airy life of the Ravens, but it would keep her closer to here, to Paris and Luna Palais, where she might someday earn enough merit to be considered for the next empty helm of a musket-class dart.

And… sure, she wouldn't have a ship of her own, but she might get a mecha out of the deal. That could be fun.

From what Treville had said, it would not have made a difference if Dana had arrived in her own antique yellow-sprayed dart, with a gleaming stainless stud at her cuff and a photo silk full of nostalgia in her pocket, but oh, she was still seething about what had happened back at Meung Station. Everything had gone wrong from there. If Dana saw that thieving bitch from the Moth again, she was going to…

But there she was.

Dana stood at the plexi-glass doors that opened from Treville's observation deck. From here, she could see across Marie Antoinette Esplanade, one of the main shopping hubs of Paris Satellite. The immense plaza was busy with people, many of them in the colour-coded uniforms of the Fleet – Red, Gold, Blue, White, Grey, Black.

Right there amongst so many short and shaven and tightly-braided heads was a woman walking quickly, her long sweep of black hair streaming out behind a violet flight suit.

Dana could still hear the voice of the pilot from the Moth drawling in her ear, the snide *'Buttercup.'*

The thief, who had taunted her into an illegal game and stolen her very identity.

Blazing hatred flashed through Dana's body, and she flung herself at the nearest escalator, running several steps at a time to get to the foot of it, dodging shoppers and customers and her fellow pilots to reach her prey.

"Hey, stop!" she yelled, but the pilot from Meung Station did not even glance up.

CHAPTER 4
HOW THEY MET AND OTHER MINOR TRAGEDIES

So far, Dana's day had been a colossal waste of time. After years of working, she had finally reached the space station of her dreams, only to have those dreams squashed by reality.

The Musketeers weren't taking new pilots.

Even if they were, she wouldn't be top of their list.

She had travelled all this way from the other end of the solar system, sold the ship her Papa had restored with such pride and joy, failed to live up to her Maman's reputation… it was all such a mess.

Dana could not let herself be angry at Amiral Treville, or even those scruffbag Musketeers who had the best job in the galaxy and wasted their time pissing about like naughty schoolgirls.

But as she stood on the gantry, looking down across the beautiful ornamental plaza and the pilot in the bright violet flight-suit, she knew who she could be angry at.

That viper with the long, beautiful sweep of hair, who had tricked Dana into thinking she wasn't a pilot, then beaten her painfully in a game of Duel, and robbed her blind. The one who called her embarrassing ship a butter-cup. Ro, if that was really her name.

Oh yes, Dana could be angry. As if there was even a choice.

She all but flew down the escalator, dodging people this way and that as she ran across the plaza. She circled around into what looked like a clear area, and nearly collided with a transport cart bringing cryo-tubes in through a large door marked Medibay.

Impatient, Dana waited until they were clear and then bolted forward, only to crash into a man as he stepped out of the medibay doors. He cried in pain at the impact, and Dana bounced off his chest, landing heavily on the ground.

"Sorry," she said breathlessly. "I'm after this villainous cow of a— Oh!"

She knew this man. It was Athos the Musketeer, still sporting his frivolous golden beard, a freshly-bandaged shoulder, and apparently bleeding once again from the chest.

Possibly that last part was her fault.

"Shouldn't you still be in the medibay?" she blurted out.

He growled at her, clutching his wound. There was no charming twinkle as he had shown back in the office of Amiral Treville. "With an accent like yours, kid, shouldn't you have better manners?"

"I didn't mean to bump you," Dana said impatiently, scrambling to her feet. "And I said I was sorry. But I must catch her —"

Athos reached out and grabbed her with his good arm,

squeezing her shoulder painfully. "If you're in a hurry now, sweetness, when will you be in less of a hurry? We have a code of conduct on Paris Satellite, and it sounds like you need a lesson in manners."

Damn it all, that was fighting language. Dana felt sick to the stomach at the thought of taking Duel again so soon after the last time, but she was anxious to get after that pilot before she lost her.

"I'm new on station," she said, shaking his hand from her arm. "Where are such things usually done?"

"Level 5, Alpha square behind the Luxembourg," suggested Athos. "1500 hours."

"Done! Fine. Whatever."

Dana spun away from him, picking up speed again as she tore on through the plaza, desperately hoping that she had not lost her prey.

There was the violet flight suit, disappearing into a narrow walkway. Dana ducked and weaved around the crowd, closing the distance between them.

She saw another Musketeer pilot from Treville's office, the curvy and cheerful woman called Porthos, still wearing that splendid custom-made coat and bedazzled belt. It was matched now with a jewelled turban to conceal her pilot's buzz cut. What a peacock! Dana could not imagine why people bothered with such fashionable fripperies when there were ships to fly. Porthos stood out from her group of friends, laughing and making expansive gestures as she shared a joke.

Dana measured the distance with her eye between Porthos and the narrow walkway and judged that she could just dart in behind the Musketeer and not lose even a second's running time in her pursuit.

As she scampered past, though, Porthos swung her arm up and around and accidentally smacked Dana in the face. Dana's arm whirled around automatically to slap her away, and the two became tangled in Porthos' coat.

For the second time in only a few minutes, Dana hit the ground of the plaza, hard enough to knock the wind out of her. As she tried to scramble up and keep going, she heard a horrible ripping sound and was smacked back down.

Her face grazed on something against the cool artificial tiles, and she lifted her head to find that several pearl studs had detached themselves from Porthos' belt and were now embedded in her cheek and neck, burrowing themselves happily into their new home.

"Thief!" thundered Porthos, lunging at Dana. It was alarming to see quite so much cleavage bearing down upon her, and the last thing she wanted was another fight.

"Ow!" Dana replied. "Take them back, I don't want them!" That was it, then. The pilot in the violet flight suit was long gone, and Dana wasn't sure she even had enough anger left to confront her, not after this. Maybe Paris Satellite was trying to tell her to stay out of fights.

Paris Satellite was not subtle.

"What do you want to go thundering around like that for?" grumbled Porthos, wrenching the studs back with far more force than necessary. They made a popping sound as they came free of Dana's skin. "What are you, twelve?"

"You hit me first," Dana protested, and one of Porthos' friends laughed.

"She has a point, Pol," noted another.

Porthos leaned her heaving bosom even more threateningly towards Dana, who wondered if it had been registered as a deadly weapon. "Want a chance to hit me back, sunshine? Since you're so keen on making friends."

Ah, so what Paris was actually telling her was that she needed to get into more fights. Without subtlety. Wonderful.

"1600 hours, behind the Luxembourg," Dana said with a sigh.

Porthos smiled, straightening her turban. When she relaxed, she looked like a satisfied cat. "The very thing, pet," she said, as if they were arranging a coffee date with shoes and gossip, or whatever it was that girlfriends did together.

"Wear your second-best coat," Dana suggested and took off before the Musketeer could swipe at her. A burst of laughter followed her as she ran off up the walkway, and she was certain it wasn't 'Pol' Porthos they were laughing at.

This place made her feel like a twelve-year-old, all scraped knees and awkward elbows. She was starting to hate Paris.

It was no use running. The walkway was empty, and Dana trudged along it, keeping her eye out for her prey despite having little hope left. Other walkways branched off every twenty metres or so, and the pilot from Meung could have vanished along any of those branches.

Dana stopped walking altogether and let the moving floor beneath her feet hum her forward, through the echoing tunnel. Signs suggested that this was a good direction to go in order to find lodgings, though she had no idea which hotels or boarding levels were any good, and which were likely to suck up her credit under false pretences.

She had been an idiot. A double idiot. Not only was she jobless and homeless, but now she was expected to fight two of the Royal Musketeers. Bare knuckles were too much to hope for – and she wasn't convinced she could take either of them – no, it had to have been Duel they hinted at.

Duel, the pilot's drug of choice. That had gone so well for her last time.

Dana's dreams of the life she would build on Paris Satellite had been royally fucked over. At this rate, she'd be on a shuttle home with her brain bleeding out her ears by supper time.

The walkway hummed directly into another brightly lit plaza, smaller than the other, though with just as many people hanging around. Lots of pilots here too, though there was a higher percentage of civilians as they got further from the space dock. This was a recreation hub, with all manner of virtual sports and games being played out in the open.

In the centre of the plaza, a sonic fountain burst forth with light and sound. Dana felt a ping in the visitor's stud she had been issued, and her senses flooded with options. She could play reality tennis, conduct an imaginary orchestra, or throw herself into an anti-grav well to practice her swimming strokes. Oh, look, Prince Alek's Zero-G TeamJoust exhibition match was going to be televised live shortly, and she could hire an implant to insert herself virtually into the body of his team's android opponents.

Everything cost credit points, and the money left over from the sale of the *Buttercup* wasn't going to magically increase any time soon. She had to find lodgings, not screw about here.

Still, if the Duel burned out enough of her synapses, Dana would either be dead or in need of hospitalisation by the end of the day shift. In that case, her lack of pre-paid lodgings would be a feature, not a bug.

A cluster of Musketeers in their bright blue-and-whites lounged near the sonic fountain with a couple of fellows in Pigeon grey, laughing and chatting together. Dana felt a tug on her heart. That should be her. It was all she had ever wanted, since she was old enough to understand her mother's madcap stories.

One for all and all for one, and all that bullshit. Everything she'd ever believed about Musketeer camaraderie was here, illustrated in blue and white.

Aramis, another of the pilots from Treville's office, stood head and shoulders above her friends, conversing with ease. She was so graceful and clever-looking, exactly the kind of Musketeer that Dana longed to be. Unlike Porthos, Aramis had not succumbed to vanity away from her ship – her hair still remained tightly pinned on top of her head, as if she was ready to launch at a moment's notice.

Athos was obviously a ruffian with pretensions to aristocracy – or an aristocrat with pretensions to ruffianity, Dana wasn't sure which – and that Porthos woman was a complete preening egotist. But Aramis was the sensible one, by the looks of it. Sensible enough to broker peace between her friends and the idiot Gascon who had an appointment to duel with them in a few hours?

Dana made up her mind to try. She was no coward, but the last thing she wanted was to get in a pissing contest over her pride.

The pilot from Mcung had taught her that.

As Dana approached the friendly group, she saw that Aramis had her boot firmly on a photosilk that must have fallen from the pocket of her flight suit. No one would knowingly tread on a silk like that – it risked damaging the fibres, and like everything else on Paris Satellite, a replacement would not come cheap.

That was her in.

"Hello again," Dana said politely, stopping a little away from the group as if she had only just seen them. "We haven't exactly been introduced, Captain Aramis. You've dropped something there."

Aramis resisted Dana's friendly overture with a chill in her voice. "You're mistaken," she said firmly. Her smoky eyes gave no sign that she even recognised Dana from earlier in Treville's office.

Oh, space dung, what had Dana done now?

It was too late for her to take it back, to keep breezily walking as if she hadn't meant to hover. One of the Pigeons gave Aramis a friendly shove and snatched up the silk which proved to display a collection of intimate images, each fading into another, of a very attractive white woman with platinum-blonde hair. In lingerie.

"Aramis you devil," he said, choking with laughter and waving the photosilk around to make sure everyone got a good look. "When you said you were friends with Captain Dubois, we didn't know you meant Just Good Friends."

Aramis sent Dana a fierce look, as sharp as a slap. "It's not mine," she said, grabbing the silk back. "It obviously belongs to Dubois, so I'll give it back to her first chance I get. She won't want you sex fiends staring at her Dyson spheres."

"I bet you'll give it to her," snorted the other Pigeon, and most of her friends fell about in fits of laughter.

One Musketeer, a sleek fellow with his head shaven clean, gave Aramis a dirty look. "Or I could pass it on to her husband," he said pointedly. "Since he's my engie."

Marriage contracts, Dana remembered. On the outer stations, such things were treated casually, as they had been in the olden days. But Paris Satellite was the hub of 'civilisation.' Church opinion counted for a lot, especially since the current Regence's rise to power. The Cardinal had supported the Regence's claim to the solar system over that of her three brothers purely because she swore the same public commitment to righteous morality that the Regences before her had so dramatically failed to maintain.

Faith, obedience and the sanctity of contracts. You could marry anyone you liked in this solar system, for as long as you liked – even aliens, if that was your kink – and when your contract ran out it was no harm, no foul. But publicly breaking a marriage contract before its time ran out was enough to ruin anyone, rich or poor, Regence or Musketeer.

A public commitment to making divorce all but impossible could not help but create an excessive rise in adultery – that stood to reason. But the political climate right now meant that what went on behind closed doors was enough to get you fired, publicly humiliated, or even arrested, if you were careless enough to be caught.

Dana had just outed two complete strangers as adulterers. So much for not making today any worse.

"Don't worry," Aramis said, her hands stiffly in her pockets. "I'll take care of it. Discreetly."

Her friends cuffed her around the shoulders, continuing to give her a hard time, but Aramis arched her neck at them and laughed it off, teasing them back about their own scandals.

Dana tried to sneak away, agonised with embarrassment. How was she supposed to know that the silk would cause so much trouble? She should never have left Gascon Station. There was no welcome for her among the Musketeers, not in the way she had craved since she was a kid sitting on her Maman's knee, listening to stories about adventures and eternal friendship.

She did not belong here. Treville had made it clear there was no place for her. Why couldn't she get it into her own thick skull?

Dana tensed as she heard sudden boot steps behind her. An arm hooked painfully around her neck.

"Well, that was a fine little scene," Aramis whispered, smiling through her teeth as if she and Dana were genuine BFFs. Her arm, which might look casually friendly to anyone else, squeezed tighter. "Who sent you after me, baby doll?"

"I'm so sorry," Dana whispered back, unable even to pretend she was not miserable. "I didn't think."

"Thinking was most definitely absent," said Aramis, flicking Dana in the ear with one beautifully manicured fingernail. "Next time you see someone blatantly trying to hide evidence with their boot, how about you leave them to it? Unless you've got an arrest warrant for me. Have you an arrest warrant? You have to tell me if I ask you directly."

"No!" Dana insisted, shocked at the very idea.

"Not a Pigeon, then. Or one of the Cardinal's Hammers?"

"I don't work for anyone yet, I —" Dana paused. "Hammers?"

"Sure, Sabres in the air, Hammers on the ground. Blunt instruments, all. The Cardinal has eyes everywhere, and wouldn't she just love to secure an arrest warrant for a Musketeer. We're loyal to the royal family above and beyond, you understand." Aramis blinked, and gazed directly into Dana's eyes as if she was searching for the answers of the universe.

Dana stared back, unblinking and miserable. She had no anger left. She had a horrible feeling that she might cry.

"All right," Aramis said after a moment. "I believe you. Just an idiot kid, then. Fresh off the shuttle?"

"I'm from Gascon Station," Dana said sullenly.

"Gascon? Oh Lord, isn't that somewhere near Freedom? I didn't think anyone lived out that far." Aramis shook her head, and the arm around Dana's shoulder relaxed into a less threatening gesture. Almost a hug. "Right, then. You're new, and you're stumbling around like a kitten on absinthe. I get it. I sympathise. Sadly, I have a moral obligation to do something about you."

Dana closed her eyes and groaned. She could see where this was going.

Aramis was still talking, her voice musical and as lovely as the rest of her. "You think we don't see baby dolls like you every other week, prancing off the shuttle all bright-eyed and innocent, thinking the only way to get ahead is to take a Musketeer scalp? We live and die on our reputations, and you have just taken the reputation of one of the finest pilots in our fleet and dragged it through the mud."

"I'm sorry," Dana burst out. "I didn't mean to embarrass you."

Aramis rolled her eyes. "Not me, you dingbat. Captain Dubois, one of the finest pilots and most indescribably beautiful women in the history of Paris Satellite. Who is in no way my secret girlfriend." She released Dana, and patted her on the head. "I'm going to have to fight you."

"Somehow I thought you might," sighed Dana. This was how the day was to play out, then. No escaping her fate.

"I know an excellent and secluded little place, behind the Luxembourg on Level 5. Do you know it?"

"I think I can find my way," said Dana. "I'm free at 1700 hours." In a manner of speaking.

"Excellent. Good chat." Aramis gave her a mighty thump on the back with surprising strength. "Nothing personal, baby doll. But, well. You pissed me off."

There was a lot of that going around.

CHAPTER 5
THE MENDING OF ATHOS

The Luxembourg on Level 5 turned out to be a Church of All. Dana had not expected that. Was it seemly to take brawling drugs and play at duels with brain-altering spaceship games so close to a house of God?

Then again, the Musketeers were up for all manner of other vices and sins, why not add sacrilege into the mix?

The Luxembourg was a lavish installation compared to the cathedral booths Dana had seen down on the main shopping plazas: a pure white structure behind a storage bay, with bright plexi-glass windows which flicked through a rotation of holy images: the solarnauts, star fields and other images from early astro-travel. There were no pointed roofs or gables in space station architecture, but the windows told you this was a place of worship.

The tourist visa stud in her collar sparked into life as Dana approached the church, informing her that if she registered her palm print at the door, the church would present her with her own personalised religious imagery, based on past preferences.

For a moment, feeling lost and far from home, Dana considered it. But she was about to take part in a highly illegal ritual, so now was not the time to be leaving a trail of her presence on Paris Satellite.

Later, there could be absolution, and comfort. For now, she had to keep alert and be ready to run if there was trouble.

Trouble other than three Musketeers waiting to burn her synapses out, obviously.

Dana had assumed the spot behind the Luxembourg that all three Musketeers were so keen to use for duelling purposes would be a spare storage space, or some other generic empty room with metal walls. Instead, she found that the corridor behind the church opened out into a meadow.

Grass. Trees. Sky. Tiny fucking daisies bursting up out of the alarming greenness of it all.

Possibly the brain damage had kicked in before she even took the dose of Duel?

But no, as Dana walked across the soft, spongy grass, she spotted the bleeding edges of the scenery. The colour degenerated into random pixels here and there, making an occasional ragged flaw in an otherwise perfect design. This meadow was Artifice all the way, the same technology they used to make churchgoers feel that they were stepping into the sacred building of their choice.

Everything about satellite or station life came down to two things: conservation of space, and the sanity of residents. Artifice helped with both, though as each generation passed, it became less and less necessary to mimic dirt-side conventions with any degree of accuracy.

When humans first came to live among the stars, they had very conventional ideas about what they needed to retain their sense of cultural identity: the romanticisation of grass and sky, for example. The first artificial environments had been too accurate; literal uncanny valleys that made the station residents feel more homesick than ever. Fantastical and creative artificial environments became popular precisely because they weren't a pale imitation of 'home.'

Dana had never before walked across an Artifice environment that was trying so hard to look planet-authentic. The rec ground that ran across the top of the power plant in the centre of Gascon Station had been hacked by generations of teenagers, so the sky was a multi-coloured jumble of graffiti tags and dirty jokes, and the ground only replicated grass during the annual Locals vs. Incomers cricket match. The rest of the time it displayed random artistry, as far as you could get from a plain old-fashioned dirtside landscape.

No one ever wanted to replicate an image of the planet of Freedom with its ice and rock and engineering installations. Dana had, however, lost her virginity in an underwater simulation of the ocean world of Truth, so she did understand something of the planetary appeal, if only as a novelty.

Perhaps Paris was different. This was the Honour and Valour end of the solar system. There might be more residents here who craved white bobbly clouds in a clear blue sky, and grass.

This meadow had to be a Valour simulation – from

what Dana heard, that terraformed planet was obsessed with recreating imaginary histories from the olden days of Honour, the planet of origin, in the days before the Warming turned even the northern hemisphere into a place of desert and bushland and dry creek beds. No one had lived on Valour further back than eight generations, so it seemed unlikely that it would have genuine stone circles – did that make this Artifice meadow a simulation of a simulation? Or another example of humans kidding themselves they belonged anywhere but the stars?

The grass made Dana's feet itch through her boots. She was certain she would not enjoy Valour at all, if was anything like this faux-medieval cartoon. Her eyes longed for the plain flat grey walls that were everywhere, back home. Gascons didn't need to pretend that grass was growing underfoot – they got on with living their lives in practical, everyday environments.

It wasn't just the meadow. Paris Satellite was trying too hard to impress her, and Dana was over it.

Her would-be murderer, the first of three, lounged against a tall grey stone. Athos the Musketeer looked less like a pilot and more like a retro burlesque performer with those long, luxuriant blond locks and matching beard.

This was so much worse than the Moth pilot from Meung. How was that hair not a major safety hazard, with all the cables and plug-ins required for basic flight conditions? Dana glared at him as she approached.

"Ah, the girl from Gascon," Athos said with a vague wave, not bothering to stir himself. "Forgive me for not rising to the occasion, but my latest medipatch still needs two minutes to complete its clever work. It's not quite the hour, in any case, and I'm waiting for my seconds to arrive."

There was an open bottle on the grass beside him. Was she expected to duel a drunk? Then again, perhaps it might give him an unfair advantage, if he were anaesthetised against the sharp flashburns caused by Duel. The medipatch was a worry. Much though Dana wanted to survive this encounter, she also didn't want to end up with a dead Musketeer on her hands.

Dana drew close to him. "If your wound still troubles you, we can postpone…" she suggested.

"None of that, I have my honour to think of!" Athos sat up slightly, grimaced, and lay down again. "That wasn't two minutes yet, was it?"

"Not even slightly," she said, not wanting to smile, not at all. God help her if she started to like this fool.

"I hate waiting for things," he grumbled.

His comment about seconds only just sank in. Dana glanced around. "You invited others, did you say?"

More people to witness her shame and potentially steal her identity studs if she lost consciousness. Marvellous.

"Of course. You need a second to duel. I always invite two, because my friends are terribly unreliable, and apt to get distracted." Athos gave Dana a sharp look from beneath his lidded eyes. "You didn't bring a second?"

"I don't know anyone on Paris Satellite," she confessed.

"No one at all?"

"I just got here. I met Amiral Treville…"

A look of mild alarm shot across Athos' face. "Yes, well, don't invite her. It's illegal, you know, for us to have these little exchanges."

"I'm new, not an idiot," Dana snapped.

The medipatch made a chiming sound, and Athos leaped to his feet, making a few experimental lunges. "Excellent, all better now!" he exclaimed, then doubled over in a fit of pain. "Fuck it."

"Sit down," Dana ordered him, pushing him back down on to the Artifice grass. She flicked open his shirt and peered at the medipatch. "Where did you get this thing? Not from the official medibay."

"I may have found it lying around somewhere." Athos reached for the bottle, but Dana lifted it up quickly and moved it out of his reach. He made a low growling noise in the back of his throat.

"It's dodgy, however you got it." She tapped a few experimental codes into the flat patch. "If I put in the code for anti-inflammatory, it reads as a lung purge. There must be a crossed circuit."

"Are you a medical professional, girl from Gascon?" Athos asked her, his face uncomfortably close as she fiddled further with the medipatch.

"No, but I'm good at rewiring bad tech to make it work," Dana said, biting on her lip as she concentrated. "We have to be, out on the rim. Supply ships don't come that often, and printing anything costs – four times as much – *there*."

The medipatch chimed sweetly. "Skin and blood vessel repair continuing, complete in three minutes, twenty-eight seconds," it announced in a babyish voice.

"Three minutes," groaned Athos, swooning again. "I might as well be dead."

"You're welcome," said Dana, moving away from him so he could do up his own damned shirt. He had a tattoo of a sunflower there, not far from his wound, and she didn't want to be caught staring at it.

His eyes brightened as he looked past her. "There are my seconds now. You'll like them. Everyone likes them."

Dana braced herself before she turned, only to discover that the sinking feeling in her gut was justified. Two female pilots – one tall and slender, one short and round, strolled along the grass towards them, with the bright white shape of the Luxembourg Church looming behind.

"Excellent," said Athos. He waved cheerfully at his friends from where he remained lying on the grass. "Good news, chaps! We can get started as soon as I stop bleeding internally!"

Aramis and Porthos gave odd looks to Athos and then to Dana herself.

"A little early aren't we?" Porthos drawled.

"Quite a lot early," Aramis corrected.

"Unless —"

"You don't mean to say —"

Athos jumped in now. "Why are you two behaving like a *Love and Asteroids* double act?"

Porthos broke first, laughing uproariously.

Aramis was more reserved. "Don't tell me this is the same girl who crashed into you, Athos? And the clod who damaged your new belt, Pol? My, baby doll, three challenges in one day. You have been busy." She eyed Dana up and down.

Dana bristled at that. "I challenged no one, Captain Aramis. I simply accepted…"

"You don't mean you're fighting all three of us?" Athos broke in.

"Not all at once," Dana said impatiently. "I wasn't

expecting Captain Porthos for another hour, and Captain Aramis for two. It's not my fault no one can keep to a schedule."

"My feelings are hurt," said Athos after a long moment. "Didn't you think I'd give you a good enough challenge on my own?" His beard twitched.

Dana scowled, hating how they flustered her with their teasing. "Shall we get started? Or haven't you finished cooking yet?"

Athos tapped his medipatch. "Almost done. Fighting three of us, without a second. Aramis my love, you might as well put your feet up, it's hardly likely you'll get your turn."

"I can think of somewhere to put my feet," Aramis said, nudging him with her boot. "Are you getting up, or is the kid going to have to fight you from there?" She frowned down at him. "You are mended, aren't you?"

The medipatch beeped its approval.

"Up I come!" Athos whooped, leaping to his feet with a smoothness that belied his previous damage. He gave Aramis a smacking kiss on the mouth, then looked past her to Dana. "Good patch up, sweetness. I can see you'd be useful to have around if I weren't honour bound to give you a pasting."

"Such a gentleman," said Porthos, arranging herself against one of the stone monoliths as if it were the most comfortable of armchairs. She reached around for Athos' abandoned bottle, and took a swig. "What's your name, little one?"

Dana was sick of being talked to like she was a child. "My name is Dana Amelie Alix D'Artagnan of Gascon Station," she said between gritted teeth. "Can we get on with this?" She looked from one Musketeer to another, wondering which of them had brought the equipment with them. "Well? This is a duel isn't it?"

"So it is," said Athos in a low purr that reminded her he was more than the lazy buffoon he had pretended to be. He had to be more than that, to fly musket-class here in the centre of the solar system, even if his parents had bought him a posh accent. "*En garde* then, little one. Let's see what you're made of."

His hand flicked against his belt, catching up the baton that swung there, and to Dana's horror it flickered into life, revealing a long, silver streak of metal where empty air had previously been.

A sword. A genuine sword. These crazy bastards didn't take pilot drugs and throw imaginary spaceships at each other. They fought their duels with edged weapons. Which explained, of course, where Athos got that wound of his, and why Treville was so pissed off about it.

She was going to die here today, with a long stabby weapon impaled in her body.

It was impossible to guess what Paris Satellite was trying to tell her now.

CHAPTER 6

THE WRONG SORT OF DUEL

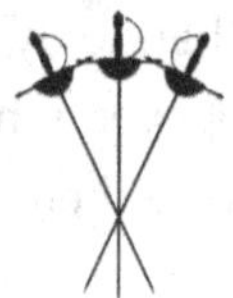

Dana stood in the Artifice meadow, staring down the tip of the Musketeer's sword. Athos stared implacably back at her, waiting for… for what? For her to draw a sword of her own?

That was only one of the many things wrong with this scenario. "You duel with swords," Dana said slowly. "That's – *why do you even have a sword?*"

"It's called a pilot's slice," Porthos contributed from where she was very comfortably seated on the artificial stone. She tossed her own baton from hand to hand. "Official issue – smartsteel. It shapes itself into any blade length or width that we require. Essential in emergencies. Designed to be our final option if we're trapped in wreckage or need to hack our ship into a rudimentary shelter."

"So of course you figured out a way to use it as a casual weapon against each other for kicks," Dana said with heavy sarcasm.

"A hundred and one uses," said Aramis with a warm

smile of her own. She sat on the grass beside Porthos, unpinning her dark hair so that it fell loosely down her back. None of them were taking Dana remotely seriously.

She was a joke to them.

"I thought you meant *Duel*," Dana exploded, looking back at Athos. He did not lower the sword pointing directly at her.

Athos glared at her along the thin line of metal. "You mean with pilot drugs and computers and seedy betting circles? Of course not. We couldn't fly straight if we were doing that to ourselves every other day." He paused in reflection. "Well, these two couldn't. They're lightweights."

"Whereas fighting each other with metal spikes, perfectly sane!" Dana snapped back. She shook her head at him, stepping back out of range. "I don't understand you. Any of you. You have the best fucking job in the world, and you act like bored teenagers in a pantomime. Metal swords, and honour duels and – that beard!"

Athos looked almost hurt, and did lower the sword this time. "What's wrong with my beard?"

"IT'S RIDICULOUS!" Dana howled. "Long hair worn out is against every military regulation there is – you can't possibly say it's not a flight hazard. But that beard of yours is taking the *piss*. It's like a mad concoction of all the other beards that male pilots shave off every morning. It makes no sense at all. You make no sense at all!"

Athos tilted his head at her with an odd sort of smile. The other two weren't nearly so restrained – Porthos laughed so hard she was nearly sick, and Aramis leaped up to smack Athos between the shoulders. "Some of us have been telling him that all year," she declared, tugging at his locks. "But only when drunk. He never believes us."

Athos stroked his long beard, frowning. "I grew it for a bet. Ten months I've had it, waiting for Amiral Treville to order me to shave it off. Someone spoiled the surprise ahead of time – thank you, Porthos…"

"Not guilty!" protested Porthos.

"…And so Treville refuses to acknowledge it, pretends she's never even noticed I have a beard." Athos sighed deeply, as if this was a great tragedy to him. "I suppose she assumed I'd get bored of it soon enough, or that I'd have strangled myself with the ship cables by now."

Dana frowned at him. "So you lost the bet?" She still wasn't ruling out the possibility that these three were making fun of her.

"Of course not!" Athos said, completely serious. "I bet she wouldn't crack. Let that be a lesson to you here in Paris. Never bet against Amiral Treville." He looked Dana over, from her own regulation shaved head down to her sturdy and serviceable boots. "You don't actually have a sword, do you," he said finally. It was not a question.

Dana shook her head slowly. "That's how you were wounded," she muttered. "You let some rival stick a *blade* into you?"

"I tried to stop him," he said as if that made it reasonable. "I'm not completely irresponsible. And I can't help it if dangerous men with questionable politics flock to me. It's a curse."

"You could stop actively encouraging them to murder you," Porthos suggested.

Athos rolled his eyes at her. "The weight of past evidence suggests otherwise."

"You're all crazy," Dana interrupted. "How do you even have time to do your jobs? I haven't got a blade. I haven't got a ship. I – washed out of the Musketeers. If this is your idea of honour, put down the swords and I'll take you on with my bare hands." She held herself in boxing stance, determined that she wasn't going to leave this meadow without hitting at least one of them very hard in the face.

There was a brief pause in which the expressions of all three Musketeers barely changed. Athos raised his blade for a moment in something like a salute, and then flicked it back into the shape of a baton.

"Well then, D'Artagnan," he said reasonably. "We'd better get you fixed up with a job, a blade and a ship before we try to kill you. It's only sporting."

They got drunk instead. Fiercely, companionably drunk. Somehow, Dana had ended up classified as a mate rather than an upstart, simply for her willingness to shout at Athos.

Surely making friends wasn't this easy? It had never been so easy for her before. She might be more suspicious if she wasn't far too drunk.

The bar was called the Abbey of St Germain, which meant the staff wore medieval monk costumes, a source of great amusement to all three Musketeers because of some joke lost in the mists of time.

Dana could not understand half of what they said to each other, but she liked that they never bothered to explain. It felt as if she was already one of them.

They had convinced Athos that the beard had to go. He resisted, until Dana pointed out that the joke had gone on so long, Treville would be more disturbed by its absence than its presence. Aramis seized upon this premise, and Porthos plied Athos with wine until he agreed to it.

"I'm sure this is an android's job," he said dourly, sitting lengthwise on the bench. Aramis sat astride the bench behind him, running the sonar clipper slowly and thoughtfully across the back of his head until only a thin layer of stubble remained.

"You don't trust androids," said Aramis, concentrating. A nearby bar android hovered, sucking up the hair that had fallen in snippets all over the polished floor.

"I don't trust *you*," Athos said.

"Liar," said Aramis, turning his head so as to tidy up above his ears. Dana watched Aramis' hands, gentle and competent as she played barber for her friend.

Athos' eyes fixed thoughtfully upon Dana. "So what did you do, baby pilot?" he asked, not slurring nearly enough for a man on his third round of a golden elixir called Valorous Grain. "To earn three duels in one day."

"It just sort of happened," Dana admitted. She had given up trying to moderate her own drinking on the grounds that being sober would make it even harder to communicate with these reprobates. "Didn't it?" she applied to Porthos and Aramis, who laughed at her.

"You offended my chest," Athos said sternly. "My poor, wounded chest."

"Your pride," Dana corrected.

"And yours."

She shrugged, slightly ashamed of herself. "Granted."

"But my two lady friends here…"

"He only calls us ladies when he's drunk," Aramis put in.

"It's the only time he remembers," Porthos added.

Aramis elbowed Athos to make him turn around again, so she could start on his beard.

"These *ladies* are the pinnacle of grace and excellence and forgiveness," Athos said grandly. "How did you make enemies of them?"

Dana looked over at Porthos, who busily poured herself more wine. "I don't need a reason," Porthos said, looking as embarrassed as Dana felt. "I fight to fight."

"We argued about fashion, I think?" said Dana cautiously. This at least was a joke she could share with Porthos, rather than watching as the Musketeers lobbed them over her head.

"Fashion, that was it." Porthos winked at Dana. "Don't tell him, pet. He'll only make fun of us."

Athos had moved on from them already. "But Aramis," he said. "No one has ever quarrelled with Aramis... she is perfectly amiable in all ways."

"You dickhead, you quarrel with me constantly," said Aramis, buzzing away at the line of his chin.

"You have the patience of a saint," Athos told her. "And yet..."

Aramis sighed. "And yet." She gave Dana a wary look before returning to her task. "Our new young friend and I argued over a matter of theology," she said. "You know me."

"Too much religion," said Athos fondly. "It always gets you into trouble."

"If you lived a more devout life, your soul would thank

you for it," replied Aramis, kissing him on the top of his head.

A dark expression fell over Athos' newly-shorn face for a moment. "The very opposite, I think," he muttered.

An attractive 'monk' cleared the empty bottle from the table and opened a fresh one for them. She tipped Aramis a wink as she did so, and managed to flash some leg despite the large brown robes.

"Oh," said Athos, cheering up. "That sort of theology. Makes more sense."

"I resent your implication," said Aramis, but she was laughing.

"Can we stop talking about this?" begged Dana. She was still kicking herself about the photosilk.

"The only proper way to change the subject is to toast the best boss in the skies," said Athos, coming to his feet suddenly. "Amiral Treville!"

"Treville!" thundered Porthos.

"You clown," snapped Aramis, pulling Athos back down to the bench. "I almost cut half your chin off."

None of them noticed that Dana failed to join in the toast. What had Amiral Treville done for her?

The door of the bar swung open, and a Sabre officer walked in, resplendent in a red and gold uniform. She was accompanied by three uniformed Red Guards – Hammers – with the Cardinal's cross shining brightly on their scarlet jackets.

Athos was a different man in an instant, his smile vanished. Aramis had left a thin layer of beard close to his chin. There was a scar running over the top of his freshly-shorn scalp, as if his head had once been cut open with an axe. He leaned into Dana as the Sabre and her underlings approached. "D'Artagnan. If the sight of them makes you want to draw a sword, or swing a chair in their faces, then you are a true Musketeer at heart."

Then he winked, one long-lashed blue eye.

Dana knew it to be true. Other children were trained by their parents to love particular TeamJoust colours, or to nurse a deep patriotism for the station or planet on which they were born. For Dana, since she was a baby, it had been Team Musketeer.

She had never met a Sabre or a Red Hammer to talk to, and yet she hated these guards on sight.

The Sabre was a short and stocky white woman with a spiky mohawk, and the bars of a major on her lapel. "Drinking at mid shift?" she said in a low drawl. "Sad, Captain-*lieutenant* Athos. You used to be someone."

"Claudine Jussac," Athos replied, lifting his glass as if toasting her health. "I note your uniform still fits. Strange, as you seem to be losing height every year. Perhaps it's the artificial gravity. You need to get yourself dirtside for a holiday. Suck in some sun, get laid, and then maybe the terrible shrinkage will abate."

Jussac scowled at him. "There's been a complaint, Athos."

"I wouldn't take it personally," he said in a reassuring tone. "Some people are simply never going to like you. I think it's because you're not very friendly."

Jussac's eyebrows drew in even closer. "Athos. You're not helping yourself here. Shut your mouth."

"Now talking is forbidden by the precious Cardinal!" Porthos interrupted, drumming her fingernails on the table. "What next, are they taking our wine?"

Aramis was deeply unimpressed with both of her

friends. "How about you state your business and get out of here, Claudine?" she asked in the calm voice of a peacemaker.

Jussac smiled at Aramis with all her teeth. "You three have been fighting again, on church property, behind the Luxembourg. In our jurisdiction."

"Lies," said Porthos immediately. "What would your mother say if she saw you hassling poor innocent Musketeers, Claudine?"

Jussac bridled. "I've been in service to the Cardinal for seven years, Pol. I outrank all three of you. Don't you think it's time to take me seriously?"

"We would, baby doll," said Aramis. "But it's hard for us to keep up with all you bright young things, with your freshly pressed uniforms and your busywork."

Jussac folded her arms, and she really did look like a sulky teenager, Dana decided. "We have security footage of Captain-lieutenant Athos baring sword behind the Luxembourg."

"We didn't even fight," Dana burst out. Aramis gave her a warning look and placed one finger to her mouth.

Athos stood up, turning to face Jussac. She came up to his collarbone, just about. "I thought it was illegal to monitor so close to a house of worship," he said calmly.

Jussac tilted her head back, obviously hating to do so. "The Cardinal has made a new ruling," she snapped. "So many unsavoury types took advantage of the Church privacy laws to play their dangerous games." She let her red jacket slide open to show the baton of a pilot's slice on one loop of her belt, and the glittering red chrome of an arc-ray on another. "Guess what, Athos Bloody Smartarse Musketeer? You're under arrest."

Dana held her breath. Athos looked at Jussac up and down quite deliberately, as if he was preparing to pick her up and throw her bodily through the nearest window. "No," he said after a moment. "I don't think I am. The Luxembourg and its grounds may be under the Cardinal's jurisdiction, but this bar is on Crown property and I'm wearing the blue and white. I'm not under arrest."

Jussac barely blinked. She flexed her hands once, and in response to that signal, the door of the Abbey of St Germain was flung open and a dozen more Red Hammers entered the bar. It all looked official, right up to the point that they drew blades instead of stunners.

The saucy monks and other customers melted back into the far corners.

"You don't have a sword," Aramis said in an undertone to Dana. "Better hide under the table until this is all over." Before Dana could react to that, Aramis was up and over the table, her pilot's slice baton extending into a wicked gleam of a sword.

Porthos roared and turned over the table in the same moment, leaping towards her friends.

Dana D'Artagnan paused in horrified amazement as the bar erupted into the most fearsome brawl.

"Fuck this for a joke," she decided, and dodged around the fallen table to punch the nearest Sabre in the kidneys and take his slice off him.

Paris Satellite, the centre of elegant civilisation. Not entirely what she had expected.

But not boring, Dana thought, grinning wildly as she ducked and punched and figured out very quickly how to get the most effective use of a pilot's slice at close quarters. Most certainly not boring.

CHAPTER 7
A ROYAL RECEPTION

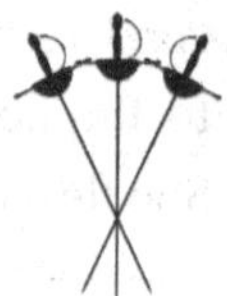

Lalla-Louise Renard Royal, Regence of the Solar System, awoke in a haze of perfumed sheets and the musky scent of her husband. Even with her thoughts already turning towards the business of the day, she always enjoyed the performance art that was the morning ritual of Prince Alek of Auster. It was the only reason she had not suggested separate bedrooms after their first night together.

The prince was slim like a cigar, and he had an endless supply of suits as beautiful as himself. Alek's eyes were modified emerald this season, to match his shoulder-length emerald hair. A man built for jewel-tones, if ever there was one. She might have enjoyed the effect more if she didn't know it was chosen to honour his TeamJoust colours.

Alek selected a suit of mint and silver, dressing himself slowly and with great deliberation. A long streak of metallic scales traced a line directly from his temple, down his neck and the side of his torso, over his bare hip and all the way down to the soft underpad of his foot. It was a common mutation for the inhabitants of the warm, desert climate of Auster, a continent in the southern hemisphere of Honour.

"I hear they fuck dragons," was a common slur, a drunken joke, and one that Lalla-Louise had steeled herself against when the betrothal was first mooted. But she liked her dragon man, and from the few times they had touched each other, she knew that his skin was soft where it was not scaled. As the metallic streak disappeared beneath layers of silk and cotton, she found herself even more fascinated by the phenomenon, peeking out as it did at his throat and ankle.

This morning, Lalla-Louise lifted herself on one elbow to watch the dressing process through lidded eyes. Oh, men. Why were they so much more attractive when their angular lines and curved muscles were covered in pretty things?

"I suppose you can't come to the match today," he said when he reached the cravat, his fingers hovering in the act of a careless knot as if he wondered whether to bother. More scales disappeared beneath that whisper of silk so that the silver flecks on the side of his face were all the more stark against his beige-gold skin.

Such a question was rare for him; she was as disinterested in the game he played as he was in her own work, and her favoured recreations.

Oh, how she longed for the Hunt. There were three opalescent ampoules awaiting her in her dressing table drawer, awaiting a moment of leisure. But there was never enough time.

"I'd adore to, dove," Lalla-Louise said lightly. "But I

have Amiral Treville to meet for morning chocolate. Some of our pilots have been misbehaving."

Alek gave her a twist of a smile. "Your marvellous Musketeers. Are they making you look bad again?"

He was sharp, her husband. She had not expected intelligence or wit from this planet-born New Aristocrat of the wrong religion, who only came alive when he was playing that zero gravity sport, but Alek had proved to be a pleasant conversationalist with occasional moments of incisive commentary. Keeping her side of the contract was hardly a chore at all. If only Lalla-Louise enjoyed the embrace of his body as much as she liked looking at it, they might have a marriage to speak of.

Another eight years. It seemed like an eternity. Ten year contracts were rare these days, even among royalty, but Lalla-Louise and her advisors had wanted to make a statement to the solar system: that the Church of All was not the only source of moral stability. By the time this marriage contract ended, Lalla-Louise would be secure in her position, but Alek? She had no idea what he would do or want or need when their time as husband and wife was done. She barely knew those things about him now.

"You have hit the nail on the head, darling," she said. "There are times when I seriously consider letting the Cardinal's Fleet take over once and for all. Let the Musketeers disappear like the anachronism they are."

Alek winced at that, she noticed. If the Cardinal gained more power than she already held, life would become much harder for those who followed the Elemental faith of the planet-dwellers. "Not really?" he asked.

"No, not really." Lalla-Louise rose naked and crossed the room. A quick bath was all she had time for, with

Treville waiting. At least Treville wasn't the stickler for punctuality that the Cardinal was. "I like to dream sometimes, of a life free from responsibility. Can you imagine how splendid it would be to have nothing to do all day?"

The bathroom door slid shut between them, and if her husband replied to her tactless remark, she did not hear a word of what he said.

Lalla-Louise wore formal silks and a wrapped star-scarf over her sleek black hair when she greeted Amiral Treville in the breakfast room, less than an hour later. She preferred modesty when discussing the Musketeers for exactly the same reason that she chose scandalous outfits for discussing Church business with the Cardinal – it was best to keep them all on their toes.

Theirs was a fractured and fragile ecosystem. If either Amiral Treville or Cardinal Richelieu believed for a moment that the other had lost credibility with her, it would go to their heads and might well translate to political instability. Lalla-Louise Renard Royal had been taught by experts since the age of five: she was a sleek weapon of the diplomatic arts.

"My dear Jeanne," she said as the fearsome commander of the Musketeers stomped into the breakfast room in full uniform. "What a week you've been having! Sit down, please. I'd hate you to overdo it."

"My job requires a steady state of overdoing everything," Treville grunted, and then gave Lalla-Louise a wary look. "As does yours, of course, your Majesty."

"Indeed," said Lalla-Louise with a very small smile

upon her lips. Her maids bustled around them in starched-perfect uniforms, presenting steaming cups of chocolate with cream and pastries.

Lalla-Louise knew for a fact that Treville detested sweets, but was always too polite to say otherwise. It made these breakfasts so much more entertaining. "My dear," she said as she inhaled the fragrant spices from her cup. "What are we going to do about your broken Musketeers?"

Treville gave her a flinty look across the delicate breakfast table. "Who said anyone was broken, your Royal Highness? My gals are as robust as they ever were."

"Ah yes," said Lalla-Louise with a secret smile that suggested that wasn't the ringing endorsement that Treville might have hoped. "But the current calamity is beyond the pale, you must agree. I spent simply hours placating the Cardinal last night. The poor darling has made herself quite ill with the strain."

Treville's expression did not alter. "I had no idea that her Eminence was so frail. Perhaps she needs an ocean holiday to blow the cobwebs away."

That was going too far. Lalla-Louise frowned. Witty side-stepping of the issues was expected at a meeting such as this one, but she was only prepared to allow a certain amount of wilful ignorance. "I don't think her Eminence is the one falling down in her duty, Amiral. How does it reflect on me to have the Royal Fleet brawling in church-yards and bars?"

Treville leaned in, giving up all pretence at drinking her chocolate. "How am I to do my job when the Sabres and Hammers are allowed to run rampant across Paris

Satellite and beyond, claiming rights of jurisdiction where none exist, and picking fights with my pilots?"

"If the Musketeers and not the Sabres had won the war against the Sun-kissed, the Cardinal would not feel so entitled!" Lalla-Louise bit into a lemon-dusted croissant the size of a peach, allowing the powder to explode prettily across the tablecloth. "This nuisance behaviour helps no one."

"I quite agree, your Royal Highness," said Treville. She reached for what appeared to be the only unsweetened pastry on the plate, and chewed vigorously on it until she reached the gooey centre of plum jam and almond *crème*. After an almost imperceptible pause, she kept chewing as if the pastry had not horribly betrayed her.

Lalla-Louise licked lemon sugar off her lips and fingertips. "Tell me about the girl. The one who was taken into custody along with your gallant troublemakers."

Amiral Treville blinked. She did not look suspicious, but Lalla-Louise knew that it was best to proceed as if Treville was thinking the worst of her at all times. "Dana D'Artagnan. Daughter of one of my best pilots from your mother's reign."

"A new recruit?"

"Hardly," Treville scoffed, then realised that Lalla-Louise was not joking. "No, your Royal Highness. Not possible with our recent budget cuts. I'd have liked to offer her something. The kid has guts, and a good flying record."

"Perhaps her Eminence could use a new Sabre…" Lalla-Louise teased, knowing that this was a sore spot with Treville; the Cardinal's pilots had not been subject to the same degree of financial restraints. Then again, the

Cardinal largely funded the Sabres herself, thanks to the ample finances of the Church of All. It was hardly the Crown's fault.

"I am on your side, your Royal Highness," Amiral Treville said sharply, out of nowhere. "You remember this, don't you? My Musketeers serve the Regence first in all things."

"Are you suggesting that the Cardinal and her Sabres are not equally loyal?" Lalla-Louise countered. She met Treville's angry eyes and sighed. "Oh, my dear. You know how it is. The balance of power is a tricky thing, and we owe the Cardinal so much."

"You don't owe her your throne," Treville snapped. After a far too long pause, she added, "Your Majesty." The rebuke still stung.

"As I said in the beginning," Lalla-Louise said, dropping the game. "Let us see what can be done. Captains-lieutenant Athos, Aramis and Porthos have been released from the Cardinal's custody and returned to their quarters. No charges are to be laid this time, given the faults on both sides of the – ruckus."

Amiral Treville's eyebrows rose almost completely up into her closely-shaven scalp. She had come prepared for a greater fight than this. "I received no word of their release."

"The matter was handled about thirty seconds after you entered this room," said Lalla-Louise. "Keeping them overnight has been enough to assuage her Eminence's outrage… for now."

"I understand."

"But let us speak of the young Gascon. I believe she felled five Red Hammers in the fight at the Abbey."

"Five and a half, according to my reports," said Treville.

"That suggests that she is very loyal indeed," said Lalla-Louise. "She had only just met these Musketeers, and yet was prepared to fight against impossible odds to defend their honour. I like that."

Treville's mouth twitched as if she had almost thought about smiling. "I like her too," she admitted. "A year ago, I'd have put her in the blue and white already."

"Is it true she fought Major Jussac to a standstill, and wounded her in the arm?"

"After the Cardinal's favourite knocked Athos unconscious with a wine bottle," Treville confirmed.

Lalla-Louise sighed. She would rather have liked to see that. She had been at school with Claudine Jussac, and found her a most irritating creature. "Time to put security cameras inside the bars, Amiral."

"As you say, your Majesty."

From the look of her face, Treville thought she had won. But Lalla-Louise had a card she had not yet played. "I would like to meet these Musketeers, Amiral. Also, their new friend. Arrange it."

Groundfall had never agreed with Dana. Even the joy of being allowed to ride in Porthos' beautiful musket-class dart, the *Hoyden*, was not enough to compensate for Dana's alarm at descending towards the moon.

Paris Satellite had been in her head for years, and Dana had not once thought about how near that would bring her to Luna Palais, the Royal Moon of Honour.

The *Hoyden* was several generations newer than Dana's old *Buttercup*, but that didn't make it new. The midnight blue paint job was less than pristine, and there were several meteor dents along the outer frame. Like all Musketeer ships, there was an elaborate and artistic tattoo splashed over the tail-fin – most of these were mono-chrome, but the *Hoyden's* tail was decorated with a multi-coloured mural of a spiral galaxy.

Inside, the surfaces were gleaming and bright, better tended than any ship Dana had seen before. She was reminded of the heavily studded belt that Porthos had been showing off when they first collided with each other. Was it professional pride or personal vanity that led her to keep her ship in such good condition? It was quite a contrast to the scratched and battered interior of Athos' dart, the positively antique *Parry-Riposte*.

"Here we go, pet." Porthos leaned over her controls with a fierce grin, guiding the dart down towards the moon as if it was nothing to her. The helm covered her shaven head neatly, with cables webbing out in all directions.

Dana longed to drag the helm off Porthos and take the ship for herself. Being a passenger made her heart beat too fast.

As they fell into the final descent and the landing gear flicked out, Dana felt the moon's gravity kick her hard in the spine. She knew it was mostly in her head – the actual gravity of the moon was going to have far less wear and tear on her body than the grav on any given space station.

And yet, this was dirtside. Dana could count on the fingers of one hand how often she had set foot on a moon or planet. There was a wrongness about solid ground that she could never get over.

Put me back in space where I belong.

Porthos let her breath out in a long, satisfied hiss as she completed the docking procedure, and the dart finally stilled. She plucked the various cables out of her head with a swish, and removed the helm. "Don't worry, peanut. Once we're under the dome, the air will be as fake as anything else you're used to breathing."

Dana scowled. "I'm fine."

"You can let go of the seat now," the older pilot smirked. "Don't fret yourself. It's only the Regence. She's a doll. Most of the time."

"Only the Regence!" Dana was wearing her best flight suit, but she felt shabby for such fancy company. "Do you think she's going to arrest us?"

"It's hard to tell with her Maj." Porthos shrugged, stretching her arms and legs as she eased out of her own seat. "She pretends she doesn't approve of our bad behaviour, but secretly she's all over it. She'd be duelling herself if the protectors would let her out more often. Still, she's unpredictable. It depends on who has annoyed her more, recently: Treville, or the Cardinal."

"Wonderful," Dana groaned.

Lalla-Louise had been working all morning, appointment after meeting after public appearance, and she was worn thin. When she retired to her rooms for a late lunch, she did not eat a bite, but instead stretched out on the large, perfumed bed, emptied an ampoule of nexus under her tongue, and plugged The Hunt directly into the port in the back of her neck.

The forest of Valour embraced her, dark and delicious, and she ran so fast she nearly flew. She could smell her prey nearby, a blend of fear and alien pheromones. Her bow flew into her hand as she tracked him, step by step, scent by scent.

Nothing could compare to this. Not her beautiful husband with his silk suits and muscles, not the thrill of politics, not food, not sex.

There was only this.

An hour later, the alarm wrenched her out of the game, sweating and shuddering at the return to reality. She used to let a servant awake her, but her reflexes were too violent when she was fresh from the Hunt, and it was so inconvenient to wash blood from her knuckles before going to her afternoon meetings.

She had not eaten, but that hardly signified.

If Lalla-Louise had only been able to stay inside another fifteen minutes, she was sure she would have destroyed the beast once and for all. It was infuriating.

On the other hand, she had already been running late for her appointment with Amiral Treville and the Musketeers when she first went under, so she wouldn't be the only one who was frustrated.

Lalla-Louise rose and tidied her hair away again, beneath the rich blue star-scarf. Walking at an unhurried pace, she made her way along the long balcony that led to the Crown Gallery.

She could hear a slash and twang of metal against metal, and halted at the very edge of the balcony so she could observe without being seen.

They had given up on her. Other subjects might have stood to attention even into the second hour, but Treville and the Musketeers had a touch of irreverence about them, and this was not the first time their Regence had kept them waiting.

Athos and the others had dumped their formal jackets on the polished floor, and were giving their new friend a sword lesson.

Dana D'Artagnan, if this was she, was a lithe young woman with deep brown skin and a pilot's buzz cut. She concentrated, frowning as Porthos demonstrated a move on Aramis. Athos leaned in and corrected Dana's grip on the pilot's slice, and then her stance.

Treville, watching them from the sidelines, glanced up and saw the Regence. Lalla-Louise pressed a silencing finger against her own lips, and Treville nodded reluctantly.

The sword lesson continued. The three of them made surprisingly good tutors, and the young newcomer had grit. Every mistake only made her more determined to work harder.

Lalla-Louise had never understood what it was that drove people to be pilots. The thought of flying through the cold of space, bound to your ship with implants and cables, had nothing like the appeal of taking game drugs in her own bedchamber.

But this – the clash of metal on metal, the elegance of duelling your way past another person with a sword. The Regence understood why her pilots never stopped fighting each other.

She cleared her throat to alert them to her presence, and descended the stairs. By the time she reached the polished floor below, they had all scuttled back into their formal jackets, and were standing at attention with the blades nowhere in sight.

"Your Royal Majesty," said Treville, clearing her own throat. "May I introduce you to…"

Lalla-Louise was already standing in front of the new recruit. "D'Artagnan," she said in her most musical, seductive voice. "I'm always glad to meet young people who are eager to serve the Crown."

D'Artagnan met her gaze with a wary deference that Lalla-Louise was used to seeing in the faces of her subjects. "Your Royal Majesty," she said. "There is nothing I want more."

"Good." Lalla-Louise smiled, and clapped her hands. "Commandant Essart, I think, is looking for new blood in the mecha squad. It will be an excellent training ground for you. And perhaps one day…"

She let the words trail off, pretending not to enjoy the look of crushing disappointment on D'Artagnan's face. The child needed to learn that dreams did not simply fall into your lap.

"Perhaps one day, the Musketeers," the Regence said finally. "But not yet."

CHAPTER 8
THE NESTING HABITS OF MUSKETEERS

t is a truth universally acknowledged that anyone with piloting experience can easily get to grips with a mecha suit within a few hours.

Dana was pretty sure that anyone who made that claim was full of enough shit to fill the mecha suit in question.

This was her life now. She was a Pigeon.

Not just any Pigeon. She was the newest recruit of Commandant Essart's Elite Mecha Squad, charged with protecting and serving the inhabitants of the Luna Palais and surrounding city, within a giant plexiglass dome on the moon.

Dirtside guard duty.

She pretty much wanted to kill herself.

"Stop complaining," said Aramis, who had (along with Athos and Porthos) sacrificed a rec shift to come and laugh at Dana's attempts to put her new mecha suit through its paces in the Mecha Training Centre, in the outer city of Luna Palais. "At least it's a job."

"This is not flying," Dana said between gritted teeth. "This is the very opposite of flying."

She had worked in a mecha suit when she was fifteen, and saving every penny for flight hours. That had been quite fun. But that was space-going mecha, for a few hours at a time, performing basic repair work in zero-g on the outside of Gascon Station.

This was hell – she could barely walk, she couldn't wrap her brain around what all the buttons were for, and once she got the hang of it, her main duties were going to be breaking up duels and drunken brawls between civilians and pilots on leave. Oh, with a side order of providing an extra layer of wall between the disgruntled masses and the royal family in the event of assassination attempts.

It was not flying.

"It's a start," said Porthos, who had brought a laden picnic basket for them all to share while they amused themselves at Dana's expense. "Not every baby pilot gets a private audience with the Regence before being rewarded with a plum position."

"Guarding her Majesty's moon is an honour," agreed Athos, who had found the bottle of wine in the basket and wasn't sharing it with anyone. "You impressed her."

"If you've all quite finished making fun of me," Dana snarled. "I only have the rest of this shift to master the controls before I go on duty. If you want to make sure I don't accidentally set fire to Luna Palais or your precious Regence, a little help here, please?"

The mecha was a lot like flying a dart. It was plugged into her synapses, the helm of the metal body connected intimately to her brain. But while it was second nature to Dana to be 'at one' with her ship, gliding effortlessly through the depths of space for days and weeks at a time, it was remarkably difficult to deal with limbs. These large, throbbing metal appendages stuck out from her giant tin can of a mecha suit, and had a tendency to lash out in any direction if Dana let a stray thought distract her.

She knew how to do this. The theory was the same as flying a ship. And yet… ships didn't have arms.

"I can't," she moaned. The mecha lowered its pigeon-grey head, and the large metal shoulders slumped. "It's not too late to volunteer for a civilian transfer."

Athos leaned towards her, rapping lightly on the visor of the mecha. "Kid," he said in a stern voice. "That's not how this works. The Regence likes you. She gave you this job as a dainty treat – as a reward for nearly stabbing Captain Jussac to death which I have to say is a box I have ticked at least three times in my life and never once been rewarded for… what was I saying?"

Aramis reached out and took the neck of the wine bottle off Athos. "He's saying, Dana darling, that you can't turn down her Majesty's reward. It's rare enough to be a favourite of hers. Believe us, you don't want to make your-self her enemy. There wouldn't be anything left of you but a pile of skin and sequins."

"I always wondered what it would be like to pilot a mecha," Porthos said thoughtfully, peering up at Dana. "Isn't it even a little bit awesome?"

Dana flexed her fingers, and one of her power arms shot a sudden burst of flame at the surface of the training room, making all three Musketeers jump nearly out of their skins. The floor melted into a pile of slag, then patiently began to rebuild itself. "I suppose there are compensations," Dana admitted.

Whenever she lay down to try to sleep in the tiny bunk allotted to her in the Squad barracks, Dana found herself thinking of the Regence, and the look on her face as she presented Dana with her 'reward'.

"And perhaps, someday, the Musketeers," she had purred.

The Regence was the most beautiful woman that Dana had ever seen. She was a sylph of a creature, all soft lines like a watercolour sketch of a weeping willow. Her lips had been painted gold to match her clinging gown and elaborate hair brooches.

Dana had previously considered Aramis to be the pinnacle of feminine grace and beauty, but Lalla-Louise Renard Royal, Regence of the Solar System, left Aramis in her perfumed dust.

Perhaps, someday, the Musketeers.

Hope could keep you going longer than anything else. Hope would have made this whole Mecha Pigeon nightmare almost tolerable, if it wasn't for the fact that Dana could not sleep on the moon. She did not understand how anyone could.

Dear Maman,

It could be worse. I think if you say something often enough, you come to believe it. I didn't come to Paris to waddle around inside a robot body, but as the weeks have passed… well, I'm almost glad of this strange reward that the Regence bestowed upon me.

After all, we had been caught duelling (the fisticuffs kind, as Athos would say, not the fuck-your-brain-up kind), and I might well have been turfed into a cell for a month or two, or given my marching orders from this sector of space.

Yes, I'm billeted on Luna Palais on a permanent basis, and if I think too hard about that word 'permanent,' I would scream at the walls. Dirtside is not where I want to be. But there is work for Pigeons up on Paris Satellite, and once the first probationary month passed, I started getting as many shifts Up There as Down Here.

Things that are good about living on the moon:

1. Leaving the moon on a regular basis.

2. Attending Zero-G TeamJoust matches at the Andromeda Bowl, especially with Porthos, who knows more about the game than any sane human being should, and has colour coded wigs to match the three different teams that she supports depending on which stream you're following… you know what, I'm not even going to try to explain.

3. Earning credit, which means I can pay for my own meals instead of sponging off my friends – and they can sponge off me when they're out of pocket (which seems to happen a lot, it's amazing how easy it is to spend money on having a good time in Paris).

4. Commandant Essart is way less scary than Amiral Treville, and even cracks a joke sometimes.

5. It's not forever.

I don't love my mecha suit the way I'm supposed to. It's nothing like the relationship I've formed with even the most basic of practice ships. But it's getting better. I didn't accidentally set fire to anyone this week, which reduces the risk that I might do so to the Regence or the Prince Consort.

After my second month in the Mecha Squad, I was able to

request shifts flying shuttles back and forth between Luna Palais and Paris Satellite to transport equipment and some of my fellow Pigeons. The shuttles are bulky and ugly just like the mecha suits, and I always want to throw up when I make moonfall, but flying a ship is better than anything else. Always and forever.

It's not planetside, at least. The shifting green-brown, gold and blue orb that is the over-heated planet Honour looks pretty from up here, but I'm happy to keep my distance from the wretched place. Bad enough that I'm supposed to sleep on the moon. It's been months and I'm pretty sure that I'm not going to adapt.

I used to manage an hour or two in barracks, when I was exhausted, but it wasn't enough, and I was starting to worry it might get me seriously hurt, or worse. I don't know if it was my stupid brain or my stupider body or some gravity shit that I was never going to figure out, but sleeping on the moon was just impossible.

Aramis noticed it first. "You look like shit," she told me when we met for a drink not long after my first shuttle job to Paris. "Have another drink," she added.

At that point, I was facing a black spiral inside my own head. "I don't think I can," I told her. Drink wasn't going to help. Nothing helped.

"Sleep, then," she urged me.

"If only."

Then – I think I collapsed in the corner of the booth in the Abbey of St Germain sometime later. Athos and Porthos had joined us by the time I woke up – the three of them ordered wine on my credit stud for hours, the bastards!

After that, one or other of them always insisted I crash in their Paris digs when my shift ended. And after Porthos had a word with one of her boyfriends who apparently works in Sched-

*uling and Admin (sooo convenient I can't even tell you),
suddenly I get all these double shifts which happen to end on
Paris Satellite instead of Luna Palais.*

*I have friends, crash space, and my credit is increasing at a
slow but positive crawl. Life could be worse.*

*Thanks for not telling Papa about the Buttercup – and for
being so understanding. I hated not telling you both from the
start, but I most of all didn't want to hurt his feelings. I know
you're steel-coated, like me. D'Artagnan women can handle
anything.*

Love, Dana.

Dear Maman,

*What, really? You want to know more about these Muske-
teers I'm hanging out with? I thought I talked about them too
much already!*

*Let's start with Athos, the one I know least about. Aramis
says he has a tragic past, but she never provided details – all
three of them are loyal to the point of sheer stupidity, so that
doesn't surprise me.*

*Athos lives in two rooms beside a grimy bar on 4th Level, the
only drinking hole in Paris that he refuses to patronise. I think
that means it's pretty bad.*

*He shares digs with his engie, Grimaud, who is much older
than I expected, and the perfect roommate because she's
constantly plugged into headphones, and never talks.*

*"She doesn't laugh at my jokes," Athos said the first time I
unfurled my trusty bedroll on his floor. "She also doesn't chatter
through my hangovers, or suggest I call my mother more than*

once a year. Love you, Grimaud!" he yelled in the direction of the tiny kitchenette.

She gave him the finger, which I took to mean she loves him too, but won't put up with his bullshit.

Grimaud wears a star-scarf all the time, but I don't think she's especially religious – I suspect the scarf is there for the same reason as the headphones – blocking out the universe. Or maybe blocking out Athos.

"The Sabres keep trying to steal her," Athos told me once. "Best engie in Paris. But she likes my ship too much to let me go. There's no artistry involved in keeping a fucking Sabre in the sky: they replace each part the second it fails."

Grimaud's children are convinced that Athos is secretly married to their mother, and they always send him brandy at New Year. I suggested this might be an elaborate assassination plot on their part, as everyone knows Athos is the Musketeer most likely to drink himself to death. There may be a formal betting pool on that one. Athos rejected the idea on the grounds that it wasn't especially good brandy. I'm not convinced...

Apart from his cheap habits, his silent engie, his perverse sense of humour and his formerly ridiculous beard, Athos the New Aristocrat remains a mystery. I've learned not to try to match him drink for drink, not to talk to him at all when he gets a certain maudlin look on his face, and never to tease him about lovers, not even when Porthos does (she teases everyone about everything, and gets away with it somehow).

He doesn't have friends apart from Aramis and Porthos and now me. The others have wider social circles, but I think sometimes Athos would prefer to have no one at all.

He has, however, been teaching me to use a pilot's slice for recreational fencing, which is not the same AT ALL as illegal duelling, so don't freak out. I'm getting good.

Porthos, or Pol to her other friends, is the polar opposite to Athos. She has a large apartment somewhere over in Gilles Section — was it as trendy in your time as it is now? Popular civilian sector, all fashion emporiums and cafes. Her rooms are lush, and she never stints when it comes to food, drink or treating her friends. I have no idea where the money comes from.

She has at least four casual boyfriends that I know of, and I'm not entirely sure if any of them knows about each other. I can't bring myself to ask.

Porthos rooms with her engie, Bonnie — it's still traditional for pilots to provide board for engineers because accommodation up here is bloody expensive, and engies get paid so much less than pilots. That goes double for the Musketeers. Can you have double of less?

Bonnie is a dab hand at cooking as well as patching up spaceships, and she has Porthos' rooms smelling and looking like heaven. She's happy to do all the cooking and cleaning as long as she has the freedom to dip in and out of the treasure trove that is the Wardrobe of Porthos. Apparently if you're a lady of short stature and large bosom, regular access to designer outfits that fit you is more useful than actual currency.

Whenever I crash with Porthos, it's on a comfortable sofa bed with the promise of croissants in the morning. The only reason I don't do it more often is because Bonnie disapproves of me. Not sure if it's personal or if she feels I make the place untidy.

Still, when picking which of my friends to stay with, it's hard not to lean towards the option that means warm cinnamon milk at bedtime, and a pillow that feels like a marshmallow dream made by silkworms.

Finally, Aramis. I'm still figuring Aramis out. When we're out in public she's all about wine, women and general debauch-

ery, but at home she's a lot more quiet, introspective and — yeah, religious.

Her rooms are stark apart from a collection of antique theology texts, a brilliant selection of herbal teas, and virtual windows dedicated to the weirdly green and storybook-pleasant country scenery of the planet Valour.

The main view in her salon is a rolling hillside with an old-style Church of All.

"I like to be able to see the church from my home town," she said once. "Someday I'll have one of my own." She really does seem to believe that she'll do it one day — leave the Musketeers to join the Church. Why would anyone want to be anything but a Musketeer?

The weirdest thing about Aramis' rooms is Bazin. He's a church android that she picked up in payment for a gambling debt, and reprogrammed with engie functions. His original program remains, and serving a human who isn't part of the priesthood is a constant cause of distress to him.

Which makes him the most passive aggressive android I've ever met. He delays all but the most necessary functions, except those involving religious activity, and he pointedly hates all of Aramis' friends, especially those who stay over. I always half expect to find that I've been neatly moved out into the corridor during my sleep, bedroll and all.

Aramis writes, all the time. Letters and articles on theology or the state of the soul, which she gets published in journals. Some of the letters are private, ongoing debates with other theorists. Some of them are elaborate flirtations, others are foundations of future essays. If she could only give up her habit of seducing unavailable women, she would do fine in the Church.

But there's that pesky morality contract thing, you know.

"I am moral," Aramis insists, when challenged on this point.

"Who am I to seduce if not women who are attached elsewhere? If I sleep with someone who has expectations of a future with me, I'd be bound to disappoint them when I leave Paris to become a priest."

She suggested once that if/when she leaves the Fleet, I could have her spot. We were worse for wine at the time, and I confessed that I didn't want to be a Musketeer without her. We hugged and there might have been a few tears. Athos and Porthos laughed at us.

(Yes, in case it wasn't obvious, I have a slight crush on her, it's fine, I'll get over it)

I've never had a group of friends like this before. I understand now, what you used to say about being a Musketeer and the friends you had at your back. I have this, and it's good.

I wouldn't sacrifice any of them to reach my dream, not one.

(Perhaps, someday, the Regence suggested to me. A tease, not a promise.) It's easier to return to the dull grind of Mecha Squad Essart, knowing that I have friends like these waiting for me when my shift is done.

Love, Dana in Paris

CHAPTER 9
MADAME SU'S BED AND BOARD

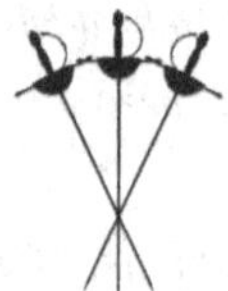

Two months after her arrival on Paris Satellite, Dana could finally acquit herself with a minimum of embarrassment when it came to her duties for Mecha Squad Essart. She almost never blew things up unintentionally. She had made a few mates here and there, amiable chaps you could chat to while you checked your gear and ran through safety drills, or shared a long shift of guard duty in the dodgier areas of the Luna Palais dome.

Home was still Paris Satellite, and despite Porthos, Aramis and Athos' mostly successful attempts to draw her into their gambling-drinking-screwing-around habits, Dana had managed her credit well enough to afford digs of her own.

It would be nice to have a berth where she could sleep without worrying that she was getting in the way of Grimaud or Bonnie, or risking the state of Bazin's soul. Not to mention that she preferred not to wear out her welcome with her friends.

Quite by accident, while searching for somewhere to live, Dana also found herself an engie.

After flooding her brain with unnecessary ads for luxury accommodation she could never afford, Dana's info stud finally locked in the filters she needed. Unfortunately, all the other temporary vagrants on Paris Satellite were better at this than she was. Every time she made her way to an address she thought she could afford, it was only to discover that someone else had got there first.

At least Dana was learning her way around – or so she thought until she set out to locate a boarding suite on level thirty-eight, only to find herself in a small warehouse full of machinery for hire – games devices, clothes printers, art tablets and transporter cubes. Everything looked second hand and well maintained but it still wasn't what she was looking for.

"Damn," she said aloud.

A teenager with pigtails slid out from under a small air skimmer. "Hello!" she said cheerily. "Can I help you?"

"I'm in the wrong place," Dana said, consulting the map in her stud. "Or this is glitching again."

"That depends on what you're looking for." The girl, who had improbably red hair, light skin and freckles, leaped to her feet and wiped oil on to her coverall.

"This isn't Madame Su's Bed and Board, is it?" Dana asked. Tiredness washed over her. This was almost enough for her to give up and return to the rent-free bunk waiting for her on the moon. Almost, but not quite. She'd still never managed to sleep through the night Down There.

"Of course it is," said the girl with a cheery smile. "Madame Su is out looking for her husband. I'm her assistant." She stuck out a hand that was still slightly oily.

"I'm Planchet. Hey, you're not a Pigeon, are you?" Her eyes lit up at the realisation that Dana wore the Royal Grey uniform. "Do you have a mecha? That's beyond extreme. Do you need an engie? I qualified all my certs last year, but I can't get a spot."

"We're not the Musketeers," Dana said, as if she needed a further reminder. "We don't hire our own engies."

"Oh," said Planchet, her face falling. "I knew that. I applied to the Pigeon pit crew last year, but they want more experience. It's hard to get experience on mecha up here, you know."

"Yes, I can imagine." Dana looked around the messy warehouse. "You said this is a boarding house?"

"Not a house exactly," said Planchet. "There's a spare room over the workshop, though, and Madame Su doesn't charge much." She looked a little embarrassed. "I work my board. But that won't be necessary for you. You have a real job!"

"You'd think," Dana muttered. Her credit was only creeping very slowly into the black. While she had gained many benefits from her friendship with the Musketeers, she found their excessive socialising quite expensive to keep up with.

This did not look like a place that would charge through the roof, but the workshop noise might cancel out any orbital benefit to her sleep patterns.

"I suppose you can tell Madame Su I was here," she started to say doubtfully, when the landlady herself appeared.

Madame Su was a stocky woman, perhaps fifty years old, with shiny black hair entirely lacking in grey. She wore a fashionable suit of orange silk and eye-blindingly green embroidery, and had several pearl studs running up both arms from wrist to elbow.

"Planchet, it's worse than I thought!" she declared, then stopped and looked Dana over. "Can I help you, pilot?"

Pilot, Dana thought, warming to the woman straight away. "I was hoping to see the room?"

Madame Su sniffed at her. "Got many things? What's your job? You'd better have pay coming in regularly or I'm not going to let you in at all. Valuable stuff here, you know."

Dana touched the collar of her grey uniform. Did the woman think this was a fashion statement? "I work for Mecha Squad Essart. Royal guard and ferry duty, out of Luna Palais. I need a berth here in the city for occasional shift sleeping. But I'll pay full rent, of course…" She stopped.

It was when she said, 'Royal guard,' she decided later, that Madame Su's face had taken on that odd, stricken expression. After that… well, Dana had barely managed to inspect the clean but bare room above the workshop before she had a clamshell tablet shoved into her hand with a contract ready to sign, and a rent that was suspiciously low.

There was a catch. There had to be a catch. But Dana could not afford *not* to take advantage of whatever it was made the old lady so very anxious.

Now all she had to do was buy a bed, a pillow and a food printer, and wait to discover why Madame Su was so keen on having a Royal guard living above her warehouse.

It took three days, which suggested the landlady was in less trouble than Dana had imagined, or else was so suspicious and paranoid that it took her that long to build up her courage.

In any case, three days after Dana took on the little room above the warehouse, her landlady decided to call in the favour for the exceedingly cheap rent. Madame Su invited her new tenant to take tea with her in her own sitting room, featuring the same combination of lavish fabrics and gaudy fashions as her own clothes.

Today's suit was pink and striped, with a pattern of lilies on the lining of her sleeves and hems. It clashed with the orange and red Space Deco wallprint.

"Madame Su," said Dana over a cup of rather weak green tea. "Are you in trouble?"

At this, her landlady burst into messy and noisy tears.

Horrified, Dana stared at her cup, wishing she had invited Aramis along. Aramis had a soothing voice and the ability to pat people comfortingly on the shoulder in just the right way. In fact, Aramis was less than ten minutes away if she took the express walkways and the turbo shuttle, and Dana was overwhelmed by the compulsion to call her instantly and claim an emergency. Even Porthos would be more use right now than Dana herself.

Dana did not know how to be comforting. She could barely manage polite, most days.

"It's my husband," Madame Su howled. "My darling little Conrad."

"Is he dead?" was the first thing that Dana thought to say, and this led to more noisy tears, then some horrific snorting. "Sorry. Not dead. Is he –" All the things she could think of to suggest were … perhaps not things that should be said out loud. She took a deep breath, instead. *What would Aramis say?* "What's wrong?" she tried, and patted Madame Su's hand awkwardly.

"That woman," said Madame Su, hiccupping now. "That awful woman has him."

Wonderful. And now it was down to Dana to dispense advice on how to be dumped? She sent a silent curse in the direction of Conrad Su, wherever he was. "Maybe you're better off without him?" she tried.

Madame Su's back straightened, and she gave Dana a murderous look. "How can you say that? How does that help me? He might be *dead*. Or worse."

Dana found herself surreptitiously glancing around the room to see if there was any booze on display. Anything would do. Her friendship with Athos, Porthos and Aramis had taught her that cheap wine had as much to offer a thirsty pilot as the fancy stuff.

"I knew that spoiled Palace brat would be the death of him," Madame Su muttered. "Prince my freckled arse. Never let your husband play sports, it all ends in tears and treachery."

"Can we start at the beginning?" Dana asked. The sooner her landlady explained what was going on, the sooner she could get to that lovely bed that had cost her the last of her financial buffer.

Tomorrow's dinner would take her into the red, unless she could scab dinner off one of her friends, but that was tomorrow's problem.

Madame Su gave a hoarse, raspy breath. "You have a kind, sympathetic face, D'Artagnan."

No I don't. Get on with it.

"My husband Conrad works at the Palace down on Luna Palais. He's a tailor. Quite the best of tailors."

Dana resisted the urge to ask if Conrad made Madame Su's suits. They were something else.

"He works for that selfish Prince Consort," said the landlady, her face twisting up as bitterness came through in her words. "That's why he married me, of course, you're not allowed to work at the Palace without a marriage or priesthood contract to prove your morality." She sniffed at Dana. "Different for guards and pilots; they prefer you not to be hampered with spouses and families. I sponsored Conrad through his final years of apprentice-ship," she added, with a spark of something like pride. "Three years I've put into him, and now I'm finally recouping on my investment, though they don't pay him nearly what he's worth, it's tantamount to slavery, and look at him now, not appreciating what he has, not thinking about me for a second. Intriguing with his master and that Chevreuse bitch. Whispering in corridors. Getting into trouble. He's going to ruin everything for us!"

Dana was utterly lost in this sea of accusations and panic. "What kind of trouble?" she tried.

"He's been abducted," Madame Su announced conspir-atorially, after first glancing around to check no one was listening at the door. "I knew he would come to no good, but I hoped for more than twelve months of Palace pay checks before it all came crashing down!"

Dana was starting to feel sorry for darling little Conrad. "Abducted by a woman?" she ventured.

"Not for lust," Madame Su hissed. "He would never do that, he's a good boy, he knows better than to break a contract with me, another seven years and he'll be free of all obligation."

Dana wondered if she would be able to cope with ten years married to a Madame Su in exchange for her dream job. Conrad was made of stern stuff. "Who abducted him, and why?"

Madame Su patted her hand. "I knew when I saw you, that you'd be useful to have around the place," she said happily. "You're tough, everyone says so. D'Artagnan can look after herself. You did agree to help me out around the place when anything came up suited to your skillset," she added.

Yes, Dana had been well aware of that clause, and had signed the rental contract anyway, because a year of good sleep for a fraction of her pay seemed like a good deal whatever the hidden costs turned out to be.

Hello, hidden costs.

"Are you saying you want me to find your husband?" she asked finally.

"Yes, before he makes everything worse."

"Worse than being abducted?"

"He knows secrets!" Madame Su said, too loudly, then shushed herself. "Palace secrets. He's been there among them, and I think he knows too much about..." and there she pressed her lips together.

"You have to tell me everything, or I really can't help you," Dana groaned.

"Someone has eyes for someone else," Madame Su said, barely above a whisper now. "At the very highest level. Where a broken marriage contract could – be very damaging. You understand?"

Oh, Dana did not want to know about this. Adventure,

yes, intrigue, all very well. But marital scandals in the Palace? No, thank you.

"The Prince was approached recently," Madame Su said, confirming Dana's worst fears. "By someone digging for dirt on his marriage. My Conrad swears the Prince is innocent, but there must be something in it, mustn't there, or he'd just tell the Regence that the Cardinal's out to get him."

All this and the Cardinal too. Dana groaned inwardly. She had thus far managed to avoid the attention of the powerful leader of the Church of All.

"If her Eminence can prove the wrongdoing of one, then she could take the solar system from the other," Madame Su whispered loudly. "Her Majesty, may sunlight fall upon her moon, came to power on that speech, that wonderful speech."

On the Sanctity of Contracts: the speech that was heard across the solar system. Lalla-Louise Renard Royal had stepped across the fallen reputations of her older brothers to take the throne on the promise that the moral centre of the planetary alliance could be found in the royal family, as well as the Church of All.

The Church's tenets had kept humanity together as a functioning society after colonising space]. Morality, faith and the sanctity of contracts were the prime fuel of space-dwelling humanity.

It was important enough to the Regence's reign that her government might well fracture under the weight of a broken marriage contract. If darling Conrad had evidence that his master was playing away from home, this was political dynamite.

"Go on," Dana said. Once she knew, she could never unknow it.

"It was that game started it all," Madame Su said angrily. "Last Joyeux, when the Duchess of Buckingham joined their team. It happened that night, whatever it is. I don't want to know!"

Dana frowned. "Buckingham, the Ambassador of Valour? I saw her on the newscast, cutting a ribbon on her tour of Honour."

"Humph. Buckingham," Madame Su said, smacking her cup down on the table and pouring more tea. "Conrad thinks there is a trap to lure her here, to catch her in a compromising position with the Prince Consort."

Dana was suspicious now. "But if they have been warned, what's the problem? The Prince can simply stay away from her."

"Last time I saw my darling Conrad, that was his plan," Madame Su agreed, though her voice suggested she was close to breaking down again. It wobbled. "But now he is missing, and no one at the Palace will speak to me of him. I questioned the others he works with, and they said he was last seen in the company of a terrible person, a woman who is not to be trusted."

Dana sighed. It sounded like something straight out of *Love and Asteroids*. "Well, that's a start. Do you know who she is?"

Madame Su took a deep breath and lifted her chin. There was something quite stately and dignified about her. "Her name is Rosnay Cho," she said firmly. "She works as a special agent of the Cardinal, though she has no proper rank in the Church and I am certain she is a wickedly sinful woman."

"They usually are," Dana said lightly. "What else do you know about her?"

"Long hair, though she claims to be a pilot half the time. And she has a scar." Madame Su drew the pattern across her face, and Dana felt herself holding a breath she scarcely remembered taking in.

"Does she fly a brand-new Moth fighter?" she asked.

Madame Su closed her eyes and nodded quickly. "I see her when I go to the auction houses and the promenade," she said. "Watching me. I've no way to get a secret message to the Prince Consort about Conrad, not without her catching me. Could you do it for me?"

Rosnay Cho. Dana couldn't believe it. That Moth pilot from Meung, the one called 'Ro' – it had to be her. Dana shivered, remembering the spaceships flying back and forth in the air between them during the Duel, and that burst of pain…

"I'm going to get a message to the Prince, and I'm sure he'll help find your Conrad and bring him home," she promised Madame Su, patting her hand as comfortingly as she could. She was getting better at that.

If Dana had learned one thing since she left home for Paris Satellite and the Musketeers, it was that Ro was her enemy. If she was the enemy of the Crown as well, then it was Dana's duty to get in her face and, with any luck, punch her in it.

Duty, in this case, would also be pleasure.

CHAPTER 10
THE WEIGHT OF THE SOLAR SYSTEM

Dana's head was full of turmoil as she left Madame Su. A royal scandal was the last thing she wanted to get mixed up in! But if this was a chance to get one over on Rosnay bloody Cho, it was worth the risk.

She wanted to ask the advice of Athos and the others. Surely they knew more about securing a royal audience than Dana did. But all three of them were flying border patrol today, and this wasn't the sort of conversation to have over comms.

No, Dana was going to have to handle this herself. It would make a good story when she joined her friends for supper later.

The best part about this affair was the ship. Madame Su had a decade-old scout venturer stored in the civilian dock, and was happy for Dana to fly it down to Luna Palais rather than cadging a lift on official transport. The thought of having a helm wrapped around her skull again was enough to make Dana sing and dance. She missed having her own ship so badly that it hurt.

If only she had hung on to poor old *Buttercup*.

Dana made her way through rows and rows of ships on E Dock, searching for the code that matched the keypass Madame Su had given her. It wasn't here – she was too far along, and would have to go back a block or two.

As she spun around, she saw a ship that she recognised.

No. It couldn't be that – there were plenty of Moth fighters, even those of the very latest generation. The fact that it looked exactly like the Moth that Dana had docked next to on Meung Station meant nothing.

Only…

The closer she got, the more she felt certain that it was the same ship.

Dana heard voices, and backed up into the shadow of a tricked out vintage Sabre with flames painted across its hull.

There was Rosnay Cho. The pilot with the long black hair stepped out from the Moth, speaking into a clamshell tablet that was the same colour as her rose-coloured flight suit. "Don't speak to me like that," she said furiously. "Of course he's fucking secure. You're the one playing mind games. Are the friends going to prevent our target getting to the moon or not?"

Dana heard another voice, low and male and melodic, coming out of the clamshell. "With friends like these… who needs enemies?"

"That's not an answer, Milord." Never had a formal title been spoken with such heavy sarcasm.

"You put your pieces in place, sweetness, and I'll worry about mine."

Rosnay snapped the clamshell closed, gave a short scream of frustration, and then strode away from her Moth, heading for the sphere-lifts. She made another call before she got there, this time through a comm stud in her wrist. "Foy. Check in with me in three hours on the Stellar Concourse. I don't fucking care what I said about your rec-hours. Right."

The sphere-lift hissed open and swallowed her up.

Dana breathed in and out. She had no idea what any of that meant. Milord. Was that the same Milord she had seen with Ro on Meung Station, the pretty man who looked too posh to be in a dive like that? They were in this together, whatever it was.

Her eyes turned back to the beautiful, gleaming Moth. Was Madame Su's abducted husband right here under her nose? Dana didn't dare try to break in. Who knew what kind of security layers were built into a ship like that?

Planchet might know a trick or two. The kid was handy with electronics.

First things first. Dana had promised Madame Su she would fly to Paris and get a message directly to the Prince Consort. She had time to check on the ship before she made a decision about the Moth. Dana tracked back along the dock until she found the right row for the Su scout venturer.

As she approached the right zone, Dana felt her senses prickle. She leaned casually into a recharging station as if checking the instructions, and glanced around. No one in sight. And yet…

She could see the Su scout, squat and greenish-grey on

its dock platform. There, caught in the glare of the flat lighting in this area, she saw two shadows beneath it that were shaped like people.

Not just people, by their stance. Red Hammers, perhaps? Or Ro's colleagues? There was a military feel about them.

The Su family had *someone's* attention.

Dana backed the hell up. She kept walking until she was at the sphere-lifts, and then let them suck her away from the civilian dock. She didn't breathe properly until she was back in one of the shopping plazas, surrounded by people.

How the hell could she get off Paris Satellite discreetly? She didn't have a ferry shift until tomorrow.

Her brand new comm stud, the one she had been issued along with her mecha when she signed the contract with Commandant Essart, chimed suddenly with an unfamiliar code. Dana stopped at the nearest set of privacy booths and slipped into a soundproof cubicle before accepting the call. "Hello?"

Planchet's face, all worry and freckles, appeared in the air before her. "Are you alone?"

"Yes, what's all this about?" Dana remembered the scout. "You have to tell Madame Su —"

"She's been arrested," said Planchet, looking like she was about to cry. "Four Red Hammers turned over her rooms. They took her away. I hid under the clothes printer, waiting for them to leave, but they didn't! I mean, two of them left with her, but the others are still there. I don't know what to do."

Dana thought with regret of her own room, which she couldn't reach without going through Madame Su's workshop. "Can you get out of there without them seeing you?"

"There's the heating ducts," Planchet considered. "D'you think they'll arrest me?"

"I don't know. Better not find out. Meet me —" Dana gave Planchet the address of the apartment Athos shared with his engie Grimaud. "Wait in the bar next door if no one's home. I'll be there as soon as I can." She hesitated. "Do you know how to bust the security of the latest generation of Moth fighter?"

"If I download the manual." Planchet sounded delighted at the challenge. "I'll do that before I leave."

"Only if you can do it silently!" Dana urged. "Don't take any risks."

She made her away across town, heading for the district where Athos lived, worrying all the way. She found Planchet happily ensconced at Grimaud's kitchen counter, eating a second helping of freshly printed pie.

"Thanks for looking after her," said Dana.

Grimaud took off her headphones. "You're looking for Conrad Su." It was the longest sentence Dana had ever heard her say.

Dana looked accusingly at Planchet, who shrugged with her mouth full. "She asked."

"Do you know Su?" Dana asked, still trying to recover from the fact that Grimaud was acknowledging her existence.

Grimaud rolled her eyes. "Number 18," she said. "Emerald Knights."

"That makes no sense at all." No, wait. The Emerald Knights. "Are we talking about Zero G TeamJoust?" Dana said finally.

Grimaud smiled with all her teeth. "The game we conquered space to play," she said in a tone that bordered on the religious.

It was near the end of the patrol shift, and Grimaud was due down on Crown Dock to meet Athos and the *Parry-Riposte*. Before she left, she set Dana and Planchet up with a recording of the most famous Zero G TeamJoust game of the previous year.

Thanks to Porthos, Dana had taken an interest in Team-Joust since her arrival on Paris Satellite. She knew who most of the fleur-de-lis teams were, at least.

Prince Alek of Auster played in the fleur-de-lis 0 League, which pushed up the Regence's popularity ratings something shocking. Alek was fit, fashionable and fancia-ble. Dana had seen a few clips of his games – even in the unflattering padded armour he was an unforgettable figure with brilliant emerald eyes and matching hair.

Right now, she took the time to observe his teammates. Conrad Su was not just the Prince's tailor but his jousting partner. Along with a feisty female pole-defence called Laurel Slaughter who had joined the team recently, they were the Emerald Knights, one of the most popular fleur-de-lis squads in Paris.

"Everyone knows about this game," said Planchet. "The final match of the season, last Joyeux. Chevreuse – their previous pole-defence – she sprained her ankle, and the Prince called in a celebrity sub at the last minute. Drove the audience wild, and the bookies too." She nodded at the screen.

The sub was tall and statuesque, with a wide white smile and reddish-brown skin that matched her long, frizz-curled hair. Even beneath the padding, you could see the muscle on her from shoulder to thigh.

"She'd never played 0 League before, not officially, but everyone knew who she was," said Planchet.

Dana watched the helmeted woman as she bounced back and forth in the air before the cams, a large pole tilted in one hand. "She's famous?" she hazarded.

"She's the Duchess of freaking Buckingham!" Planchet's mouth was full of the sandwich Grimaud had made for her before she left – apparently her freckled face cried out to be fed. "Georgiana Villiers. Buck to her friends and the media feeds. Ambassador of Valour." She nodded at the screen like a demented squirrel, still chewing. "Gossipnode exploded when it was announced. Buck's got 11 million followers, and they were fan-tracking the game like crazy."

"I don't know what most of those words mean," said Dana. "She's popular, then." The Duchess of Buckingham. Madame Su had claimed she was implicated in an affair with Prince Alek.

"Brilliant game," said Planchet, skipping to the highlight montage. "There's Conrad, Madame's husband. He lives at the Palace."

The Emerald Knights celebrated their win with the age-old sporting traditions of bro hugs, rude gestures and the slapping of butts. Su was stocky where Prince Alek was tall, but he had the same combination of silver scales over golden skin that marked him as a native of Auster. His hair was bright blue, contrasting with the Prince's green. He had to be at least twenty-five years younger than his wife. "Go Madame Su," said Dana, impressed. Her taste in men was better than her taste in fashion and wall decor.

The cam feed scanned the crowd, capturing the hubbub of the Emerald Knights supporters.

"Slow it!" Dana said sharply.

Planchet did so, and gave her an odd look as the audience footage crawled to a near-standstill.

Dana had spotted her friends. The three inseparable Musketeers.

They sat together in a tangle, right behind the players' bench. There weren't three of them, but four. A woman with bright purple hair, an Emerald Knights jacket and fierce green face-paint was cuddled between them, her head thrown back against Athos' shoulder. When she saw the cam pass by, she screwed her face up and roared directly into the lens.

Who was she?

Dana heard a throat clearing, and looked up to see Athos in his doorway, regarding her with that flat, unblinking gaze he often used to unnerve people.

"We're watching a game," she said.

"So I see." Athos dropped his heavy jacket at the door and headed for the kitchen corner of the apartment. "Turn it off, Grimaud." His engie appeared behind him, mouth pressed shut. There was an angry tension between them.

"Don't tell her what to do," Dana objected.

"Turn it off!" Athos roared.

Grimaud gave him a filthy look, and turned off the vid. She gestured for Planchet to join her, and they went into the other room.

"Are you drunk already?" Dana demanded. "You've only just got off duty."

"Believe me, I am sober," Athos snarled. "If you'll excuse me, I plan to do something to rectify that." He began searching his cupboards. "Grimaud, where's the good whiskey?"

Silence from the other room.

"Conrad Su has been abducted," Dana said quietly.

Athos stopped for a moment. "I see. Not overly surprising."

"Not surprising?"

"He's close to the Prince Consort. Kidnapping is practically part of the job description. I'm sure he'll be returned quickly enough."

"He's been gone three days."

Athos located the bottle he had been looking for, wedged behind the food printer. "That is troubling," he admitted. The anger had dissipated now.

"His wife suspects the Cardinal is involved, through an agent called —"

"Well, yes," Athos said patiently. "I imagine so."

Dana could have hit him out of sheer frustration. She watched as he poured several measures of whiskey into two glasses, drank one, added ice to the second, and rapped a code into the food printer.

"Don't you think someone should do something?" Dana demanded eventually, while the printer hummed to life.

Athos poured a fresh drink for himself, in the glass without ice. "This is palace politics. I have been playing this game since before you were born…"

"You would have been ten," she snapped.

"I started young. You don't want to get involved, D'Artagnan."

The printer chimed, and Athos removed a roast beef sandwich from it. He picked up the whiskey glass with ice and the sandwich, and went and rapped on the inner door of the apartment. Grimaud opened it after a moment, and glowered at him.

"I am very sorry for shouting," said Athos, sounding sincere. He gave her the peace offerings.

Grimaud took the plate and glass and closed the door again.

"Now, where were we?" Athos asked as he returned to Dana and more importantly, his drink.

"You were about to explain to me what happened at a certain fleur-de-lis match last Joyeux, when the Duchess of Buckingham played on Prince Alek's team," said Dana.

He gave her a dirty look. "I was not."

"Come on, Athos!" she exploded. "You were there. I saw you on the cam. If something happened that night, you know about it."

Athos sighed. "You have no idea what you are getting into here, little one."

"I'm *not* a child."

"It was a bad Joyeux for all of us." He met her eyes. "Some nights are better forgotten."

"I agree with you," Dana said calmly. "Right up to the point that it comes back to bite you on the arse."

He regarded her steadily for a moment, then had another swallow of whiskey. "There are two different forms of TeamJoust: cinquefoil and fleur-de-lis. You know the difference?"

"We get sports broadcasts all the way out on the rim, you know." In truth, Dana had paid little attention to TeamJoust before Paris. She knew that cinquefoil was melee-style, five jousters per team, and it was brutal. Fleur-de-lis was three per side, played in a sequence of one-on-one until the final melee spar. It was considered the more civilised game, because fewer people got seriously damaged while playing.

"That game – the one you were watching – was the fleur-de-lis showdown of the century. The Emerald Knights versus the Night Witches for the final, but Chevreuse busted her ankle three days before the game."

Dana nodded. "Chevreuse was their third teammate?"

Athos' tone was almost fond. "Former minister of Public Relations. Used to give the Cardinal absolute hell on the Palace Council. Nice legs. Excellent pole-defence. And just good friends with Aramis, since you're after all the dirt."

Dana certainly knew enough to understand what 'just good friends with Aramis' meant. She reached for the remote that Grimaud had left behind, and called up the image of the cam panning the audience. "Is that her?"

The woman with the purple hair and Emerald Knights colours, pulling a horrid face into the cam feed, then laughing.

"That's her. She insisted we all go to the game – we were playing nice and waiting to see if her latest breakup with Aramis was going to stick. I had to carry the wretched woman to her seat." Athos didn't sound like he had minded much. "Chevreuse, Conrad and Alek were unbeaten that season. She practically threw herself off a balcony when she realised she wouldn't be able to play the match against the Night Witches. But – did I mention Chev was a political genius?"

Dana couldn't believe she was jealous of this woman

who had been friends with the Musketeers – her Musketeers – before she came to Paris. "No, you didn't."

"She figured out a loophole in the rules. If anyone subbed for her in that match, it wouldn't count as the same team, and they'd lose the 'Invincible' claim for the season. But the Duchess of Buckingham was an Ambassador, and there's a legal twist that allowed her to take on the duties of any member of the Palace Council, as if she were that person. Contracts are sacred in Paris." Athos' mood had certainly warmed up. He poured Dana a drink of her own. "Brilliant move. So Buck took Chev's place, they beat the Night Witches 6-3, and the rest is history."

Dana leaned in. "And?"

"There is no and."

"A few minutes ago, you were furious I was bringing all this up. The twist ending to the story is … their team won and everyone was happy? I don't buy it, Athos."

"Something happened," he admitted. "There was a party afterwards, and things got out of hand. Sometime in the early hours, Chevreuse asked me to delete some security footage as a favour to her, which I did. I assumed it had something to do with Prince Alek, but I. Didn't. Ask." His blue eyes blazed at Dana. "Even if I knew anything, I wouldn't tell you. We serve the Crown first."

"Crown first," Dana agreed quietly.

"The Regence was informed about the incident. Buck was sent on a tour of Honour, with the expectation she not return to Paris during her contract as Ambassador. Her time must be nearly up by now – she'll be heading home to Valour any day. As for Chevreuse…" Athos sighed, looking tired. "The Cardinal had been trying to get rid of her for years. Chevreuse has been living in exile ever since. Artemisia, I think."

Artemisia was one of the cities in orbit around the ocean world of Truth. Dana had visited there once – a nice enough place, but no Paris Satellite. She wasn't jealous of Chevreuse anymore.

Athos reached for the bottle of whiskey again. "Those are the stakes you're playing for, sweetness, when you get involved in palace politics."

"I don't think you'd better drink more," Dana said. "Not if we're going to rescue Conrad Su from the Cardinal."

A smile played over Athos' mouth. It looked different, with the beard so close-shaven. "I don't believe I volunteered. Madame Su isn't *my* landlady."

Dana leaned in. "Are you going to make me say it?"

"Don't, D'Artagnan," he warned. It was a teasing voice and nothing like the unexpected anger that had flown out of him when he first arrived.

"All for one…"

Athos hissed and set the bottle down. "Really? You're seriously pulling this? You're not even a…"

"And one for all," finished Dana.

He glared at her for a long time. "I'll call the others."

"Good plan."

CHAPTER 11

THE FRIAND OF ARAMIS, THE ESPRESSO OF ATHOS, AND THE CONVENIENT BOYFRIEND OF PORTHOS

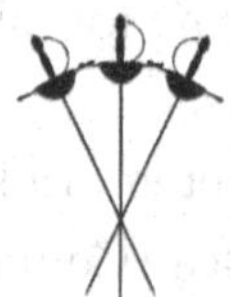

"'ve never broken into a spaceship before," said Planchet excitedly. "At least, not a spaceship that belonged to someone who might turn up at any moment and shoot us."

"Ye of little faith," said Porthos over the comm. "I'll have you know that Edwin and I…"

"Edmund," corrected the helpful and convenient boyfriend of Porthos, who worked for station security and was letting her take a few liberties with the cam feeds.

"Ed and I are on the job," said Porthos smoothly. "And I can tell you right now that the glamorous villain in the watermelon-coloured flight suit is currently drinking mocha shots on the Stellar Concourse. Her engie, meanwhile, is taking in some adult entertainment at the Ishtar Club. Oh, and the security cams on E Dock are all mysteriously glitching, and will continue to do so for the next hour or so."

"No idea why," said the deadpan voice of Ed.

Planchet consulted her clamshell tablet, checking the

manual specs one more time. "Keep watch, Cap," she said cheerfully. "I'm going in."

"I'm not a Captain," Dana sighed. Technically, her rank was Mecha Cadet, but when she was at work, she was generally referred to as Squaddie, because Essart was the sort of jolly commander who liked everything to be informal and friendly. It was horrible.

"I keep forgetting," said Planchet. "Don't worry, Cap. You'll get there in the end." She had moved capably into the role of engie, despite Dana not having a dart to offer her, musket-class or otherwise.

As Dana watched, Planchet stuck a small steel stud on the side of the Moth. When she activated it from her clamshell, a bright neon web swept across the entire ship and pulsed three times before disappearing.

"Interesting," mused Planchet, peering at the info dump as it peeled across her screen.

"Can we hurry it up?" Dana said anxiously. "The cams might be off, but anyone could walk on through…"

"There's one warm body on this ship."

Dana blinked. "Is it Conrad Su? Can you tell? Or another engie?" She had no intention of underestimating the resources that Rosnay Cho had at her disposal, especially if she was working directly for the Church of All.

"The hair colour's right," said Planchet, chewing her own lip.

"Sounds promising. How do we get in? What's the weak spot?"

"The back hatch," said Planchet. "No, wait." She ran around the back of the Moth, and Dana followed her. "Look at that!"

The beautiful curve of the ship's rear end had a gleaming, perfect surface. As Dana watched, though, it bubbled and bent outwards. "I suppose that's a weak spot," she said doubtfully. "Is there something wrong with the ship?"

"That's not the ship," said Planchet, sounding gleeful. "That's the prisoner. I think he's set off a melt-mine." She leaned forward in fascination. "I've never seen one used except in simulations, that's extreme!"

Dana pulled Planchet back beneath the landing gear. As they watched, a hole tore itself in the back of the Moth fighter, leaving ugly edges of twisted metal. On the one hand, it was a crime to cause such damage to a thing of beauty like this Moth fighter. On the other hand, the ship belonged to Ro, and that made it hilarious.

A head of bright blue hair stuck out from the twisted hole, and then a stocky athlete of a man, barely Dana's age if he was a day, catapulted out of the informal exit and rolled neatly on the ground.

"Hey," Dana called softly. She considered saying, "Hey, I'm Dana and I'm here to rescue you today," but she managed to restrain herself.

Conrad Su was not in the mood to be rescued. "Keep back," he warned, and leaped up on to the wing of the Moth. "I'm done with you bastards. If the Cardinal wants to lock me up without trial, she can bloody well do it herself."

"Your wife sent us!" Dana yelled up after him. "We have to get you to safety."

"Thanks," he laughed. "But I trust my wife about as much as I trust the Cardinal. I'm going home." He leaped from the Moth on to a nearby drone carrier, and then a venturer, and so on across the row of ships.

"Go after him," Dana said to Planchet, pushing her forward. "He should recognise you."

"I think he's too busy rescuing himself," said Planchet, sounding impressed.

"That won't last long if he heads home!" Porthos had reported back that the Su apartment was still packed with Red Hammers ready to arrest anyone who rang the buzzer.

Planchet scampered after the escaped prisoner. "Monsieur Su! Stop!"

Aramis had picked the short straw. Rosnay Cho's engineer Foy had some dubious tastes in entertainment, and the tacky shenanigans of The Ishtar Club were about as sexy as holo-cartoons.

Finally, Foy replied to a message through his comm, and stood up to leave. Aramis did the same, leaving a large tip by her drink as she followed him out.

"We're on the move," she said quietly into her own comm.

"Heading this way, or back to the ship?" Athos asked in her ear.

"He's strolling back along the promenade," said Porthos in her other ear. "Towards you and Cho."

"Order me an espresso and a friand," said Aramis. She liked the warm friands that they printed down on Stellar.

"You're paying," Athos told her, and she heard the chime that told her someone was accessing her credit.

"I should never have given you the code," Aramis groaned.

She kept half an eye on Foy as she strolled back along the promenade that overlooked the Stellar Concourse. There was Athos, sitting at one of the cafes on the lower level, his Musketeer jacket a bright blue beacon. From where he sat, he had line of sight on his own mark, the infamous Rosnay Cho.

Aramis had heard a lot about the Cardinal's special agent over the years, but had never actually set eyes on the woman. Athos had failed to mention how spectacular Cho was to look at, from her confident body language to the long scar across her face accentuating her raw beauty. Trouble in a flight suit that fit well in all the right places. "I'm starting to see why young D'Artagnan has taken such a *close* interest in this woman," Aramis murmured into her comm.

"Behave," chided Athos. She watched him reach out and take something from the food printer embedded in the table. "Get over here, or I will eat your cake."

She ran down the stairs lightly, and kissed him on both cheeks as she joined him at the table, as if they hadn't seen each other in years. "Next time, you can take the part of the mission that means sitting in a strip club." She bit into the friand, still warm from the printer.

"Fun afternoon, was it?"

"I've never been so disinterested in naked boobs in my life before. All the pink lights and cheesy peep-hole costumes and glitter *everywhere*." Aramis shuddered. "I wanted to wrap the women up in cardigans and take them all home with me."

Athos raised his eyebrows.

"Not like that," she growled. "I wanted to feed them

soup and rub their feet. Those shoes look so uncomfortable."

"As would be the glitter."

"Don't remind me." Aramis concentrated on her cake and coffee for a moment, letting Athos observe Cho and the engie.

"Aramis," he said after a moment.

"Mmm?" she said with her mouth full.

"Do you remember the parties after the big game, about six months ago? The fleur-de-lis final during Joyeux?"

Aramis finished chewing, and blew on her coffee. "I remember getting wasted because Chevreuse and I had broken up. There were some really good drugs and excellent music and possibly it snowed indoors unless that was a side effect of the drugs, and oh yes, you got up to something suspicious with my ex that got her exiled, so thanks for that."

"I had very little to do with it," he said sourly.

Aramis missed Chevreuse. She had been a good friend as well as a lover, and a fun time all around. Conveniently, the distance they had between them now made it possible to forget all the blazing rows they had shared in between the fun nights out and long nights in.

"That's the night I'm thinking of, yes," Athos went on, and apparently they were still talking about this. Huh.

Aramis set down her coffee and peered at him. "Is that what all this is about? The same old – scandal that never was?" Did that mean they were going to have that other conversation about Chevreuse, the one Athos only ever started when too drunk to remember it the next day?

"Perhaps." Athos glanced briefly over at Rosnay Cho. "Porthos, how is D'Artagnan getting on?"

"A snag or two," said Porthos in their comms. "But she found the fella she was looking for."

"A successful mission, then," said Athos, ordering another espresso. "I loathe surveillance."

"I know," said Aramis, patting his hand. "You think such deep thoughts when you're left on your own. It upsets your stomach."

"Why do you think I surround myself with people who never shut up?"

"This sounds promising," Porthos broke in, patching Rosnay Cho's clamshell into their comms.

"The wife should be comfortable in the Armoury," said Cho, as clearly as if she were sharing the table with them. "Our guest might change his mind about talking once he knows that the Church has her in custody." She drummed her fingers on the table.

"What's the word from Milord?" asked Foy.

Aramis glanced at Athos with curiosity in her eyes. "Milord," she mouthed.

Athos shrugged in response. It meant nothing to him.

"Bastard likes to tease," said Cho. "But he'll come through. He always does." She checked her clamshell, and frowned. "There's one loose end I don't like. The Su family have a lodger, and no one's seen them all day. Why does the name D'Artagnan sound so familiar?"

Athos and Aramis went very still.

"Don't you remember?" the engie guffawed. "Back on Meung Station. The buttercup?"

Cho laughed, too. "Don't suppose it's the same kid. But

I'll stroll up to the Su residence to see how their mousetrap is going. Anyone who calls on that family over the next few days gets taken in for questioning. If the lodger *is* our little buttercup, I'll enjoy the look on her face when she gets arrested." She got to her feet. "Go check that the Moth is charged up, file a flight plan for 20:00 hours. I need to be down on Luna Palais before midnight, to report to her Eminence."

"D'Artagnan," Aramis said softly into the comm. "Engie coming your way. Get out of there."

"Already out," came the muffled voice of Dana. "How long?"

"Ten minutes or so, maybe fifteen if there's traffic on the spherelifts."

"I can make extra traffic," Porthos volunteered. "Can't we, Ed?"

"You're enjoying the power a little too much, darling," observed Ed, but he didn't object.

"Do you want to take the bloke with the locs or the lady in the angry trousers?" asked Aramis. Rosnay Cho was already walking away, in the opposite direction to her engie.

"You take the engineer," said Athos. "I fancy this mousetrap of theirs. If Cho and her Red Hammer friends are looking for a D'Artagnan, maybe they should find one."

Aramis didn't like the sound of that. She gave him a hard look. "Planning on convincing a bunch of Hammers that you're a short, black Gascon with girl parts?"

"A physical description will make things harder, if they have one." Athos admitted. "But I can be very convincing."

"As long as there aren't any Sabres there who recognise you."

"I don't know if you've noticed, but someone cut my hair recently. I could be anyone." He had a mischievous light in his eyes.

Athos smiling while sober was rare, but Athos allowing himself to enjoy something other than wine and swordplay was a thing to behold. "You should probably take off your Musketeer jacket," Aramis suggested. "If you're serious about pretending to be someone else."

"That sounds like cheating."

"We have more fun since she joined us, don't you think?"

Athos gulped down the last mouthful of his espresso. "It's better than being stabbed in the chest," he conceded. "But the day is young."

When she first set out to rescue Conrad Su, Dana had not envisaged ending up with him flat on the floor beneath her, caught in a secure headlock. "Planchet, how do you know this hellcat?" Conrad hissed, arching his back up as if trying to throw her off.

Dana was small, but sturdy and strong. She held firm, squeezing him a little tighter around the throat. "Do you want me to explain it again?"

"No," Conrad snarled. "I want Planchet to explain."

Planchet loomed into view over them both, grinning all over her freckled face. "Dana's a pilot!" she said brightly. "I'm going to be her engie when she's a Musketeer."

Dana should correct that 'when' to 'if', she knew, but

she couldn't bear to dampen the kid's enthusiasm. "That's not relevant," she said instead.

"She is Madame Su's new lodger," Planchet added. "We came to rescue you. Was that a melt-mine on the side of the ship? That was amazing!"

"A piece of tech I picked up from a friend," said Conrad, lying still now. "Dana, then."

"D'Artagnan," Dana corrected.

"I think as long as you're sitting on my back, I can call you by your first name. Swear by your honour and your ship that you're not working for the Cardinal."

"I don't have a ship," Dana sighed. "But I'll swear on my honour and all future ships."

"Your loyalty is to the Prince Consort?"

"To the Crown," Dana said. She sat up, allowing Conrad to do the same. He didn't look quite so preternaturally pretty in person as he had on the holo screen but that could be because he had been captive in a ship for a couple of days. "My loyalty is to the Crown."

Conrad rubbed his neck, and winced. "It'll do. I can't go home?"

Dana shook her head. "They're waiting at your place, to detain all visitors." Porthos had patched the table conversation to her comm as well, which may have made her explanation to Conrad more confused than she intended, since she was listening to them at the same time. "Including me, as your wife's lodger."

"They don't know about me, though!" Planchet said cheerfully. "Madame Su pays me in bed and board, and she's always kept me off the books."

Conrad gave the young engineer a friendly shove. "Don't say that like it's a good thing. My darling wife's not taking gross advantage of you for your own protection." He looked seriously at Dana. "Here's the thing. Prince Alek is my employer and my teammate. I'm the closest friend he has left on Luna Palais. That means I've been picked up for questioning, and subjected to security checks more times than I've made silk coats. And trust me, I've made a lot of silk coats. There's a standard routine to it — they let me go about my business after an hour or two. But this time was different."

Dana nodded. "Is this the first time Rosnay Cho was involved?"

"The first time she's got her hands dirty," Conrad muttered. "Though I'm starting to think she was behind other incidents in the past. I thought she'd let me go once I convinced her there was nothing compromising I could tell them about his Highness. Luckily, Cho favours psych drugs and brain cables for interrogation…"

"You surprise me," Dana said dryly.

"I happen to be one of the 5% of the population who can't be influenced that way," Conrad went on. "My brain won't take adjusting, mechanical or chemical. One of the reasons people in power share so many bloody secrets with me. I would have waited for Cho or her employers to lose interest, but I ran out of time." He paused, looking at Dana as if he was still wondering how much to share with her. "I have a vital appointment later today, down on the moon. That's why I risked the melt-mine to get out. I have to reach the Prince Consort in the next couple of hours, or he is going to get himself into so much trouble. Seriously. Cities burning, solar system crumbling, shit is going down."

Of course she was going to help. She had come this far.

"You can't go by civilian shuttle," Dana said immediately. "Too many Church zones to cross between here and there – they'd pick you up as soon as you moved through their surveillance coverage."

"I can take him in my dart," Aramis said in her ear.

Dana shook her head. "You and the others have done enough, and your ships are too recognisable. No point in advertising the involvement of the Musketeers, not unless we have to."

"Athos won't be needing his ship for a while," pointed out Porthos in her other ear. "Since he's about to…"

"Shh, don't distract her," Aramis cut in. "You have a plan, don't you, Dana?"

Dana found herself grinning. "Conrad has an appointment Down There, and I'm a pilot. All we need is a ship. Ideally one that we already know we can hack."

Conrad gave her an odd look. "You want to steal Rosnay Cho's Moth?"

Dana felt as if her insides were full of lightning. "You have no idea how much I want to steal Rosnay Cho's Moth."

"But I blew a hole out the back of it," Conrad reminded her.

"I can fix it!" Planchet said excitedly. "I can!" she patted a small satchel on her belt. "I've got my box of tricks, including sealing glass and rotor-connectors. The self-repair system on board should do the rest once I log Dana into the system."

The sphere-lift beside them beeped suddenly, and irised open to reveal Aramis with an unconscious man at her feet. "So what you're saying is," she said calmly. "It's a good thing I just gave Cho's engie a dose of Pentasleep and stole his ID stud." She opened her hand, revealing the small metal stud that she had removed from Foy's wrist.

Conrad raised a hand. "Can we stuff him in the sonic shower compartment and feed him protein bars through a slot? No particular reason."

"How much longer do you need to keep E Dock in a security blackout?" Porthos broke in over the shared comm channel. "Because Ed is going off shift in about twenty minutes, and I owe him two steak dinners and some amazing sex."

"Three steak dinners," corrected Ed. "And dessert."

"Baby, I have all sorts of ideas about dessert…"

"Twenty minutes will be fine!" said Planchet, blushing hard. "It only takes ten to backdate a flight plan into the system."

"Interesting," said Aramis, gesturing for Conrad to help her pick up the unconscious engie. "Dana, your talent for human resources is spot on. My own engie is far too moral to endorse a caper like this."

Dana gave Planchet an encouraging smile. "I think we're going to work well together," she agreed.

CHAPTER 12
ASSIGNATION AT THE MECHA GRAVEYARD

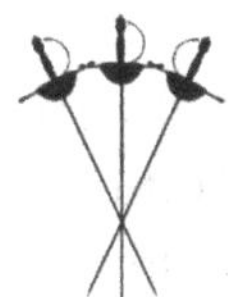

"We're actually doing this," said Dana, sixteen minutes later as they prepared to roll the Moth out of E Dock. She had twelve separate cables plugged into the back of her helm, three of them feeding threads of data directly into her brain. Thanks to Planchet's hacking skills, the Moth had welcomed her as an old friend and trusted pilot.

Fly, darling, come fly with me, we'll see the solar system together...

"*Bon chance,*" said Aramis over the comm. She had elected to remain in Paris. She had also slipped a pearl stunner into Dana's pocket before letting them go. "I'd come along for the ride, but Porthos has her hands full, and I have a feeling I might need to save Athos from himself."

Dana frowned, her hands stretching over the smooth controls. "What's up with Athos?"

"Don't get distracted," said Aramis' honey voice. "I've

been rescuing Athos since you were a teenager. So, last week, basically."

"Hey," Dana protested.

"Fly straight, baby doll," said Aramis. "The moon is the big white thing you'll spot on your scanner once you're in the air." She signed off the comms with an electronic trill.

This ship felt amazing inside Dana's head.

"Two minutes," said Porthos in her ear. "Get out while the going's good. We want to see nothing but a clean, empty space when these cam feeds hum back to life."

"A clean, empty space I can do," breathed Dana.

Oh, she loved this ship. It felt warm beneath her hands, and inside her head.

Dana had learned on darts, musket-class and otherwise, and could fly just about anything up to and including the very slow venturers that were used to ferry personnel back and forth between Paris and Lunar Palais. She had tried out a few fighters here and there, usually for testing purposes, but had never flown a Moth fighter of this quality before. The Moth was roomier than the dart, while still being streamlined enough to cut beautifully through the atmosphere.

It was like steering silk. Dana barely had to think her commands, and the ship responded with a light touch, reflecting subtleties of thought she didn't even know that she had.

Space wrapped itself around the Moth, and pulled them in.

"Luna Palais Tertiary Dock, this is Control," repeated the helm inside Dana's head as they made their approach. "Identify."

This was the hard part. But Planchet had a hack for every occasion, in this case turning the ID chip stolen from Rosnay Cho's engie into a profile avatar and voice simulator.

"This is Engineer Chretien Foy, Moth 286921," Dana said, reading off Planchet's clamshell tablet.

"Where's your pilot, Foy?"

"Maintenance run only, regulation 68A." Engineers could fly ships solo for freight or service as long as they were travelling distances of four hours or less, within chartered space. "Just put in a new set of power spheres, running tests in all atmospheres," Dana added, on impulse.

Conrad was smiling at her from the co-pilot's seat. He had a good smile. It made his eyes brighter than his hair, and that was saying something. Dana found herself captivated by his hair. It wasn't just the artificial neon blueness of it, it was the spiky texture and the silver tips to those spikes, that matched the scales that ran naturally down both edges of his face. "Don't embellish," he mouthed at her.

She gave him a rude gesture in reply, and he laughed.

"We can't give you a spot for another hour, Moth 286921," said Control. "Can get you a berth on Secondary Dock much sooner. How long will you be on the surface?"

"Triple shift if you have it," said Dana.

"I can do you a double."

"I'll take it."

Dana muted the comms and prepared for landing. "Well done, Planchet," she tossed behind her.

"I think she's asleep," said Conrad, amused.

Dana craned her neck behind her. Planchet was strapped into one of the aft seats, her head lolling against the humming wall of the ship. "She deserves it," she said. "Saved my bacon at least three times today. Will you make your appointment?"

Conrad tapped the blazing sapphire stud that he wore implanted on his ring finger, checking the time. He then leaned over Dana's arm to call up a map of the dock they were heading for, and transfer it to his stud. It was odd to have someone seated beside her. She hadn't flown with a co-pilot since first year training. "Barely," he said. "I'll have to hustle along the Triumph to make it. The Secondary Dock is closer to the Palace, but I won't have the benefit of the bullet train."

Dana longed to ask what it was that was so important, but she kept the thought tight inside her chest. Curiosity was a bad thing, when state secrets were concerned.

Conrad touched her shoulder briefly. "Thank you for helping me, Dana. If I had a vote, you'd be in Musketeer blues already."

She ignored the compliment, which made her feel strange, and set about the landing protocols instead.

As they descended through layers of airlock, Dana felt the familiar leaden weight settle in her stomach. Lunar gravity was all the worse after flying a real ship.

Fly again, pleaded the Moth in her head as she executed a textbook perfect landing in the allocated berth. Her shoulders sagged. She didn't want to let go.

Gentle hands came around to disconnect her from the helm, one cable at a time.

"That's Planchet's job," she protested dimly. "She needs to practice…"

"I'm sure she is capable of doing it in her sleep," said Conrad. "But I'm closer." He leaned around Dana, releasing the catch on the helm. "Easy does it."

She felt bereft as he lifted the helm up and set it into the correct module, ready for its real owner to reclaim it.

Conrad came back to Dana, feeling her pulse and staring intently into her eyes for a moment, to check her pupil size. Routine checks, performed as if he did them every day.

"I thought you were a tailor," Dana said.

"I have many skills," said Conrad, and then proved it by kissing her.

Dana's senses were already firing wildly after that short, glorious flight in a ship that knew how to sail the stars instead of slowly chugging through them. The loss of helm response had been like a cold bucket of ice water over her brain, and here she was heating up all over again.

Conrad was warm and confident and confusing. Not to mention, married to her landlady. But Dana kissed him back. His warmth was more than welcome.

Leaving Planchet to clear up the last of the crime scene (including record deletion, strapping an unconscious Engineer Foy in the pilot seat, and faking records for Dana and herself on a civilian shuttle), Dana and Conrad made a speedy path across Lunar Palais to the Palace.

They caught a tram along the Boulevard Triumph, which had been deemed of too great historic and artistic value to be spoiled by a bullet train, despite such trains having been invented long before a city was built on the moon.

Conrad grew nervous and agitated as they neared the Louvre. He had not tried to kiss her again. Dana stuck with him, to make sure that he made it as far as the Palace without being abducted again.

Rosnay Cho was going to spit chips when she realised her ship had been stolen, and Dana grinned at the thought of it. She wished she could see the look on the other woman's face, and wondered idly if Porthos' Ed could arrange that via security cam.

"This is our stop," said Conrad, and flung himself off the tram. Dana caught him up, and they plunged together through a gateway into the maze of gardens that surrounded the Palace.

Commandant Essart's Mecha Squad were housed on the East Side of the city. Dana had got to know the Palace grounds pretty well in her time here – but not the private gardens, which were indulgent and sprawling, concoctions of carefully designed Artifice mixed with genuine, delicate flora from every habitable planet in the solar system.

Each garden led into another, open-air rooms within rooms, and every one of them was spectacular. Still it was a blur to Dana, moving at speed through it all. Finally, Conrad drew to a halt. "Better clear off," he said. "You shouldn't be seen at the Palace. If you head back to barracks now, can you set up an alibi for yourself?"

"Well I can," said Dana, a bit hurt. "Are you sure I shouldn't see you inside?"

"There are live cams all along Moonflower Walk," Conrad said, gesturing to the arch up ahead. "That takes me directly into the Council chambers, and no one will touch me there. I'll be fine. My Prince needs me."

Dana was superfluous, then. "Look after yourself," she said sternly. "You might actually need rescuing next time."

"Let's not pretend you didn't rescue me," he said, with that smile that lit up his face. "I'd be locked up in a cell with my wife right now if you hadn't got involved — and no one wants that."

Dana had forgotten about Madame Su. What on earth were they going to do about her arrest?

"Watch your back," Conrad warned. "You've made some dangerous enemies today, whether you know it or not."

This is what I always wanted, Dana thought in a rush. *Adventures, and adrenalin, all in service to the Crown.* Her heart was still beating fast from all that hurrying through the gardens. "I'm dangerous too," she said.

To his credit, Conrad did not laugh at her. He looked at her for a long moment, and then nodded. "I wouldn't want to get on your wrong side," he agreed, and strode away along Moonflower Walk.

No more kissing. That was probably for the best.

What followed was highly embarrassing. Dana had been so hasty in following Conrad, she failed to take note of the route they took through the private gardens of the Palace.

Either that, or the Artifice glitched and scrambled the order of the garden rooms when she wasn't looking.

Maybe this was actually a cunning security system, to dissuade thieves and assassins.

Dana spent the next hour getting thoroughly lost. So much for returning quickly to barracks. She couldn't activate any of her studs without pinging her identity all over the Palace proximity systems, and she knew for a fact that there was no detailed map of the private gardens available to any but those of highest rank.

She was going to have to find her way out by old-fashioned means. If only she had a ball of string.

Dana had given up on ever escaping these wretched gardens alive, and had draped herself over a large ornamental rock to think through her options, when she heard voices. One very familiar voice.

She sat up, and crept over to a wall of bright peach Freedom roses, a famously ugly flower that managed to grow to twice its native size here with all the primping and water it had been allotted.

Dana peered through the web of thorns and saw, of all people, Conrad Su walking along a marble path. He had changed his suit and showered, his blue hair forming damp spikes. His formal coat was deep blue velvet with gold embellishments, which made him look far more like the professional courtier he was supposed to be.

Still pretty.

"Last chance to turn back from making the biggest mistake of your life," he said clearly as he passed Dana. She thought for a moment that he was addressing her. But she heard another male voice respond to his, close by, though Conrad was alone.

"Shut up, for God's sake," said Conrad, sounding

completely fed up. "I sacrificed sleep in my own bed for the first time in days for this, don't forget that."

Dana let Conrad and his invisible companion pass, then followed quietly.

She was curious about this mysterious appointment which had agitated him so much that he burned his way out of a ship that had been his prison for days. And, she had to admit to herself, she also needed him to lead her out of this maze of an ornamental garden.

If there were other reasons for following the attractive athlete with blue hair, she would not admit to them, not under bribe or torture.

It was getting dark, which was inconvenient. Dana was used to a shift-based lifestyle. Space was always dark, and if you wanted day, you turned the damned light on. Being subject to the whims of planetary bodies was still not something she felt was natural, even after several weeks of work shifts on Lunar Palais.

But these paths were lit with hidden lamps and glow-stones, and having this much shadow did make it easier to follow without being seen.

Finally they were out of the formal gardens, walking past rec hubs and a large private dock of Royal vehicles. There were a few people working here and there, so Dana kept to the dark, shadowing Conrad. He acted as if this kind of stroll was normal for him.

Where was he going? Why hustle all the way to the Palace only to turn around and leave immediately?

They emerged on the East Side of the Palace, and now she had her bearings quite clearly. She was only a few minutes from the Mecha hub where her barracks were located. No excuse to keep following Conrad to his mysterious appointment.

He headed past the practice yards, and towards the tunnel that led to the mecha graveyard. That fired up Dana's curiosity even more.

When Lunar Palais was first built, hundreds of years earlier, it was considered too dangerous to have ships zooming in and out of the main dome. The original space dock was set up in a secondary, smaller dome, with a tunnel connecting the two. This secondary dome was disused now, except as a storage space for abandoned tech that had not yet been pillaged for recyclable parts. Old spaceships, building units and especially rundown old mecha clotted the area.

Mecha Squad Essart and their engie crew sometimes held drinking parties here, among the debris and broken-down vehicles. When a suit was smashed beyond reasonable use, there would be a ceremonial drag-and-ditch, in which all members of the Squad were expected to participate. Dana had also sneaked in here once or twice on her own, so she could get extra mecha practice away from the kind but mocking eyes of her friends and/or the other squaddies.

There had been no terraforming here, nothing to disguise the surface of the moon as anything but what it was – a pitted, rocky landscape that looked like death. Dana liked it out here better than within the proper dome of Luna Palais – it felt more honest, somehow. More *moon*.

She had not thought about the fact that, as a former spacedock, the dome must be fully-functional.

Up ahead of her, past a heap of severed steel heads and giant armour, Conrad stopped in a recently cleared patch of ground. He stood in the flickering pool of light from a neon beacon, swaying with exhaustion. The light caught the occasional movement that should belong to a person, despite whatever shielding Conrad's "invisible" companion was using. Dana hid in the shadows of a disused hangar. Guilt stung her as she caught a glimpse of despair on Conrad's face. Did she have a right to spy on him because she had partly rescued him today?

Dana was about to turn and leave when she heard a sound so familiar to her that she could not move her feet.

The plexi-glass above them shifted and rotated out in layers, allowing for a ship to descend. Dana caught her breath as she watched it come down. It wasn't just that it was a musket-class dart, which automatically made it beautiful in her eyes. A scrolling pattern of fleur-de-lis and sacred constellations tattooed its back fin, clear enough that Dana was able to identify the ship. It was the *Morningstar*.

He belonged to Aramis.

If Dana had learned anything from her time in Paris it was that the Musketeers had their own secrets, many secrets, and a history she did not share. Whatever covert assignation was happening here, Aramis was involved, and she had said nothing about it even while helping with the escape back on Paris. Humiliation burned through Dana as she stared at the ship.

The pilot emerged first, wiping flight gel from the white-blond stubble of her scalp, and stretching her legs. A Musketeer, but not Aramis. This was Captain Tracy Dubois. Dana had seen more of that particular pilot than she should thanks to a certain personal photosilk belonging to her friend, but they had never met in person.

Dubois wore a full Musketeer uniform, but you would have to be a long way away to mistake her soft pink face for Aramis's honey brown tones.

Captain Dubois spoke briefly to Conrad on the ground, and they shared a handshake of forearms gripping each other, colleague to colleague. She used greater deference in greeting Conrad's companion, the one that no one could see. Then she opened up the side hatch of her ship.

Another woman stepped out, in a silver flight suit. Her hair was long and braided in loops – no longer purple, but a violent pink colour. Dana recognised her, if only by vid-image and reputation. This was the exiled former Minister of PR and Emerald Knight, the one called Chevreuse.

Another of Aramis' lovers. Dana held her breath, waiting for her friend to emerge as part of this blatantly conspiratorial group. Instead, a different woman emerged from the ship, bronzed and beautiful in a scarlet flight suit.

The Duchess of Buckingham. She had not been formally exiled from Lunar Palais but she was most definitely not supposed to be here.

A conspiracy against the Crown. It had to be. Dana had helped Conrad set up this illicit gathering! She was in so much trouble already. Time to get out of here.

Dana turned and ran across the pitted surface of the moon. In this charged, silent atmosphere, she could not help her feet scuffing the ground, and the noise of it sent echoes in all directions.

Not fast enough to escape. She heard the heavier footsteps of pursuit, and ran faster.

CHAPTER 13
CONSPIRACY IS BAD FOR THE BLOOD PRESSURE

onrad caught Dana before she reached the hatch. The gravity was softer than in the main dome, spongier underfoot, and it slowed her down. He was a Zero-G athlete. He slammed into her back, one elbow crunching between her shoulder blades.

Dana fought back, tucking and rolling, jabbing at his legs with her feet. She didn't think about drawing her stunner, not that he gave her time to do so.

His head took her in the stomach, and she clawed the side of his face, struggling to be free of him. His arms grappled hard around her waist, though, and when they hit the surface of the moon with only a slight bounce, Dana was underneath.

For a man only a little taller than her, Conrad had a lot of muscle to him. He also had an arc-ray beneath that soft civilian shirt of his, and he now drew it, pointing the bead directly into her face.

An arc-ray, not a stunner. Lethal.

"Who sent you after us, Dana?" he whispered.

"No one sent me," she snarled, shifting her weight to see if there was any give in the hold he had her in. "You know who I am."

"I know you convinced Planchet you were on the side of the angels, but if a burning comet promised that girl a spaceship to play with, she'd follow it like a puppy." Conrad breathed slowly, in and out, his hand steady on the arc-ray. "Who are you really, and why did you follow me?"

"Who are you?" Dana hissed. "What the hell have you got yourself into? Whatever the three of you are doing here, it's hardcore treason. And you made me a part of it."

"I didn't invite you!" he said incredulously. "You made yourself part of this." He stared at her, as if he could read her intentions from extremely close eye contact. Whatever he saw, it made a difference.

Conrad rolled off her and stood up, holstering the weapon beneath the concealing swing of his royal blue coat. "For the Crown," he said, testing her as he had before. "Everything I have done here tonight is in service to the Crown. God help me."

Could she honestly say the same? Had she followed him out of curiosity, jealousy, or genuine patriotism? Dana felt vaguely ashamed of herself. He was right. She had invited herself into this mess.

"For the Crown," she replied sullenly. "Always."

Conrad held out a hand, and helped her to her feet. "Come and join the Royalist pity party. We have coffee."

As they walked back towards the dart, his fingers remained tangled in hers. She did not pull her hand away.

Dubois and Chevreuse had made themselves comfortable on the surface of the moon, beside the ship. Now she came to look more closely at it, Dana was not certain it was the *Morningstar* after all. There was a shimmer about the tail fin that made her wonder if another sight-shield illusion was in play here. Could they do that, make a ship tattoo look like another?

If they could make a person invisible, why not?

Speaking of invisible, there was no sign of the Duchess, or the sight-shielded Prince.

Dubois sipped coffee from a thermos cup, and Chevreuse produced a pack of cards that she dealt in an elaborate pattern on the white rock beneath them. They both glanced up as Conrad and Dana approached.

"Absolutely," said Chevreuse, shifting from suspicious to sarcastic with barely a second's pause. "That's an excellent way to keep a low profile, Conrad. *Bring a date.*" She was pregnant, with a large dome of a stomach visible as soon as you saw her at an angle.

"This is Dana D'Artagnan," said Conrad. "She helped me get away from Special Agent Cho earlier, and she's reliable backup. Aramis would vouch for her, they're friends."

Both women raised their eyebrows at that, and Dana remembered she was looking at Aramis' current secret girlfriend as well as her ex.

"Actual friends," Dana said with more emphasis than was strictly necessary. "Does she know you've got her ship?"

"Pretty, isn't it," said Captain Dubois fondly. She touched a stud at her wrist, and the tail fin of the dart shimmered suddenly, the pattern shifting from stars and fleur-de-lis to a different image of sword hilts tangled in vines, with the silhouette of a mountain range high across the top of the fin. It was the tattoo from the *Parry-Riposte*. Athos' ship.

"Don't do that," Dana growled. "You're implicating them in whatever's going on here."

"Aramis owes me a favour, she can wear the inconvenience," said Dubois, her hand going back to the stud.

"Athos owes me nine," said Chevreuse. "Leave it as it is." She surveyed Dana thoughtfully. "You don't know why we're here. Would you prefer it to stay that way?"

That was a good question. Conrad's hand was warm in Dana's. She was well and truly compromised now, even without knowing what she was compromised about. "I assume if you were merely conspiring against the Cardinal, or the Regence, or the Musketeers, you could do it somewhere more comfortable," Dana observed, waving a hand around the mecha graveyard.

Dubois laughed at that.

Chevreuse wore a grim expression. "Oh for a warm tavern and a *simple* conspiracy."

Dubois finished her coffee, eyeing up Dana like she was working something out. "D'Artagnan, you said? I have heard of you."

Dana fervently hoped that whatever the glamorous pilot had heard did not in any way involve a photosilk. "You're taking the Duchess of Buckingham home," she blurted. "To Valour. Isn't that right?"

"Ten out of ten," said Dubois. "An official assignment from the Crown, no less. I'm not the one breaking rules to be here. Well, mostly," she added with a slightly ashamed look at Chevreuse, who made a rude gesture in her direction. "Coffee?"

"And me," said Conrad, finally letting go of Dana's

hand. "Lots of sugar, Trace. It's been a long week." They both found seats on the pitted ground. Dubois handed around more coffee, while Chevreuse flipped cards back and forth in a game of her own devising.

"A simple mission," said Dubois. "Buck has been playing diplomacy across the various continents of Honour ever since the Grand Exile…"

"Less of the grand," said Chevreuse, screwing up her nose. "Can we call it the Shit Exile? Captain Dubois here was given the job of taking our worthy Ambassador back home now her term of service is up. Implied in that order, of course, was to make sure she bloody well went home by a direct route. Do not pass Lunar Palais, do not collect 200 credits." She gave Dubois a dirty look.

"Given how much the well-being of the entire solar system relies on Buck getting home without being caught in the presence of his Royal Highness, the Prince Consort…" Dubois continued, returning the dirty look with one of her own. "We thought that the best possible chance we had was for Chev to travel to Honour, meet Buck on the ground and keep damned close to her for the entire trip, while Conrad stayed on Lunar Palais to prevent the Prince from making contact."

"It was a workable plan, right up to the point that I was abducted, and incommunicado for several days," groaned Conrad. "Guess who took the opportunity to make a bunch of subspace messages to his 'family' back on Honour?" It was his turn to shoot a dirty look, this time to Chevreuse. "I don't know what the excuse at your end was."

Chevreuse's eyes glittered dangerously. "Forgive me

for assuming Buck wasn't completely self-destructive," she said. "I won't make that mistake again."

"So many bad decisions," sighed Dubois, leaning her head back against her ship. "And here we are. Champions of the fucking solar system, with an emphasis on *fucking*."

Dana looked from one to the other of them. "Is that it?" She was almost shocked at the simplicity of the explanation. "Not some big political conspiracy, it's just an affair?"

All three of them groaned and shook their heads.

"Of course it's big and political," Chevreuse said. "It's the Prince Freaking Consort."

"It's technically treason," muttered Conrad.

"This would be the perfect excuse," explained Dubois. "To get rid of Prince Alek, at the very least – the Cardinal has never been happy about the Regence marrying an Elemental New Aristocrat. It could bring down the Regence, too. If one of her brothers turns up at the right time, putting on a moral front in the face of her scandal…"

"There had better not be a scandal," said Chevreuse between gritted teeth. "Oh, I *hate* this. I need to be at the Palace, doing my bloody job. That big-toothed hologram they hired to replace me will never save the Regence from this catastrophe."

"He's in there with her right now, isn't he?" Dana said carefully. She had figured that much out. Dubois's ship was the site of the dangerous liaison, while the Prince's friends sat outside and complained about it.

"I can't refuse his orders," Conrad explained. "That's the curse of serving the Crown." He sighed heavily. "I brought him here under a sight-shield. No one will know. We can do that much. Chevreuse is right. There doesn't have to be a scandal, as long as…"

"As long as they don't get it in their thick heads to elope," Chevreuse whispered, not even wanting to speak the words. "That's what we're really here to prevent. There will be no evidence that they spent the night together – clearing up that kind of mess is what I do best – and as long as they go their separate ways, we're done."

"How do you make sure of it?" Dana asked. "I mean – is it enough that Dubois has her orders to get Buckingham home?"

"Yeah," Dubois said, looking just as sick as the rest of them. "Except that Buck is an Ambassador. That gives her royal privilege. The flight contract specified she was not to be allowed to land on Lunar Palais, through any of the three docks. But —" She waved a hand around the barren landscape of the secondary dome. "Loophole. Maybe they should give her your old job, Chev. She's sneaky. No one's given me orders to make sure the Prince Consort stays on the moon. If he chooses to leave, I can't stop him – I have to grit my teeth and fly the ship."

Dana frowned. "If all of you working together couldn't keep them apart tonight, what on earth makes you think they won't keep trying to see each other?"

There was a long, painful pause.

"You need to find him someone else," Chevreuse told Conrad sternly. "A nice sporty mistress with a good rack and no political status. Which I told you six months ago."

"My job description does not include getting my boss laid," Conrad snapped back.

"Tonight suggests otherwise."

"Wouldn't that add up to more treason?" Dana suggested. They all turned cynical expressions on her that made her feel about twelve years old.

"It wouldn't be so bad if it was anyone but Buck," said Conrad. "Too political. She's not just aristocracy back on Valour – if they get their referendum through to secede from the system, Buck is prime candidate to be their First Minister, maybe even their Regence. She's Elemental, on top of it, so there's the religious shit in there too. Any hint of an alliance between Alek and Buck reads like a conspiracy, even if it is just two people who fancy the hell out of each other."

"Fancy," Chevreuse teased, mocking him.

He leaned forward, and punched her lightly on the arm. "All we can do is hope they get it out of their systems tonight."

"Cheers to that," said Dubois, and they clinked coffee cups.

There was no more talk of politics after that. They talked TeamJoust, mostly, with Chevreuse interrogating Conrad about the 'lamb' who had replaced her in the Emerald Knights.

Dubois joined in, knowledgeable about the sport, and Dana found herself able to follow most of the chatter thanks to the games she had watched with Porthos. She was even able to contribute a comment or two when they discussed an upcoming cinquefoil game between Serpentin and the Mousers which promised to be especially violent thanks to an emotionally fraught team line up.

They no longer felt like conspirators who had failed to save their master from falling into the wrong bed; it was a gathering of friends. Dana found to her great surprise that Aramis, Porthos and even Athos had trained her, somehow, over the last couple of months, to make comfortable friendly conversation. It was a skill that had eluded her, back home on Gascon Station.

Conrad slung an arm around her shoulder at one point, and she leaned against his shoulder, choosing to forget that he was married to her terrifying landlady.

It was nice.

The hatch opened and their prince emerged, concealed beneath the sight-shield again. He and Conrad made their farewells to Chevreuse, who tipped Dana a mocking salute before she joined the Duchess of Buckingham inside the dart that still bore the same fin tattoo as the *Parry-Riposte*.

They were all equally relieved that the prince was parting from his lover. The alternative had been terrifying.

"Don't worry," said Dubois in a low voice to Dana, before she returned to her helm and harness. "I've left a deliberate error or two in the illusion – if we've missed any security feeds, and someone collects a screen grab, it will be an obvious forgery. I wouldn't actually screw Athos over like that."

"You're so reassuring," Dana said dryly. She rather liked Dubois.

"In fact," Dubois said cheekily, and made an adjustment to her wrist. Her musket-class dart shimmered and took on an entirely different skin: gold instead of pearly white, sprinkled with scarlet stars in a regimented pattern. The engines and fin looked a different shape, for all the world as if the dart was sabre-class.

"*That's* a better look for you," Dana said, with a laugh.

Dubois winked, and let herself into the ship.

Conrad stood a little way away, having a polite argument with thin air. He broke off as Dana approached. "This is Mecha Cadet D'Artagnan," he said. "Extra security detail."

There was a shift to the air as the prince turned towards her – the artificial scenery rippled a little, though he remained invisible. "My thanks, Mecha Cadet. If Conrad trusts you, I am sure that I can do the same."

Dana tried to look as official as possible. "We should move," she said.

The three of them made their way back through the mecha graveyard, and the tunnel that led back to the main dome. Conrad led them through into the gardens of the Palace. "We should wait until we're closer to the living quarters," he said. "Before we…"

But the Prince Consort had already shrugged off the sight-shield, as if sick of the deceit. Alek of Auster looked just like he did on the holovision, only more dishevelled. Dana had only ever seen him in beautiful suits before, or TeamJoust armour. Today he wore the trousers of a beautiful suit, with a rumpled shirt over the top.

Conrad rolled his eyes. "Didn't you come out with a coat, your Highness?" He shrugged his own royal blue velvet garment off, and threw it over the Prince's shoulders. The Prince accepted this as his due, strolling amiably along the paths.

"I gave it to a friend," he said carelessly, grinning at nothing in particular.

If Dana had been in any doubt about what had been going on in that spaceship tonight, she would have known from that shit-eating grin. She dropped behind them both, playing the silent bodyguard.

Conrad was furious – he carried it mostly in his shoulders, but it spilled over into his voice. "That's all we need," he muttered. "Never mind the paper trail of tonight's activities, you left a clothes trail as well." They walked along in silence for a moment. "Which coat?" Conrad suddenly asked, as if it had been weighing on his mind.

The Prince was drunk on happiness. "You're not going to begrudge me a coat, my friend?"

"I make all your coats!" Conrad said impatiently. "Each one takes weeks of design, and is hand-printed as a one-of-a… no, never mind. It doesn't matter. Whatever your Highness needs."

A pause, as they circled the Fountain of Tranquility, a majestic stone formation from the surface of the moon, which had been enhanced by sprays of Artifice water, dancing in loops and rivulets. It was a common sight on tourist posters of Luna Palais, though Dana had never seen it in person before. There was no time to do more than glance in its direction.

"Yes, it does matter, actually," exploded Conrad, on the verge of being extremely rude to his Prince. His exhaustion from the days of captivity frayed his diplomacy. "What were you *thinking*?"

Prince Alek patted him. "It's all going to be fine."

Conrad looked utterly defeated. "As long as it wasn't the peacock coat."

The Prince kept walking along the path of marble tiles.

"The one you haven't even worn in public yet?"

"You can print another copy," Prince Alek said airily.

"Princes aren't supposed to wear copies," Conrad

huffed. He turned around, miming his frustration to Dana, who hid a laugh.

They walked through room after room of exquisite garden art, Dana making a mental map as they went so that she did not get lost again.

Conrad stopped. The Prince walked a few steps before he realised, and turned back with one beautifully arched green eyebrow. "Conrad?"

It wasn't a joke any more, or a minor costuming inconvenience. Conrad looked like death warmed up. "You removed the diamonds first, didn't you?" he asked with a shudder in his voice. "Before you took the peacock coat for a casual night-time stroll in the Palace gardens? You removed the twelve diamond studs loaded with the culture bank of Honour? The ones your wife gave you for your birthday last month?"

The Prince just looked at him.

"I'm going to be executed," Conrad whispered.

"They made her eyes sparkle," said the Prince. "You wouldn't understand."

Conrad made a sputtering sound.

"I wanted to give Buck something nice, something important – you know she's going back to Valour and they're never going to let us see each other again? My marriage contract lasts for eight more years!"

"Yes," said Conrad. "I know that, Highness, that's why I risked life, limb, my reputation and my career to let you have this meeting."

They looked at each other for a long time, and then the Prince smiled casually and turned back towards the Palace. "Lalla-Louise has bought me many gifts over the years. I am sure she won't even notice."

Conrad stayed where he was standing, for a few moments later, as the Prince went on without him.

"I should go back to barracks," Dana said awkwardly. "I bet you're wishing right now that I didn't overhear any of that."

"You're not the one I'm worrying about," said Conrad, and reached out to her hand. "Though maybe that makes me as much of an idiot as..." he stopped himself, and shook his head. "He's usually smarter than this," he added, plaintively. "You're not seeing him at his best."

Dana nodded. "I believe you."

"You don't sound like you believe me."

"I'm trying really hard." It was obvious that Conrad cared deeply about the Prince despite the other man's idiocy.

Conrad laughed. "You know, if he had decided to go with her, not one of us would have had the power to stop him."

"Wars have been started for less," she agreed.

"I know it looks like Chev and I made a disaster of things tonight, but... it could have been worse." Conrad groaned, and buried his face in Dana's shoulder for a moment. "I'm so tired. There should be a law against how tired I am."

Dana patted him on the head. "You should catch him up before he accidentally proposes to a potted plant or blurts out his night's activities to the Regence over late night cocoa."

Conrad laughed into her shoulder. "Love makes people stupid."

"I wouldn't know." Dana was having a terrible urge to thread her fingers through his bright blue hair.

Conrad looked up, and met her gaze with his. "You're young," he said. "You've got time."

That would be the moment for her to tease him – who couldn't be more than a couple of years older than her – about being such an ancient married man, but Dana couldn't bring herself to make a joke about that.

"We're done?" she asked, instead.

"You're done," Conrad said firmly. "My drama continues."

"If I can ever be of help again —"

He nodded once, and then turned away to leave her, following his Prince.

"Wait, Conrad," she called after him, feeling like an idiot. "Which is the quickest way to the mecha barracks?"

Conrad came back for a moment, and pointed down an avenue of Artifice roses bursting out of floating teacups. "Keep going down that way until you reach the glow in the dark daisy clock, and take the hedge path past the seahorse spheres. They come out near the croquet lawn, and there's a gate in the wall on the other side that leads directly to the East Wall."

She would never have found that on her own. "Good night."

Conrad blew her a kiss, jogging backwards along the path. "You're spectacular, Dana D'Artagnan. I owe you."

Dana had not stayed a night at the barracks for weeks, but she had arranged to meet Planchet there once they were both done with their parts of the adventure. She found the young engie fast asleep on her bunk, surrounded by snoring mecha cadets. The girl looked worn out, but peaceful.

Dana sat on the edge of the bunk, and Planchet stirred. "Did we save the day?" she asked drowsily.

"Yes," Dana lied. "That is a thing we did." Apart from being sworn to secrecy, there was no way she ever wanted Planchet to know what a massive waste of time their 'heroic mission' had been.

Still, the Prince Consort hadn't actually run away with his lover to a planet that was making rumblings about independence. That counted as a win, right?

"Was fun," Planchet muttered, turning over to make room for Dana. "Can we do it again?"

Dana paused, and then lay down beside her, balancing precariously on the edge of the narrow bunk. She would just close her eyes for a minute. "Sure," she said. "Any time, Planchet."

It's hardly worth lying down, it's not like I ever sleep on the Moon, was Dana's last thought for the next twelve hours.

She dreamed of flying, and peacock coats that scattered diamonds through space like a pattern of falling stars.

CHAPTER 14
THE MADNESS OF THE DUCHESS OF BUCKINGHAM

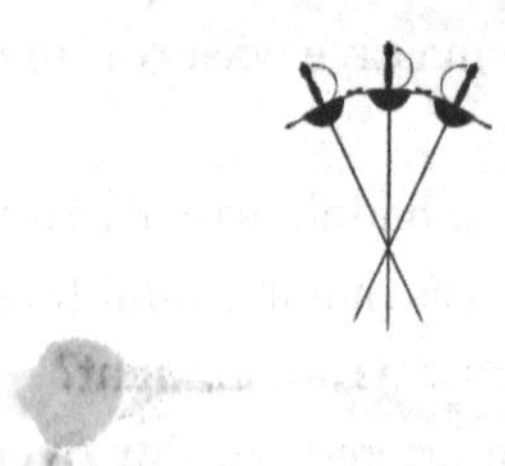

ONE WEEK AGO.

Georgiana Villiers, Duchess of Buckingham and Ambassador of Valour ('Buck' to her friends), was ready to go home. The planet of Honour was appallingly hot from one end to the other, and the southern hemisphere was worst of all. If you were going to spend this much time in air-conditioned bars and hotels, you might as well be on the moon.

Except, of course, she wasn't allowed on the moon.

It was worse in Auster than it had been anywhere else. For this entire Grand Tour Of Stay Away From The Regence's Husband, she had mostly been able to relax and enjoy herself, visiting different cultures and communities across the nine continents.

Here in Auster, though, everything reminded her of Alek, and the unholy mess they had made for themselves last year when a fun flirtation turned into something far too serious. So many of the local inhabitants had trails of metallic scales on their light gold-brown skin. They wore the scales like beauty marks, and damn it if they weren't exquisite, every single one of them.

A whole country full of Aleks. *Spirits save me.*

The other New Aristocrats, the top families that Buck mixed with socially, all either knew Alek or had heard of him. Half the men and most of the women she had danced with at the Government Ball upon her arrival were related to Alek's family. Since Buck had been up on Lunar Palais only six months ago, they constantly dug at her for gossip about his health, happiness, hair colour, fitness regime, and of course his beautiful wife who ruled the solar system.

Local boy makes good.

Buck was not going to tell them all the truth, of course – there would be no confession of a flirtation gone too far, a potential PR disaster of epic proportions, or that she still couldn't stop thinking about him. No one wanted to hear that the eight years left on Alek's marriage contract to the Regence had become a millstone around all of their necks.

She would tell no one that Alek and Buck were still exchanging texts, discreet little conversational snippets on the subspace comms, on a daily basis.

He wanted to see her again, before she went home. And oh, she wanted to see him. There were no words to describe how much of a bad idea that was, but they both *wanted.*

A week to go before a Musketeer pilot arrived to escort her back to Valour, and Buck had still not decided what to do.

Meanwhile, with almost all of the formal events finally done, there was beer. Cold beer was the best thing about

Honour in general and Auster in particular – the locals took great pride in keeping it as cold as possible, despite the inhospitable weather.

Buck had only tried 30 of the Austerian Top 40 Local Beers in the bar nearest her hotel, and was determined to complete the list before that damned ship arrived to escort her home like a naughty teenager who had been caught kissing a boy from the wrong school.

She was settling down to a glass of something called Griffin's Sweat when the door to the bar opened, and a Raven sauntered in.

He recognised Buck immediately, and came over to her. She took a mouthful of the beer, savoured its chill, and wondered what she had done wrong now.

"Your Grace?" the messenger said. He had a black cap pulled down over his head, which accentuated his pale skin and stone-grey eyes. "I have an urgent message from Madame Marie Chevreuse."

That, Buck had not expected. She reached her hand out for his clamshell, but instead he offered her a stud on his wrist to scan with her own. The ID code confirmed he did, indeed, come directly from Chev.

"Vocal message only?" Buck said, raising her eyebrows. "This should be fun."

"I have permission to cover the drinks tab," said the Raven. "If that helps."

"It does indeed." Buck waved him towards the bar. "Have them print me a glass of Desert Daughter's Old Peculiar, and they can pull me a draught of that hand-brewed ale they make in the back shed, while we're at it."

Buck finished the Griffin's Sweat while she was

waiting for her messenger to return. It tasted better than it had any right to, with a name like that.

"Okay," she said when the black-capped Raven had returned and the drinks were lined up before her. "Break it to me. What is my sweet Chevreuse up to, over in whichever of the floating cities of Truth she got exiled to?"

"She's waiting at your hotel," he told her.

Buck spluttered into the Desert Daughter's Old Peculiar, and slammed the glass down. "What the f —"

"She wanted me to break it to you gently," said the messenger, with an apologetic smile. "I'm not very good at gentle." He was attractive, especially when he smiled like that. Buck wasn't so stupidly lovestruck that she couldn't appreciate a fit man in uniform, even if it was the rather dull uniform of the independent messenger corp. "She's here to join you on your flight home to Honour."

"She doesn't trust me," Buck muttered. "Even my friends don't trust me." Damn it all. Guilt rose up in her throat like bile. Buck had been inconvenienced by the events of That Night six months ago, but Chevreuse had been destroyed; exiled formally from Honour space. This planet was the last place she should be. Chev could be arrested if anyone pinged her identity, all because Buck couldn't be trusted not to throw the last shreds of her own personal honour and diplomacy away for one night with Alek.

Chevreuse was, unforgivably, always right.

"I'm going to need more beer," Buck muttered.

"That I can help with," said the Raven.

"What's your name?" she asked, when the messenger returned with further examples from the Top 40.

"Slate," he said, giving her an odd look. Perhaps

people didn't ask his name very often. Ravens were Ravens – you saw them flitting about from place to place, but you didn't need to know about them as individuals.

That was sad, Buck decided. Far too sad. "Are you married, Slate? Ever been in love?"

His eyes, if possible, became a frostier shade of grey. "I was married once," he said. "It ended badly."

"Oh, endings," Buck slurred, waving her glass at him. "Love affairs, marriages, all end badly. All badness. It's the good bits you start out with, those are the good bits." She was drunker than she had realised, drunker than she had intended. Thoughts bubbled up into her mouth like they wanted to be free. "Would you wait eight years for the man you loved?"

Slate the Raven gave her a strange smile. "That would depend on what I was waiting for him to do."

Buck felt the first prickle of danger, but it was too late. The bar dissolved around them. He stood out, clear and sharp against the fog, this man with a lovely face, all cheekbones and grey eyes and sad, sad smile underneath the black cap that didn't suit him at all.

"You're not a Raven," she said as the pieces fell into place. "You're… I don't think you work for anyone."

"Oh believe me, sweetness," Slate said, and his voice was different now, smooth like silk underwear and vintage brandy. "I'm getting paid."

"Something in the beer," Buck muttered, trying to stay awake.

"A little something," he admitted.

"What's your name? Your real name. Not Slate."

He leaned back in his chair, regarding her thoughtfully.

"You can call me Winter, if you like. It doesn't signify, as you won't remember this when you're awake."

"I am awake. Aren't I?" Buck looked wildly around her, but the bar was frozen in amber. Her senses were fuzzy, blurring into each other. Nothing felt real.

"In one manner of speaking, yes, but in another… it's complicated. I put a micro-stud in your drink that is burrowing its way into your brain stem even as we speak. That means you're going to be susceptible to anything I tell you." Winter leaned in, and tapped Buck sharply on the side of the head. "I actually left the bar ten minutes ago. Urgent appointment back on Valour, you understand. Politics waits for no one. But look at me, sitting right here inside your head. I will see everything you see, hear everything you say, and if you follow a path I don't like, I can simply… correct you. Convenient, yes?"

Buck gazed at him, taking in every plane of his face, cheekbones, jaw. "It's treason, then," she whispered. "That's the only reason anyone would go to so much trouble."

"Georgiana, that's hilarious." He neither laughed, nor smiled. Winter was a good name for him – he was cold all the way down to his veins. "What a lack of imagination you have. The beautiful things we are going to do together are far more sophisticated than mere *treason*."

"What, then?"

Winter's eyes blazed into hers, like an ice comet powering through space. "Love first, then war. They go together so nicely, don't you find?"

Buck forgot about the man called Winter who now lived inside her head. He was gone from her memory before she stood and left the bar, making her oops-too-many-beers way back to the hotel.

She continued to not remember his existence when she discovered Chevreuse in her hotel room, and they had a blazing row about promises, exiles, and whether or not either of them could be trusted to keep it in her pants.

They both conceded moral high ground on that one.

Later, once the friends had called a truce and the heavily pregnant Chevreuse was fast asleep on one side of Buck's spacious bed, Buck's clamshell chimed with a text from Alek.

Are you asleep? he asked.

Too hot to sleep, she sent back.

I want to see you before you head home, he said next. No flirtation, no pretence.

Buck stared at the message for a long time.

"Yes," breathed a voice. She looked up and was startled to see Winter sitting at the end of her bed. He was not in disguise any more – his hair was silvery, falling around his face. He wore grey and white pyjamas, a soft blend of silk and cotton that showed their quality and expense in every shimmery movement. His feet were bare, but he looked every inch an elegant New Aristocrat. There was an arch, moneyed confidence to him, like every other man she had known growing up, except for the hard edges around his lovely face. Oh, and the fact that *he was living inside her head*.

"You," Buck said, remembering all at once in a wave of anger and nausea. "Is this it? The peace of the solar system hangs on this one moment, me texting yes or no to the Prince Consort?"

"One moment," Winter scoffed, stretching out like a cat on the covers. He pushed Chevreuse's foot out of the way, and she did not stir. Of course, he was not really here. "As if we would bank everything on a single moment. A chess game is full of moves and moments and decisions. Right now, my job is to get one particular piece to one particular place and time. The rest is up to you."

Buck stared down at her clamshell again. Yes, no, or maybe. She typed **Yes** and **I have a plan**, sending them both before she could change her mind.

Winter tilted his head back, smiling winsomely at her. "That's my girl."

"I might have said yes anyway," Buck said angrily. "You didn't have to do all this."

"Oh, Georgiana," he said as if sorry for her. "The people I work for pay a lot of money to make sure there's no such thing as a maybe."

A FEW HOURS AGO.

"You can still change your mind," said Chevreuse for the tenth time as the *Colin Guillaume*, piloted by Captain Tracy Dubois, prepared for descent.

Buck and Chev sat in the seats against the back of the cabin, bickering in an undertone so as not to distract their pilot. Dubois was another old friend, who could be trusted to be discreet no matter how much she disapproved of what they were doing.

"We've covered everything," Buck insisted. Alek, she was finally going to see him again, probably for the last time while his marriage lasted. A lot could happen in eight years. "Dubois has shielded her fin, so no one will connect my flight from Honour to Valour with a ship that touched down briefly in the old dome on Luna Palais. Conrad will make sure no one sees Alek leaving the Palace…"

"We haven't heard back from Conrad in two days," Chevreuse snapped.

Buck wasn't sure whether it was the pregnancy or the possibility of arrest that made her friend so irritable. "You know why I'm doing this."

Chev laughed at that. "I know why you *say* you're doing it."

"Alek is a wild card. Cooped up in that Palace, hardly any of his own supporters left. Do you know how many people there are down on Auster who care about him?"

"Enough to start a war, I expect."

"Everything that happened last time… it was out of his control. Our control. If he never sees me again, he'll resent the Regence and their marriage contract forever. He'll be a sitting duck for any petty conspirator who figures out what buttons to push. But maybe, if I can talk properly to him, I can repair some of the damage."

Chevreuse looked at her with heavily lidded eyes. "It's fascinating the way you manage to make this sound patriotic."

"I'm impressed too," said Winter, draping himself over the helm. He wore a flight suit this time, but his feet were still bare. Those feet of his. They curled like cat paws against the cool metal floor of the *Colin Guillaume*. Winter played with Dubois' cables, and tweaked at her flight suit, but she did not react to his presence. "I thought I was the master of compartmentalisation, but you leave me in the shade, sweetness."

Buck sighed, turning her eyes away from the bastard that only she could see. "You have no jurisdiction on this flight, Chev. You can't stop me."

"I know," said her friend in a low voice, her hand resting on the curve of her stomach. "I was hoping you'd stop yourself."

NOW.

They didn't talk.

Alek stepped up into Dubois' ship, and let the sight-shield fall away so she could see him standing there, all gold and silver and green. He wore a peacock-coloured coat that glowed with diamond studs, not exactly a subtle outfit for a secret rendezvous. He looked sad and uncertain, beneath that fall of bright emerald hair. Everything that Buck had convinced herself that she would say to him fell away with the sight-shield.

She didn't speak. She kissed him, and he kissed her back, holding her face in his hands as if she was precious, unbreakable. He rubbed his cheek gently against hers and she felt the gentle tugging rasp of his silver scales against her soft skin.

"You don't have to fuck him," said Winter.

Buck gasped with the shock of it, the remembering. It happened that way every time, like a bucket of cold water, reminding her that she wasn't here by choice.

Except, of course, she was. She was right here, doing exactly what she had promised she would never do. *They had a witness.* A sarcastic, barefoot witness who had burrowed himself into her brain.

Alek kissed down her neck, burying his face in the swell of her breasts as he lowered the zip of her flight suit. "Buck," he moaned.

Buck stared over his head to Winter who sat on the helm, feet dangling off the edge. He wore an Emerald Knights fan shirt now, over silver jeans. He waggled his bare toes cheerfully at her.

How could she communicate with the invader without Alek hearing her, and thinking she was crazy? Not that Alek was interested in anything she had to say right now, his mouth hungry against her ear, and his hands catching hers, squeezing their fingers together.

"I mean it," said Winter. "All that matters is that enough people think you're banging away in here. It doesn't make a difference to the Crown or the realm or the chess game whether you actually let him into your knickers."

"No one will say anything," she said in a whisper.

"I know," said Alek, thinking that she spoke to him. He came up for air, gazing into her face. "We have good friends, Buck. They are all trustworthy —" He kissed her mouth deeply and she kissed him back, inhaling the scent of him, the taste. *I will never have this again.*

"Oh very trustworthy," Winter said, and Buck was too busy tasting her prince to see him, but she could hear the smirk in his voice. "Still, secrets get out, Georgiana. One way or another, you and your man here will pay for tonight's deed."

I won't remember this, Buck told herself desperately. *I won't remember this. I won't remember that he was here, ruining everything.*

Alek knew something was wrong. He stepped back, not knowing why she hesitated — or, perhaps, thinking of a hundred reasons why she would. "Buck," he said softly. "Have you changed your mind about me?"

"Never," she said fiercely, and threw herself at him. "No one else matters. Not right now."

His mouth on hers was hot, and hungry. They had waited for so long, to be together.

Winter laughed.

A moment later, Buck forgot that he had ever been there.

"Take that coat off," she hissed, pulling the peacock garment roughly from Alek's shoulders. "Take it all off."

"Keep the coat," whispered Winter in her ear, a final command before he disappeared completely. "Whatever happens, Georgiana, hang on to that coat for me. It will come in very useful indeed."

LATER.

"I could come with you," said Alek. They lay wrapped up in each other, mostly naked, on the floor of the small spaceship. Buck wore his jacket, bright with peacock colours and diamond buttons, and nothing beneath it. She never wanted to take it off.

"No," she said softly. "We're not that stupid."

"Are you sure?" He nuzzled against her, his mouth

making soft kisses against her shoulder, her collarbone. "I feel that stupid."

This was why Chevreuse was here, Buck realised. Not to stop this one night of passion, but to make sure that was where it stopped.

Conrad and Dubois served the Crown. Their contracts ensured that they had to obey, if Prince Alek gave them a direct order. But Chevreuse was already in disgrace, in exile. As a mere citizen of the solar system, she was obliged to obey a reasonable demand from the Crown, but not to obey unthinkingly.

Chevreuse had spent her whole life cleaning up the messes left behind by the Crown. Buck had no doubt she would break a thousand rules to stop this particular catastrophe from becoming a reality.

Buck owed Chevreuse more than she could ever say. Their bonds of friendship could only take so much before they shattered. There was another life waiting for them both, elsewhere in the solar system.

"Shh," she said, and stopped Alek's mouth with a deep kiss. "We have this, right now. We can't take more. Don't be greedy."

In this one thing, at least, she could be selfless.

MUCH LATER.

Valour. Finally, Buck was home.

Dubois put the *Colin Guillaume* down discreetly at the smallest space dock in southern Castellion, at the border between the county of Triomphe and the duchy of Buckingham. Normally Buck's homecomings were more dramatic, with a party atmosphere and crowds of paparazzi chronicling her antics.

Perhaps she was getting old, because the thought of that made her want to drown herself. Quietly slinking on to the planet felt about right.

Her highest security comm stud filled with alerts as soon as she entered Valour space – messages, appointments, requests for her attention.

She was home. Being in Valour space meant being bombarded all over again with the political issues of the day: the referendum on planetary independence, the ethical question of terraforming the last unclaimed continent and, of course, the ongoing religious tensions between the Church of All and the Elementals, who were growing their support here on Valour.

There was the election, coming up in a year's time, the one where Buck was expected to run for First Minister of Valour now that her political credentials had been bolstered by her term as Ambassador. If only the media knew how much of that term had been spent sampling the beers of Honour. Would that make her more or less popular with the voters?

If Alek had abandoned his wife to come with her – he would have only found himself tied to another woman who was expected to dedicate every hour of every day to politics.

Buck was tempted to wear the peacock coat through the space dock, one final rebellion. Instead, she hid it deep in her luggage, not wanting Chevreuse to know about the gift.

"Your skimmer should be here shortly," Chev told her

now. "And your entourage, " She checked her comm stud. "Through here." She led Buck to a small, bleak meeting room. "They'll meet us in a minute – ugh."

Chevreuse folded up like a piece of broken furniture, and Buck lunged for her, only just catching her in time. Slowly, she lowered the other woman to the floor. "Oh, shit. Is it the baby? Chev, wake up."

Her friend's skin was very cold and too pale, contrasting against the bright pink braids that framed her face.

"Chevreuse!" Buck said insistently, raising her wrist to call for help through the comm stud.

A man cleared his throat. "My apologies for the inconvenience, your Grace."

"Not now, we need —" Buck's protest died in her throat. "You!"

It was the man in her head. That bastard Winter. But it wasn't quite him – he seemed different. Shoes, actual shoes for once, covering those pretty feet of his. He wore a discreet grey suit, like he was one of the hundreds of bureaucrats she had to deal with every day in her usual life. Instead of the wild silver tendrils falling around the sharp planes of his face, he had dull brown hair that made him look like no one in particular. Even his grey eyes were muted.

Same cheekbones you could cut a sandwich with, though.

"Your Grace," he said in an officious voice. "Allow me to introduce myself properly, now I am no longer wearing my Raven disguise. I am Milord de Winter, brother-in-law to the Countess of Clarick. I am also the newly appointed

Private Secretary of the Interior. I hold the portfolio for covert intelligence."

Buck blinked, for a moment seeing double as that other Winter appeared behind his real life double, barefoot and blowing kisses at her. He wore black pyjama pants and a copy of the peacock coat that Alek had given her, over a bare chest. His hair was sleep-rumpled and silver. It was quite easy to tell one Winter from another. "What do you want?" Buck said, still holding her friend in her arms. "Is Chevreuse..."

"Please don't worry about her, your Grace," said Milord de Winter. "She will not take serious harm for this brief spell. I thought it best that we speak alone." He smiled politely. "You're going to open your case and show me the diamonds that the Prince Consort gave you."

Buck closed her eyes tightly. Would this ever be over? "And then?" she snarled. "What happens after that?"

"You know the answer to that, sweetness," said the silver-haired Winter that lived inside her head. "You're going to forget all about me, as if I was never here. And our real work begins."

CHAPTER 15
WHATEVER HAPPENED TO MADAME SU?

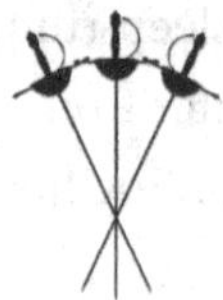

While Dana D'Artagnan and her new friend Conrad Su were entangling themselves in the politics and love life of a nation, and the Duchess of Buckingham had been entangling herself with the Prince Consort of the Solar System, one person's fate had – until now – been somewhat forgotten.

Have no fear; we shall learn her story now.

Jingfei Su was a straightforward woman. She ran her businesses with a tight hand and a shrewd attitude to the bottom line. She made most of her decisions based on what was practical – though like most people, she also appreciated the luxuries that life and a successful business afforded her. A silk suit, a gold necklace, a pretty young husband with a prestigious position at the Palace.

She had no interest in politics, apart from the fact that it often deprived her of Conrad, because his closeness to the Prince Consort made him a regular target of investigation.

Up until now, however, the inconvenience had been minor, not directly affecting her.

But here she was, under arrest, deep in the holding cells of Church jurisdiction on Paris Satellite, an installation referred to often as the Armoury because, of course, it was full of Sabres and Hammers.

The guards who had arrested Madame Su were raw recruits, which explained why Madame Su's regular bribery of her local Red Hammers to keep them from looking too closely at her business affairs, had made no difference.

After many long, miserable hours alone in the holding cells, Madame Su was dragged out to face the Commissary, whose task it was to interrogate her about the activities of her husband.

The Commissary was a short, squat woman who looked like a tortoise. Her attempts to discreetly discover what political conspiracies might involve Conrad Su were overwhelmed by Madame Su's personal need to complain about the terrible effect that sporting loyalties had upon husbands.

Madame Su had a lot of complaints to make about her husband, and they had been building up to a critical level. They all came spilling out of her now, and the Commissary was obliged to listen, though she stopped taking notes when it became obvious that few of these complaints had anything to do with Church or Crown.

Finally, the Commissary raised the subject of Madame Su's lodger. "I believe you have a D'Artagnan staying on your property?"

"Oh," said Madame Su, taken aback by the change of subject. "Yes. It's good to have a strong pair of hands around, what with never seeing my husband, and the business relying on me being at my absolute best…"

The Commissary coughed. "We have brought D'Artagnan in for questioning."

Madame Su froze for a moment. "You have?" she said in alarm. "That's no good, she was going to find my wretched husband for me. She can't do that if you have her in here!"

"We plan to locate your husband, don't worry about that, Madame Su," said the Commissary, before the other words sank in. "She? You mean he."

Madame Su looked confused. "I do?"

The Commissary made a mental note to apply to the Cardinal for a pay rise. "Let's get our prisoner in here, shall we?" She spoke into her comm stud. "Sergeant, bring D'Artagnan up from the cells to join us."

The man who was brought in by two of the Red Hammers was a blond, bearded pilot in a battered flight suit and bright blue Musketeer jacket. He bowed politely to them both.

Madame Su stared blankly back.

"Now perhaps, we can get somewhere," said the Commissary. "Sit if you like, D'Artagnan. This may be a long night."

"I'd prefer to stand, if you don't mind," said the Musketeer with a polite bow in the direction of Madame Su. "The holding cell was so small that I could barely stretch my legs."

"Fine," sighed the Commissary. "We have invited you here to help us with our enquiries about the whereabouts of Monsieur Conrad Su. Do you think you can shed light on this matter?"

"I can't think how I could," said the Musketeer, leaning against the back wall of the interrogation room, and stretching his arms and legs in slow succession. "I've never met the man."

The Commissary turned to Madame Su. "Is that correct, Madame? Has D'Artagnan ever met your husband?"

"I don't know," said Madame Su, looking at the Musketeer in confusion. "I don't think she had, before I sent her to find him… you do know that this isn't D'Artagnan, don't you? My lodger is female."

"That's quite correct," said the Musketeer. "Apologies for the interruption, but I am not D'Artagnan."

"You mean that you are not the D'Artagnan who pays rent with Madame Su, but you are… her husband, then?" asked the Commissary, paddling furiously.

"I have no wife," said the Musketeer, and for the first time his tone was less than light. "And my name is not D'Artagnan."

The Commissary blinked twice and looked at Madame Su. "Who is this man?"

"I thought *you* knew!" she exploded. "He's not my lodger, that's for sure." She gave the Musketeer a dirty look. "If she has been hiding a husband, I am certainly going to charge her double and backdate the rent!"

"Madame, I assure you, I have not been sharing D'Artagnan's apartment," the Musketeer said. "I have quite reasonable rooms elsewhere in Paris."

"So who are you?" the Commissary demanded.

"Captain-lieutenant Athos of the Royal Musketeer fleet." He smiled politely at her, and raised his wrist. "You can scan my ID if you like. I tried to suggest this when I was first brought into the cells, but for some reason the guards were very keen to keep my presence here off the records."

"That happened to me too," said Madame Su thoughtfully.

"What an astounding coincidence," said Athos of the Musketeers.

Early retirement, the Commissary decided. It was the only reasonable response to a farce like this. "You identified yourself as D'Artagnan," she growled.

"Did I?" said Athos. "I was minding my own business, approaching my friend's new quarters, and suddenly I was surrounded by a group of somewhat young and inexperienced Red Hammers. One of them asked if I was D'Artagnan in a very fierce voice…" He held up his hands, as if helpless. "I didn't like to embarrass them by pointing out the obvious."

"The obvious," repeated the Commissary.

"Madame Su here can help iron out the details of the obvious differences between myself and Mecha-Cadet D'Artagnan," said Athos.

"I can think of a few," muttered Madame Su.

The door of the interrogation room burst open, and a woman stood there in a bright pink flight suit that marked her as a civilian. She had a long sweep of black hair, a nasty scar slashed across her face, and she looked like she was about to murder someone.

"Return to the front desk immediately," blustered the Commissary, getting to her feet. "You have no right to interrupt this interrogation!"

"I wouldn't be too sure about that," said Athos, his eyes on the intruder as if she were the most dangerous thing in the room.

"My credentials," snapped the woman, holding her wrist out to the Commissary, who scanned her stud with the clamshell on her desk. **Special Agent Captain Rosnay Cho, Security Level 22**, rattled across the screen.

Level 22 meant that the agent reported directly to the Cardinal herself. With visions of her early retirement disappearing into smoke, the Commissary bowed her head. "I cede these prisoners to you, of course, Special Agent Cho."

"Only the woman," said Cho. Her eyes flicked briefly over the Musketeer who called himself Athos. "This one can rot in your holding cells for as long as you like." She held out one hand to the terrified Madame Su. "You are coming with me, madame. My employer has some very important questions to ask you about your husband."

The journey that followed was the most terrifying time of Madame Su's life. It was particularly fraught when Special Agent Cho discovered that the ship she had intended to use to transport them to Luna Palais was missing, along with an engineer, and that there were no security records of how this had happened.

After further delays and quite a lot of enraged shouting, they were eventually packed into a borrowed red and gold sabre-class dart, bound for the moon.

During the journey, Madame Su thought about every insulting thing she had ever said about the current Regence and her good-for-nothing husband the Prince Consort. Was this her fault? Had she been recorded somewhere, saying something she shouldn't? It was a relief when the dart docked a good distance from the Palace, and she realised they were going somewhere else altogether: a private residence, which contained no angry members of the royal family.

Special Agent Cho let herself in through the front door, spoke briefly to a servant, and then dragged Madame Su along with her until they reached a botanical atrium at the centre of the residence.

The greenness and realness of the plants was something of a shock to Madame Su, who preferred her vegetation pre-packed in plastic pouches, with salad dressing.

Special Agent Cho pushed her way through several fronds of greenery, dragging her prisoner along with her, until they found a corner of the atrium that was occupied.

The woman was younger than Madame Su herself, perhaps forty years old, and greying at the temples. She wore a thick apron and gloves, her dark hair tied back in a bun as she concentrated on snipping stray flowers from a strong vine with a pair of vicious-looking secateurs.

"Hello, Rosnay," she said, sounding quite serene. "How is it all going, then?"

"Mixed results," said the agent through gritted teeth. "Brought you a present, Eminence."

"So you have." The woman looked Madame Su over, as if perusing fabrics in a warehouse. "I think we're going to require tea, don't you?"

"I'd rather find my missing Moth," Special Agent Cho said angrily. "You won't believe what those cunning bastards have…"

"Tea," said the gardener in a very firm voice, not to be denied. "And little sandwiches, with lots of butter. Our guest looks tired and hungry."

Madame Su, who was not entirely stupid, and knew what the title "Eminence" meant, did her best not to burst into tears. This was Cardinal Richelieu. Chances were very low that she was going to get out of this alive.

"Tea would be nice," Madame Su managed in a small voice.

"Jolly good," said the Cardinal, snipping another dead-head. "Tea, sandwiches and a nice cozy chat."

It was the most awkward tea party in the history of the solar system. Madame Su did not dare say anything without being asked directly. Special Agent Cho vibrated with fury over whatever had happened to her spaceship. The Cardinal was pleasant enough but remained terrifyingly formal. She regularly received messages upon her clamshell in between sips of tea and bites of toast point.

The sandwiches and the tea were excellent, but there is nothing like the fear of immediate execution to make even a splendid spread taste like dust on the tongue.

"Your husband, Madame Su," said the Cardinal after a long moment. She still did not look like a grand religious leader, with only a small solar star hanging at her throat to mark that she belonged to the Church of All. She wore black flight fatigues, as if she were a soldier rather than a priest. Her hair was dressed with a constellation of pearl pins. "You are aware that he is a conspirator?"

Madame Su did not dare argue this point. "My Conrad was always such a good boy," she whispered, clutching her teacup as if it might fly away into space at any moment. "But the Palace... there are temptations."

"Indeed," said the Cardinal. "Treason can be a terrible temptation, to one so young and vulnerable."

"I knew nothing about it!" Madame Su burst out. "I only wanted my husband back safe, I didn't —" She broke off, and buried her face in a biscuit, nibbling like a mouse.

A new message came in. The Cardinal read it, her eyes flicking across the words incredulously, and then she smiled. "Tell me, Madame Su, of everything you know about your husband's connection to his former teammate, Madame Marie Chevreuse-Montbazon."

Madame Su pressed her lips together in fear. That woman. That athletic goddess with her winning smile and decadent, corrupting ways. "I have not had sight of that bitch since she was exiled, and good riddance," she spat.

The Cardinal did not say 'indeed' again this time, but she smiled a warm and reassuring smile. "You think Chevreuse a likely ringleader?"

"Trouble from head to toe," Madame Su grumbled. "A husband-eater."

Special Agent Cho received a call through her comm, and she leaped to her feet, asking the Cardinal for permission to take it outside. Her Eminence agreed with a graceful nod of her head.

Madame Su began to think that she was misplaced in her fear – the Cardinal had made no move to accuse Madame Su of being complicit in her husband's dealings.

"Why, I could tell you a story or two about that Marie Chevreuse," she volunteered bravely.

A light sparkled in the Cardinal's eyes. "Please do."

It was as if a dam had burst inside her. Madame Su barely paused for breath as she rattled out all of the disreputable, flirtatious instances she had witnessed over the last

several years. She only paused when Cho returned, interrupting without any manners at all.

"Your Eminence," she gasped. "It's done."

The Cardinal's face changed, from the politely encour-
aging lady to a sharp, incisive politician. She turned to
Cho, forgetting Madame Su was even there. "The *Colin
Guillaume*?"

"En route to Valour, with enough time missing from
their flight log to account for an unidentified ship that
docked briefly at the mecha graveyard."

The Cardinal shone from within like a diamond. "Evidence?" she purred.

"On board, with the Ambassador." Cho smiled with all
her teeth. "Milord will collect the data when they touch
down on Valour."

"Excuse me, Madame Su," said the Cardinal, sweeping
to her feet. "My breakfast meeting with the Regence has
taken on more than its usual importance. You may return
to Paris Satellite."

Madame Su blinked, surprised at the sudden release. "I
may?"

"I hardly wish to detain you."

"But —"

"Your husband escaped his abduction, and has since
returned to his bed at the Palace. I am sure he will be in
contact with you when he awakes. But it is late, of course.
After such a trying day, you should get some rest."

Madame Su stood, and was guided to the door by
polite servants as if she were the visitor who had chosen
such an unwelcome time to be paying calls. "But," she said
again, before she found herself standing alone on the auto-
matic pavement in front of the residence. It hummed

beneath her feet, drawing along the avenue of one of the wealthiest areas on Luna Palais.

"Oh, Conrad," she sighed. "What have you got us into now?"

Her credit stud chimed discreetly, informing her that she had received a substantial payment from the Cardinal's office, 'in compensation for your inconvenience, and for the rendering of future intelligence.'

At some point during the night, Madame Su had become the Cardinal's spy.

CHAPTER 16
CINQUEFOIL FOR BEGINNERS

A week after the events that Dana D'Artagnan had mentally filed away as That Night, she came off a double transport shift at Paris Satellite to find Athos waiting for her at the gate. He tilted his head at her expectantly.

She had been avoiding him, and he knew it.

"I am so sorry," Dana blurted out when she got close enough to speak.

Athos shook his head, took her arm and hauled her along the concourse, heading for Marie Antoinette Esplanade. "Not here. Practice rooms."

Dana knew discretion was necessary, but it was all she could do to stop herself from rolling out a dozen more apologies between here and their destination.

Finally they reached the entertainment hub, where Athos paid for a rec space with a credit swipe of his stud. Only when they were inside the sleek and empty white practice room did Dana realise that he had more than one baton hanging from his belt. What was the plural of a pilot's slice?

"You want to fence?" she asked as he tossed the second baton to her, then stripped off his Musketeer jacket.

"Porthos said you'd keep avoiding me until I let you get some stuff off your chest, and I thought that sounded like a waste of time, but she's generally right about these things." He frowned at her. "At least this way, we'll be doing something productive."

Dana scowled. "Porthos should keep her nose out of everyone else's business."

"See, D'Artagnan? That is why you and I are friends." Athos called up a screen in the wall and tapped a few print commands into it. "Did you get fitted for the practice gear I told you about? You need your own pattern to print from."

"I haven't had time."

He rolled his eyes at her. "Preventing bruises saves on medipatches. Make the time. This will do for now."

Athos' own fencing jacket, pre-programmed into the system, printed first. A generic woman's jacket followed, which he tossed to her. He had ordered water bottles and towels, too. "By next time, you'll need your own strip and mask. For now, concentrate on not stabbing me in the face and I'll resist the urge to do the same. We won't go at full speed."

Dana did not retort that she might have been better prepared for this session if he'd given her any warning. They both knew that if he hadn't sprung this on her, she might have kept dodging him for at least another week.

"I'll do my best," she said, struggling into the stiff jacket. She had hoped for a lie-down and some dinner at the end of her shift, but she knew better than to argue with Athos in a mood like this. Besides… she owed him.

"Stop looking at me like you drowned my pet," he snapped, setting his own pilot's slice to the thinnest, lightest setting, with a blunted tip. The SmartMetal was springy that way, best for practice bouts. When Porthos played blades with Dana, she encouraged her to go for a heavier weight of sword, but Athos was all about technique.

"Athos, you went to prison for me." Dana wouldn't even have known about it if Aramis hadn't let it slip a few nights ago. Athos was so furious that Aramis opened her mouth, he stormed out of the bar where they had been drinking. Dana had been too embarrassed to look him in the eye ever since.

"Hardly prison," he scoffed, doing a few experimental lunges with the sword. "The holding cell at the Armoury is an old friend of mine. I was only there a day or so, and it gave me a chance to catch up on the newest graffiti. Are you ready?"

"Just about." Dana stretched first. Last time she had allowed Athos to lead her in 'a little light sword practice' she had spent a whole evening massaging painful cramps out of her calves. Athos never did anything lightly.

He was waiting for her now, sword at the ready. They began with a few gentle taps, measuring distance, watching each other. "Besides," Athos said finally. "I didn't do it for you. I did it to piss off the Cardinal."

There wasn't much time to talk – not with his sword flicking at her, and Dana mustering up all her concentration to accept the lesson for what it was.

If fencing was a conversation, then Athos had all the

nouns, adjectives and verbs. It was all Dana could do to grab the occasional punctuation mark. Whenever she failed to defend herself against one of his moves, he stopped and checked himself, then did it again at half or quarter speed, so she could work out what she could or should have done to counter it.

"This is so much better than talking about our feelings," Dana said breathlessly when they paused to slug water from freshly-printed bottles.

"Don't tell Porthos," said Athos, with half a grin.

"Did Amiral Treville really go to the Regence herself to get you freed?"

He shrugged with one shoulder, wiping the back of his neck with a towel. "Someone had to. The bastards were keeping me out of the system, so there was no trace of my ID."

"Treville trusted Aramis and Porthos' word that they had you in the Armoury?"

Athos reached out and tapped Dana on the nose with his fingertip. "Treville may be scary as all fuck, but she's loyal to her pilots, and she knows we wouldn't bullshit her about anything really important. Remember that, D'Artagnan. She's worth letting into your confidence, if you've anything worth protecting. No one is more loyal to the Crown or the Solar System or the Musketeers than our Amiral Treville."

Dana hesitated, but nodded. Athos didn't trust many people, so this was worth knowing. "So Treville marched into the Palace…"

"And interrupted the Regence at her morning chocolate – with guess who?"

Dana laughed at that, a sudden shout of noise in the muffled practice room. "I bet that went down well."

"The Cardinal knows which side her bread is buttered on. She's always the first to suggest that her enemies be forgiven. It's the dart she slips in while agreeing with everyone that poisons the trough." Athos flexed his sword a few more times. "Ready for another bout?"

"It doesn't count as forgiving me if you take it out of my body in sweat and blood," Dana protested, but she dropped her water bottle to the floor and headed into the centre of the space again, sword in hand.

"Nothing to forgive," he told her. "But if you haven't got a touch on me three times by the end of this session, I expect you to grovel."

They threw themselves back into it: flick and slide, parry, defend, lunge, and endless footwork drills.

This must be what it would be like to have a brother, Dana thought as Athos corrected her stance for the fourth time, literally kicking her feet into the proper position. She grinned stupidly at him. He looked confused, then prodded her in the pit of her stomach with the blunt tip of his sword. "Again. Do better."

Aramis pounced upon them both when they emerged from the practice room, sweaty and exhausted. "Kidnapping you!" she announced, flinging an arm around Athos' shoulders and making a face at him. "So wet. Bleh."

"Can we go back to my place and shower before the kidnapping?" Athos asked, butting her with his damp head. Aramis squirmed and kept him at arm's distance.

"Ugh, yes. Though that is against the philosophy of kidnapping, so I may insist upon a forfeit."

"What are we doing now?" Dana gave into the inevitable, that her time would not be her own until the next work shift. Who needed sleep and food anyway?

Aramis shook her wrist, calling up three virtual tickets that glowed in the air before them and then disappeared back into her credit stud. "CINQUEFOIL!" she howled. "Serpentin versus the Mousers, it's going to be brutal."

"I would," said Athos calmly, "actually rather eat glass."

"I know, darling, that's why it means so much to us that you're going to overcome your appalling bias against the game of gods and join us," said Aramis. "Porthos has royal escort duty, which means three tickets going begging. Luckily, there are three of us right here."

"Give mine to Grimaud."

"She has her own. You bought her a season ticket to the Mousers last Joyeux, because you are a selfless and thoughtful person and she would have dumped your arse years ago if you didn't come through with the bribes."

"I'm beginning to regret the error of my generosity," said Athos.

Aramis ignored him, as she so often did. "Dana, you in?"

Dana had not managed to see a game of cinquefoil in Paris so far. Porthos' preferences were firmly for fleur-de-lis. Athos' distaste made her all the more curious. "Of course," she said.

"You'll regret it," Athos warned.

"And you have spent far too long in your own

company lately, my friend," said Aramis lightly, her eyes back on him. "Did you think we wouldn't notice?"

Athos strode ahead, avoiding her steady gaze. "Fine. At least with all the blood spatter and inane commentary, I won't be expected to make conversation with either of you."

"So what you're saying is, I win?" Aramis called after him, then winked at Dana. "I usually win."

ARTOIS: Here we are back for the local derby, both of Paris Satellite's homegrown teams facing off for the first time this season: that's Serpentin in green and white, and the Mousers in grey. Your commentary team today is me, Charlemagne Artois, sitting alongside three-times Solar Cup winner Renée Olympe, how are you this evening, champ?

OLYMPE: I'm excited, Artois, It's always a grudge match between these two teams, but you only have to look at the lineup to know that this is going to be a tough game. Serpentin are playing their brand new chevalier, Thierry Degas, only months after his controversial transfer back from the Freedom League who poached him from the Mousers themselves two seasons ago for a record transfer sum of 28 million credits.

ARTOIS: Yes, Olympe, you can see from the banners that the Mousers fans are still furious that their former captain returned to Paris only to sign up with their most fierce local rivals. And the team aren't any happier about it. Even before gameplay begins, the current captain and chevalier of the Mousers, Samir Olivier, has refused to include Degas in his pole salute, that's quite a snub.

OLYMPE: Who can blame him, Artois, Olivier was one of many young players who came up through the youth club with Degas, and it's always a blow to find out that your heroes care more for financial incentive than team loyalty – not that I'm bitter, as a long-time Mousers fan myself.

ARTOIS: Not that you're biased either, Olympe!

OLYMPE: Of course I'm biased, Artois, the Mousers are the best team in the Solar League.

ARTOIS: Five years without winning the Cup suggests otherwise…

OLYMPE: AND IT'S KICKOFF!

Thirty seconds into the game, Dana conceded Athos' point about cinquefoil. This was the most distressing spectator sport she had ever witnessed. There was a controlled chaos to fleur-de-lis, a dance between the Jousters and their opponents. There was technique, skill, a fierce elegance to the whole thing.

Cinquefoil appeared to have no formal rules. The large zero-gravity tank (the same size as was used for the other game) was surrounded on all sides by the audience stands. The higher up you were, the more you could see of the game – and because everyone sat about thirty centimetres from the plexi-glass walls of the tank, it was entirely possible for a player to crash into the wall right in front of your face, blood spiralling out in tiny floating globes.

ARTOIS: That's a beautiful leap from Henri of the Mousers, he's got a fierce turn of speed on him as he propels himself directly in the path of Valentine.

> OLYMPE: Always up the north side, of course, but even when they know it's coming, he's – and it's first blood in the fourth quadrant, with both Serpentin pole attacks making a vicious double play against Bradamante!

ARTOIS: She's made of nails, that player, it's like she hasn't even noticed that her nose is broken, look at that shoulder work as she shoves Valentine directly into Lola Chang's path and OH THAT HAS TO HURT!

Dana considered herself tough, but she had her hands half covering her face for most of the game. Athos was several drinks ahead of the rest of them, having started well before they even reached their seats. Aramis, the optimist of the three, genuinely enjoyed the vicious mechanics of the game – or she had, right up to the moment she had spotted Captain Tracy Dubois sitting in a private box with her husband, on the far side of the tank.

Porthos might have lightened the mood, but she was in full uniform, on duty near the royal box from which the Regence and Prince Consort viewed the spectacle, accompanied by several friends and ministers.

Dana realised that the stately older woman who sat to one side of the Regence in a plum-coloured gown was the Cardinal herself. She did not look especially religious, though there was a chilly gravity to her.

Dana shivered for a moment, when the Cardinal looked in her direction. The last thing she wanted was that kind of attention.

OLYMPE: Believe me, Artois, a broken nose hurts just as much in zero gravity as it does anywhere else, but don't take your eyes off the second quadrant, where Olivier has kicked his way past the pole challenges of St Girard and Serpentin captain Millefleur, I think we know where he's going, don't we?

ARTOIS: Millefleur isn't going to let her
chevalier get grabbed that easily, look at
her hauling Olivier back down into third
quadrant and away from his target… and
she's used BOTH HANDS, that's a foul.
Meanwhile, Anjelique 'the Angel' Anjou
just used St Girard as ballast to rocket her
halfway across the tank, and she's the
first of the Mousers to get a tip challenge
on Degas.

OLYMPE: They're in formal jousting mode
now, jet packs engaged, and OH THAT'S
NASTY!

Dana could not stop glancing over at the royal box, not
only because it kept her eyes averted from the upsetting
violence of the cinquefoil, but because Conrad was there,
in a bright sky-blue jacket that matched his hair. He sat
with the Prince, the two of them watching the game avidly,
pointing out every move and player to each other with
grins and laughter.

Aramis dropped her head to Dana's shoulder, nursing
her wounded heart from seeing Dubois on such good
terms with her husband. Even in a morose state, she was
far too observant. "I hope it's not the Prince that you can't
take your eyes off, little one," she said in a low voice, her
mouth brushing Dana's ear. "We only just finished
cleaning up the last scandal in the making…"

Dana elbowed her, turning her eyes back to the game,
just as two Serpentin players slammed themselves hard
against the Mouser captain, one from above and one from

below. The entire audience sucked in a sympathetic breath in unison, and the Mouser supporters around Dana and the others started booing and yelling angrily, some of them physically banging their hands on the tank in protest.

"Of course not," Dana hissed back at Aramis. "Don't even think things like that!"

Aramis chuckled to herself. "Such pretty men, these New Aristocrats. Not my type, of course, but I see the appeal."

"Can you stop right now?"

"I'm only teasing, Dana," Aramis said seriously. "I know it's the tailor you have eyes for."

"I hate you!" Dana muttered, slumping lower in her chair.

Aramis reached over her shoulders to catch Athos' attention by smacking him on the head. "Athos, Athos! Dana likes a boy."

"They grow up so fast," Athos said without missing a beat, though he was ordering another drink, and wasn't properly listening. "Is the game over yet?"

"Quarter time," said Aramis as the whistle went and the players retreated to have the worst of their wounds bandaged.

"Give me strength."

The second quarter was just as vicious, with both teams down to four players each by the end of it, and at least four poles swapped out due to breakages. The zero-gravity well inside the tank had to be sluiced with air pressure to remove all the globules of blood and floating splinters before the next round.

Athos wasn't interested in anything but drinking, and Aramis continued to dart searching looks at Dubois and her husband, so it was down to Dana to fetch supplies from the noodle stand down on the main deck. She returned with her hands full of damp paper containers and egg rolls, to find that the audience had quietened down to hear a royal speech.

"Just in time," Aramis groaned, snatching at the food. "I will bury my heartbroken melancholy in sticky prawns."

"There aren't enough sticky prawns in the world to bury your heartbreaks," Athos drawled.

They hushed as the Regence stood and began her speech.

Dana was impressed all over again by the Regence's grace and beauty. Lalla-Louise Regence Royal had an extraordinary public presence, her charisma shining out of her face. It was easy to see how she had won the propaganda battle, and why the people believed every promise that she made to hold the system together instead of allowing it to fracture into a series of planetary rulerships.

"You should know, my people, that I would never lie to you," she said, her low and melodic voice picked up and piped into every chair, every comm channel, so it was as if she spoke directly into every row of seats. "Many of my advisors suggested that I deny the rumours that have arisen in recent days. Rumours that the Sun-kissed are on the move, and that recent provincial attacks might well be the work of our old enemy."

Dana felt the reactions of Aramis on one side of her,

and Athos on the other. Their backs straightened, and their chins lifted. There was a tension to them, as if they were about to be called to arms.

"…no matter the distress and panic it may cause, I need you to know that I trust you all with this knowledge. If the Sun-kissed try to march against us again, let them come, for we are strong. Strong in faith and strong in arms. The Sabres, the Musketeers, the Mecha Squads, the Red Hammers: regardless of whether they are Royal Fleet or Church Fleet, all serve the Crown and the Solar System. We will always defeat those who test our faith, whether they come from within or without our own species."

The Cardinal stood with the Regence, and the Prince Consort on her other side. It was a powerful image of unity in strength.

Dana felt something soft drift past her shoulder blades and realised that Aramis had reached around her, one hand brushing lightly against the back of Athos' neck. His eyes bore fiercely into the Regence and her supporters.

Had they fought against the Sun-kissed in the war? It ended eight years ago. Dana did not know how long it was since her friends had joined the Musketeers. They could have been in the service, fighting against the aliens who almost destroyed the solar system.

Athos' hands trembled. Dana pretended not to notice.

The Regence lightened the mood with a joke, and a merry smile. The audience relaxed around her, responding to her upbeat tone.

"Because cheer is as important in times of peace and faith as it was in our darker times, I have a joyful announcement to share with all of Paris!" the Regence announced. "At her Eminence's suggestion, we are to hold a ball for my wedding anniversary to my beloved Prince Alek." She squeezed her husband's hand, and smiled adoringly at him. "It shall be televised live to the populace, and I'm sure you will be greatly entertained by our frivolities and our costumes. The theme is Diamonds and Peacocks!"

Dana spat out a mouthful of her drink. Athos automatically confiscated her cup, and swallowed half of its contents.

The royal couple were besieged by applause and well-wishers, as their assorted hangers on demonstrated their pleasure at the idea of a ball. Reporters were let loose to ask questions about which celebrities were expected to attend.

The Prince Consort's smile, however warm it was in the presence of his wife, lacked something as he turned away from her. The cams captured his faltering face, throwing it up on the larger screens. Conrad, sitting right next to the Prince, looked as if his world had ended.

"Damn it all," Dana murmured beneath her breath.

Aramis and Athos turned to her. "Trouble?" asked Athos as if a distraction was exactly what he needed.

Dana nodded. It couldn't be a coincidence. The Regence – or the Cardinal – or both of them, knew about the peacock coat and the diamond studs and the Duchess of Buckingham.

"Trouble," she said grimly. "But I don't think there's anything we can do to stop it now."

"Haven't you heard?" said Aramis lightly, tossing a food carton from hand to hand as if there had been no discussion at all today of aliens and war and a possible return to the darkest time that their people had ever faced. "We're Musketeers. Trouble is what we do best."

CHAPTER 17
PORTRAIT OF A MARRIAGE

ana had been thinking about Conrad Su and his employer ever since yesterday's cinquefoil game, and the Regence's announcement.

It was none of Dana's business. She had no right to involve herself. And yet – the safety of the realm might well depend on how the Prince Consort chose to handle the matter of the coat and the diamonds and the ball.

If the Sun-kissed were returning, if it was really true that another intergalactic war was on the horizon, then this was the worst possible time for the government to take a hit.

Dana flopped down on her narrow bed in the room above Madame Su's workshop. Sleep. She needed sleep. But every time she closed her eyes, there was a clanking noise from below. The rooms were heavily soundproofed, which meant the noise must be fearsome indeed.

Finally, she let herself out of her room and leaned over the balcony to see what was going on down there.

The workshop had been half-cleared of its usual

printers and other paraphernalia, to make room for three large mecha. They were basic orbital suits, designed for space repairs and other tasks outside the station. They were also, for the most part, in bits.

Another pallet of limbs and casings arrived on a packing trolley steered by two Pigeons, and Madame Su directed the lot to be unpacked on the workshop floor.

Planchet sat among the mechanical debris, looking as if all her birthdays had come at once. When she saw Dana, she waved merrily up at her. "Look what we got!"

Madame Su darted a glance at Dana and looked away again. She had been doing that since her release by the Red Hammers, as if she didn't want to acknowledge that they even knew each other. If it meant Dana would not be included any new Palace plots, she was okay with that.

Madame Su turned swiftly and withdrew into her rooms.

"You have to see this!" Planchet squealed, diving into the new pile of mecha bits.

Dana came down the steps to her. "Where in space did you get it all?" Her thoughts flitted to the mecha grave-yard on Luna Palais and that odd night she had spent out there with Conrad, Chevreuse and Dubois.

"Auction," said Planchet, diving into one of the pallets and pulling out handfuls of circuits. "Madame Su has a contract to supply cheap mecha for the *Calais*," she added, referring to the solarcrawler civilian transport that ran regularly between Honour and Valour. "I'm going to build and fix them from this lot, and she's paying me a percentage!"

Dana frowned at that. "I hope it's a big percentage, if you're doing all the work."

Planchet's expression fell slightly. "It's… a percentage," she said.

Dana sighed, and patted Planchet on the arm. "Do you really think you can get entire mecha suits up and running from scrap?"

"Oh yes," said Planchet, brightening. "Look at that one, the chassis is mostly complete, it's only the internals that need to be completely remodelled, and that one over there will be solid once I get the head reshaped and buffed down to size, and find it some new internal circuits. And arms."

Dana should go back to her room and sleep. She really should. Rest was important. But this looked like fun. Taking things apart, putting them back together and recycling scrap into working tech had been a massive part of her life back on Gascon Station, and while she appreciated the ease with which you could access anything you wanted here in Paris, she did love a challenge.

Besides, if she built a mecha from the inside out, she might do better with the damn things in the field. She needed all the help she could get on that score.

"Can I help?" she asked, and was rewarded by a brilliant grin from Planchet.

An hour later, Dana sat inside the most complete of the broken mecha suits. The pilot's nest was the easiest position from which to run a full diagnostic. Next to this bucket of bolts, the mecha that Dana used for her work with Commandant Essart was looking pretty damned shiny.

"I have to deliver some contracts for Madame Su," said Planchet, speaking loudly from outside the casing. "It'll only take half an hour. Are you all right in there?"

"Yep," said Dana, who had checked twice that she was able to release the opening mechanism from the inside. "It'll take me nearly that long to get this done."

"That doesn't sound promising," said Planchet, her smile dimming slightly.

"He's a fixer-upper. There's a lot more wrong with the internals than a few burned-out circuits."

Not even that report could get Planchet down. "I wouldn't want it to be too easy, that'd be boring!"

"This is why I will never become an engineer," Dana groaned.

Planchet laughed and ran off on her errand, with all the energy of a robot puppy.

Dana continued with her diagnostic. The view screens worked, which was something of a miracle as she wasn't entirely sure what they were connected to. She was about to prise up a panel to see the state of the wiring when a familiar figure walked straight past the front of the mecha.

It was Conrad Su. She had never seen him here before, though of course it was technically his home. He stopped before the door to his wife's office, about to knock, then walked away a few paces instead.

Dana felt odd, not letting him know she was here. There was no way to reveal her presence that wouldn't be extremely awkward. At least this way she could be awkward on her own without him knowing about it.

Conrad returned to the door and knocked quickly, before he could change his mind. "Jingfei?"

Madame Su emerged, staring at him in a very

unfriendly manner. She closed the door behind her, not inviting him inside. "It's you."

Conrad dragged a hand through his spiky blue hair — a nervous habit of his. "How are you? I mean, after —"

"I am somewhat recovered from being imprisoned, threatened and scared half to death, thank you so much for asking," she hissed.

He reached out, touching her arm. "I am sorry about all that. I never meant to bring it down on you."

Madame Su crossed her arms. "You never think, do you? This is what I get for marrying such a boy. It's all games and sports and friends and danger, without a thought of those who get hurt along the way!"

They looked at each other for a long moment, and then Conrad hugged her, murmuring apologies. Madame Su scowled darkly, but allowed him to comfort her, angrily wiping a dash of tears from one eye so he wouldn't see them.

Dana had never felt more like an intruder in her life. At least the mecha was disabled and so every embarrassed twitch she made would not be reflected by its giant limbs flailing around. She would have given anything to be able to sidle away, unseen.

Conrad drew back from his wife, kissing her once on the forehead. "Jingfei, I'm sorry, I really am, but I need your help. I can only ask someone that I trust."

Madame Su pushed him away. "What trouble have you got yourself into now, brat?"

"It's nothing bad, or even difficult. But I need you to carry a letter to Valour for me."

Valour. Dana hissed beneath her breath.

"Valour?" Madame Su said in astonishment. "You want

me to travel to another planet as some messenger bird? I have a business to run here!"

Conrad was showing his anxiety now. "There's no time to waste. I can't go myself, the Palace —"

"Oh yes, your precious Palace," Madame Su mocked. "I have a new contract to fill for the *Calais*, and more coming from a very important new patron. I don't have time for your little intrigues. Hire a Raven if you can't send a text like a normal person."

"Jingfei," he whispered, pleading with her. "It's important. For the Crown."

His wife arched back as if he had said something shocking, and then she smiled an oddly cruel sort of smile. "Conrad, darling. Not everyone serves the Crown first."

There was a pause as he took in her words. Then he straightened, nodding as if she had said something polite and completely uninteresting. "My mistake. I'm sorry, Jingfei. I won't bother you with this again."

Madame Su held her cheek out to him. Conrad kissed her dutifully, and walked away, his boots making a muffled sound against the metal floor.

Dana let out a long, painful breath. She wished she had not seen that. A moment later, what she saw was fifty times worse.

"Is he gone?" asked a voice from inside Madame Su's office.

"Yes," said Madame Su in a shaky voice. "Did I do the right thing?"

To Dana's horror, when the guest emerged from the office, it was the familiar figure of the Moth pilot from Meung — Special Agent Rosnay Cho. Today's flight suit was a pale green, with two matching hair combs in the same colour, glittering with jade studs. "I would have preferred it if you had thought quickly enough to take the letter," Ro drawled. "Then we'd know what his master was up to. But this will do nicely for now. Thank you for your help." She patted the other woman on the shoulder.

Madame Su straightened with pride. "The Cardinal is a good woman. I know she has everyone's best interests at heart."

Ro sent her a jagged smile. "She pays well, too. Enjoy your new contracts, Madame Su. I think you'll find them generous." She left the workshop in that long, confident stride of hers, hair sweeping out behind her.

Dana waited until she was sure that Madame Su was back in her office. Then she slowly let herself out of the mecha, stretching her sore limbs when she was free of confinement. She dashed out of the workshop only to run smack bang into Planchet, who was carrying a box of pastries.

"Aaaargh!" Dana yelled, her nerves already jangled beyond their limits.

"Aaargh!" Planchet replied. "Why are we yelling? What's —"

But Dana did not let her ask any more than that. She grabbed her by the collar and pulled her along. "Did you see Conrad on your way over?"

"Yes, he's mooching over near the Promenade, looking cross. I didn't like to —"

"Shush!"

Dana hurried along the nearest walkway, which came out above the Promenade. She spotted the still figure of Rosnay Cho leaning on the rail, watching Conrad Su from a distance. He sat at a cafe table on the lower level; his shoulders slumped in defeat. He had no idea that he was being so closely observed.

"He needs a pastry," Planchet said sympathetically.

"No," said Dana. "You know who needs pastry? That one." She pointed at Ro. "She's the woman who abducted him."

Planchet wrapped a protective arm around her pastry box. "If that's true, I don't feel she deserves pastry."

"I need you to cause a distraction. Then I will buy you a new box of any baked goods you like. Promise."

Planchet's eyes lit up. "Is it another adventure?"

"The same one, actually."

"That's even better! The last one was brilliant."

Dana managed to position herself down on the Promenade, as close as she could get to Conrad Su without being in Ro's line of sight. She waited for her moment.

There was a commotion up on the balcony as Planchet pounced, making loud declarations about how her boss had sent these for Special Agent Cho, and she hoped she liked them, and *oh!* she was so sorry, she didn't mean to get sugar all over her feet, and so on. It was a good distraction, involving flailing arms, pastry crumbs and at least three other passers-by, not even counting the crowd who stopped to watch the disaster.

Conrad Su glanced up, his head tilting as he took in the full extent of the scene being played out above him. Dana ran forward and grabbed his hand. She dragged him along with her until they reached a row of privacy booths, and shoved him inside an empty one.

He went willingly, if still confused. Once she had closed the door behind them, Dana peeked out through the view screen. The special agent was still wiping powdered sugar off her green flight suit, which made Dana think they had got away with it.

It was a small booth, so they were practically jammed together. Conrad had an odd sort of smile on his face. "This is unexpected," he said. "You could have just called, if you wanted to see me."

Dana shoved him hard in the chest, wanting to make that flirtatious look on his face disappear fast. "This isn't a seduction!"

"Good," he shot back, giving her a bit of a shove back, though his hand connected with her shoulder instead of her chest. "Because you're terrible at it!"

"Your wife is working for the Cardinal," she warned him.

Conrad groaned, and pulled his hand through his spiky blue hair again. He wasn't going to have any left by the end of the day. "Yes, I'd worked that out for myself, cheers. I'm screwed, because I need someone to take the Prince's letter to Valour. Someone who is completely trustworthy, and I've got nothing."

Dana lifted her eyebrows at him.

Conrad's eyes brightened. "Hey, you know the Musketeers. Which of them is the least likely to be in the pocket of the Cardinal?"

Dana blinked in astonishment. "None of them!"

"Oh, come on," he said skeptically. "Everyone has their price, Dana."

"You haven't asked me mine."

It was insulting, how astonished he looked. "You?"

"Don't tell me you don't trust me," she scowled. "You gave me enough to sink the government ten times over, last week."

"I know, but." He hesitated. "You're not even a Musketeer."

"Oh thank you very much! Do you want your letter delivered or not?"

Conrad crossed his arms over his chest. "I don't want to see you killed. You might have got away with that pantomime out there, but this is serious shit. People could end up dead for this letter."

"Do you want to explain its contents to anyone else?" she hissed at him. "I *know* already, Conrad. It's the coat, isn't it?"

He slumped against the walls of the privacy booth. "That fucking coat. I can make a new one in time for the ball, but we daren't risk trying to replace those studs. We could manage one or two, but the whole set? Too much could go wrong, and it's obvious that they know, which makes it worse."

"Is that why you didn't give the letter to Dubois?" Dana asked in a low voice. "Or is it me you suspect?"

Conrad sighed, shaking his head. "I don't think either of you are in with the Cardinal. For all we know, her goons wired the whole fucking mecha graveyard for sound. But Dubois already turned me down. She's trying to fix things with her husband, and after her last trip to Valour she's washing her hands of Alek and his – well, you know. Everything."

"So trust *me*," said Dana.

"You don't have a ship. Or time – don't you work for the mecha squad?"

"I can ask for leave." Dana remembered what Athos had told her, not so long ago. *No one is more loyal to the Crown or the Solar System or the Musketeers than Amiral Treville.* "I can go to Amiral Treville, take her into our confidence."

Conrad raised his eyebrows. "You have the ear of the Amiral?"

"If she agrees to help, I won't be on my own. She could square my absence with Commandant Essart, and it — would be an official mission."

It couldn't hurt to show Treville the level of Dana's commitment to the Crown and the Musketeers. For future reference.

"Fine," Conrad said at last, with great reluctance. "If you can get Amiral Treville on side, I will trust you with the Prince Consort's letter. But it has to be today, Dana."

Dana nodded, and on impulse reached out and kissed him on the cheek. Conrad leaned into her for a moment as if he needed the physical contact. "To Valour and back, for a handful of diamond studs," Dana said cheerfully, leaning all the way back so she wouldn't be tempted to kiss him again. "Piece of cake."

CHAPTER 18
KISSING AT AIRLOCKS

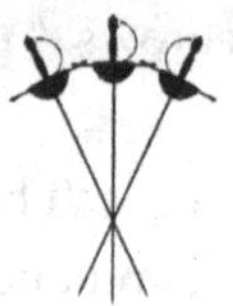

This time around, Dana only had to wait an hour and a half before she was waved in through the plexi-glass doors to Treville's office.

Treville dropped into the seat on one side of her sitting desk and waited for Dana to join her. "Timing is everything, kid. I just got off the subspace with Alix."

"Maman?" said Dana in surprise. She had barely heard her mother's voice in months. Subspace communication was an extravagance she could not afford. "Is everything all right back on Gascon Station?"

Treville shrugged her large, muscular shoulders. "It's classified. But you're family, so you might as well know. Your mother's security team uncovered three Sun-kissed agents on Gascon, disguised as tourists. We believe there are more, among the miners down on Freedom."

Dana shivered. "The Sun-kissed didn't bother with Freedom or Gascon Station last time around."

"And yet," said Treville evenly. "So you catch me on the cliff edge of a crisis, young D'Artagnan. The old enemy are moving against us and they're still too damned good at hiding in plain sight. Thank God and All for the vigilance shown by your mother and the Gascons. But what's your news?"

Dana hesitated for only a moment, then straightened her back and met Treville's gaze. If she didn't have confidence in herself, how could she expect anyone else to believe in her? *Even Conrad needed some persuasion*, she thought sourly to herself. "I need you to authorise a mission to Valour."

Treville's face did not move. "Last I noticed, chicken, you weren't working for me. Remember Commandant Essart? Appallingly chipper old duck, but good at her job."

"This isn't a Mecha Squad matter," said Dana desperately. "It should have gone to a Musketeer, I know that. But – chance brought me into the path of a secret, and now I'm in the confidence of the Prince's tailor, and they've said they will entrust me with a letter…"

"Hey," said Treville, reaching out a surprisingly soft hand to grip Dana's shoulder. "Breathe."

Dana felt like a child. She had meant to be so cool. But she took the Amiral's advice, sucking in a slow, deep breath and letting it out again.

"So," said Treville, a moment later. "This is about the Prince Consort?"

"It's a matter of great political and personal sensitivity to his Highness," Dana said in a small voice. "He needs someone to take a letter secretly to Valour, and collect an item for him before the ball. They know I'm talking to you – I can tell you what the letter will contain."

"No," Treville said. She stood up, pacing back and

forth. "Keep your damned secret, D'Artagnan. If his Royal Highness needs this, that's good enough for me. You'll need backup."

Dana nodded slowly. "And passage on the *Calais*, I thought?"

Treville looked amused. "You're not negotiating for your own dart?"

Dana's face felt hot. "I wouldn't presume!"

Treville picked up a clamshell and tossed it from hand to hand before tapping notes into it. "I'll need to arrange leave for you with Commandant Essart, and move the schedule around to release some Musketeers to accompany you. What do our three inseparables think about all this?"

Dana felt a stab of guilt. "They don't know about it yet – about the mission. I came to you first. They know a little of the rest."

"You know," said Treville. "Porthos has been a bit off colour lately. Perhaps she needs some dirtside air to pick her up. Aramis is well overdue for some personal leave, though I'm not going to admit that I've heard enough gossip around the traps to know she's eating her heart out over some woman or other. And I'm sure Athos has picked up at least one duel-related injury this week." Her mouth twitched, and she tapped a few more commands into her clamshell. "They could do with a holiday."

It was an odd feeling for Dana, to be taken at her word. "You're putting a great deal of faith in me," she said.

"Yes, I am," said Treville in a firm growl of a voice. She looked Dana up and down. "I like your initiative, D'Artagnan. Athos speaks well of you, and a week doesn't go by without one of my gals bending my ear, hinting that you're worthy of service to this fleet of ours."

Dana hadn't known the Musketeers were doing that. Part of her wanted the floor to open up and swallow her from embarrassment. But she wanted to grin stupidly, too. They believed in her.

"More to the point," said Treville calmly. "You came to me first with this. You're not so swept up in the romance of being a Musketeer that you dodge proper procedure, like some people I might mention. And…" She looked uncomfortable. "What I'm going to say to you right now will not go out of this room. I don't like what's happening on Luna Palais. I don't like that her Eminence takes every damned chance she can to fuel tensions between the Regence and her husband. It's a nasty business, and it undermines the stability we were promised with their alliance. If Prince Alek needs discretion, I'm going to give him my best people. Got it?"

"Got it," said Dana, allowing the stupid grin to take over her face.

"So get the hell out of here, and take that letter where it needs to go. I'll handle the rest."

Stunned, Dana left the office. Next time the others raised a glass in honour of their precious Amiral Treville, she would be shouting along with them.

Dana went to Aramis' place first. She had not seen her in a few days. Unusually, the android Bazin let her in immediately without first quizzing her on her recent religious observances, or whether she had wiped her feet.

"Captain-lieutenant Aramis will get dressed, if her friend is here," he said with an unhappy trill, his metallic head tilting to one side.

Aramis lay on her couch with a large volume of theological poetry balanced on her stomach, and a towel over her eyes. Her hair, usually bound up in a topknot for duty, fell in a dark wave over the arm of the couch. "Bazin, shut up and make me coffee."

"Captain-lieutenant Aramis did not attend church this morning," Bazin said in his usual monotone, with a hiss against his words that made a bemused Dana think he was perhaps trying to whisper.

As Bazin trotted away to make coffee for them on the other side of the room, where the food printer was sandwiched between two bookcases, Dana sat on the edge of the couch near her friend. She reached out gently and took the towel off her face. "Are you drunk?"

"Heartbroken," sighed Aramis. She did look miserable, and her eyes were red and sore. "Also, overdosed on poetry."

Dana eyed the large book skeptically. "Does it help?"

"Not today." Aramis sat up and leaned her forehead against Dana's shoulder – not so much a hug as a droop. "Why do I always feel so bad when they return to their real partners? I knew I was only borrowing her, but it *hurts.*"

Dana had fairly limited experience with sleeping with men or women who were contracted elsewhere – and she refused to connect Aramis' current misery to the flirtation she had going with Conrad Su. She patted her friend's back and gave her a proper hug, glad that her crush on Aramis had long disappeared into platonic friendship.

Friendship was better. It had the potential to last longer, especially where Aramis was concerned.

"What you need is a mission to take your mind off it," Dana said, trying to sound cheerful and encouraging.

"Captain-lieutenant Aramis has received notification of two weeks personal leave beginning today!" announced Bazin from the food printer. "It will allow her the time she needs to contemplate the many ways in which she can nourish her soul."

Aramis came alert at the news, pushing Dana out of her arms. "Leave? Why am I on leave? Has someone been gossiping to Treville about my love life?" She swayed for a moment. "Ugh. Too much poetry. Take it away before it poisons me."

Dana hastily levered the enormous book off Aramis' lap and dropped it on the floor, then pushed it under the couch with her foot. Hopefully that would be far enough away. "I requested the leave for you. But we have to go to Athos' place right now. If you're up for an adventure."

The old spark lit Aramis up, if only briefly. "An adventure. Why didn't you say so?"

Grimaud answered Athos' door, her headphones securely fastened beneath her star scarf. She said nothing as Dana and Aramis trooped in, carrying the coffee cups they had brought with them at Bazin's plaintive insistence.

Athos stood at his kitchen bar, with a clamshell sprawled open before him. "Funny thing," he said. "According to Treville, I have been given two weeks leave to improve my health. Do either of you know something I don't, or does she finally agree that I need to devote myself to full time drinking?"

Dana bit her lip. "Actually, Treville wants you – all of you – to follow me."

Athos' eyebrows looked at least twice as skeptical as the rest of him, and that was saying something. "To take the waters at Truth? A holiday spa on one of the Daughters of Peace? D'Artagnan, I didn't know you cared so much about my aches and pains."

"Valour," said Dana, and watched his face close over. There was something about that planet, she knew, that disturbed Athos greatly. It couldn't be helped. She needed him for this. She needed all of them.

Porthos burst into the apartment, not bothering to hide the fact that the entry code to the door had not even slowed her down. "Leave!" she exclaimed. "Since when do we get personal leave without asking for it? Is Treville cracking up at last? Is someone trying to get us out of the way?" She gave Aramis a very pointed look. "*Someone* hasn't been shagging pretty politicians again, have they?"

"I don't know why you look at me," said Aramis, tossing her hair. "I haven't seduced anyone political for months. I'm nursing a broken heart."

Porthos turned to Dana, who tried not to look guilty. "It's you, isn't it?"

"Secret mission for the Crown," Dana admitted.

"And does this have anything to do with —"

Athos raised a hand, and the other two went very still, watching him. "Treville thinks we should follow you, D'Artagnan?"

"You're the reason she trusts me," Dana said, feeling

defensive. "All three of you. She refused to even ask for the details once I told her it was a royal secret…"

"We won't ask questions either," Athos said steadily. "This is your mission. Tell us only what we need to know."

Dana felt warmth spreading from her stomach. It was a good thing, to be trusted. "I will receive a letter shortly," she said. "To be delivered to an old acquaintance of yours on Valour."

Athos flinched at that, but it was Aramis who said, "Buck?" in a low voice.

Dana nodded. "She received a token from the Prince Consort which he needs back here, urgently. Before the anniversary ball."

"That's a tight time limit," noted Porthos.

"We can do it faster in the darts," said Athos. "But too showy. They'd make us in an instant."

"I don't have a dart," Dana pointed out.

Athos shrugged, as if that was a minor detail. "You could ride with one of us."

"He's right, though," said Aramis. "The three of us setting off in our darts is too obvious. I presume we'll be followed?"

"Her Eminence won't want me to get to Valour," Dana admitted.

All three of them nodded, as if this was what they had expected.

"Special Agent Cho will have her eye on you now," Porthos added.

"I thought the *Calais*," said Dana.

Athos winced. "I don't like the idea of us trapped on that damned solarcrawler. Too many ways to get boxed in."

"We could take a getaway ship as freight," Porthos said thoughtfully. "Or one of us could follow the *Calais*, ready to patch in if we have to."

Dana had a thought. "Do you know how to use a sight-shield, to conceal or change your ship's tattoo?"

All three of them blinked at her.

"Where did you learn a trick like that?" Aramis asked.

"Your girlfriend," Dana admitted. "Um. Your most recent girlfriend."

Aramis' eyes narrowed, and she hooked one arm around Dana's neck. "Is it time for you and I to have a chat about information is best shared sooner rather than later, baby doll?"

"Later," said Dana. "The *Calais* leaves in two hours. I already booked our tickets."

The *Calais* solarcrawler was the slowest way to get from Paris Satellite to the planet Valour, but it had the benefit of being too damned big and too damned populated for anyone to hijack.

It looked like an articulated earthworm made out of steel armour and plexi-glass, and ran a steady transport service between Paris and Dover Satellite, the largest orbital city of Valour.

Three days there, 24 hours planetside to find the Duchess of Buckingham and reclaim the diamond studs, and three days back. Grimaud was parked in freight guarding Athos' disguised *Parry-Riposte*, while Bazin and Bonnie crewed Aramis' disguised *Morningstar*, which would discreetly follow the solarcrawler and allow them to scan for any other ships which might be following. Porthos' *Hoyden* remained in Paris, to make it less obvious that the three Musketeers known as the 'inseparables' had bugged out at the same time.

Planchet reluctantly agreed to stay out of this particular adventure, as someone had to keep Madame Su from suspecting that Dana had gone anywhere.

Planchet had loaned her clamshell to Dana, fitted out with an app that assimilated all network, broadcast and social media references to the Duchess of Buckingham. This would hopefully help her locate and communicate with Buck as efficiently as possible.

Dana, standing on the crowded platform near the airlock, had not yet received the letter from the Prince Consort. They were running out of time.

Athos and Aramis were already on the solarcrawler, staking out the four-person cabin that Dana had booked for them. Porthos was at the other end of the platform, making a very public farewell to one of her boyfriends who conveniently worked as a baggage handler here at the dock. This worked as a perfectly reasonable 'we are ordinary people not on a secret mission' cover, as it turned out that the departures platform was a place where a lot of people did a lot of kissing.

Dana stood there, surrounded by travellers and their friends and families, and so much kissing. Her thoughts were full of Rosnay Cho, and she jumped every time she spotted a colour that seemed deeply inappropriate for a flight suit. The Cardinal would certainly send her special agent after them, if she knew that this mission was taking place.

The Cardinal, Dana was starting to learn, knew bloody everything.

A hand caught at hers, dragging her back off the platform. Dana resisted only for a moment when she saw a spiky lock of blue hair sticking out from beneath a black cap like the ones that the Ravens wore. "I like your disguise," she said breathlessly.

"I worked on it specially," said Conrad Su, with mischief alight in his eyes. Before Dana could ask a question or even mention the letter, he tugged her towards him, and she fell upon his mouth.

It was a good kiss, a more thorough combination of tongue and heat than they had exchanged before, and Dana would have been lost in it entirely if not for the sting of a stud burrowing into the lining of her cheek. "Romantic," she said as their mouths parted.

"It's what all the cool kids are doing," Conrad said, with a gesture at the couples and families around them. The crowd had thinned, as they were only a few minutes from final lockdown. Only the hardcore kissers and huggers remained on the platform.

"I have to go," said Dana.

"Obviously," Conrad said, ducking his head slightly as he smiled at her. He almost looked shy for a moment. Another reason to find him attractive, as if she needed it. "Good luck," he offered.

Dana was feeling confident again. "Kiss me again before I go," she said impatiently.

This time, when their mouths came together, there was no exchange of information studs. Just tongue.

✤ ✤ ✤

By the time Dana found the carriage where Aramis and
Athos had begun the first card game of many,
the *Calais* was already detaching from the airlock.

"Here's to a boring and uneventful journey," said
Athos, not looking up as Dana slid into the seat next to
him. Porthos joined them a few minutes later, sitting
beside Aramis and opposite Dana. "Three obvious intelligence agents in the cheap seats," she said. "A couple more
I'm not sure of in first class. More Hammers than I've seen
on Calais duty – but most of them are doing security
checks for Sun-kissed spies."

"That's a good cover," said Athos, dealing the cards.
"Though increased security is to be expected after the
Regence's speech. Blood scans?"

"Psych too."

He nodded. "D'Artagnan, if they ask you, choose the
blood scan. You don't want to give anyone an excuse to
look inside your head."

"Got it," said Dana. She wormed the stud that Conrad
had given her out of her cheek with her tongue. High-
grade platinum, very fancy. It would look out of place in
the line along her wrist. This was where having hair longer
than a centimetre would be useful. She hesitated.

"Ankle," said Athos without looking at her. "Stings like
a son of a bitch, but it's amazing how often an interrogator
forgets to check inside your boots."

"That's true," said Porthos as Dana slipped her fingers
inside the soft leather of her boots, and ground the stud
into the flesh just above the bone of her ankle. "I used to
keep an arc-ray down there until that time I accidentally
burned off two of my toes."

"To Valour, then," Dana said breathlessly. She didn't

have the words to say how grateful she was that her friends were willing to come with her on this, without even knowing the details of the mission.

She was grateful to them, full stop.

"To Valour," Athos echoed, in a far less enthusiastic tone.

Aramis nudged him with her knee. "Cheer up. Dana's the only one who has to make it in one piece to the planet. Chances are, the three of us will be collateral damage along the way, and she'll abandon us dead and floating in the freezing wastes of space."

"Promises, promises," replied Athos.

CHAPTER 19
HOW THEY LOST PORTHOS AND ARAMIS

Dana had thought that she had got to know her three Musketeers well over the last couple of months. But you don't really know people until you are forced to spend several days in close confinement with them.

They were dressed as civilians. For Athos, this meant a grey flight suit and matching jacket. Aramis joked that if you cut off Athos' arm, you would find blue blood dotted with the fleur-de-lis in his veins, so the lack of uniform was fooling no one. At least his new jacket was long enough for him to carry his pilot's slice concealed.

Athos also had an ancient and battered dark grey hat, which he pulled down over his face to pretend he was asleep, when he wanted no one to talk to him. This was most of the time.

Porthos wore a fiery red wig, blazing gold earrings, and silk pyjamas in a swirling ocean pattern on the grounds that a touch of glam made her more comfortable — and as the only one of them who had left their ship back on Paris Satellite, she didn't have to worry about being ready for the helm. Every six hours or so, to prove how bored she was, she changed her outfit and her wig.

Athos had threatened to set fire to her suitcase.

Aramis wore a dark green flight suit, gathering her hair at the nape of her neck instead of the usual tight topknot. "If I have to fly in a hurry, I'll probably strangle myself," she noted. "But at least it looks casual."

The first day on the *Calais* solarcrawler consisted of card games, nervous tension, and Aramis and Porthos telling loud, scandalous stories about each other's sex lives, which had the bonus effect of scaring away the travellers who attempted to share their carriage.

It allowed them to spread out more, so that Athos could sulk quietly on the far side of the aisle from his more raucous friends. Aramis sometimes joined him, reading poetry to herself and sighing loudly about the desertion of Tracy Dubois.

Dana spent her time stalking the Duchess of Buckingham via Planchet's very convenient app. At least this meant she grew annoyed at the dissolute lifestyle and irritating public habits of someone other than her three friends.

By the second day, all four of them were just about ready to kill each other. They took turns sleeping in the bunks above the seats, never more than two at a time. They prowled the aisles of the other carriages in the guise of visiting the food printers, and they developed new and interesting ways of getting on each other's nerves.

It was third shift of the second day, and the train lights were low. Dana slept for a few hours, to the soothing sound of Aramis and Porthos muttering at each other beneath her bunk. Athos, in the bunk on the far side of the carriage, had been lying still for a long time.

As Dana awoke, she heard a name, and then another, and frowned as it seemed that Aramis and Porthos were speaking in code.

"Londres," said Aramis.

"Ngyeng," said Porthos.

"Petronova."

"Dee."

Dana turned, irritated, to see Athos' bright blue eyes shining at her from across the carriage. "They're trying to work out which of them has shagged their way through more of Paris," he said, and there was something about his disapproving tone of voice that broke Dana completely.

She laughed out loud, and Athos' mouth twitched as if he wanted to laugh too. Just like that, their friends were less annoying again, which came as a relief.

"The peanut gallery can stay quiet, or we will entreat them to put their money where their mouths are," Aramis said from below.

"Oh, I'm definitely not playing," said Athos, rolling on to his back.

"You could bet on the outcome," suggested Porthos. Gambling was always an option where she was concerned.

"Not doing that either," Athos said firmly. "It's going to be a tie."

"Smartarse," said Porthos. There was a long pause. "It is a tie. Inconceivable. I *know* Aramis is more of a tart than I am."

"My affairs are sequential rather than simultaneous," Aramis said, sounding smug.

"Be thankful you have divided Paris so neatly between

you both," Athos yawned. "Aramis takes the women, Porthos the men – no need to squabble about it."

Dana arched an eyebrow at him, and asked the question she would normally not dare to speak aloud. "And what about Athos?"

He huffed quietly at the ceiling and said nothing.

"Ah," said Aramis, as if she was discussing a great tragedy. "Athos fucks no one. It is a great source of frustration to us all."

"Not true," said Athos from his bunk, shifting again so that he had his back to Dana. "I hooked up with a Sabre three months ago. You got into a duel over my honour."

"Oh yes," Aramis said sourly. "How could I have forgotten?"

"The truth," said Porthos in a mocking voice. "Is that Athos fucks no one who could ever make him happy."

"Thank you!" said Athos, sounding approving. "Far more accurate."

There was a long pause, and Dana wondered if he was asleep or only pretending so that the conversation would end.

"And Dana?" said Porthos cheekily, from below.

"Oh, me," Dana said, glad at least for the low lights so she wouldn't have to meet any of their eyes. "Paris is full of beautiful women and irresistible men. I'm sure I'll catch up with you all eventually."

Athos snorted. "If you could try not to attract a political conspiracy with *every* affair, it would be easier on my nerves."

Dana grinned at the ceiling, thinking of the beautiful Conrad Su. "No promises."

A few hours later, Dana was awoken by a touch of Aramis'
cool hand on her cheek. "Time to start paying attention,
baby doll," the Musketeer whispered.

"How long?" asked Athos, rolling out of the other
bunk and landing lightly on his feet.

Dana took longer, sighing before opening her eyes
properly. "How long for what?"

"There are three points on the route where
the *Calais* crosses Church Space," said Aramis, helping
Dana down from her own bunk. "If they're going to jump
us, it's going to be in one of those windows of opportunity.
The first one is due in about twenty minutes. But it's a
short run. They'd have to be confident they could arrest
and have us packed away in under an hour. The second
window is next shift and much longer. That's the one
they're most likely to take."

"Unless they lose their nerve and strike early," said
Athos.

Dana felt disgruntled. They hadn't mentioned any of
this to her before. This was supposed to be her mission!
Then again, she should have researched the route herself –
it had never occurred to her that she would need to check
for pockets of Church Space. "Where's Porthos?"

"Porthos is in the bar lounge, creating a false sense of
security among the Red Hammers," said Aramis, with a
sly smile.

"Is that code for gaming and drinking?" asked Dana.

"I'm hoping for gaming and pretending to be much
more drunk than she is," said Athos. "But you can never
be entirely sure, with Porthos."

"Spaceship calling the sword silver!" Aramis coughed pointedly. "She's not the only gambling drunk in this party."

"I never said she was." Athos replied.

Aramis spoke into her stud, connecting all three of them to Porthos. "Darling, you need to pull back. Dangerous territory ahead."

Dana heard a buzz of conversation and static in her ear for a moment, then the clink of glasses. After a long pause, they heard Porthos speak in a low voice. "May have miscalculated. I keep winning."

Aramis frowned. "So lose some of it and get back here."

"I've been trying," Porthos insisted. "But I *keep winning*. They're seriously pissed off. If I leave the table now I think they're going to kill me."

"So you're gambling with Hammers," Athos said between gritted teeth as he joined the conversation. "And now you've given them an excuse to jump you."

"I've bought drinks for the room but that's only going to take us so far," Porthos whispered. "They're calling me back to the table, hang on."

"Cheat to lose," Aramis hissed. "I don't like this."

"Fuck that," said Athos in a voice harsher than Dana was used to from him. "Leave the money and run. Porthos, get the hell out of there. This smells like a trap."

Silence from Porthos.

Aramis took her pilot's slice from her bag and hung the baton from her belt, giving up on any pretence that she was a civilian. She pulled an arc-ray Dana had never seen before from one of the deep pockets in her flight suit. "I'm going to get her."

Dana took the opportunity to check on her own weapons – the pilot's slice baton that Athos had given her, and the pearl stunner from Aramis.

Athos was already at the door of the carriage, but Aramis grabbed his collar and hauled him back. "No! I'm going to get her," she insisted. "You and Dana make for the *Parry-Riposte* in the hold. Porthos and I will make contact with the *Morningstar* and get out that way."

"Aramis," Athos said in a pained voice.

"Go," she said, smacking him on the shoulder. "You have to get Dana to Valour." She blew Dana a quick kiss and then threw herself through the rattling connecting door and was gone.

For a moment, Dana could not breathe. Then Athos moved, lifting himself up into the bunk he had most recently slept in. His fingers, and then the sharp edge of his pilot's slice, worked quickly against the ventilation panel in the ceiling, which sprang open as if this was a trick he had prepared earlier.

"You've done this before," Dana accused.

Athos gave her a swift, fierce grin. "Memorising the blueprints of public transport vehicles is never a waste of time. We chose this particular carriage for a reason." With a fluidity that would only surprise those who had never fenced against him, he slid up and into the opening he had created, climbing into the narrow space beyond.

Dana did not hesitate to follow, pulling the ventilation panel closed behind them.

Their journey through the inner fittings of the *Calais* was long and tiring, though they covered a remarkably short distance for the effort it took. By the time they had made their way down into a service corridor, Dana was grimy and short of breath. Athos looked more cheerful than she had seen him in ages.

"Another short cut," he revealed, hacking the electronic lock of a freight lift. "Act like you own the place."

"Pretending I own an entire solarcrawler won't arouse suspicion at all," Dana griped, but she restrained herself from saying more. What would she have done without her Musketeer friends and their experience to get her this far?

She had never felt so young in her life.

The freight lift took them down to the storage bay in the belly of the *Calais*, which was packed with crates and containers. Running alongside the enormous bay were the separate cells containing ships under transport to Valour. Each opened out into its own airlock, for ease of loading and unloading.

Dana's stomach untwisted with relief as she saw the *Parry-Riposte*, its fin tattoo covered in a neutral pattern of geometric shapes instead of its usual display of sword hilts, vines and mountain range. For the first time, Dana wondered about that mountain, and what it meant to her friend.

Athos hissed between his teeth, and Dana responded to his warning, stepping back to conceal herself behind a pile of bright orange storage tanks.

Dana did not have an arc-ray of her own, only the pearl stunner. When Athos slid his own hand out from under his grey jacket, she was mildly surprised to see that he was also armed with a stunner.

How many? she mouthed to him.

He showed her four fingers.

Two each, then. Perfectly manageable. If she could overcome the pounding of her heartbeat in her ears long enough to aim.

The comm silence from Porthos and Aramis was terrifying. She couldn't think about that.

Athos counted to three silently by tapping his boot lightly against Dana's own. Then he swung out on the far side of the tanks, and Dana moved the other way. She immediately saw two Red Hammers standing sentry at the hatch of the *Parry-Riposte*, which hung open. A pair of Sabres had hold of Grimaud's arms and were marching her away from the ship.

Dana shot fast, first the one holding Grimaud's right arm, and then the guard on the left of the hatch. Athos had taken out the guard on the right of the hatch already, but tried for a double shot on the guards holding Grimaud, which set up a fierce buzz of bright white stunner feedback.

They ran across to the ship, coming to a halt at Grimaud's unconscious body.

"Is that why you're not allowed a real gun?" Dana demanded.

"Results are what matter," Athos growled, scooping up his engie and throwing her over his shoulder. "Let's get on board."

"You didn't trust me to cover two of them," Dana spat.

Athos gave her a weary look. "Don't take it personally, D'Artagnan. I don't trust anyone to do anything."

But it wasn't true, Dana thought sourly as they made for the hatch and closed it behind them. If Aramis and

Porthos had been here, Athos would not have hesitated to assume they were each capable of stunning two guards.

The *Parry-Riposte* had a standard internal layout for darts, with a secondary engie seat beside the pilot's harness, and a couple of jumpseats at the back of the flight deck for passenger transport. Like Dana's old *Buttercup*, there was a tiny cabin at the back with a bunk and other basic features.

Instead of putting the stunned Grimaud on the bunk, Athos strapped her into one of the jumpseats and then took his own place in the pilot's position, arranging harness and helm with a deliberate precision that made it clear he had done this many times, without the assistance of an engie.

Dana would have offered to help, despite being pissed off at him, but he didn't even pause as he snapped the cables into his own neck port, and clipped the straps of the harness firmly around him.

"Request emergency burst exit," he ordered her, inserting another cable into his scalp as he secured the helm. "They won't open the airlock for us otherwise."

Dana took the seat beside him and leaned into the ship's comm, glad she could have something practical to do. Something to take her mind off worrying about their friends, if only for a few seconds. She summoned up a casual drawl as she spoke. "Calais Control, this is civilian storage ship reference A309458, requesting clearance for emergency airlock release."

"Reference 309458, this is an irregular request," came the tinny voice from Calais Control. "Full passage will not be reimbursed."

"Sorry, Calais Control, family emergency. We need to

bug out earlier than expected. Terms and conditions understood."

"Safety protocols enabled, airlock will release in three minutes."

"Thank you, Calais Control." Dana glanced over at Athos. "Three minutes."

"A lot can happen in three minutes," he said grimly, flicking between security screens. He rolled the ship forward a little, to put more distance between the crumpled Hammers and Sabres, and themselves.

It was at the two-and-a-half minute mark that reinforcements arrived. Half a dozen more Hammers ran into the storage bay, arc-rays at the ready.

Athos immediately fired up the main thrusters, sending a wave of heat back in the direction of the fallen and active guards.

"You'll kill them," Dana said in a low voice.

"Better them than us," he said calmly. "Or did you forget that your mission is for the Crown?"

"Reference 309458, detecting life signs too close to your ship for standard safety parameters," broke in Calais Control.

Dana reached for the comm, but Athos took over. "They're nothing to do with us, Calais Control, but if we move fast, the rogue element won't be coming into the airlock with us."

"Understood, Reference 309458," said Calais Control, and to Dana's surprise the airlock seal slid open. Athos ran the ship forward just enough, and the seal closed behind them, to the dismay and fury of the Sabres and other red guards.

"Thought it was you, Athos," added Calais Control in a far more casual voice. "Pol with you?"

"She's still on board, Marc," said Athos. "Keep an eye out for her? She was in trouble, last I heard."

"Understood 309458, fly safe," said the voice, back to its business-like and almost robotic formula. The final seal of the airlock gasped open, propelling the *Parry-Riposte* out into cold space. They drifted for several hundred metres before the distance was safe enough for Athos to fire up the engine properly and draw the dart away from the *Calais*.

"Was that another one of Porthos' boyfriends driving the damn solarcrawler?" Dana said after a moment.

Athos shrugged. "I'm not even surprised anymore."

Dana concentrated on breathing, trying to calm her thoughts down. They were clear, for now. She was on track for her mission. But it had been one hell of a cost.

Athos' hand nudged against hers, and he pointed to one of several screens showing the spacescape outside the ship. Dana could see the long, sinuous shape of the *Calais*, running along the virtual rails that traced glowing, only-detectable-by-computer silver lines from Paris Satellite all the way to Valour and ensured there was no deviation in the flight path.

There, attached to the side of the train like a leech on a miner's leg, was the *Morningstar*. Like the *Parry-Riposte*, Aramis' dart was in disguise, with a pattern of suns and moons tattooed across its fin instead of the more devout imagery that Aramis preferred.

Athos activated his comm, pulling Dana into the same call. "Bonnie, Bazin, what's happening?"

There was a pause, and then the anxious tones of Bazin

the android filled the comms. "Captain-lieutenant Aramis is aboard, but wounded. She is not currently conscious. Engineer Boniface has boarded the Calais to secure Captain-lieutenant Porthos."

Athos nodded grimly, as if this was about what he had expected. "Give Bonnie and Porthos as much time as you can, but if any Sabres or Hammers approach the hatch, detach immediately and get Aramis to a medibay. Meung Station is the closest."

"Those instructions are compatible with my orders from Captain-lieutenant Aramis," Bazin said. "Godspeed, Captain-lieutenant Athos."

"Godspeed, Bazin," said Athos, and closed the comm.

Dana was shaking. She had no idea what to do with any of this. "Aramis and Porthos."

"They'll be fine," Athos said. "Worry about us. We're the ones with the precious cargo. They're out of it." He glanced at the screens. "We can outstrip the Calais and make it to Valour in the next eight hours at maximum thrust. Nine or ten hours if I take the route to avoid crossing pockets of Church Space. But if they send pursuit ships after us, there's nothing to do but fly fast and hope for the best."

"Not if," Dana said in a small voice. "When."

Athos nodded, hands steady on the controls. He always looked more at peace in helm and harness of his dart than at any other time. "Not if," he agreed. "When."

CHAPTER 20
PIECES OF ATHOS

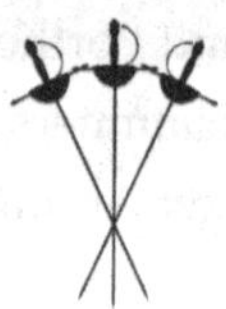

ana checked her comm stud for the twentieth time. No one had made contact – not Aramis or Bazin or Porthos or Bonnie. At this stage, she would almost welcome a notification that she was about to be personally arrested by Cardinal Richelieu.

"Stop it," Athos said in a low voice. "You're driving yourself crazy. It won't help."

"Can I just –"

"No." He refused to let her make contact again.

"But –"

"They know how to get in touch if they can. Filling their comms with anxious queries is not going to help anyone, and it will provide far too much information to anyone who might have them in custody."

"You think they're under arrest?"

"It's not an unlikely scenario."

"Aramis was wounded," Dana moaned beneath her breath. "And Bonnie hadn't even found Porthos!"

"I know, all right? Shut up about it."

"*Athos*," she said, knowing she was whining like a child but unable to stop herself.

"I can't fly if I'm frantic," he snapped at her. "Stop talking about them. Think of something calming."

That was the dumbest thing Dana had ever heard. "Who can be calm at a time like this? How do you do it?"

"Fencing," said Athos. "Fencing is calming. Do those footwork routines I showed you. In your head, if you please, I don't want you prancing around the flight deck."

"You want me to do footwork in my head?" Dana said incredulously. Another thought occurred to her. "Hang on, is that what you're doing when you get that pained expression on your face?"

"If I say yes, will you *stop talking*?" He was tense, and his hands were trembling slightly on the controls.

Dana subsided. He needed a calm frame of mind to pilot the ship. The least she could do was not sabotage him. "Footwork, got it."

She filled her mind with fencing exercises, her feet wriggling as she took herself through her paces. To her surprise, after a while, it did make her feel as if she could relax…

Dana blinked rapidly, looking around the small flight deck in alarm. "What was – hey, was I asleep? What the hell happened?"

The stars were different. She hadn't blinked or zoned out for a moment. She had been properly asleep. She could see the bright circle of Valour up ahead, and the blur of orbiting stations. They were a lot closer than they had been.

"That was some good calm right there," drawled Athos. "Nice and quiet, except for the snoring."

Dana gave him a suspicious look. "Did you drug me because I was talking too much?"

"No, you genuinely fell asleep," he assured her. "It was a beautiful thing. When I am old I will look back on that time with fondness."

She couldn't believe it. Asleep. "I don't even have Grimaud's excuse."

"Could you check on her? I'm concerned she hasn't come to yet."

Dana nodded and let herself out of the seat. Grimaud sat strapped against the far wall, her head drifting to one side. Dana ran through the usual response checks, everything short of putting a medipatch on her chest. "Her vitals are fine," she reported finally. It was rare for a dose from a pearl stunner to last more than an hour or so on a victim, but Grimaud had received a double blast. They were lucky she hadn't gone into coldshock.

"I hate stunners," Athos growled.

"She wouldn't have got it from both of us if you'd trusted me to hit my marks," Dana pointed out again.

"I know," he admitted. "Sorry. I don't trust easily."

"I'm shocked by that revelation," she said lightly. She hadn't expected him to apologise. "Shocked, I tell you."

Athos' hands might be busy at the helm, but he still took the time to give her the finger.

Dana grinned.

⚜ ⚜ ⚜

Valour loomed ahead of them, and still there were no messages from Porthos, Aramis or their engies.

Not even mental footwork calmed Dana down this time. She checked and rechecked her comm. She found herself reaching out for Athos' wrist, just to see if anything had come in on his comm without him noticing, but he pulled his arm away from her with a growl.

"They're *fine*, D'Artagnan. They'll get in touch when they can. And if not – if they can't get to a communicator because they've been taken, we'll just have to go collect them when we're done with this mission of yours."

This mission of yours. That stung harder than it should have done. Dana didn't need reminding that she was the one who had brought them here.

Athos sighed impatiently. His eyes were still on the screens, his hands busy on the controls, but Dana knew that sigh. It was closely related to the 'Porthos wants us to talk about our feelings' huff.

"Do you really need me to reassure you why they're going to be all right?" he said finally.

"Yes," said Dana. "Whatever you've got. I'll take it."

"Fine. Years ago, not long after the war when I still lived on Valour, I was – in a bad way. A drunk, for the most part, and don't interrupt to tell me what a drunk I am now."

"I didn't say a word," she murmured.

"Worse than now, if you can imagine it. I travelled halfway around the damned planet to get away. Bought a bar in the middle of nowhere on the side of a fucking mountain, and I climbed so far inside a bottle that I couldn't even remember my name. Which was fine, because I'd left that behind with everything else."

Athos was silent for a while, his fingers dancing across the dashboard as he made minute manual adjustments. He used his hands more than any other pilot Dana knew. Almost as if he didn't trust his brain.

After a few minutes of concentration he returned to his story. "A woman walked into the bar, and I knew she was a spy. The war was over, but the Sun-kissed continued to infiltrate the solar system with covert agents. I had – personal experience at recognising them. I was less than impressed with how the local militia handled that first instance, so after that I contacted the Fleet directly when I had useful information."

"Treville?" Dana asked in a low voice.

Athos smiled briefly, and she saw the warmth in his eyes. "Treville. I forwarded information directly to her over the next couple of years. It's amazing what you can learn in a bar, especially one at the crossroads of several travel routes. It was quite a game – I started drinking less and listening more. Then one day, a local criminal gang who had been profiting from Sun-kissed kickbacks figured out what I was doing."

Dana winced.

Athos nodded. "I was captured, and carted halfway up that damned mountain so they could decide whether they were going to ransom me or make me disappear. I convinced them that I was worthless."

Dana gave him a dirty look. "Did you have a death wish?"

"Something like that. I certainly had no desire to reveal who I used to be. There was no one to miss me. The thought of disappearing so thoroughly was – something of a relief."

He did not look at her. Dana did not dare try to meet his eyes, and not only because they might end up crashing into an asteroid. Athos had never revealed so much of himself before, and she did not want it to stop. "What happened? Obviously you survived."

"The Musketeers happened," Athos said flatly. "Two darts arrived in the nick of time. My abductors were arrested, and taken to Paris Satellite for questioning. I wasn't given a lot of choice in coming along. My rescuers patched me up, fed me, talked nonstop until I enlisted formally, and I haven't got rid of them since." He offered Dana a brief, biting grin. "It's going to take more than a compromised solarcrawler and a handful of Sabres to get Porthos and Aramis off my back, believe me."

Dana considered his story in silence. It was comforting to hear his confidence in their friends. More than that – it meant something that he had been willing to share these pieces of his history.

"Isn't there a mountain on Valour called Athos?" she said finally, picking up on a detail of the story that he might not have wanted her to notice.

"It's possible," he grunted.

"You named yourself after a mountain?" She turned to him, alight with curiosity. "What was your name before?"

But that was one question too many, and she saw his face close over. "Story time is over, D'Artagnan."

"That's not fair."

"Life is unfair."

She considered pouting, but that would just annoy both of them. "How long until we reach Valour?"

"We should pass Meung Station in an hour or so.

Entering Valour atmosphere shortly after that, if we make it in one piece."

She looked at him in alarm. "Why wouldn't we make it in one piece?"

"Largely because of the six pursuit ships that have been gaining on us for a while now. We also have to consider the possibility that there might be more lying in wait for us, when we reach the planet."

"Porthos and Aramis really aren't the ones I should be worried about, are they?"

"Nope."

Grimaud woke up about twenty minutes out from Meung Station, when Athos slowed the ship down for planetary approach. She coughed and shifted uncomfortably in her harness.

"Stay where you are," Athos barked at Dana, but she slipped her harness and went to check on Grimaud, taking her a flask of water.

"How do you feel, engie?"

Grimaud swallowed down some water with shaky lips, her reflexes slower than usual. "Like someone shot me."

"They're vile, those Sabres!" Athos called from the front of the flight deck. "Can't trust them an inch."

Dana gave him a dirty look. "You're not going to wriggle out of it that easily."

"You don't have to live with her!" he protested.

Dana continued to glare at his back. He gave in after thirty seconds of studied silence.

"Oh, fine. Grimaud, best of engies, you were caught in

a friendly fire of pearl stunners. I will make it up to you, if we survive this. Speaking of which — D'Artagnan, get the fuck back into a harness before I flip you through the viewscreen. Things are about to get bumpy."

Dana had barely made it back to her seat before the *Parry-Riposte* jolted violently. Athos spun them off into a hard spin, then straightened them. "What is it?" she asked, fastening the last snaps of her harness.

"Those pursuit ships I mentioned some time ago ? The ones that have been closing in over the last couple of hours but haven't otherwise given us any trouble?"

Bright flashes of laser light exploded across the right side of the view screen, and the *Parry-Riposte* shuddered around them.

"I get it," Dana said breathlessly. "Trouble."

Three shots rang across the sky in quick succession; Athos managed to get the dart under two of them, but the third skimmed the hull with a vibration that made Dana's teeth rattle.

Athos swore twice. "Damage?"

Dana thought at first that he was talking to her, but Grimaud rapped out specs from behind them and she realised that the engie had access to a diagnostics panel from the rear seat.

There was one here, as well, right by Dana's hand. She called it up without asking permission. "Another three pursuit ships approaching from behind Meung Station."

"Of course there are," Athos bit out. He wiped something from the other side of his face and she saw a spatter of blood on his hand. Was that coming from his ear? "We know what they're after. We've got to get you down to that planet."

Another burst of light crossed Dana's field of vision, but Athos slung the ship through a series of fast manoeuvres, avoiding the blast. "If we get close enough to the station, they'll stop shooting," he said. "There are three cathedrals on Meung, and twelve more across the other orbital stations and satellites."

"We still have to lose them."

"That I can do."

Dana stared at the blood on his hand. "Athos... how deeply are you tapped into this ship?" It was different for different pilots and ship combinations. The better a pilot, the longer they had been flying the same ship, the more intimately woven their brain was into the controls. The more likely they were to take actual damage when their ship did.

"It's just flashburn," he said dismissively.

"You didn't answer my question."

Grimaud cleared her throat, and said nothing. The nothing she said was big enough to fill the flight deck.

Dana concentrated on the pursuit ships: the pattern they made across the diagnostics panel. Another wave of blasts came at them, from two different angles. Athos ducked and rolled the dart, but he shuddered under them with the force of another impact.

"The good news is they're not trying to destroy us," Athos said under his breath. His eyes were glassy with pain. "Orders to take us alive, or we'd be in pieces already. Hold on to something, both of you." The *Parry-Riposte* took on a turn of speed that Dana didn't know this generation of dart was capable of. They weaved around the pursuit ships and skimmed directly under Meung Station, then punched directly into Valour space, breaking through the atmosphere with a blinding flash of light.

"It rains a lot on Valour," said Dana, using the diagnostics panel to search their region more widely.

"That's what they say," said Athos flatly, his hands and eyes busy on the controls.

"So," she said, navigating a fast route and skimming the panel over to his central screen. "Cloud cover. Lots of it. Get in."

He gave her a biting smile, and followed the route she had given.

"We're draining the power spheres. Ten more minutes of this speed and we're in real trouble," Grimaud warned.

"I know," Athos told her. "We've got other problems. D'Artagnan, ever flown doubles before?"

"Sure, once or twice in training," Dana said without thinking. And then – "*What?*" He couldn't be serious.

"I wouldn't ask," he said, and for the first time she realised that there was an uneven quality to his voice that had nothing to do with the vibrations of the damaged ship around them. "But there's a good chance I'm going to lose consciousness in the next five minutes. Care to hop aboard?"

Doubling was a dangerous technique, only hauled out in training and dire emergencies. Having a second pilot keyed directly into the ship provided backup, yes, and in the best cases a merging of skills. But it meant merging thoughts, too, and it had never occurred to Dana in a million years that Athos of all people would be willing to open himself up like that.

Bloody hell. He must be dying.

"Come on, D'Artagnan," Athos roared, eyes fixed

firmly ahead. "I can use Grimaud if I have to, but you're the better pilot. Make a decision."

"I will. Of course I will." Dana glanced back, but Grimaud was already in motion, dragging a secondary helm and cables out of a panel in the side of the ship.

Dana had doubled with her mother, once or twice, before she was old enough to fly solo. It had been a strange, dissociative experience, to touch the mind and memories of a woman she thought she knew better than anyone. The first time she did it, her mind was assaulted by the memories of Maman's first battle. It had taken years before she could go near a spaceship helm without thinking of corpses floating in space.

This helm fitted snugly over her head, and the snap of the cables plugging into the base of her neck felt like home.

"Why is this affecting you so badly?" she asked Athos. There was something about this that didn't add up.

"He's on nexus," said Grimaud, leaning around Dana's chest to make the last few connections.

Dana blinked. Nexus was the most powerful of the psychic drugs – it was used for gaming and other civilian cocktails most of the time because only a complete idiot would use it as a pilot drug. It was too bloody strong. "All the time?" she demanded. "Why?"

"Because I drink too much," Athos muttered. "There comes a time when all the Sobriety patches in the world don't stop your hands shaking at the helm and harness."

"Fuck," Dana breathed. That meant he wasn't just directly wired into the dart. Athos' mind was wrapped in and around the *Parry-Riposte*. Every shot on target was hitting his system directly. She remembered the pain of the flashburn she had experienced during the duel with Rosnay Cho. It had been nearly unbearable, and that didn't even involve real ships.

"Hence the need for a co-pilot right now. Which, by the way, is one of the most humiliating requests I have ever had to make." Athos wasn't looking at her. His eyes and hands were all over the controls. Not a tremor in sight.

She wouldn't have known he was in trouble until the last moment, not if he hadn't confessed. Dana was used to thinking of Athos as invulnerable.

"I reserve the right to yell at you once we're on the ground," she said, shrugging her shoulders into the harness and making a mental check as the cables and connections stung her synapses. There he was, the *Parry-Riposte*, ready and waiting for her. "Ten minutes should do it. After that we'll never mention it again. Grimaud, I hope there's another ampoule of nexus left."

"No," Athos snapped. "You don't need it."

"We've never practiced this together, Athos, this isn't fencing footwork," Dana snarled back at him. "Do you really think we're going to hold it together raw? I'd prefer a controlled dose of something milder like Flight but something tells me you don't have it in stock."

Grimaud already had the ampoule out, which she now placed on Dana's tongue.

She hadn't taken psychic drugs since Meung Station. *What goes around comes around.* As the nexus swamped her system, Dana wondered if Rosnay Cho was captaining one of those pursuit ships.

"Now," she said quietly. "Let's do this."

Grimaud made the final connection, and the *Parry-*

Riposte reached out to Dana, pulling her roughly into the mind of the ship.

Thoughts and memories flooded her, a jumble of dream images and impulses. Dana clawed through it all, resisting the urge to stop and sift through what belonged to Athos and what was her own. She had a ship to save.

She was the ship. Dana's mind reached out to her co-pilot, and she felt his thoughts brushing hesitantly against her.

The screens filled suddenly with a fierce, blinding purple light, and Dana felt her tenuous connection to the ship and Athos shatter into a million pieces.

CHAPTER 21
CRASHING AND BURNING

They were falling. Of all the things you could possibly do with a spaceship, falling had to be one of the worst.

Dana could not move. Her brain was swallowed up by the *Parry-Riposte*, and he was damaged in so many places. Dana's thoughts were consumed by it: the cracking of the hull, the spark of broken wires, the painful burn of the defence shield as the last precious layer peeled away from the hull.

This was not good.

She could not find Athos. Had he already lost consciousness? If she reached out a hand or opened her eyes then she would see him beside her, but she wasn't willing to lose her cerebral connection to the *Parry-Riposte* to confirm what she already knew.

He was there. But he wasn't *here*.

There was no cheerful song of flight and joy coming from the *Parry-Riposte*. Even the ship himself was frozen in fear. Dana reached out with her thoughts, remembering the first time she had ever piloted a ship in space on her own, not piggy-backing on the flight controls of her mother. She was fourteen, and invincible.

From that moment on, she had never wanted anything but flying spaceships.

The memory buoyed her, kept her upright while she reached deeper into the ship, searching for his power spheres, his thrusters, anything to stop this horrible, stomach-churning descent.

Her memory of first flight collided with another, a memory of hands on the helm and a screen full of stars, and a first ship, a ship she had never flown before, patient and loving under her hands.

It wasn't her memory.

"Athos," she breathed, and pressed in deeper. His memory was so close to hers – first flight, the sickening joy of it, the knowledge that nothing else in life would ever be quite this good or simple or right.

In the real world, on the flight deck of the *Parry-Riposte*, she felt Athos' boot nudge against hers.

Footwork, Dana thought, wanting to laugh hysterically. That was what they needed after all. A routine to perform in unison until they became properly aligned.

But there wasn't time for that, because they were falling out of the sky.

She pushed her memory fiercely against his, smashing them together. Her thoughts fractured at the pressure, one memory bleeding into another. Other data filled her head, shattered images of space and ship and thrust and metal. Memories broke into pieces and reconnected. She couldn't tell where she ended and Athos began.

Bare feet, walking across polished floorboards. She was stupidly in love with those feet. Who did they belong to?

They reached out together, Dana and Athos as a unit. Holding together they drew the ship upwards, out of its sheer drop. Up and up, through the blueness and into the comfort of grey.

Cloud cover again?

she asked inside their shared mind, not wanting to unsettle the balance by speaking aloud in the real world.

We're over the ocean

he sent back.

Could put her down here, but it won't help your mission. Need to head for Castellion, get as close to Buckingham as possible before we

Land?

Crash

Such an optimist.

The cloud should affect their instruments

And ours. I can't see a damned thing. The pursuit ships

We haven't lost them yet

They flew straight and even, a perfect motion of speed

and grace. Everything was going to be all right, if they could fly like this for long enough.

Dana opened her eyes. The *Parry-Riposte* settled calmly in the back of her head as if this was normal. She finally felt stable enough to check for herself, via the physical screen.

Athos' eyes were open as well. He had a savage grin across his face, and blood running from his nose. "Catch me if you can," he said aloud.

They darted from cloud to cloud, surfing the sky with occasional bursts of speed followed by long slow glides that used almost no power at all.

"Here," Athos breathed. "Like this." A stab of pain roiled through him and the ship fell from his grasp.

Dana caught it, taking the lead, skimming the ship along the inner edge of the cloud. Navigation. That was what she was here for. Being his double meant more than steering the ship. "Still with me?" she murmured.

She felt a warm glow inside her head, like a handshake or a formal salute before the fencing began.

They didn't speak after that, but took turns handing the ship back and forth between them, taking point and then falling back. It was like a game, if she pretended she wasn't aware he was badly hurt. They were going to have to do something about that.

Damn you, Athos. Nexus was for emergency situations and for early training, not for everyday use. Dana hated to think what kind of damage it had done to him. Did they have enough medipatches on board to deal with this? What medic training did Grimaud have, or would it be down to Dana?

Assuming they were all still breathing when they hit the ground.

Crash, not land. They didn't feel like they were crashing now, but Dana had a suspicion that the *Parry-Riposte* was concealing the worst of his damage. Like ship, like pilot.

There's Castellion

Athos said to her, and Dana felt a burn of complex emotions attached to that simple word, the name of a continent.

They weren't her emotions. Athos was the one who had baggage when it came to this planet. For one horrible moment Dana was tempted to poke into his mind and see what came spilling out.

He'd know. She should be ashamed of herself, but she only held back because she didn't want to get caught.

What's the plan?

she sent to him.

For when we crash

Land

Athos corrected, as if he had never put the idea into her head about crashing.

Have faith.

Always.

She took control off him and sped ahead, refusing to toss it back to him.

Have a nap, old man

Put your feet up

Athos' mind melted around hers, blurring them together, so his hands and hers worked together in perfect sync.

None of that, pup

I'm not dead yet

Dana was overwhelmed by a vision of green grass. She smelled lemons and rain; blinked the grass away only to be caught by the sight of crisp white sheets in a bright bedroom. She saw the curve of a perfect shoulder blade; a mess of hair that looked silver in the sunlight. She could not see the man's face, but his presence made her warm all over.

"A hundred and one reasons to hate this planet," said Athos in the real world.

Dana shook her head, blinking. "That seemed like a good memory."

"Not from this angle."

She threw him a memory of her own, of the miserable months she had spent on Freedom, fixing comms equipment for the miners to raise credits for her final flying accreditations. Even the rain was grey on Freedom, grey and opaque like the minerals they dug out of the planet, and the skin of the miners who had worked the surface for too long.

Athos shook his head and smiled.

I'm not playing memory chicken with you

So, I win?

There was a snap inside Dana's head, hard and sharp. The *Parry-Riposte* fell from her control, and Athos did not reach out to catch him.

What the hell?

That was our second last power sphere

Damn

Going down, D'Artagnan. Any last words?

Tell Aramis that you were right

I hate cinquefoil

Athos laughed at that, a shout of a sound in the silent flight deck, almost buried beneath the terrifying sound of the ship's vitals disintegrating around them.

Down they went.

Dana's first thought as she awoke was

empty

They lost the final power sphere sometime before the emergency landing which was as close to a crash as made no odds. The *Parry-Riposte* was silent in her head, and when she reached out to tug the ship back inside herself, her senses thrumming thanks to the nexus in her bloodstream, she felt nothing from him.

alone

She forced herself outside her own head to take stock of her physical state. The harness and the chair had protected her from the worst of the damage, though she was stuck in a coffin of twisted metal.

The roof of a spaceship should not look like a sagging canopy.

Dana released herself from the harness and helm, shaking her scalp free of the connections. Thank goodness Athos had let Aramis cut his hair before getting into a crash like this, or he'd have been…

She couldn't see Athos. She could not see most of the ship, as his hull had buckled around her. Her feet were jammed up against the remains of the console, which was crumpled into an ugly shape.

Athos should be there, but all she could see was the very edge of his seat, and a sharp-edged wall of metal that had separated them.

Dana's feet were wet. More than wet. Water sloshed through the ruined ship, up to her ankles. "Missed the continent," she groaned. "That's embarrassing — such a big target."

For a moment she thought one foot was trapped, but it was only her boot caught on a ragged edge of metal. Dana pulled it free, glad she didn't have to remove the boot, and then paused for a split second to run her fingers inside and check that the stud was still burrowed into her ankle.

It would be disastrous to lose it, after all this.

The *Parry-Riposte* creaked around her as Dana slid out of her seat and crawled under another piece of wreckage. The water levels dipped higher, wetting one of her legs up to the knee.

Sinking was bad. Sinking a spaceship was up there with falling and crashing. At least nothing had exploded yet.

Dana made her way through the damaged dart. She found the main hatch but it had crumpled inwards and would not respond to her touch. Further on, she found the slashed remains of Grimaud's seat. The *Parry-Riposte* lurched under her, flinging her into a hip-deep pocket of water.

What did she have to work with here? No arc-ray. A pearl stunner was only good for use against people, not metal. Her fingers went to the baton that hung on her hip. So there was that.

This situation was exactly what the slice was for. But something about the feel of the hilt against her fingers made Dana check Grimaud's jumpseat again. Those slashes were too even to be accidental. Someone had already been here with a pilot's slice.

There was a tilt on the ship – the further back Dana went, the deeper the water got. That was promising – he wasn't filling up completely which suggested the water wasn't as deep as she had suspected.

And maybe… yes, there. Dana saw a twisted bunk, the soft silver mattress pulled aside, and beyond it a gouged shape in the wall, mostly submerged in water.

She had located where the water was getting in, at least. The escape route Athos had left for her.

Dana took a deep breath and plunged forward, through the smooth lines of sliced metal, and into the water. She swam down into darkness and then up, to the fluttering pattern of light she could see on the surface.

Up and out, gasping in air that tasted like planet. They had landed in a freshwater lake.

It took her a few strokes to reach the edge and haul herself out into a day that was strangely warm considering how much cloud they had flown through to get here. The sky was blue, an intense shade that Dana had never quite seen before, not on Freedom or Truth, the only planets she had visited. Tufts of cloud swam through the sky above them, some white and some grey.

The grass was so green it hurt the eyes. They were surrounded by picturesque scenery: mountains and trees like something out of a children's fairy book. Dana didn't have time to gaze at the pretty. Athos was there on the grass, only a few metres from the edge of the lake and their part-submerged ship, leaning over the body of Grimaud.

He was soaked to the skin, one hand tangled in Grimaud's wet star-scarf as he applied the medipatch to her neck. Dana approached him, letting her hand brush his arm only slightly to let him know she was there.

"I was coming back for you," he said in a low voice.

"Didn't need you." She glanced back at the ship. He had made the right call. The wreckage was floating in the water, and had only shifted at all once Dana started moving. "How's she doing?"

"Breathing. Stable. She has a gash in her arm but didn't lose too much blood." Athos pushed away from Grimaud and buried his face in his hands. That would be the shock catching up with him.

"Any landing you can walk away from…"

"Don't. Even." There was despair in his voice.

Dana gave him a swift hug from behind, her arms wrapping around his shoulders for a moment before she released him. "Breathe. We're down. We're in one piece. All of us."

It was more than she had expected, during their descent.

"And a brilliant story to tell Aramis and Porthos when we catch up with them," Athos said, his voice sounding far away.

"That too." Dana didn't want to think about Aramis and Porthos.

A light spray of water spattered across the back of her skin. She stared at the droplets for a moment. The heat of the day had given way to a cooler breeze, and the clouds had more grey than white in them. There were more of them. Dana watched, fascinated as blue bleached out of the sky.

"Now it's raining," said Athos, sounding sullen about it. "I've been on this planet for five minutes, and it's raining on me."

Rain. Dana had felt it in virtual simulations, but never in real life. The air had a breathless feel about it, as if the world was about to fly apart into pieces of water. It was lovely.

Dana wanted to laugh. At Athos, at the scenery around them, at the delicious realisation that they were alive when they should have died in a crash like that, surely. "Did you and this planet have a bad break up with each other? Is counselling required?"

"I hate this sodding planet," he growled. "I hate being rained on. I hate – are you dancing right now?"

"Maybe a little," Dana said, spinning around on the spot with her fingers and arms flung wide. "I want to see if I can move faster than the raindrops."

"D'Artagnan," Athos said, keeping his voice even. "You are enjoying this planet far too much. Should I leave you two alone together?"

"Jealous that I'm getting on so well with your ex?" Dana threw herself to the ground. The grass still felt warm from the sunshine that had disappeared behind the grey clouds. "I've never liked a planet before. This is new."

"It won't last," Athos warned, but there was less resentment in his voice. "Rain might be a novelty now, but wait until it's been going for seven days, so you can't go out, can't walk or ride anywhere…"

"Ride?" Dana said, lifting an eyebrow. "Are we talking about live animals? What kind of fucked up New Aristocrat hijinks did you and this planet get up to together?"

"I refuse to answer that question on the grounds that – shut up," Athos said, turning back to Grimaud as she sucked in a sudden, sounding-awake breath of oxygen. "Engie? Still alive?"

Shakily, Grimaud raised one hand and gave him the finger.

"Thank God for that," Athos said, reclaiming something of his usual poise and snark. "Getting my revenge on this entire planet would have been time-consuming."

⚜ ⚜ ⚜

Grimaud was going to need to rest, and she couldn't be left alone. Athos refused to admit he needed medical attention himself. When Dana finally slapped a diagnostic medipatch on him it took a full fifteen minutes to list all of the recommended treatments.

Dana wanted to stay with them while they mended, but there was the mission. The platinum stud was all but burning a hole through her ankle.

"It's not even a choice," Athos insisted. "You need to get to Buckingham and get that bloody stud off your ankle. If you manage to collect the item you came for, you're heading straight back to Paris *without* collecting us first."

That was the worst part.

"But if I –"

"D'Artagnan," he said sharply. "If the Sabres catch up with Grimaud and me, we won't offer any resistance. Arrest is a short cut home for us. If our clever 'ditching in the lake' plan works, and they don't find us, the two of us can make our way back by the slow path. Neither of us possess incriminating evidence. We'll be fine."

Dana screwed up her face in frustration. She knew he was right. This was her mission. "If you're not back in Paris before me, I'm coming to get you," she vowed. "All of you. Aramis and Porthos too."

Seated beneath a temporary shelter he had rigged from the contents of the ship's emergency locker, with Grimaud lying on the grass beside him, Athos gave her a salute that was not entirely sarcastic. "We would expect nothing less," he told her. "Get the hell out of here, D'Artagnan. You're wasting time."

And that was how, having already lost two Muske-teers, Dana finally abandoned the third. It felt like a terrible mistake even before she was out of his sight.

Dana was really starting to hate this mission.

CHAPTER 22
THE MAKING OF ALIX CHARLEMAGNE

It took six hours for Dana to find civilisation – a large enough town to have a bullet train node – with the assistance of Planchet's clamshell.

From there, it took several hours of travel and changing connections before she reached the duchy of Buckingham. It was surreal, to be surrounded by people and white noise and all the amenities of a heavily populated planet, so soon after ditching into a lake in the middle of nowhere.

Athos had done a good job, getting them this close to the right region before they made planetfall. If Dana thought too much about that, she might cry or hit something and break her hand, so she concentrated instead on what an idiot he was to be taking nexus for every flight. Did Aramis and Porthos know he had been doing that to himself?

They had to know. The three of them were the insepa-rables. Dana was the stray puppy they had adopted. She couldn't let herself wonder too deeply about why these close friends had even bothered to let her into their tight group in the first place.

On this damned bullet train, there was too much time to think. It took no effort at all to locate the Duchess of Buckingham, thanks to Planchet's app which consolidated all Gossipnode references to the political, sporting, celebrity dynamo that was Buck.

Buck had addressed the Elemental Separatist Union earlier in the day, signing autographs outside the Hall of Communications in the largest city in Buckingham, and then returned to her country estate where she had been hosting a house party all week.

Dana was underdressed for the occasion. But there was no going back now.

It rained again, as Dana approached Villiers Manor. A light mist of water descended from the sky in a haze leaving droplets clinging to her eyelashes and stubbled scalp. Villiers Manor was twice the size of the palace on Luna Palais. Obviously it was the way of decadent dirtsiders to sprawl across the planetary surface as if they had all the room in the world.

The gravity felt better to Dana than her previous dirt-side experiences, and she put that down to Valour's history of being terraformed. Perhaps the planet had been designed to appeal to the needs of the spaceborn.

There was nothing else about Valour that felt familiar, for a person who spent most of her life encased in metal. The scenery continued to be fresh and green. For the first time in her life, she thought she could see what the dirt-sider fuss was about.

The mountains surrounding Villiers Manor were grey and looming in their rocky formations, which reminded Dana of Freedom except for the green fringing around every peak.

A servant allowed her in through the front door, as Dana claimed to be a messenger. Her plain black flight suit was obviously not a formal Raven uniform, but the servant was polite enough to not point this out. Dana hovered awkwardly in an entrance hall about the size of Marie Antoinette Plaza.

Paris was home. That thought was enough to make Dana smile for a moment. Her face was still holding the expression when a woman dressed like a mermaid hurled herself down the staircase.

Buck trailed copper silk and sequin scales behind her, in a long train that formed a tail. Her impressive bosom was clasped in two bronze seashells, picking up the high-lights of her reddish-brown skin and bright golden eyes. Her hair was braided into metallic chains that fell almost to her feet. "You have a message from Alek?" she asked, her voice warm and inviting. Before receiving an answer, she hurled herself into Dana's arms.

Dana had been unprepared for an armful of duchess, but that wasn't nearly as off-putting as the other woman's wide, blown pupils. Georgiana Villiers, Duchess of Buckingham, was high as a kite.

"It's an urgent message," Dana said firmly, setting Buck on her feet before she felt it was safe to let go. "Do you have a dose of Sobriety handy?"

Something like fear flitted briefly across Buck's face.

"Can't do that," she said, and put her finger to her lips. "Ssssh. Worked very hard on this chemical balance. He can't see me when I'm like this."

"Do you mean – the Pri –" Dana started to say, but Buck lurched forward and pressed both of her perfumed hands across Dana's mouth.

"No no, don't say it, walls have ears. Come on."

Dana allowed herself to be dragged up a staircase that could have housed about ten Musketeers, and into a room that might be a library because the walls were covered with antique books from floor to ceiling.

"I only come in here when I'm flying," said Buck, her pupils so large that there was no other colour visible in her eyes except for the tiniest streak of brown. "So he doesn't see. He mustn't know that I've worked out how to –" she paused, unsteady on her feet. "He doesn't know that I remember him when he's not here. I forget sometimes, and then – I come here to remember."

She reached out a hand to a touch-sensitive light on the wall, which illuminated the room more brightly.

"It keeps me from losing all the pieces," Buck whispered, and there was a tremor of fear in her voice as she looked up.

Dana followed Buck's gaze, and saw a single word blazing across the ceiling, spelled out in golden light from the wall panel.

WINTER.

"He got into my head," said Buck. "He sees everything I see. He made me betray–" Tears were bright in her eyes all of a sudden. "I have to remember, or I can't fight him when he gets inside my head. He's not here now, though. Be quick. Give me the message."

Hesitant, not knowing if Buck would even remember this once she had sobered up, Dana reached down to extract the stud from her ankle. It had been burrowed there so long that it felt like part of her.

She passed it over, and waited as Buck pressed it into her own wrist and listened to the message within, her eyes closed. She swayed a little as she all but inhaled the sound of her lover's voice. Then her eyes snapped open again. "The coat. It never made any sense that I took the coat. Come on."

Dana followed Buck to her private quarters. Duchesses required multiple wardrobes in which to keep their many outfits. Every room on this floor had one or more cupboards dedicated to fancy dresses, boots, hats, trousers, jewellery and other trinkets.

So much space. So much wastage. On Paris Satellite or any other station, even the most dedicated party animal would have most of their clothes dissolved and reprinted based on the needs of the day. Why would you need to keep so many things?

Dirtsiders were crazy, and wealthy New Aristocrat dirtsiders were crazier than most.

"Here!" Buck crowed, diving into yet another room full of massive antique furniture and lush carpets that made Dana's feet feel like they were being softened up for bad news.

The duchess pulled a garment out from under her bed: a soft heap of purple silk shot with gold, green and midnight blue. An embroidered pattern of feathers covered the silk in an intricate design. This had to be the peacock coat Conrad had made for his Prince – Dana had never actually laid eyes on it before, but what else could it be?

Diamonds glittered ferociously from the lapels of the coat. Dana blinked as she took them in. Prince Alek had tossed the coat away as an impulsive gift to his lover, not thinking about the value of the studs or the danger if it turned up in the wrong place.

"I shouldn't have taken it," said Buck, handing it over. "Of course I shouldn't. But Winter was in my head and – I don't remember." She sighed deeply, and sat on the bed. Her voice was steadier. "I don't know why he didn't take it off me at the spaceport. You know there are two Winters? The silver and the brown. The silver lives inside my head, but the brown – he's the dangerous one. You won't even see him coming."

Dana smoothed the silk between her hands. "It's all right now. I will get this back to Conrad and the Prince in good time for the ball…" But then she stopped, and laid the coat out on the canopied bed, stretching it flat so that she could count the diamond studs. "Ten. There are only ten here."

Buck frowned, a gleam of intelligent thought passing briefly across her glazed, drugged-up expression. "No. There were twelve. Of course there were twelve. For the twelve continents of Auster."

Dana wanted to shake her. "Has anyone touched this coat? Since you left Dubois's ship?"

"Winter," Buck moaned, and slid down on to the floor. "He must have taken them. He's going to use them against Alek." She buried her face in her hands. "I am too high for this. Can't think straight. But if I get straight, he'll come back and he'll *know*."

"Okay," said Dana, thinking fast. She was apparently the only person in the room who could be trusted to make plans. "Assuming that you're right about having a spy implanted in your head – and I'm taking a *lot* on trust right now…"

"Agreed," Buck said softly.

"If Alek wears it at the ball, with only ten diamond studs showing, it will be a disaster. Especially if your Winter has passed on the other two diamonds to someone in a position of power." The Cardinal, Dana thought with a shiver. The Hammers and Sabres who jumped them on the *Calais* were working under her orders, and they weren't the only ones. Rosnay Cho. That mysterious Milord. Perhaps more agents that she didn't even know about.

Dana's brain finally caught up with her mouth. "We need to replace the diamonds. Conrad didn't want to risk it on Luna Palais or Paris Satellite, but that was when he thought we might have to replace all twelve."

You couldn't print diamond; it was one of the few substances that couldn't be artificially replicated. But if the Duchess was willing to bankroll them, and they had the right craftsperson, they could perhaps have a couple of studs made from scratch in the time available.

Buck nodded, caressing the coat with one hand. "I know an electro-jeweller in Liberte who should be able to – do a thing." She waved her hand vaguely.

"Can I use your credit?" Dana had no shame in asking. This was Buck's mess and Dana was already doing more than enough to clean it up.

Buck waved her hand again, to indicate that she didn't care.

Dana cracked open her clamshell, plotting a course.

The bullet train could get her to the nearby county of Liberte. It wasn't even going out of her way – from there she could travel on to Arguerinne, the largest spaceport in the region. There were closer ports, but she needed a crowd to get lost in.

She would miss the connection with the *Calais'* return trip, but that was just fine with Dana, especially if she could use Buck's credit for passage on a venturer instead. She had no doubt that the Hammers would be well aware now of the name Dana had been travelling under with the Musketeers – better to use a new identity and let the *Calais* passage stand as a false trail.

"Won't this Winter of yours be able to see everything we've planned when you sober up?" was the next thing Dana thought to ask. Hopefully Buck's plan was not to never sober up; that didn't seem sustainable.

The duchess reached for her locket, which snapped open to reveal a cornucopia of pharmaceutical delights. "This little black pill is Oblivion. Can knock me out for a day or two. Should lose – about a day of memory. I'll forget all about you, brave little Musketeer. Also that incredibly boring conversation I had with Madame Pinquenot this evening. So win-win." She preened a little, looking delighted with herself. "Winter will never see what we talked about here today."

Dana didn't correct Buck about being a Musketeer. She liked the assumption.

She reached out to close the locket before the duchess got too enthusiastic about popping pills. "Let's get that

credit line and travel pass sorted out first, yes? And—"
This last request was deeply embarrassing, but she had to
ask. "I think I might need to borrow a frock."

Two days later, a woman whose travel pass named her as
Alix Charlemagne waited impatiently on the platform to
catch the bullet train from Liberte to Arguerinne. She had
spent most of the day pacing up and down the sales floor
of a high-end electro-jewellery emporium so exclusive that
it didn't even have a name. An elderly self-described
genius called Mr Emil took seven full hours to blast-cut
and engrave two diamond studs to match the others on
the Prince Consort's coat.

They had decided to fill the studs with ancient opera
tracks, cave paintings and century-old social media
memes, to complement the content of the other studs that
were apparently stocked with the 'culture bank' of
Honour.

Emil's work was excellent, and it would pass, but Dana
was pretty sure she had lost ten years off her life waiting
for the studs to be ready.

The dress wasn't helping. Thanks to the over-enthu-
siasm of a drugged-up Buck, Dana had come away from
Villiers Manor with a suitcase full of frocks, shoes, baubles
and even a cosmetic wand, which made her feel like an
alien playing dress-up. But she needed to look as different
as possible to Dana D'Artagnan.

The fashion among New Aristocrats on Valour was for
retro-glamour: long sweeping skirts and jewelled collars.
Dana had come *this* close to putting a corset on under this

particular travelling gown but decided at the last moment that there was only so much internal outrage she could stomach.

Athos might crack a smile if he could see her now. Assuming he recognised her. The other two would be rolling on the floor — Dana had muttered enough about Porthos' vanity when it came to covering her pilot's buzz cut with elaborate wigs that she was due for some ribbing of her own for this piece of gender performance.

Alix Charlemagne had long black curls spiralling around her ears, a pearl choker wrapped around her throat, and a jade green gown covering her from muscular shoulder to pearl-buttoned ankle boot. Dana had never dressed so femme in her life, and she felt like a complete idiot. Especially when she tangled the back of the gown in the automated doors, and needed two of her fellow passengers and a conductor to help her free it without ripping.

All she wanted to do after that was to throw herself into the nearest seat and nurse her embarrassment quietly, but the conductor caught sight of her travel pass and waved her all along the length of the train to the first-class carriage.

Cheers, Buck.

The other occupants of the carriage were a white couple who were ignoring each other. The man had untidy brown hair, a rumpled business suit and a near-permanent frown. He leaned against the window with all his attention fixed to a gleaming chrome clamshell. Dana didn't dwell on him despite a vague sense of *deja vu*. Where had she seen him before? Perhaps they were celebrities, like those yahoos in Buck's photostream.

The female passenger, who wore her auburn hair with pearl-clustered hairpins, and actually *did* have a corset beneath her own tailored silk travelling gown, was delighted to see Dana. "Finally, someone to gossip with!" she exclaimed, all but clapping her hands with glee. "I'm Bianca, Countess of Clarick, and I just *know* we're going to be the best of friends!"

Dana considered it a personal triumph that she didn't turn tail and run instantly. Time to suck it up and become Alix Charlemagne, as convincingly as possible.

Oh, God. She might have to talk about shoes.

CHAPTER 23
SOMETHING POLITICAL

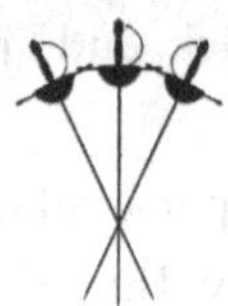

Dana – or rather, her cover identity, Alix Charlemagne – learned more about her travelling companions over the next few hours than she ever needed to know about anyone. The charming Bianca was just as interested in Alix's story as she was in her own, which meant that Dana had to busily invent all kinds of details and then try to remember them.

It kept her awake for the journey to Arguerinne, and the venturer that would take her off this planet and home to Paris Satellite.

Bianca, Countess of Clarick, forbade her new friend from ever referring to her title. She embodied everything that Dana had ever heard about New Aristocrats. Bianca was an elite hobbyist sportswoman who occupied her days attending parties, travelling for shooting competitions, and duelling in the back streets for kicks.

Relieved, Dana confessed her own taste for the sword. The profile she had built was that of a spoiled daughter of a wealthy family on a Grand Tour across the solar system.

She incorporated an unnamed Athos in her tales as an extremely grumpy swordmaster. Aramis, likewise unnamed, became Alix's poetry tutor, while Porthos, mentioned only as 'Madame Polly,' was her governess.

After a while, she realised that she was enjoying herself. Bianca had a talent for card games as well as gossip. It was the first time Dana had relaxed since she was last with her friends.

Vaniel was more of a mystery. Bianca described him as 'something political in the city' and he offered nothing to add to that, busily working away and ignoring them both. The only time he interrupted their conversation was when he threw himself half across Bianca's lap to call up a newscast on the back wall of the carriage.

"Oh, not now, Vaniel," Bianca moaned. "Turn it down. I don't have the least interest in whether the Marquise De Wardes is running for office or if she's been named Best Dressed Politician for the third week in a row. Your obsession is boring."

"Put a cake in it, Bee," was all her charming companion replied. He stood in the aisle watching the newscast with an odd, burning hunger in his face.

Later, when their sumptuous supper was delivered, Dana nodded towards the other side of the carriage where Vaniel had exiled himself as part of his ongoing interest in the political ramifications of whatever it was that this Marquise de Wardes had said in her public address. "Will your husband want to eat as well?"

Bianca stared at her in open-mouthed shock and then all but killed herself laughing. "Oh, that's *priceless*, Lexie," she bellowed. Alix Charlemagne had become Lexie somewhere round about the third hour of the journey, and

Bianca demanded she call her Bee in return. "Vaniel, she thinks we're married! Isn't that a kick?"

"How precious," said Vaniel in a light drawl that almost, but not quite, reminded Dana of Athos.

"He's my brother-in-law," Bee said when she had herself under control. "Widowed, when my poor sister died a few years ago. I keep him around since he had the good taste to sire the Clarick heir – saved me the trouble of birthing my own children! Who can be bothered with that nonsense?"

Dana saved herself from answering by filling her mouth with a smoked salmon blini.

"Of course," said Bee thoughtfully, eyeing Dana up from head to toe. "It would make us very happy if he married again. I don't suppose you're in the market for a husband?"

"Bee," said Vaniel warningly from the corner, which showed he was keeping at least half an ear on proceedings. "Don't marry me off to strangers on the train."

"Fine," Bee said, and mimed 'we'll talk later' to a horrified Dana.

By the fifth hour of the journey, even Bee had exhausted all topics of conversation. She collapsed against the window with a selection of fashion magazines she had managed to apply to Vaniel's tablet. Only minutes after she started flicking through the images, she was fast asleep.

To Dana's surprise, Vaniel surfaced from his work long enough to order tea from the food printer, and then offered to play a game of chess. "Clears my head," he said with a rare smile.

He beat Dana twice in quick succession, all the while explaining to her why the political aspirations of the Marquise de Wardes were important – she was a staunch loyalist to the solar system, and had announced today that she was in the running for First Minister. Her platform was based on opposition to planetary independence for Valour, supporting the continued rule of the Regence Royal.

The Marquise's talent for personal PR and her reputation as a fashion icon had helped to establish her massive popularity among the all-important demographic of voters who hated politicians.

To Dana's surprise, once she realised that the Duchess of Buckingham was the other proposed candidate for First Minister — running on a platform of planetary independence based on an upcoming referendum — she became rather interested in the matter, and was more than happy to listen to Vaniel's spiel.

He enjoyed having someone to bounce his thoughts off, and the two of them spent a pleasant hour or two batting politics back and forth in a manner that might or might not have been flirtatious.

It was late at night when they finally arrived in the city. Dana rose with her suitcase full of frocks and peacock coat and diamond studs. The venturer on which Alix Charlemagne had booked her passage would leave at midnight.

"Perhaps our paths will cross again," said Vaniel, his political face restored and his hair combed neatly. "You're on your way to Paris Satellite?"

"I've always wanted to go," said Dana with a smile that she didn't have to fake. Home, she was going home.

"I'm sure you'll find many amusements there." Vaniel shook Bee awake with a brotherly carelessness, and the other woman hurled herself at Dana with apologies and lipstick-smearing kisses and promises to keep in touch.

Dana had already half-forgotten the Claricks when she stepped on to the platform. The sooner she got back to Paris and completed her duty to the Prince Consort, the sooner she could reunite herself with Porthos, Aramis, Athos and their engies.

A delegation of secretaries and assistants were waiting to greet Vaniel and Bee. Several of them swiped wrist studs against Vaniel's to share files instantly, while one lurched ahead of the rest to perform a formal greeting. "Milord de Winter, the press conference has been pushed back an hour, but the Freedom delegation has priority depending on…"

Dana almost lost her footing and fell under the train.

"Goodness, darling," said Bee, leaning back to clasp her elbow. "You look like you've seen a ghost."

"Dizzy," Dana whispered. God and All. *Milord de Winter*. Winter. This charming, chess-playing political obsessive was the man who had put a psychotic copy of himself inside Buck's head, to spy on the prince. It was worse than that, because with that title 'Milord' she realised where she had seen him before.

He had been dressed differently, acting differently, that night in the bar on Meung Station: all silver hair and lazy drawl. But it was him. The agent working with Rosnay Cho.

You know there are two Winters? The silver and the brown.

The silver lives inside my head, but the brown – he's the dangerous one. You won't even see him coming.

Dana had liked Vaniel. She had played chess with him, and his sister-in-law had tried to set them up and OH GOD she had the diamonds here in her suitcase, only metres away from him. She had escaped right under his nose.

He wasn't looking in her direction as she drew away. She wasn't interesting to Vaniel de Winter now that he had people around him who actually understood the Valour political system. Still dazed, Dana exchanged a final air kiss with Bee and fled the station, heading across the city she didn't know to reach her berth on the venturer.

Home, she was going home. Away from politicking Milords and drug-addled Duchesses and charming Count-esses and the sodding planet that was capable of making Athos furious merely by raining on him.

Home, to Paris. Everything was going to be all right.

Lalla-Louise Renard Royal, Regence of the Solar System, was surrounded by peacocks: a host of beautiful people in bright, preening colours. She had never been so bored in her life.

The Hunt called to her, as it often did. But she pressed down the urge to flee this crowd and bury herself in her beloved chemicals. She had a duty to perform tonight. She had to find out if the terrible thing that the Cardinal believed about her husband was true.

Not that Cardinal Richelieu had said anything at all to condemn the Prince Consort. She implied it with the occasional word, or gesture, or sympathetic glance. A hint in the wrong place could bring down her government, and Lalla-Louise could not let that happen.

The Cardinal knew best. Lalla-Louise had always believed that, even when 'what was best' meant taking power and funding away from the Musketeers who had always served the Crown so diligently.

The Regence of the Solar System maintained her independence from the Church. She shared breakfast chocolate with Amiral Treville as often as she did with the Cardinal. She listened to many advisors, not just the diplomatic priest who had been there since the beginning. Lalla-Louise had even married against the advice of her Eminence, thinking that she knew better.

No, she *had* known better. Maintaining good relations with Honour and the Elemental faction was important, no matter what the Church of All said about it. Lalla-Louise married Alek to prove to the solar system that she could unite everyone: Church and Elementals, dirtsiders and space dwellers.

If they had an heir by now, even the Cardinal would drop her resistance to Alek's role as Prince Consort. A baby would have been the perfect way to unite the most divisive groups in the solar system.

Lalla-Louise was going to have to put her foot down about that soon. Alek's religious and cultural beliefs made it hard for him to accept the idea of a capsule-born baby, but he must realise by now that they were not going to get an heir any other way.

Assuming, of course, that the marriage did not dissolve first.

It was unthinkable, that the Cardinal might be this

wrong about something. But if the Cardinal was right, then Lalla-Louise's marriage was more of a lie than she had ever imagined. Alek – her sweet, beautiful husband was not hers after all, but another conspirator working against her.

Lalla-Louise heard the chime that indicated that the Prince Consort had entered the ballroom. She rose to stride through the crowd of masked beauties. Her guests gleamed in peacock colours, scattered with diamonds and diamanté beading.

The ballroom was decked out as a glorious, jewelled garden, with crystal hover-chandeliers lighting every corner. The hover-chandeliers were equipped with cam feeds, capturing the outrageous costumes and elegant dancing of the Regence's chosen guests so that the party could be broadcast live across the solar system.

Lalla-Louise was garbed as a huntress of olden times, with a gilded bow strung across her back and long trousers made of deep green suede. Instead of her usual army of dressmakers, she had summoned Alek's own tailor Su to make her a long silk coat that would perfectly complement the one he had made for her husband's birthday.

She had taken the opportunity to examine Su's face for any hint of betrayal, but his hands were calm and his manner pleasant during their fittings. Apparently, he knew of no reason why that coat might cause her pain or public embarrassment.

Lalla-Louise cut through the crowd and finally, *finally* saw Alek. He stood in polite discussion with a group of political types from Valour. Of course, he was not surrounded with friends. He had so few left on Lunar

Palais, with most of them exiled for political reasons, or distancing themselves from him for their own protection.

He was as handsome as ever, a prime example of Austerian beauty. And yet, Lalla-Louise felt a chill as she approached him.

Alek wore black from head to toe. His hair had been recoloured so that it fell in feathery locks of purple, green and gold like the fanned tail of a peacock, and he wore diamond beads that hung from each ear. But there was no sign of the peacock coat, nor the diamond studs. Lalla-Louise burned with a fury so hot that there was no air left in the room.

It was true, then. She had made a mistake with him. The Cardinal would hold this over her head forever.

"Husband," she said, ice dripping from her voice. "How plain you look this evening."

"Wife," he said politely, taking her hands to kiss them both. "I hope you don't mind that I chose to dress simply tonight. How can one peacock stand out in a crowd of hundreds?"

"On the contrary," Lalla-Louise snarled. It was rare for her to feel any emotion outside her beloved game, but this made her so angry she couldn't see straight. "I particularly chose the theme of this ball so that you could display the diamonds I gave you. I chose my own outfit to complement yours." She sounded like a petulant child. If she had a glass of champagne in her hand, she would throw it over him.

Alek's face changed, as he realised the extent of her anger. "My darling, forgive me. I did not wish to risk eclipsing your own appearance." He kissed her hands again, more passionately. "I shall change at once."

"See that you do," she said, barely getting out the words. Her husband made his exit with a polite bow that infuriated her as much as everything else about this evening.

The moment that Alek was gone from her sight, Lalla-Louise turned to see Cardinal Richelieu regarding her with warmth and sympathy.

She wanted to smash everything. But instead she smiled and nodded and accepted the congratulations of her guests as if this party was everything she had ever hoped it would be.

CHAPTER 24
HOVER-CHANDELIERS ARE FOREVER

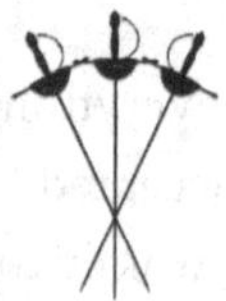

ana leaned back against the arm of an embroidered couch in the Prince Consort's dressing room. She was not asleep – she could not imagine herself managing to lose consciousness yet – but she was nearly home and that was wonderful.

Conrad was the opposite of relaxed. He was dressed for the ball, in a beautifully cut but undecorated black suit much like the one that the Prince had insisted upon wearing. The simple shade and lines of the suit showed off the golden-brown glow of Conrad's skin and the metallic scales that trailed down the side of his neck.

Conrad's shoulders were tense. His long tailor's fingers drummed in an anxious pattern against the back of the couch. His blue hair was a shade too long now, and kept falling in his eyes, forcing him to brush it impatiently away every few minutes. Dana could see that his thoughts were entirely on Alek, and the scene playing out right now in the ballroom.

"Can't go out there like a normal person, he has to

make a performance of it…" Conrad muttered, mostly to himself.

Adrenalin still burned through Dana – the long venturer journey back from Valour had not dampened the excitement of the mission, especially as she had spent most of her time fidgeting in her seat and recounting the adventure in her head, when not using Planchet's clamshell to research any information she could find about Milord Vaniel de Winter. She had not been able to find out much except that he was Private Secretary of the Interior and had something to do with government intelligence.

Ha. Something political. Hilarious.

As Milord, he had been working with Rosnay Cho for the Cardinal. As Winter, he had apparently taken up residence inside Buck's tortured mind. But what did any of that actually mean?

Dana didn't want to think about it. What she wanted was to lean over and lick a wet stripe up Conrad's throat. If he could stop being irritated by the Prince's antics for five seconds, she might get her chance.

Conrad pressed both hands over his eyes now as if he was actually in pain. "He could have worn the damned coat and the damned studs in the first instance, now he's just drawing attention to the whole mess, and…"

"Conrad," Dana said in a low voice.

"It drives me up the wall, if subtlety was a gene his was removed at birth, maybe it's some kind of subtlety disorder…"

"Conrad."

"You don't know what I put up with, Dana, you really don't –"

Dana crawled along the couch and straddled his lap. "Conrad."

He opened his eyes, huffing out a startled breath. Then, very slowly, he smiled. It was an exceptionally charming smile, and it warmed her all the way down. "Hello there," he said, his attention finally on her.

"Hi," said Dana, shifting in his lap.

"Have I mentioned how grateful I am that you saved my idiot boss's hide?"

"I'm sure you were about to mention it."

Conrad walked his fingers up the back of her bare neck, drawing their mouths closer together. His lower lip made a teasing swipe against her own, a preliminary touch that made her shiver. More. She wanted more. "I was definitely about to do that."

The door to the dressing room slammed open, and Alek marched in. "Don't mind me," he snapped, heading for where the peacock coat hung, freshly pressed, against the wall.

Conrad drew back from Dana with an apologetic look, and she climbed off his lap so he could get on with his job. "Ready for Stage 2, highness?"

"Stage 2," Alek agreed, holding out his arms.

Conrad slid the peacock coat on the Prince. The cut was perfect, of course, swinging against his hips in a fierce statement of bold beauty. The lapels of the coat glittered with twelve perfect diamond studs. Even knowing that two of them had been replaced very recently, Dana could not tell the difference.

"Still don't know why you needed to bother with Stage 1," Conrad said, coughing as he spoke so that the Prince could choose to ignore the insubordinate tone.

"Yes you do," Alek said calmly. "I had to see if my wife chose to test me. I wanted to give her a chance to trust me." He sighed, giving no sign of being pleased at the effect of the peacock jacket in the mirror. "Not that I have any right to complain."

"We all know that the Cardinal's objections to you have nothing to do with what you do or don't do in bed," Conrad said, brushing the coat one last time for the sake of professional pride.

"Still," said Alek, his face set hard. "I have a second chance to make this right. I'm not going to let my own weakness get the better of me again. I knew the deal when I signed the contract. Time to start making the best of this bloody marriage."

He turned to Dana on his way out, clasping her hand for a moment. "I can never thank you enough, Captain D'Artagnan."

Dana blinked with shock at the title. "That's not – that's a long way off," she said finally, embarrassed at the thought of it. "I'm not even a Musketeer."

"We'll have to see if we can do something about that," said the Prince Consort with a cheeky grin. "In the mean-time, accept this token of my appreciation." He pressed something small and sharp into the curve of Dana's palm and then swung away, striding back to where the Regence was waiting for him in the ballroom.

Dana looked down and saw a jewelled stud in her palm. It gave off a very expensive gleam of white, shot through with coloured veins that swallowed the light around it. "Oh," she breathed.

Conrad came to see, his blue hair falling in his face again as he peered over her palm. "That's an opal," he said. "Very rare. Only found on Auster. The prince likes you." He looked up, then, his dark eyes catching hers before he smiled. "Not as much as I like you."

Dana arched an eyebrow at him. "You admit I was the right person for the mission, despite my lack of credentials?"

Conrad laughed at that, dropping back on to the couch beside her. His hand trailed up and down her wrist, a casual touch that nevertheless made her pulse pick up speed. "You can't blame a fellow for being careful."

"Careful is good." Dana leaned back against the couch. "I suffered a lot for this mission. I wore a dress. Me. An actual dress." She had changed back into a plain flight suit as soon as she reached Lunar Palais. The thought of swishing one of the Duchess of Buckingham's gowns around here where people knew her was enough to make her howl with embarrassment.

"I'd like to have seen that," Conrad said, his eyes lighting up.

"It was horrible. A crime against humanity."

"I don't believe a word of it." His hand stroked her arm, all the way up until his fingers brushed against her collarbone. "Dana, I can't – you know about palace contracts, right?"

She leaned into him, her own fingers combing through his spiky blue hair. If he was allowed to touch, then so was she. "Are we talking about morality clauses?"

"No one cares about that stuff, not really, you know what palace types are like, all so sophisticated you want to smack them in the face. But I can't afford to give anyone ammunition against me, not in the middle of all this. If I get myself exiled, Alek will have no one left in his corner."

Dana nodded, her fingertips drifting lower to trace the muscular ridges of his shoulder blades. "Are you saying we can't, or that we have to be discreet?"

Conrad leaned into her, nuzzling her neck. His breath was warm against her skin. "Discreet. Not the other one. The other one is a *terrible* idea."

"Where?" she whispered. She didn't want to stop touching him, but he was right – the Prince's dressing room was not the place for this. Discreet. She could do discreet.

"I need to be here tonight. What are your plans for tomorrow?"

Dana sighed, and pulled away from him. Her brain worked better when she wasn't thinking about the warmth of his skin against hers. Tomorrow was so far away. "I have to report to Treville – and then check for any sign of communication from my friends. If there's no word from any of them or their engies, I'll have to retrace the trip and see if I can find out what happened to them."

"Will you still be in Paris tomorrow night?" Conrad moved back against the other side of the couch, putting distance between them. Dana wanted to pounce on him, but she could be a grown up about this. She could wait.

"It should take a day or so to get everything sorted before I'm off again," she said slowly. "So yes. I'll still be here."

Conrad gave her a hopeful smile. "I have tomorrow evening free, and I know somewhere we can go. Will you meet me at the Fountain of Tranquility, at 19:00 hours?"

"Yes," Dana breathed. She tried to make herself stand up and walk out of here with her dignity intact, but she couldn't help herself. She moved forward, just a slight arch of her back, and Conrad met her in the middle of the couch.

They caught at each other, one hungry kiss turning into another, and another. One of them was going to have to be strong enough to pull away.

As Conrad's tongue grazed against her teeth, Dana was certain it wasn't going to be her. She curled her hand into the fabric over his hip and tugged him closer.

The Marquise de Wardes had embraced the peacock and diamonds theme more thoroughly than any other guest at the ball. Her thick, black corn-rows were adorned with ribbons and silk peacock feathers, fanning out as if she was about to take flight. She was wrapped in a gown that sparkled pale and gleaming against her dark skin, giving the effect that it was made of actual diamond.

The hover-chandeliers, programmed to capture the most visually interesting moments of the Regence's ball, clustered so intensely around the Marquise that they almost caused a collision.

All the media representatives who had been allowed into the ball (a very exclusive list) clustered around her as devotedly as the hover-chandeliers.

Lalla-Louise Renard Royal watched the scene – the Marquise's glowing smile, and her self-deprecating laugh as the party began to orbit around her. The Cardinal was right. This was the woman that they – Church and Crown alike – needed as First Minister of Valour. The Regence needed the support of the Marquise, with her sharp wit, her talent for PR, and her unswerving loyalty to the idea of a united planetary government.

It was almost as good as having Chevreuse around again. Lalla-Louise frowned at that thought. She had never found a good enough replacement for Minister Marie Chevreuse-Montbazon. But of course she had to go. A Minister of PR who cared more about the Prince Consort than the Regence Royal was not someone to be trusted.

The Regence resolved to invite the Marquise de Wardes to extend her stay on Lunar Palais. They had much to discuss, and she wanted to make it clear to everyone that the other woman had her support and friendship. If that meant sabotaging the Duchess of Buckingham's attempts to win the Valour election and Lalla-Louise's husband in one blow, then so much the better.

"Your Highness looks sad," said a voice. Lalla-Louise looked up into the calm eyes of Cardinal Richelieu: the one person who was always on her side. The Cardinal wore formal silks and a long star-scarf that entirely wrapped her hair. It was rare for her to dress so traditionally out of church services – though in a nod to the theme of the ball, the scarf was purple with a peacock pattern picked out in gold embroidery thread.

"Your Eminence should not be so concerned about me," Lalla-Louise replied softly.

"How can I not? The solar system rests in your hands, my dear. Your wellbeing is vital to us all." This was the Cardinal as foster-mother and devoted longtime friend, then, and not the sharp-tongued, ruthless political advisor. It was not always easy to tell the difference.

Lalla-Louise made an effort to smile. "This anniversary ball hasn't gone quite as we hoped."

The Cardinal arched one perfect eyebrow. "I think it's going splendidly. But perhaps we had different outcomes in mind."

Lalla-Louise became angry at Alek all over again. What in space was he thinking, strolling in wearing clothes that were barely formal enough for dinner? Had she lost his respect as well as his loyalty?

She had hoped that by now they would have become a powerful team working in sync with each other, a partnership that strengthened her ability to rule the solar system. Something like the robust, businesslike relationship her grandparents had enjoyed. She should not be worrying about any secret alliances his family on Auster might or might not have been making with the New Aristocrats of Valour behind her back.

It all came back to Chevreuse. The Duchess of Buckingham going rogue was one thing, but if Buck had Marie Chevreuse on her side… that woman was diabolical.

"You will forgive me, Highness," said the Cardinal. "But I have a gift for you. As you know, I am always thinking about the Crown."

"Yes," said Lalla-Louise absently. "Of course you are."

"I know that your Highness has been concerned about my recent… theories about Prince Alek's loyalties. I was startled – no, dismayed, when a recent rumour reached me, and sent one of my best agents to investigate. I think you'll find that the answer to all our questions lies here." And the Cardinal spread her gloved palm wide.

Two perfect cut diamond studs gleamed beneath the light of the hover-chandeliers.

Lalla-Louise stared. "Those are the studs that my husband should be wearing tonight."

The Cardinal smiled sadly. "I hate to be the one to break it to your Highness, but this is an important reminder that even those with whom we are most intimate can become compromised." She tipped the diamonds into Lalla-Louise's palm.

"You'll excuse me, Eminence," said a smooth voice breaking into the sudden buzz that Lalla-Louise heard in her ears. "But I would like to dance with my wife."

She was numb all over, and yet she felt Alek's arms come around her. He drew her into the dancing with that same fluid grace they managed at no other time in their lives. Dancing. They had always been good at dancing.

Three of the hover-chandeliers broke away from the Marquise de Wardes, and tracked the royal couple as they moved in perfect synchronicity across the ballroom floor.

"I'm sorry," Alek said, and as Lalla-Louise leaned back in his arms she saw that he was wearing the coat, finally. The colour looked gorgeous over the plain black suit, and he had put some kind of gold glitter gel in his emerald-green hair that made him sparkle beneath the lights. "I was feeling rebellious, and took my anger out on you. It was unfair of me. It won't happen again."

He took her breath away with his beauty. Lalla-Louise rarely craved physical touch, even that of her husband, and yet she could look at him all day. "Angry?" she said in a softer voice than she had intended. "What on earth made you angry?"

There was a different energy about him tonight. Alek danced with her like he played that zero gravity game – as if there were a winner and a loser, and one of them was about to be struck by a pole. "I got the distinct impression that I was being tested," he said with an edge to his voice.

"I did not like it. I don't think it was your idea – but that doesn't make me feel better."

Even as her wrist rested elegantly on the back of his neck, Lalla-Louise's hand was still curled around the two diamond studs that the Cardinal had presented to her. She was not entirely sure what they meant. "I'm sorry, my dove. I had convinced myself that you were involved in – something political."

Alek twisted his mouth in exaggerated distaste. "Have you met me? I leave the political to you, dear heart. I'm sports and entertainment."

She laughed, and let him sweep her onwards with no further words. The dance could speak for them now. More hover-chandeliers clustered above them, capturing their warmth and happiness from every angle. Finally, the song ended and they came to a stop near Cardinal Richelieu. Time to be brave. "Did you lose these?" Lalla-Louise asked, opening her hand and pressing the new diamonds against her husband's chest.

Alek looked down, counting exaggeratedly. "All present and correct." Sure enough, there were six diamond studs weighing down each of the long lapels of his beautifully tailored jacket.

Lalla-Louise was confused. "Your Eminence, am I missing something? We should have twelve diamonds, and we appear to have fourteen."

The Cardinal looked as if someone had poisoned her precious atrium garden, and burned down her favourite cathedral for good measure. Then warmth shone out of her eyes, and she smiled like the proud mother figure she had always been to Lalla-Louise. "A gift, your highness. Consider them tokens of my esteem for the Prince Consort on the occasion of your anniversary. May you celebrate many more."

Lalla-Louise did not believe a word of it, and she was certain Alek did not either, but they were all friends here. The hover-chandeliers were broadcasting every moment to the solar system at large, and smiles were called for all around.

"Surely it is not appropriate for me to outshine my beautiful wife," said Alek, and promptly took the new diamonds out of Lalla-Louise's hand, pressing them to the lapels of the jacket she had worn to match his. "We are quite out of balance, my love," he added, and seized more diamonds from his own jacket, pressing them to hers, then pulling them off and rearranging them so that it was impossible to tell which were the new and which belonged to the original set.

Lalla-Louise laughed in a moment of pure delight. When the music struck up again, she let him lead her in another dance. The hover-chandeliers trailed above them, capturing every secret smile and casual touch and diamond gleam between husband and wife.

You could not save the solar system by dancing in public, but here and now on the brink of another terrible intergalactic war, it could not hurt.

It could not hurt at all.

CHAPTER 25
A LOVE LETTER TO ABSENT FRIENDS

Dana was lightheaded as she left the Palace by the front steps, heading for the Mecha shuttle in the hope of catching a ride back to Paris Satellite. Sleep was what she needed. Sleep, and a message from each of her three best friends telling her they were alive and well.

But she would settle for sleep.

She could still feel the imprint of Conrad's fingers upon her, the rough press of his tongue against hers, and the painful ache as they dragged themselves apart from each other again. She wanted him so badly, and now that she *had* him, she did not want to wait.

Sleep was unlikely.

Dana swung out of the main doors and clattered down the steps, happily invisible among the glamorous peacock and diamond guests who didn't even look twice at her with her battered flight suit and pilot-short hair. She was no one of importance, and she liked it that way.

Dana dodged several frocks lined with feathery collars,

only to collide fully with a man in a dark purple evening jacket and light grey shirt. "Oh!" she exclaimed as she had the breath knocked out of her, and then again, more quietly, as she realised in whose arms she had accidentally thrown herself. "Oh. Milord."

Vaniel de Winter had his arms around her, to stop her falling down the steps, and he made no move to release her. His serious gaze roamed over her in curiosity. Grey eyes, she realised. Dana had never noticed them before, but they were the same shade of grey as his shirt. She imagined they looked even more piercing when he wore his hair bright silver as he had on Meung Station. "Miss Charlemagne," he said in greeting, and there was a note of question in the name.

Did he know? she wondered in a panic. If Milord was as devious and powerful as Buck had implied, surely he knew everything by now.

"Uh, yes," she said, and smiled brightly, remembering the carefree persona she had taken on during their ride on the bullet train. "Fancy seeing you here."

"It's a flying visit," he said, drawing back so that he was not holding her quite so intimately, though his hand still brushed her waist. "Bee wanted to attend the ball, and I heard that the Marquise de Wardes was likely to be here, so… two birds with one stone."

"Of course," Dana said. "Politics," she added with a wry smile.

Vaniel returned the smile, and for a moment it was easy to believe he was exactly what he had seemed to be, in the first-class carriage with his chattering sister-in-law. "You have not dressed as formally as everyone else," he added.

She didn't look at all like the Alix Charlemagne he had met on the bullet train. He had recognised her without the wig and fripperies.

"I'm in disguise," she said, twinkling at him. It was a source of great shame to Dana that she had discovered her inner twinkle, when pretending to be Alix. But that didn't mean she wouldn't use it when there were no other weapons within reach.

"Ah." Vaniel – no, Milord – looked amused. "I won't ask."

"Better not."

They looked each other over for a moment more, and then the formal politician in him took over. He stepped aside, and gave Dana an officious nod. "I did not think our paths would cross again so soon, my dear."

"You never know what the solar system has in store for us," she said, trying not to let any of her nervousness show in her face or her voice.

"Indeed," replied Milord de Winter.

They bowed to each other again, and then Dana moved awkwardly around him so that he could head up the steps and into the Palace.

If de Winter had anything to do with the matter of the Prince's diamonds, he was far too late to do anything about it. Dana had beaten him, and Rosnay Cho, in a single night.

Smiling to herself, she hurried off to catch a tram back to the nearest space dock. The sooner she was back on Paris Satellite in her own bed, the better she would feel.

Even if Paris without her three Musketeers was not Paris at all.

Dana slept for twelve hours straight. She had not meant to, but the adrenalin and stress and frustration finally caught up with her. One moment she was clenching her fists tightly with the memory of how much she had wanted to forget about Palace protocols and morality clauses in employment contracts and just suck Conrad Su's cock into her mouth, and the next she was lost in the strangest dreams of fencing footwork and crashing spaceships, and memories that did not belong to her at all.

When Dana awoke in her little box of an apartment, she stared for a moment at the blank white ceiling, not sure if she was on a solarcrawler, bullet train or venturer. She was not even convinced that she was Dana D'Artagnan.

It took some minutes to believe that she was in her own bed, above Madame Su's workshop. She had seven hours before she was due to meet Conrad at the Fountain of Tranquility, and she had to make those hours count.

No more distractions or regrets or heated fantasies. Today was about the loyalty she owed to her friends.

After a brief sonic shower, Dana headed out to the workshop. Madame Su was nowhere in sight, but Planchet tinkered away at her heap of mecha that looked a lot closer to completion than they had a week earlier.

"Hey chief," Planchet said, her face open with joy as she saw Dana emerge. "Back in one piece, then?"

"I am," Dana said, leaning on the balcony and stretching her neck. "I lost track of the others. Can you help me collect them?"

"Of course, what do you need?"

Dana's eyes flicked to the closed office door.

"She's not here today," Planchet said cheerfully. "Appointments down on Lunar Palais."

"That explains why you're calling me 'chief' while standing in the workplace of your actual employer."

"Exactly!" said Planchet. "So I can help, right?" She set a large metallic arm down on the floor, eager to start.

"First things first," said Dana. "I need to trace Porthos, Aramis and their engies. Which means finding out if any of them got arrested along the way to Valour, or if they're hiding out. I need a new comm stud that can't be traced to either you or me, access to the private databases of the Church as well as the Royal Fleet and any medibays between here and Valour. And I need a lot of coffee."

"Is that all?" said Planchet. "That doesn't seem like a lot."

"Good," said Dana, trying not to be cynical in the face of Planchet's exuberance. "You start with that list, and I'll go around to their apartments and see if they've made it home under their own steam." It would be embarrassing to set off on an entirely unnecessary jaunt back to Valour just because she hadn't bothered to use the high-tech method of knocking on doors.

Dana had spent far too much time sitting in recent days – first the train and then the venturer. Walking off her nervous energy across Paris was a good place to start.

Dana had not expected Athos and Grimaud to be home yet, given the shape of the *Parry-Riposte* when she had last seen him, so she went to their apartment first to get the disappointment out of the way. Aramis was possible. Surely if she hadn't been too badly wounded, a medipatch or two would have her back on her feet by now, and she would have travelled back to Paris…

Porthos was the wild card. Dana had absolutely no idea what had happened to her after the *Calais*. Perhaps she had been arrested? Or wounded, like Aramis? Or…

The lack of comm contact between them all was distressing Dana more than she liked to admit. Once she had a clean stud, she could risk getting in touch even if they were in Church custody. But why had none of them reached out to Dana yet?

Athos' apartment was empty. Dana had the entry code – Athos' drinking habits meant that all of them had needed to help him get home at some time or another.

Inside, Dana looked around, feeling guilty about being here. But not so guilty that she didn't steal one of his jackets – a blue one that looked even more like a Musketeer jacket than the grey 'disguise' jacket he had worn on their mission. You could almost see the outline where there should be a fleur-de-lis symbol on the back.

She would return the jacket when Athos had proved to her satisfaction that he hadn't managed to get his stupid self killed.

No one replied at Aramis' apartment. Dana couldn't bring herself to leave straight away, and she didn't have the code for entry. She leaned her forehead against the door, willing her friend to be inside, complaining about her broken heart, or inhaling too much poetry.

Dana had not gone this long without talking to Athos, Porthos or Aramis since they first dragged her into their company. She missed them so much. While she trusted in their sense of self preservation, she couldn't help worrying that at least one of them might be lost for good thanks to her mission.

Could she forgive herself, if Aramis or Porthos had been fatally wounded? Or their engies? Athos had been so worried about Grimaud. What if she didn't make it?

Guilt set in, good and proper.

As Dana turned to leave Aramis' door, she heard boot-steps nearby. Her heart lifted for a moment as a Musketeer rounded the corner in full dress blues. But the short blond hair and light skin was a dead giveaway that this was not Aramis.

It was Captain Tracy Dubois. She looked equally disappointed to see Dana. "Oh," she said. "I had a proximity alert placed on Aramis' door so I'd know when she got back. She's not with you, then?"

"No," said Dana, taking a moment to marvel at the level of stealth technology that Aramis' girlfriend used to keep an eye on her. Only, weren't they supposed to be exes now? Interesting. "She's not back yet. I'm setting out to collect her shortly."

Worry flickered across Dubois's face. "What went wrong?"

"I can't talk about it."

"Of course. I know the score." Dubois probably knew exactly what the mission was about. She had been Conrad's first choice to take the letter to Buck, before he even asked his wife. Still, it was in both of their interests not to say anything aloud in an unsecured corridor.

They stood there for a moment, equally awkward.

"Would you give Aramis something for me?" Dubois blurted, her pale cheeks flaring red with embarrassment. "A letter."

"Of course," said Dana, holding out her wrist to accept a shared file, stud-to-stud. Instead, Dubois reached into her own flight jacket and pulled out a flat, crinkling object. The envelope felt brittle in Dana's fingers as she accepted it.

"Aramis likes paper," Dubois said, shifting back and forth on her feet.

"Yes, she does," Dana smiled, remembering the heavy poetry and theology books that smelled like dust and dryness.

"Don't let her burn it or anything, before she's read the contents. She can be dramatic." Dubois had recovered her snark, and even managed to roll her eyes. "I was wrong, to end things like I did. I miss her. Will you tell her that, if you get the chance?"

"I'll do my best," said Dana, tucking the letter securely in the pocket of Athos' jacket.

Porthos' place next. Dana had her hopes up far too high that she would be welcomed by the scent of freshly brewed tea, and bread warm from the oven.

But neither Porthos nor Bonnie replied to her chime. Dana called through to Planchet through her comm. "Can you crack a door code for me?"

"Sure," said Planchet without asking why. There was a pause, and a tapping sound, and then a high-pitched whine filled the corridor. Every door within Dana's sight buzzed open, all at once.

"Just this one," Dana hissed, hurling herself inside Porthos' apartment and slamming it behind her. "Just this one!"

"Oops," said Planchet. "Fixed, sorry. I have the other things you needed, by the way."

"Brilliant. That was fast." Porthos' apartment was usually warm, with music playing and spices in the air. Today, it was cold. Dana felt a stab of loneliness. "Planchet, are you due any leave from Madame Su? A few days, perhaps?"

"I've got a couple of months banked but she's good at thinking up reasons why I shouldn't use it," said Planchet. "Why – hey, do you want me to come with?"

"I'll need your hacking skills," said Dana. "And... I'm going to need an engie." Porthos' apartment had an entire kitchen as a separate room. Dana had found what she was looking for, a small crystal keysphere hidden in a bowl of lemons.

"You've got a dart?" Planchet asked, her voice going up into a shrill tone of excitement.

"Yep," said Dana, pocketing the keysphere to Porthos' *Hoyden*. "I have a dart. We're going to use him to bring the Musketeers home."

Late shift rolled around. Dana lingered in the palace gardens of Lunar Palais, waiting for a rendezvous with a married man. She felt like she had a fully-charged power sphere in her chest, vibrating with anticipation.

Dana had to admit, her head was hardly in the game for flirtation and sexytimes. She kept checking her comm for updates from Planchet. They had mapped several possible medicentres where Bazin might have taken Aramis. Planchet had delved far more deeply into the Church arrest records than any civilian ever should. She determined there was no arrest record for any of the missing Musketeers or engies.

The lack of data didn't have to mean anything. When Athos had been arrested as 'D'Artagnan,' they kept him from pinging his true identity. Records could always be faked or erased.

Planchet located the city on Valour where Athos and Grimaud had been most recently, thanks to the salvage records of a ship that had to be the *Parry-Riposte*.

That gave Dana the idea to track Aramis (and possibly Porthos) via the *Morningstar*. Planchet was working on it. All in all, it was a lot to keep in Dana's head. The sensible thing would be to ditch Conrad.

But this thing that the two of them had going, the flirting and the kissing and the hands all over each other, it was more of a distraction to Dana than if they had shagged their brains out already. Getting laid could only simplify things for them both. They could burn it out of their system and get on with their lives. Right?

Conrad was half an hour late. Had he changed his mind?

Dana had flight plans to review and Planchet's comms to monitor, and what with one thing and another, she was able to distract herself while she waited to find out whether she had been stood up.

The time clicked on toward 20:00 hours, and there was

nothing left to review or check. The Fountain of Tranquility was aptly named. For the first time in a week, Dana had absolutely nothing to do. There was something calming about sitting in the shadow of the dramatic rock formation, watching the Artifice water spray in careless, perfect patterns across the shadows and smooth lines.

She would give him another hour. She had nowhere else she needed to be, until tomorrow morning.

Dana fiddled with the studs along her wrist, trailing up her arm to the one she kept near her elbow, covered by the sleeve of her flight suit or fatigues. The Prince Consort's opal was empty of information, except for a certification-file of authenticity that marked the location and creator of the jewelled stud. It was worth a lot, she knew, even without getting it formally valued.

The Sun-kissed were rising again, and Dana knew she was more likely to get a commission in the Musketeers during wartime. Especially if she could finance her own helm and harness. The opal's value was equal to a substantial downpayment on a new dart.

Dana's dream was closer than ever, but it meant nothing without Athos, Aramis and Porthos to share it with.

She heard footsteps, against the quartz pebbles of the nearby avenue, and a wave of warm relief and desire surged through her. He was here. He had come to her, finally.

"Dana D'Artagnan," said a low, husky voice. "Fancy meeting you here."

Every warm cell in Dana's body turned cold, as if the atmosphere had been sucked out of the lunar dome. That was not the voice of Conrad Su.

Instead, a woman approached from the shadows, stepping into the light of the fountain that illuminated the ragged scar that carved through her beautiful face.

It was Special Agent Rosnay Cho, radiating smugness.

This did not look good.

CHAPTER 26
RENDEZVOUS AT THE FOUNTAIN OF TRANQUILITY

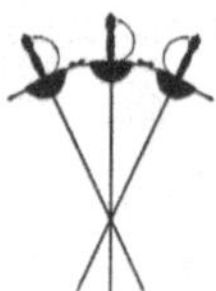

Dana's body reacted to the other woman's presence as if they were about to fight to the death, though Rosnay Cho made no move to attack. Instead, the Moth pilot from Meung leaned a hip against the glorious rock formation, as if she had all night for Dana to think up something intelligible to say.

It might take longer than that.

"I suppose we should start with the little tailor that could," said Ro in that low, confident drawl of hers that had driven Dana to the point of rage back on Meung Station. Now it made her want to curl into a ball of embarrassment. "I'll admit, I was expecting to find him here with his pants around his ankles. Any thoughts?"

Dana lifted her chin. Oh yes, there was the sting of anger that Ro usually aroused in her. "I haven't seen him today."

"Stood you up," said Rosnay Cho, almost sounding sympathetic. "That's a damned shame."

"What are you talking about?" Dana couldn't be

standing here in the Palace gardens having a conversation about her love life with Rosnay freaking Cho. It was impossible. She must have fallen asleep. Spacelag could do that to a person.

"He's not in the Palace," said Ro with a brief shrug of her shoulder. "And it wasn't me who abducted him this time. Bad news for Conrad Su – my orders have always been to keep him alive."

Dana's throat caught at that. "You think he's dead?"

"I haven't the faintest idea. But nothing short of abduction would have kept him from this cute little dance you two have going." Ro made a descriptive hand gesture that was just short of filthy. "The Cardinal doesn't know where he is, the Prince Consort doesn't know where he is, his wife *never* knows where he is, and you are here alone, every bit as clueless as the rest of us. That's a worry, don't you think?"

Dana gave up on trying to make sense of the fact that Rosnay Cho was here, talking like they were allies. She dropped to the ground, stretching out her legs. Sitting meant she was less likely to lose her temper and punch the special agent in the nose. "Any suspects?"

"One or two ideas," said Ro, looking down her nose at her. "A rogue agent, most likely."

"Why are you telling me this?"

Ro joined Dana on the ground, crossing her legs neatly under her as if she sat on garden paths every day of the week. "There's a subtle form of interrogation that they teach us about at Special Agent Academy. Not sure if you've heard of it. It's called a conversation. I thought perhaps we could have one. I'm sure you'll get the hang of it as we go along."

Dana searched Ro's face for some kind of clue as to what was going on here. She saw nothing. Ro met her gaze without hesitation. She did not look or feel like an enemy.

This was wrong on so many levels.

"We're not friends," Dana said finally. She couldn't access the anger she had felt at Ro in the past. The combined loss of Athos, Aramis and Porthos, followed by the revelation that Conrad was missing… it left her numb. But that didn't mean she was going to be an idiot.

"We don't have to be friends," Ro told her. "We're professionals. Whatever you think of my employer and me, we serve the Crown."

"The Church," Dana corrected sharply.

Ro's smile only widened. "The Church serves the Crown."

"Does it really?"

"Kid, let's try to keep the treasonous paranoid conspiracy theories to a minimum, shall we? For once?"

"I haven't committed treason!" Dana said hotly.

Ro looked at her for a long moment, her smile shifting into something thoughtful and not altogether nice. "That's good," she said. "Because I haven't arrested you for treason. It would be a terrible thing for both of us if we turned out to be wrong."

A long silence stretched between them. It made Dana's shoulder blades itch, but it didn't seem to worry Ro at all. She relaxed into the silence and brought that smile of hers back into play. It should be classified as an intergalactic weapon. "By the way, the trick with the pastries? That was adorable. Amateur as hell, but that's why it worked. I never saw it coming."

Amateur as hell shouldn't be a compliment, but in Ro's

mouth it sounded exactly that — and Dana was struggling to get past the implications of 'adorable.' "How much do you know?" she asked finally.

"Oh, buttercup, don't show your hand too soon," Ro said, laughing at her with her eyes. "I know more than you'd like me to know about the shit you've been up to since you got to Paris. But I know less than I would like. That's why this conversation is necessary."

This felt more like a duel than a conversation, and Ro was winning, hands down. "What is it that you really want to say?" Dana demanded. "You'll forgive me if I don't want to banter with the bitch who flashburned me unconscious, and stole my ID and credit the first time we met."

"Interesting attempt to take the moral high ground from the scrappy little cunt that stole my Moth and abducted my engineer," said Rosnay Cho, the words coming out as calmly as if she was saying she preferred lemon in her tea. The warmth bled out of her face, leaving her cold and professional. It was an impressive shift. Dana wished she could control her own features so readily. "This is what you need to know, kid: I could have destroyed you by now, if I thought you were a serious threat."

"Does that mean you don't think I'm a threat or that you don't take me seriously?" Dana didn't know whether to be relieved or insulted.

Ro laughed once, a short and sharp sound. "Both, but I can't help being *fascinated* by what you'll do next. It's like watching a spaceship crash."

Okay, now Dana knew she was being insulted.

"You're dangerous," Ro conceded. "But you're so

bloody new at this, you don't even know what the rules are. Shutting you down would be like kicking a puppy for peeing on the floor."

Definitely, thoroughly insulted.

"But if the Cardinal asked you to — shut me down," Dana pushed. "You would, wouldn't you?"

Ro looked exhausted. "Her Eminence is not your friend right now, D'Artagnan. But that doesn't mean she is your enemy. If I were you, I'd make an effort to keep it that way."

"Milord de Winter," Dana blurted.

Rosnay Cho's face went very still. "Go on," she said. "What about him?"

"He's one of the Cardinal's agents, isn't he? He works with you."

Having Ro's full attention was worse than she had imagined. Dana tried not to swallow or blink or reveal in any way how nervous she was in the face of that steely gaze. She didn't want to provide further entertainment. *A puppy that pees on the floor: that's what she thinks of me.*

"I'd classify Milord as freelance, if anything," Ro said finally. "He's done work for the Church, some work for the Crown. I've never managed to parse his loyalties. He's ruthless and he's useful, and he always has his own agenda running in the background."

"Could he be — the rogue agent?" It was a thought that had been in Dana's head since Ro told her that Conrad was missing. Vaniel de Winter was here; he had been at the Palace last night. Was that a coincidence? Was he really here because of his sister or the Marquise de Wardes? If he knew Dana's true identity and her previous mission — if he knew as much about Dana and Conrad as Rosnay Cho obviously did —

Ro pressed her lips together, giving the matter some thought. "Do you have any reason to believe that?" she asked finally.

"I met him, that's all. When I — recently." She was not going to admit to the matter of the diamonds, not even if the secret agent knew every single detail. "He didn't know who I was."

"Oh, buttercup," said Ro, as if she felt sorry for her. "If you believe that, you're greener than I thought."

Dana's comm trilled. She tapped it, hoping to hear Conrad's voice.

Instead, Planchet's voice sounded in her ear. "Chief! I have a location for Porthos now. And a ransom request."

Dana blinked. "Ransom for Conrad?"

"No, for Porthos. Has Conrad been kidnapped again? Madame Su's going to be so pissed off."

"Maybe. Don't tell her yet. I'll be back as soon as I can. Flight plan filed?"

"Done and done," said Planchet, sounding gleeful. "I told the Madame I was going to visit my mother for a week. She threw a wobbly but I let her dock my pay and she cheered up."

"Good, thanks. Sorry about the pay thing. See you soon." Dana stood up, stretching her legs. At this rate she was going to have to become a Musketeer purely so she could ensure someone was providing Planchet with a salary. "I have to go."

"Of course," said Rosnay Cho, letting her shoulders rise and fall in something like a shrug, but far more elegant. "Find your friends, bring them home. I'm not going to stop you."

"Why not?" Dana asked.

Ro rose to her feet. "No one's paying me to stop you, kid. Not yet, at least. Move fast. You never know when that might change." Her politeness was doing Dana's head in. Rosnay Cho piled on the surreal by extending a hand towards Dana as if they were respected colleagues.

Dana shook her hand, feeling a tingle of warmth at the connection. Tonight could not get any weirder.

But no, that wasn't true, because Ro leaned in, brushing her mouth against Dana's cheek in an intimate gesture that felt a lot like a kiss. "If Milord has your boyfriend," she whispered near Dana's ear. "I'm sorry, buttercup, but you're not getting him back."

She released Dana's hand, and walked away across the palace gardens without another word.

"So," Dana muttered to herself. "That was a thing that happened."

CHAPTER 27
PAYING FOR PORTHOS

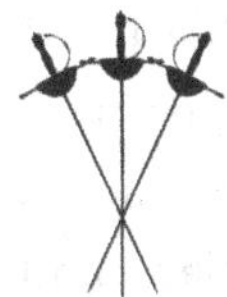

ana had flown a lot of ships lately that were not hers. The crew shuttle didn't count, not really. But Rosnay Cho's Moth and the *Parry-Riposte* had clawed themselves into her head. In both cases she had been high on stress, terror and excitement – with the *Parry-Riposte*, she had been dealing with the added pressure of Athos nearly dying and the colossal mindfuck of blending their brains together with nexus to keep the damn boat in the air.

The *Hoyden* was like a cool breath of lemon-scented oxygen, by comparison. Of course Porthos' ship would be the most comfortable, inside and out. This was going to be a cruise made of cake.

Getting away from Paris Satellite was the difficult part. Dana had left her digs well before Planchet set out for her 'holiday' so that Madame Su did not suspect that Dana was stealing (borrowing!) her mechanic.

Still, the travel pack that she swung over her shoulder apparently smelled of guilt, because Madame Su was out and about suspiciously early, getting in Dana's face about her comings and goings.

"Hardly here but you're off again, Mecha Cadet, they work you hard down on Lunar Palais, don't they?" she said, barring Dana's path out of the workshop.

"You know all about hard work, don't you, Madame Su?" Dana replied, polite as anything. She couldn't afford to lose her temper and give anything away, even if she wanted to shake her landlady and demand to know if she was aware her husband had been kidnapped. (Again.)

Dana could still feel Special Agent Rosnay Cho's breath on her cheek as she whispered those last few words to her.

If Milord has your boyfriend, you're not getting him back.

Damn it, she had no idea where to even start looking for Conrad Su. She needed Athos, Aramis and Porthos back in her corner. They had to be her first priority.

After she finally shook off the suspiciously curious Madame Su, Dana's next stop was to Amiral Treville. Dana had to report the loss of all three Musketeers and her intention to fetch them back as soon as possible.

Without mentioning the specific details of the mission, such as the diamonds, Buck and Prince Alek, not to mention her own romantic interests, Dana did her best to share what she could with the large, intimidating Amiral. She also confessed about her confusing conversation with Special Agent Rosnay Cho, about Conrad's disappearance, and the possibility that her landlady was operating as one of the Cardinal's spies.

Dana was concerned that she sounded like something out of a holo-soap, but Treville nodded and listened and took her seriously.

"Leave the Su matter with me, D'Artagnan," she said

as Dana's report wound up. "I'll have a quiet word with his Highness at our next meeting, and we'll see if we can't find out what's happened. Chances are, once this latest kidnapper figures out that the tailor can't be brain-drained, he'll be dumped back on the streets. Bring back my Musketeers, and we'll reconvene in a week or so to pool our findings."

Dana smiled at that, comforted by Treville's confidence. "You don't think they're dead?"

"Dead drunk, maybe," Treville scoffed. "Not one of those three would give me the satisfaction of coming to a bad end. They'll be the death of me, more likely. You, though, kid," she added with a rare smile as she issued another travel pass and credit transfer to D'Artagnan for the journey: for ransoms, medibay bills and expenses that the three Musketeers might have incurred. "I have a feeling you may outlast us all."

Now Dana was at the helm of the *Hoyden*. She allowed Planchet to fasten her into the harness, opening her mind to the smooth inner workings of the ship.

PLEASE ENJOY THIS FLIGHT. I KNOW WE'LL
BE SPLENDID TOGETHER.

Dana hadn't known what to expect from Porthos' ship computer; with a name like *Hoyden* she hadn't expected a voice like warm marmalade and an encouraging, paternal air.

THAT'S RIGHT, PET, YOU'RE DOING
WONDERFULLY,

the ship added as she pulled them out of the dock and into open space.

WHAT REFLEXES!
I AM IMPRESSED

It was embarrassing how nice it felt to have the ship praise her, even though she knew it was an egotistical quirk of programming. She was going to have to tease Porthos about it, and the thought of that made Dana grin all over her face. "Let's look at those ransom demands," she said once the flight was underway and the ship's glowing compliments had eased off to a gentle, encouraging murmur.

Planchet tapped her clamshell and called up the text exchange to one of the Hoyden's navigation panels so Dana could read it easily.

987ss3Xunknown: To retrieve Capt Porthos: Chantilly Station, Grand St Martins, Room 308. Bring 1500 credits.

029PlanchetCS: May we speak directly to Capt. Porthos or Eng. Boniface to confirm their location and identity?

987ss3Xunknown: Planchet don't be an idiot

this is B

Do you have the funds?

Lives & sanity may depend!

029PlanchetCS: We'll be there.

What is the status of Captain P?

987ss3Xunknown: Driving me up the
fucking wall, that's her status

"That does sound like Bonnie," Dana agreed. "I
wonder why they need so much credit."

Planchet frowned. "Isn't Grand St Martins a casino?"

Dana did her best not to beat her forehead upon the
dashboard of the smooth-talking ship. Somehow, she had
fallen into the trap of thinking that Porthos was the
sensible one of the three. That certainly wasn't true when
gambling was involved.

Even a 'sensible' Musketeer was a Musketeer. Ratbags
and reprobates, all of them.

Dana missed them so much.

"We'll see soon enough," Planchet said cheerfully. At
least she was enjoying herself.

Chantilly Station was very different to Meung Station.
Meung was primarily a refuelling stopover, packed with
engies and mechanics and seedy, one-night entertain-
ments. Chantilly was a high-end tourist zone and shopping hub. Dana was no longer surprised at the size of
Porthos' ransom – the number of digital stings and adverts
that poured into her comm on the short walk from the
space dock to the central plaza was so overwhelming that
she wouldn't have been shocked to find Porthos stuffed
and mounted in a fancy department store.

Everything was for sale in Chantilly.

Grand St Martins was not a casino. Worse: Grand St
Martins was, quite obviously, the most expensive hotel on

the station. It oozed class, and charm. You could practically smell the price tags rolling off it in a perfumed haze.

The windows were made of real stained glass, and the
entrance door was original polished wood. Dana was
starting to think that the ransom for Porthos was suspiciously low.

They stepped into the hotel lobby, and Planchet let out
a short breath of amazement. There was another pertinent
detail about this place that had not been evident from the
outside. It wasn't for humans.

Oh, the staff were human enough, for the most part,
but every guest from reception to the dimly-lit bar restau-
rant at the far end of the foyer was a Mendaki. Dana had
always got along rather well with the aliens she had met in
pilot bars and similar dives, on Gascon Station as well as
on her various stopovers across the solar system. But they
had been comrades, able to speak the common language of
ships and beer and spare parts.

These Mendaki were from the richer end of the
intergalactic alliance. They wore flowing robes and
jewelled piercings instead of flightsuits and pornographic
tattoos. They spoke their own language in bell-like trills
instead of using dodgy translator units to approximate
speech in Standard.

The staff waited on them hand and foot, with the kind
of polite servitude that always irritated Dana, no matter
who was doing the serving and who was being treated
better than everyone else. Still, there was no getting
around the fact that this was a hotel for the Mendaki and
their comforts. What on earth was Porthos doing here?

"Brilliant," whispered Planchet. "I've never seen so
many all in one place. Aren't those outfits amazing?"

"Let's stroll towards the sphere-lift," Dana said quietly, her eyes on the circular door to the left of the front desk. "As if we've been staying here all week. Casual as you can."

"Oh we won't stand out at all, do you think?" asked Planchet, and it took Dana a moment to realise that the young engie wasn't even being sarcastic.

"Maybe we'll get lucky," Dana sighed. Shoulders back, they headed for the sphere-lift.

They didn't make it. Two staff members in tailored uniforms cut them off and led them back to the front desk with such deference and politeness that Dana was hardly aware it was happening.

"Can we help you, madame and madame?" asked one.

"Are you guests of the hotel?" asked the other.

Dana lifted her chin. "We're visiting a friend on the third floor," she said, using a tone of relaxed confidence that reminded her of Aramis and how she was always wrapping complete strangers around her little finger.

It didn't work so well for Dana.

Both staff members sucked in a breath and looked at her with suspicion. "And the name of your friend?" said one.

"For security reasons, you understand," said another.

Their voices were not nearly as deferential.

Dana's smile came out as more of a grimace. "It would be most indiscreet of me to tell you."

"Ah," said a soft voice behind them. "You would be Madame Porthos' friends, I think."

Dana and Planchet turned to see a tall blue-green Mendaki approach. Her head was smoothly puckered, and her tendrils fell from the lower part of her face down almost to her knees. She wore a smart suit in the same colours as the staff uniforms, though better tailored. Most importantly of all, she spoke excellent Standard rather than relying on a translator unit.

"And you would be?" Dana asked sharply, not even caring if she came across as rude. She wanted to see Porthos alive and well. Pretence had never come easily to her.

"I am Madame Gsaoid, manager of this establishment," said the Mendaki. "May I assume that you are here to take custody of Madame Porthos?"

Take custody was an odd phrasing. "I am here to see her," said Dana. "Is there any reason that I should not visit her room?"

"Not at all," said Madame Gsaoid with a quick bow of her head. "I would be most pleased to escort you there personally if I did not fear for the life of myself and my staff."

"Excuse me?" Dana said disbelievingly. "Who has threatened you?" Did this have something to do with Porthos' ransom? What the hell kind of trouble had her friend got herself into? Thoughts of space mobsters and casino crime, or the Red Hammers, or something worse than that, all flitted through her head at once.

"Why, Madame Porthos," said Madame Gsaoid, with a jerky inflection of her mouth that Dana had learned in her experience with other Mendaki not to mistake for a smile. "She has threatened the safety of any of my staff who attempt to approach her room."

Dana folded her arms. "What did your staff do to her, to provoke such a threat?"

"There is the matter of the bill," said the manager.

"Madame Porthos has firmly discouraged any attempt to negotiate on what is currently owing. I very much hope that your presence will smooth these matters over." She gave that totally-not-a-smile expression again.

Dana hesitated. She could probably cover the bill right now, but she wanted to hear what was going on with Porthos first. "I will visit with my friend," she said. "And then I shall discuss her account with you. In about an hour. How does that sound?"

"That would be most satisfactory," said Madame Gsaoid. This time, when she made the expression that was not a smile, her tendrils all stood to attention as if everyone in the hotel should be very, very afraid.

"Dana!" howled Porthos in delight, grabbing her friend around the neck to haul her into the hotel room. "You're here! Finally. Something to eat?"

For a moment at least, Dana put aside her worries and enjoyed the fact that Porthos was alive and in one piece. "Are you drunk?" she asked as Porthos tugged her on to a couch made of several circular tiers. Perhaps it was designed that way so the Mendaki could rest their tendrils across multiple levels.

"I am so drunk it's not even funny," Porthos announced, burying Dana in a deep, bosomy embrace. "There is nothing else to do around here, and the food printer keeps making these lovely cocktails just for me."

"Hi, Bonnie," Dana said, barely able to disentangle herself from the hug with Porthos. Her friend wore bright green silk pyjamas, and a slightly askew beehive wig with jade hairpins.

Porthos' engie, sprawled out on an enormous heart-shaped bed, glanced up from her clamshell. "About time," she said. "I want to get back to my kitchen and my real life. Have you paid the bill yet?"

"Not yet," said Dana. "Porthos, what in space happened after the *Calais*?"

Porthos immediately pulled up her pyjama top to show off a flawless, round brown stomach. "Got stabbed," she said proudly. "Twice, with swords. And arc-ray burn here, under the ribs. Hurts like a bastard, arc-ray burn."

"You look all right now," Dana said, reaching out to tug Porthos' clothes back into some semblance of order.

"The hotel sent up medipatches," volunteered Bonnie. "Our credit studs were scoured by the Red Hammers in the fight, so we couldn't pay for an official medicentre."

Porthos nodded, looking sadly around the hotel room. It was obviously designed for Mendaki and not humans – the surfaces were smooth and cool. The bathroom that Dana could see through the doorway was twice the size of the bedroom, with a sunken pool. "A close friend of mine used to own this place," she said. "Thought we could hole up for a week or two, and not have to worry about the bill."

"By the time we realised it was under new management, we already owed them too much," Bonnie chipped in. "It didn't help when Madame here slipped out to an underground gambling den and ran our debts up even higher."

Porthos looked guilty. "Champagne?"

"No more drinking!" Dana chided. "Or gambling. We've got work to do, and two other Musketeers to find."

Porthos leaned against her happily. "Missed you, pup. Where's my Aramis? Missed her too."

"I don't know," Dana sighed.

"And Athos. Is he sad without us? He gets grumpy when he's left alone too long. I bet he's grumpy and sad."

"I hope not." Dana extracted herself from Porthos' octopus-like embrace and went to the door, calling up the final bill for the room. "This has gone up since the manager spoke to me in the lobby!"

"Needed more champagne," said Porthos, looking guilty.

"What you need is a Sobriety patch."

"Way ahead of you," said Bonnie, holding up an ampoule between finger and thumb. "I had this printed three days ago, ready for our exit. Got the good stuff because I don't think a basic patch will hit her sides."

Porthos sulked. "I'll take it when we're about to leave."

"If we don't leave right now, I may shoot you," her engie replied.

"Damages," Dana read out of the extensive list of items. "Porthos, really? You damaged the lift, a mirror *and* a bar stool?"

"They may have asked me to settle the bill at a tactless time," Porthos admitted. "And my trigger finger was – triggery, after the *Calais*."

"You threw a tantrum in the sphere-lift when that rich boyfriend of yours refused to settle your bill," Bonnie put in.

"Shut up, you. I also owe ninety credits to a local loan shark," Porthos said helpfully. "Harry the Hand. Lovely bloke. Showed me pictures of his kids and promised not to break any of my limbs for at least a month as long as I stick to the payment plan."

Dana finished reading off the damages, and sighed loudly. "I hope we're not going to need much credit to get Aramis out of wherever she is. You're blowing my budget."

"I tried contacting Bazin," said Bonnie. "But all he sent me was some quotes about service to God."

Porthos' eyes went wide and she held out a hand urgently in Bonnie's direction. "You never told me that. Sobriety, now. Gimme."

Bonnie handed over the ampoule and Porthos snapped it open with her teeth, swallowing the dose hard. "Aramis is alone with Bazin, away from Paris Satellite," she said, her eyes already more alert. "This is bad. We should have expected this, the little rat fink weasel."

"I don't understand," Dana frowned. "He's her engie, and an android. Surely we can trust him?"

"He's had a week to work on her without the rest of us around," Porthos hissed. "She's probably a bloody Abbot by now."

Dana blinked. "Aramis wouldn't throw away her service to the Musketeers to join the Church." Her friend often talked about her time in the Musketeers being temporary, but Dana had assumed the day Aramis would leave was a long way off.

"Not unless she was feeling especially sad and lonely and oh I don't know, maybe someone else's wife had broken up with her recently?" Porthos snapped. "When Aramis gets dumped, she wallows in self-pity and theological poetry and then, if Athos and I aren't around to stop her, she tries to quit the service to become a priest. Every. Single. Time."

Dana groaned. "Fine. I'll pay the bill and we'll get out of here as quick as we can. Planchet, do you still have that trace on the *Morningstar*?"

"It hasn't moved from Meung since I first located it," said Planchet.

Meung Station. Dana shuddered at the idea of returning there. But this time, she would have friends at her back. She had a sudden memory of Athos at the helm of the *Parry-Riposte*, with pursuit ships coming at them from all sides.

"There are three cathedrals on Meung Station," she said.

"Bugger it," said Porthos, pushing her aside from the door. "We'd better move fast, before Aramis gets herself all spiritually enlightened."

CHAPTER 28

FOR LOVE OF ARAMIS

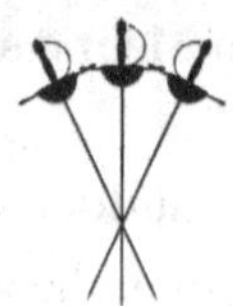

Their plan to find Aramis ran aground on Meung Station. Dana, Planchet, Bonnie and Porthos searched the station, checking every cathedral and religious zone before admitting that she was likely not here at all. She had spent several days at a medibay on Meung, but disappeared off the grid shortly after checking herself out.

"I'll meet you back at the dealership," Porthos said gruffly.

They had located the *Morningstar* earlier that day, in a corner of a dodgy spaceship dealership reserved for crafts in hock. Aramis must have been in desperate need of funds to pawn it at such a disreputable establishment.

"The manager said he couldn't release contact information," Dana protested.

"Yes," said Porthos in a voice so chilly that it might have belonged to Athos. "And I was happy to respect that when I thought we might find her at one of the nearby cathedrals. But we're running out of options."

Porthos slapped on pearls and a high scarlet beehive of a wig before returning to the dealership and spinning a yarn about a fake husband (whom she always called 'my darling Coquenard') who had promised to buy her the perfect spaceship. Dana trailed after her, making the occasional apology on behalf of her 'boss' as Porthos readjusted every screen and seat in the place, and managed to smear lipstick on nearly every smooth surface.

The salesman, who was more junior than the manager who had been on duty last time they swung past, was very aware of his responsibility for any damage that this troublesome customer might inflict upon the vehicles.

Porthos' epic distraction prevented him from noticing Planchet and Bonnie as they broke into the back office with a handful of connection cables and a pack of empty data studs.

"Let's try the red one again!" Porthos shrieked, playing up an accent that tilted between 'New Aristocrat' and 'Holo-soap Diva'. "My darling Coquenard loves to see me in red, and I have the perfect shoes to match."

"There aren't any red ones, madam," said the salesman, sounding desperate.

"That's a terrible state of affairs, my good fellow. Which ones can we make red?"

The coffee printers on Meung Station made every liquid taste like they had a faint film of oil on their surface. Porthos refused to even try printing tea until they were back on the *Hoyden*.

"Aramis used a false name to pawn the ship," revealed

Planchet, cracking open the clamshell to show the files she had cloned.

Porthos placed a large, genuine china teapot and several small cups on the floor of the flight deck. "Oh no, sweet pea, R. de Herblay is her birth name." A look of distress flitted across her face. "That's bad."

"Why is that bad?" Dana asked, pouring tea for everyone. She was sure Porthos would have done it herself by now if she wanted it to be done perfectly.

"Aramis hates her original name. If she's using it, that means – she needs her legal identity."

"Probably to sign a contract with the seminary," said Planchet, helping herself to a cup. She rocked back, startled as Porthos and Dana turned identical looks of fury upon her. "Sorry, what did I say? Help?"

Bonnie prodded both Porthos and Dana back a few inches so that they loomed less threateningly over the engie-in-training. "Breathe," she commanded them all.

Porthos took a few deep breaths, then swallowed half a cup of scalding tea. "Why did you say that about a seminary? What seminary?"

"The contact information Aramis gave the dealership is Crevecoueur Abbey," said Planchet, shuffling back awkwardly to add more distance between them. Dana didn't blame her. Porthos looked positively murderous. "It's on Dover Satellite, attached to the university there. It's a seminary for new priests."

The words that came out of Porthos' mouth next were anything but religious.

"Are we bad people?" Dana asked, a few hours later. They had flown the *Hoyden* from Meung Station to Dover Satellite and found a cheap dock to hire. Bonnie and Planchet elected to remain on the ship.

Dover Satellite used almost as much Artifice as Paris Satellite, perhaps more. Dana and Porthos stood on a wide, grass-lined avenue underneath a starscape that gave the illusion of being dirtside, except for the visible rotation of the stars.

Porthos had changed from her usual civilian glamour into Musketeer battledress – blue flight suit and fleur-de-lis jacket, with her shorn hair bare to the false sky. She had even wiped off her lipstick.

Dana wore Athos' not-a-Musketeer blue jacket over her own charcoal grey flight suit. Both of them wore their pilot's slice batons slung from belts, and sensible boots. Ready for action.

"I have no idea what you mean," said Porthos. She leaned against a wall, staring at the pretty, fluted tower of Crevecoueur Abbey. The Artifice was so detailed that it included green ivy clambering over the pale golden stonework.

"I mean," Dana sighed. "If Aramis really wants to sign herself up to the priesthood — she's always talking about how she plans to someday — shouldn't we let her get on with it? Are we bad people for stopping her doing something that might make her happy?"

Porthos' eyes went darker than usual. "I don't care if it's selfish," she said after a long moment. "I don't give a flying frig if it makes us bad people. I want her back. She's my best friend, and they can't have her. Also, she owes me money."

Dana felt relief wash over her. "Okay," she said with a biting grin. "Let's be terrible people."

"It's what Musketeers do best," Porthos replied.

Crevecoueur Abbey would not let Aramis go without a fight. Their opening salvo consisted mostly of nuns. Several elderly, sweet-faced old dears met Porthos and Dana at the door, politely explaining why it was that 'Novice de Herblay' could not receive visitors during the period of contemplation, as she was in consultation with several advisors about the thesis she was to present to the Abbott. The Abbott would then decide on her suitability to join the Church.

Every time one of them referred to Aramis as Novice de Herblay, Porthos gritted her teeth and corrected them with 'Captain' until she looked about ready to explode.

"I'm afraid you don't understand," Dana put in when there was finally a gap in the conversation. "We have brought some papers for Captain Aramis that she greatly needs to reference in her thesis proposal."

"Oh, that's all right then," the nuns said happily, and offered them fresh-brewed tea.

"Maybe later," said Porthos. It was a sign of how desperate things were that she turned down the offer of tea that had been brewed instead of printed.

One of the more elderly nuns led the Musketeer and her friend up a winding staircase, and along to a library. Bazin the android stood to stiff attention, guarding the door of his mistress.

As he saw Porthos and Dana approach, the android

looked more dismayed than Dana had thought was even possible, on the face of an artificial person.

"Please, Captain-lieutenant Porthos," he moaned. "It's so calm here, and no one ever tries to shoot at us, and Novice de Herblay is planning a most excellent thesis that will confirm her brilliance in the scholarly arts of theology…"

"Modesty in all things, Bazin," said the nun, chiding him. "We have no need for pride here."

The android's stiff metal shoulders slumped. "Yes, Sister," he sighed. "I would prefer not to allow these people in to interrupt Novice de Herblay."

"We serve God and All, Bazin, not our personal needs," said the nun, moving him aside.

"I dislike spaceships so much," the android engineer muttered. "A few centuries of religious contemplation and not being shot at, is that too much to ask? We were *so close.*"

Porthos gave him an unsympathetic clap on the shoulder as she was ushered into the library by the elderly nun. "We'll have a talk about loyalty to the Royal Fleet later, Bazin."

"Yes, Captain-lieutenant Porthos," Bazin sighed.

Dana slipped into the library after Porthos, and almost crashed into her back because her friend had stopped still.

There, at a table strewn with antique books, was their Aramis. She wore a flowing black robe and a full star-scarf wrapped around her hair. Her eyes were alight with animated intelligence as she argued with two priests about the nature of God and All.

"But surely it is not heresy to acknowledge one's reluctance at choosing to serve God…" In that moment, Aramis saw her visitors. She broke off her earnest debate, and smiled with dazzling warmth.

Dana's old crush on her friend smacked her hard in the chest all over again. She had somehow lost her immunity to Aramis' beauty in the time they had been apart. Aramis glowed with happiness, still fired up from the intellectual debate.

"Oh, we're *terrible people*," Dana whispered.

"I can live with it," said Porthos.

"My friends," said Aramis, her joy filling the room. "I am so glad to see you are unharmed."

"Mostly," said Porthos. "I took a wound or two but it's all fixed up now, and Dana's barely dented. How about you?"

Aramis pressed her hand to her chest and smiled. "You'll tease me for giving God the credit and not the medibay, but this time I do believe I was saved for something more, Pol."

"Something more than being a Musketeer," Porthos repeated. "Something more than Paris and friendship and serving the Crown?"

"I hope you don't mind the interruption, superiors," Aramis added to her new companions, who eyed Porthos and Dana as if they had rolled in drunk from the nearest tavern. "I have not seen my friends in a long time. Porthos, D'Artagnan, perhaps you can bring your perspective to the debate."

Porthos let out a short laugh, but pulled up a chair to the table. "If it's about your thesis, darling, I doubt I can contribute much."

Dana followed her lead, sitting beside Porthos. "Unless your thesis is about swords or spaceships," she added, happy to play along. "We're good at swords and spaceships."

Aramis' eyes gleamed, and she continued with unironic enthusiasm for her topic. "Ah, but you see, it's all about dogmatism versus idealism, and I am sure you have an opinion as to which most accurately reflects the kind of priest I should become upon my ordination…"

Dana saw Porthos grip the chair arms, her knuckles standing out as white against the brown skin of her hands.

"You mean to go ahead with this?" Porthos asked softly.

"It is the life I have always wanted, dear heart," Aramis replied, breaking off further discussion about dogmatic theory to smile at her friend. "And — it is the right time, for me."

Dana realised the exact moment that Porthos gave up: her face pulled itself into an 'I am happy for you' expression instead of the more expected 'if you do this I will burn this abbey to the ground' expression.

"I think perhaps," Dana broke in. "Before you make the final decision about this thesis of yours, Aramis, you should consider *all* the relevant source material."

The priests blinked at her. Aramis had an odd smile on her face. It lacked the warmth she had turned upon her friends earlier. She was still so beautiful that it made Dana want to cry. "Did you have something in mind, pup?"

Dana slid the letter from Captain Dubois out of the inner pocket in Athos' jacket. "Like this, for instance." The paper crackled as she handed the envelope across, placing it into Aramis' outstretched hand.

Aramis gripped the envelope firmly. It crumpled in her fingers with a sharp sound before she seized control of herself and flattened it out against the surface of the table. After contemplating the envelope for a moment, she tore the letter open and read it silently to herself.

Dana did not dare look at Porthos. She stared at Aramis and waited, well aware that everyone in the room was also staring at Aramis and waiting.

No pressure, or anything.

"Superiors," Aramis said after a moment. "You will excuse me, please. I must — commit myself to private contemplation for an hour or two. May we pick up this discussion after Matins?" She rose, ushering the priests to the door. "Bazin, see I am not disturbed," Aramis added, and then closed the door behind the representatives of the seminary.

Porthos turned to look at Aramis, hope alight in her eyes.

Aramis pressed the letter to her chest and grinned the wickedest of grins. "She loves me. Tracy Dubois loves me."

Dana let out a long huff of air in relief.

"Well, of course she does," said Porthos, as if she hadn't doubted for a minute.

"How quickly can we get home to Paris?"

"That depends," said Dana. "Do you want to collect your ship before you go? Because we might not have enough credit to get the *Morningstar* out of hock."

Aramis laughed carelessly. "We'll work something out."

Porthos leaped to her feet and gave Aramis a rough hug. "You scared me for a minute there, you rotten cow."

Aramis kissed her hair. "All for one and one for all, you silly bitch." She looked over Porthos' head to Dana. "Where is he?"

Dana might not be smart enough to contemplate a pre-ordination thesis in theology, but she knew exactly who Aramis was talking about. "Athos is on Valour. We crashed the *Parry-Riposte* more than a week ago, and I had to leave him and Grimaud to salvage the ship while I completed the mission."

"He's down on the planet?" Porthos exclaimed. "You never told me that. That's not good, Dana. We should have collected him first."

Dana wanted to point out that they might have lost Aramis to the Church forever if they hadn't picked her up today, but she knew better than to protest.

Aramis paced back and forth in front of the door. "This is bad. Athos and Valour do not cope well with each other."

"I'm aware," Dana said sharply. She wasn't an idiot.

"Either he's dead, or there's no wine left on that planet," announced Aramis. "I know which option I'd bet my money on." She tucked the love letter from Tracy Dubois inside her flowing black robes. "Let's find out where Bazin has hidden my flight suit, and bring home our boy."

CHAPTER 29
THE HUSBAND OF ATHOS

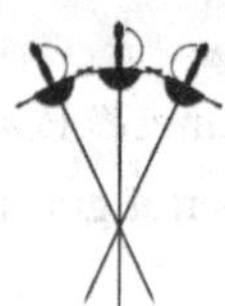

"And I thought *my* ship was in bad shape," Aramis said sadly, looking at the crumpled heap of metal that remained of the *Parry-Riposte*. Planchet had tracked the salvage code to a shipyard in the city of Amiens, north of the lake with which Dana had recently become acquainted.

"What are you doing?" Dana asked as Porthos climbed up on top of the nearest charging hub, planting her booted feet astride it.

"I'm noting all the drinking establishments that are visible from this yard," said Porthos, her eyes slowly sweeping the area from her new high vantage point. "He wouldn't have walked any further than he had to."

"Grimaud was wounded," Dana said, feeling that someone had to defend Athos at this point. "I'm sure the first thing Athos did after getting credit for salvage wasn't to buy a drink."

Aramis and Porthos simply looked at her.

Dana sighed. "Fine, okay. But what makes you think he's nearby, and still drunk? It's been a week."

Porthos patted her arm as if she was a child. "It's not that we're deliberately thinking the worst of him, Dana. But we know him really, really well."

"Spread out, take a street each," said Aramis, cuffing Dana lightly across the back of her head. "I hope he hasn't run out of credit. Athos shouldn't have to deal with this planet sober."

"Hell," said Porthos. "If we have to deal with Athos dealing with this planet, I don't want to be sober."

Athos being sober was the last thing they had to worry about. Dana was assigned to the Rue de Souveray, which sounded far grander than the cobbled alley that it turned out to be. The surfaces in this city were cracked and uneven, another aspect of dirtside life that Dana was glad she would never have to get used to.

It was mid afternoon in this time zone, with the sun already losing its enthusiasm for the day. The bars were not open yet, catering for the nightlife of Amiens. Dana did find a bakery that turned out to be not much help because they didn't serve wine. She then went further up the street only to discover a dance club. Athos would rather cut off his arm than drink there.

Dana frowned, staring back down the street. To find Athos, she had to think like Athos. Where would he have chosen to drink?

She returned down the sloping street to look more

closely at the closed establishments. What about that pub down on the corner? It looked shabby and comfortable; the kind of place where people didn't ask questions about where your credit came from.

It shouldn't be closed. A place like that got half its income from serving hearty lunches and letting customers linger at tables long into the afternoon. *The Gilded Lily* was scrawled on a sign that swung off an iron hook on the corner of the street.

As Dana watched, two customers approached the doors and knocked. They shouted their protest through the door, and eventually sloped off, looking unhappy.

Dana pressed her lips together. There was something going on. She headed down and knocked for herself, peering in through the glass panel (real glass!) in the door.

A man with a broom passed in front of the door and made a vague 'fuck off' gesture at Dana, then ignored her. She knocked again, more forcefully.

Finally, the landlord came to the door, holding his broom aggressively. "Not open!" he grunted. "Can't you read?"

Dana cupped her ear, pretending she could not hear him through the glass.

He opened the heavy door about four inches. "We're not bloody open, okay? Not today, not tomorrow at this rate." He paused, staring at Dana's jacket. "Are you one of them?"

Dana had considered shoving her foot in the door to prevent him from slamming it in her face, but with the size of the landlord and the vibrating anger coming off him, that would be a good way to lose a foot. She backed up from the door. "Am I — one of what?"

"You're a bloody Musketeer," snarled the landlord.

Dana squared her shoulders, tired of correcting the world. "Yes, I am," she lied between her teeth. "I am a bloody Musketeer."

"Thank Earth and Fire for that." He reached out and seized her, physically lifting her inside the pub. "Get that sodden, wine-soaked bastard out of my cellar before he destroys everything I have left."

Ah. This was what professionals would call: a clue. "Wine-soaked bastard?" Dana said innocently.

The landlord shoved at her shoulder. "He's yours, aye? The maniac with the sword and the woman who looks like a good religious sort but is basically as bad as him?"

Tact was called for here. Tact and subtlety. "Does the wine-soaked bastard have a beard?"

The landlord grabbed Dana around the arms again, propelling her across the floor. "You have to get him out of here. I can't run a business like this. Can't even sleep because I keep expecting the arsing sot to set fire to my pub in his ravings. Get him out."

Dana found herself facing a large, barred doorway. "I can do that," she said. She should call in Aramis and Porthos. She knew that. And yet — she was the one who had left Athos on this planet. It was up to her to rescue him.

The landlord wrenched the bar off the door. "You'll be settling his bill before you leave," he growled.

"Consider it done," said Dana confidently. She wasn't sure there was enough credit left for that even with the funds she had received from both Treville and Bucking-ham. Porthos had been expensive, and Aramis insisted on leaving a generous donation to the abbey as well as getting the *Morningstar* out of hock. "Can you tell me what happened?"

"Church guards," the landlord said, and then spat on his own floor. "Hammers. Never liked letting that sort in, especially in red uniforms and spouting Paris accents. But when they give me orders, I know better than to do otherwise, you know?"

Dana didn't like the sound of this. "Go on."

"When your man came in, he was quiet enough – the kind who doesn't want anything to get between him and his glass. The lady wasn't any trouble either. But a couple of them churchies came in, shouting about how they'd caught him — claimed he was a credit fraud, and the governor himself wanted him in custody."

Dana nodded grimly. It made sense — they wouldn't have wanted to admit the real reason to arrest Athos.

"He turned fierce, and the lady too — they fought off the guards and killed them right here on the floor, then barricaded themselves in my cellar. I sent word to the governor about it all, expecting him to send some more men to dig the criminals out of my place."

Dana looked from the door to the landlord. "How long ago was this?"

"Three, four days."

"And he's still down there?"

"The governor didn't know nothing about it," the landlord stuttered. "Local enforcement took the bodies but no one wanted to claim them — they weren't churchies at all, turned out, let alone from Paris. The credit fraud they'd been talking about, he was arrested three provinces from here."

"So Athos — my friend — was innocent," Dana said

darkly. "And you've kept him imprisoned down there for days."

"Imprisoned!" the landlord protested. "I've tried to give him his damned freedom. I've offered it to him on a silver platter. But he and that engineer of his, they refuse to come out. Tried to shoot me last time I put my head around the door, and ordered me to bar it closed."

Dana did her best not to smirk. "And uh, he's all right down there? Does he have access to food and medipatches and —"

The landlord turned a furious face upon her. "Food? He has all my bloody printers. My stores. My wine. I can't open up without them. He's going to ruin me."

Dana clapped him on the shoulder. "Don't worry. I'm taking him home."

"Raving nutter, he is. They go funny sometimes, you know. Them who fight in the wars. It's not good for a person."

"Open the door," said Dana, steeling herself for the worst. "I'm going in."

The landlord unlatched the door and stood well back. "None of your shooting!" he yelled down into the darkness. "Brought a mate of yours, gonna take you home!"

There was a long silence. Then the bright white light of a pearl stunner flashed in the darkness. Dana ducked fast, going down to her knees.

"Don't trust you, little man," called Athos, his New Aristocrat accent ringing out clearly from beneath them.

The sound of his voice made Dana's stomach tighten. She felt exactly as she had looking upon Aramis' face for the first time, back at the Crevecoueur Abbey, and at Chantilly Station when she saw for herself that Porthos was alive.

It was all going to be okay now.

"Athos," she yelled down the stairs into the blackness within. "What did we agree about you and pearl stunners? Stick to the sword, and maybe you won't hurt yourself."

There was a silence, and a soft choking sound. "Is that D'Artagnan?"

She was glad it was dark so that he couldn't see the stupid smile that broke out across her face. "Are you going to invite me into your creepy man-cave, or what?"

"Come on down," Athos called out, faking the same cheerfulness. "Mind the stairs in the dark, don't want you breaking your fool neck. Grimaud took my last medipatch. But no one else, D'Artagnan. I don't trust anyone else." His voice trembled, and it chilled Dana for a moment. He sounded far from okay.

"Close the door behind me, but don't bar it," she said softly to the landlord. "I'll have him out within the hour and all this will have been like a bad dream."

"Expensive fucking bad dream," muttered the landlord, but he did as she asked.

Dana descended the stairs, her hand trailing along the wall to keep her steady. "Have you been in the dark all this time, Athos? No lights down here?"

"Didn't want to waste candles," said Athos. A light flared somewhere in the cellar: a flame in a genuine lantern.

"Kicking it old school," Dana said, looking past the yellow blaze of light to Athos' face. He looked like shit. "What have you done to yourself?"

Athos raised a half-full wine bottle in an uneven salute. "Gave myself too much time to think."

Grimaud moved into the circle of yellow light, throwing a blanket off her own shoulders on to Athos' lap. "And on that note," she said, her eyes holding Dana's for a brief moment. "I'm going for a bath. I presume you can keep him from offing himself for an hour or so? I'll meet you outside."

The engie stomped up the stairs. "You," she called sharply to the landlord, just before the door shut behind her. "Hot water. This is an emergency."

Dana sank down on her knees beside Athos. She had to move a couple of empty bottles out of the way to sit down. "Want to tell me what she meant by that?" she asked softly.

"She was joking," he said, his hand still circling the neck of the bottle. She wanted to take it away from him, but even wrecked his reflexes would be better than hers.

"I don't think she was," Dana sighed. She reached out an arm, giving Athos a rough hug around the neck. He smelled like sour wine and engine oil. He didn't shrug her away, but leaned into her neck, like he was actually willing to take comfort from her touch.

Valour had broken him, then.

"You came back," Athos sighed, half asleep.

"Someone had to save you from yourself." She shoved him with her hip. "I told you I would. Porthos and Aramis are here, too. We've been looking all over. Should I get them in here?"

"No, not yet." He shuddered under her arm.

Dana curled around him, her other hand smoothing

over his until the tremble lessened. "Athos, you're a mess," she sighed. "What's wrong? Can you tell me?"

"They don't know. Never wanted them to know."

"How is there anything those two don't know about you?"

Athos shoved her away, then. He rocked up on his heels, disappearing into the darkness, and stumbled back with another bottle. Not wine this time. It smelled like some kind of brandy, when he uncapped it. When he collapsed, he pushed the lantern between them to keep Dana at a distance. "They don't know that I'm not worth saving," he said flatly, and necked the bottle.

Dana resisted the urge to smack the bottle away. At this rate, getting him to drink himself unconscious might be the only way to drag him off this bloody planet.

She considered her options. Porthos and Aramis were both capable of flying everyone home between them. There was no law that said she had to do this sober.

Dana held out a hand for the bottle of brandy. "Give," she ordered. Athos handed the bottle to her, and she took a deep swig. It had a smooth heat to it that warmed her all the way down. She couldn't remember when she had last eaten anything. "Bullshit you're not worth saving," she added, and held on to the bottle as long as she could before Athos motioned for it back. "I call double bullshit on that."

"You've been running towards the Musketeers for your whole life, D'Artagnan." He sounded defeated. "Arms outstretched. Haven't you noticed that the rest of us got here by running away from something?"

She let him take one swallow, then dragged the bottle back for herself. "What makes you special, Athos? What makes the demon you're running away from so much more dramatic than everyone else's?"

He made a noise like a sob. She realised he was laughing and that was actually worse. Dana had never heard him laugh like this before. She would be quite happy never to hear it again.

"I am worse," he said. "You saw it when the ship came down."

Silver hair tousled over the back of a neck. Bare feet on soft grass. "The happy memory that made you sad," remembered Dana.

"My beloved husband," said Athos, with sarcasm hovering around the word *beloved*. "Before I killed him."

Dana handed him back the bottle of brandy. "You know you don't get to leave the story there, right?"

He huffed out a long breath, his fingers curling and uncurling around the neck of the bottle. "You're welcome to drink with me. But you're not entitled to anything else."

Time to call in reinforcements, to contact Porthos and Aramis and Bonnie and Bazin and Planchet and gang up with them to drag Athos' sorry drunken carcass out of here. It was amazing Grimaud had lasted as long as she had in this cellar without using the pearl stunner on him and dragging him out by his feet.

But the words 'my beloved husband' hung in the air and Dana knew, she knew that once they left this cellar, he would seal himself up again like a barrel.

The mystery that was Athos had been nagging at Dana for a long time, and this revelation that there was a story from his past that even Aramis and Porthos did not know … that was too intriguing to be ignored. Selfish, but she wanted to know.

So she drank. They drank together, gulp after gulp, and Dana told him of the adventures he had missed, of Buck and the replacement diamonds and the mysterious Milord de Winter.

As the brandy dipped low in the bottle, she confessed about Conrad, his disappearance, and the ominous conversation she had shared with Rosnay Cho. Her voice broke as she repeated the words, *"I'm sorry, buttercup, but you're not getting him back."*

Athos shrugged.

"Seriously?" Dana howled at him, snatching back the bottle. "That's all you've got?"

"Either the lad went back to his wife, or his own meddling in politics got him killed. If you want sympathy, Aramis will hug you until the end of time. Porthos is good at tea and kindness. I don't give a fuck."

"Are you dead inside?" Dana snarled.

Athos gave her a thin smile. "Basically."

"Because you killed your husband." A low blow.

"Not even that." He reached for the bottle. Dana held on to it stubbornly. Athos growled. "I have no interest in epic love stories. Even yours, sweetness."

"How did you end up on that mountain, miserable out of your skin, the day that Aramis and Porthos rescued you?" she challenged him. "What *happened* to you on this planet?"

"It didn't happen to me," Athos said, tugging more forcefully on the bottle. Dana held on to it, using all of her muscle to keep the brandy in her lap. "It happened to someone else."

Dana felt the cellar tilt around her. She was drunker than she had meant to be, and she wasn't sure about anything except that she was not going to let Athos swallow another mouthful. "Who?"

Athos gave a last desperate lurch, and Dana gripped the bottle harder. The glass cracked between their fingers, and the brandy leaked out over their boots.

"It happened to the Comte de la Fere," Athos snarled, barely noticing that the glass had slashed a bloody line into his palm. "He's dead, and good riddance."

CHAPTER 30
IN THE CELLAR OF THE GILDED LILY

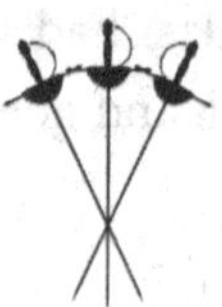

"You're wearing my jacket," Athos observed, as Dana picked slivers of glass out of his shaking hand by lantern light.

They had to get out of this cellar. Athos had drunk enough of the Gilded Lily's printstock of wine and brandy to poison him. Dana felt half-poisoned herself, even if the bottle they had shared most recently was of exceptional quality.

Right now, she was trying to make sure he did not bleed too badly.

"Gauze strips in the inner pocket," Athos added, which was lucid of him. "Why are you wearing my clothes, D'Artagnan?"

Chances were high he would never remember this conversation. "I missed my friends. Shut up."

He laughed softly.

"I hate you," she told him.

"As is only right and proper."

Dana made a huffing sound. "You are the king of self-pity."

"I wasn't the one complaining that the Cardinal's mysterious secret agent and/or political advisor kidnapped my boyfriend before I got a chance to jump his bones."

"That is not how I phrased it at all," she said, smacking a gauze strip over Athos' cut much harder than necessary.

"Ow."

"Time to sober you up." She brought out her trump card, a Sobriety patch she had tucked into one of the many useful pockets in this jacket.

Athos' eyes widened as he saw it. "Fuck no. I've been working on this bender for most of the week, D'Artagnan. You wouldn't be so cruel."

"Come outside with me now, and I won't sober you up until we're off planet. This is my final offer." Never mind his tragic past. Removing him from this cellar had to be her priority.

Athos gave her a searching look. "Open another bottle and I'll tell you the worst story you've ever heard."

Dana refused to give into temptation. "Athos, another bottle might kill you."

"Half a bottle. I'll share."

"Half a bottle might kill me."

His blue eyes were so very intense in the dim light. "I told you that I murdered the man I loved, and you don't want any more details?"

"Wine, not brandy," Dana whispered. She was dirt. Curious, weak dirt.

Athos reached out without looking, his hand closing

around the neck of a new wine bottle. "I'm sure the land-lord won't mind."

"He's going to call the local militia if we don't pay your tab," Dana replied, but she let him unseal the bottle. "Start talking, or I'll break that one too."

Athos took a long, steady swallow and wiped his wet mouth with his unbandaged hand. "There was a Comte who lived in the far North of this continent, who fell in love," he said. "Which was the first stupid thing. But they were young, and stupidity was his elemental privilege. They were students together at the university, and they were going to change the world."

"Students of what?" Dana asked. She took the bottle off him and tasted the wine. It mixed badly with the brandy already sloshing around in her stomach.

"Philosophy. Politics. If you could get a degree in being wide-eyed and idealistic, these two young idiots would have signed up without a second thought. The Comte was a New Aristocrat through and through — he wasn't supposed to have a purpose beyond keeping his lands from burning down around him, and solving the disputes of his province. That had been the Fleet's excuse for not allowing him to sign up for service when he came of age during the War against the Sun-kissed. An excuse he had accepted all too readily."

"But now he wanted more," Dana prodded.

"Because *love*," said Athos. That word had never been spoken with such venom in the history of the solar system.

"I'm sensing this story doesn't end well."

"Oh, you think?" He paused, his breaths slow and steady. "The second stupid thing the Comte did was to marry his lover after university. They were on fire together, determined to use the power and privilege of the New Aristocracy for something good. The war was over, and the Valour government had played lapdog to the Crown during the conflict, in exchange for keeping their brightest and best out of the war." His head drooped, and Dana thought for a moment he had nodded off. "There might have been poetry."

Dana almost laughed at the sheepish, despairing way Athos said that. *He needs to tell someone*, she insisted at the spark of guilt that she was taking advantage of his drunken state. "Poetry," she repeated.

"It's traditional, in love affairs," Athos said, so pompous that it was all too believable that he had once been a baby-faced, politically charged New Aristocrat who ruled a province, rather than a drunken Musketeer who couldn't fly his ship without chemical assistance.

"Poetry, philosophy, politics… and love," Dana said lightly. "A heady cocktail."

Athos nodded grimly. "For a happy marriage. Right up to the point that the Comte's husband fell ill. He contracted a midwinter fever that no medipatch could cure. A burning fever that lasted for three days and nights. During that time, he spoke of — secrets, awful secrets. And that was how the Comte learned that his husband was a fraud. He had spent all that time thinking himself deliriously happy, but here was genuine delirium, and the cruel truth."

"What truth?" Dana whispered.

"He was so fucking beautiful," Athos said in a ragged voice. "Pale skin, like moonlight. That hair. And — I never saw how false he was until it was all too late."

Athos tipped the bottle up to his mouth and Dana let

him take a drink before she reclaimed it. "Why was it too late?" she asked.

Athos matched her question with another. "What do you know about the Sun-kissed?"

Hardly the time for a history lesson, but she went along with it. "They're ruthless. Alien. They hide in plain sight, because…" The words faded on her tongue. Dana stared at her friend in horror, suddenly realising how this story fit together with the other story, the one he had told her when they were crashing and burning. "No."

"They hide because they can look like us," Athos agreed through gritted teeth. "They can look like any fucking thing they want. But after three days of fever, of genuine illness, he couldn't hold on to the transformation any longer. So the Comte's beautiful husband rolled over in the sheets and his skin turned dark red like he was sunburned, and the war tattoos spilled across his back, line by line, and light poured out of his eyes and mouth, and it turned out that it didn't matter that we thought the war was over and that Valour had made it through untouched. The Sun-kissed were still among us, hiding spies in plain sight. Placing them near people they thought could be of use."

Athos was bitter and tired, and Dana wanted to take all the hurt away from him. She had not imagined something as awful as this. She was sick at the thought of it — of discovering you had shared a bed with an alien and an enemy. Of being deceived so vilely. She could guess how the story ended. Athos had already told her that part.

"The Comte — executed his husband personally?" There was only one way to ensure that a Sun-kissed was dead, Dana knew from school. She had been twelve years old when the war ended, and it had all seemed so theoretical. *You take their head, and you burn the remains.*

"It was his duty," said Athos, closing his eyes and leaning back against the nearest barrel. "Damn," he added. "That's a good wine, that one. Too drunk to do it justice. We should take a bottle or two when we leave."

"We should go in," said Porthos, bouncing impatiently on the soles of her boots.

She and Aramis had waited outside the tavern for over an hour. A little while earlier, Grimaud had emerged into the late afternoon sunshine with damp hair and sonic-scrubbed clothes. Aramis made a token payment towards the landlord's exorbitant bill with the last of the credit they had and pledged Amiral Treville to cover the rest. They sent Grimaud back to the *Hoyden* and the *Morningstar* with Bonnie and Planchet, to file the flight plans and ready the ships for the long trip home.

"Give them a little longer," said Aramis. "We don't know what state he's in."

"Dana's a puppy. She doesn't know what she's up against." Porthos had seen Athos at his ordinary worst a hundred times or more, but his rock bottom was something she had only glimpsed twice, and had hoped to never see again.

Aramis squeezed Porthos' shoulder. "She's not that young. It's good for him, to have someone other than you and me to pick him out of the gutter from time to time. With Dana — he might manage to summon some pride."

Porthos gave her a filthy look. "That's not fair on her. He's her hero."

"And today she gets to find out that he's human," Aramis said serenely. "It will be good for both of them."

"I hate when you're spiritually calm," Porthos muttered.

Aramis gave her a gentle hug. "Isn't it nice, though? Just a little. To share him."

"He's not a food parcel."

"My shoulders are feeling lighter."

"Probably the love letter burning a hole in your pocket."

"Could be," Aramis smirked.

The door to The Gilded Lily opened. Athos walked out, blinking in the light of the sun. It came in at a piercing angle, about to descend into the mountains beyond Amiens. Athos looked rough, his beard back to the long, untended horror it had been before Aramis last got her hands on him with a sonar clipper. He had lost some weight, probably from drinking too many meals, and he was unsteady on his feet.

He carried Dana slung over his shoulder like a dead weight. "Kid can't hold her drink," he muttered as he approached them.

Porthos wanted to hug him, but she feared any sudden movements would pitch them all on to the historically authentic cobblestones at their feet. "Credit's covered," she informed him. "Grimaud gave the landlord an approximation of the damage in the cellar."

"Let's get moving before he discovers how much she was underplaying my consumption," said Athos.

The three of walked down the street together, falling into step as they always did.

"Can I claim a favour?" Athos asked after a long moment.

"Try us," said Aramis.

"Wait until we're in orbit before you attack me with that Sobriety patch D'Artagnan has in her pocket. I don't want to be sober on this fucking planet."

Aramis and Porthos exchanged a glance.

"Fine," said Porthos. "But if you throw up in my beautiful ship, I will toss you out an airlock."

Athos winced as they turned a corner and that setting sun pierced his vision again. "Didn't know being thrown out an airlock was on the table. That's actually my preferred option."

Aramis squeezed his arm. "Do you want us to get what's left of the *Parry-Riposte* out of hock before we go?"

Athos shifted slightly, preventing Dana from sliding off his shoulder. She moaned as his arm bumped against her stomach. "No. Sometimes you have to leave rubble behind and start over."

Porthos bumped against his other side — the side holding Dana — with her hip. "Sounds like good advice, Athos. Maybe you should take it someday."

"Bite me, Porthos."

The Musketeers allowed the engies to pilot the *Hoyden* and the *Morningstar* back to Paris. Planchet was sent on the *Morningstar* to practice astronavigation with Bazin, and

Bonnie took the helm and harness of the *Hoyden* with Grimaud snoozing in the jumpseat beside her.

Dana woke up four hours out of Meung Station, pressed against the wall in Porthos' bunk. A Sobriety patch burned a perfect triangle into her right shoulder. Aramis sat beside Dana, her long legs tangling with those of Athos, who was propped up comfortably against the other end of the bunk reading from a tablet, with Porthos tucked under his arm.

There were three Sobriety patches visible along the length of Athos' neck.

"I can't believe we all fit in one bed," Dana said as she yawned herself awake. Her own feet were pressed against Porthos' knees.

Aramis elbowed her. "Economy of space is the most important skill we have as a species," she said, quoting a long-ago prophet who had taken their people to the stars.

"This bunk is larger than regulation," added Athos.

"I like to be comfortable," said Porthos defensively.

"No complaints here," he said with a quirk of his mouth, and head-butted her gently. She poked him in the ribs with a finger.

Dana pulled herself up upright, sitting with the wall behind her. "This is nice," she said. She wanted to grin stupidly at all three of them, but she settled for letting her head fall on to Aramis' shoulder so she could doze again.

When Dana awoke the next time, Athos and Aramis were no longer there. Porthos sprawled out at the end of the bunk, watching a cinquefoil game on the same tablet Athos had been reading from earlier.

"They're checking on Grimaud's injuries," Porthos yawned, before Dana gave any indication she was awake. "Or rather, Aramis is checking on her injuries, and Athos is being extra sarcastic so that he can pretend he's not fussing over his engie like a mother hen."

Dana grinned at that. "He's protective."

"Oh, honey, you have no idea." Porthos muted her game, laying the tablet aside. "It was bad down there, huh?"

She meant the cellar, of course.

Dana frowned. "I've never seen him like that," she confessed.

"Not many do."

"He was so lost. Is he that unhappy all the time?"

"Pretty much," Porthos sighed. "He hides it well. Too well, most days." She flicked a curious expression at Dana. "You're burning to ask questions. I wouldn't, if I were you."

"No questions," Dana muttered, looking away. She had enough of Athos' secrets now; she didn't need more of them.

"Oh," Porthos breathed. "Well, that's new."

Dana scowled. "What are you talking about?"

"He told you, didn't he? About his husband."

That earned a startled glance from Dana. "What?" She double-checked that the door to the flight deck was firmly closed. "He said you didn't know," she hissed.

Porthos looked guilty, and sad. "I found out on a very bad day," she admitted. "He was out of it, he doesn't remember telling me. Aramis knows too, the shape of it at least."

Dana was relieved. She was not cut out to be anyone's support person, least of all the complex bag of angry spiky space weapons that was Athos' inner turmoil.

"How much do you know?" she asked finally. She wasn't going to assume all Athos' secrets were fair game because Porthos had an excellent poker face.

Porthos tilted her head at Dana, regarding her. "I know his husband is dead," she said softly. "He blames himself. Sometimes he's so eaten up about it that he sabotages everything good in his life."

Dana nodded at that, thinking of the business with the nexus. Athos was a brilliant pilot, but he didn't trust himself. "Except you," she said after a moment. "You and Aramis. Having you as friends, it's the best thing that he has."

Porthos laughed at that, not an overly cheerful laugh, but deep and honest. "Believe me, he's sabotaged that plenty of times. We won't let him go, though." She leaned in and scritched Dana's short buzz of hair on her scalp, as if she was a puppy dog. "If you know as much as I do, about the husband and the deep dark misery and all that, I'm impressed."

"It's not —" Dana said awkwardly, because she knew more, a lot more than Porthos was saying. *She* was the one Athos had chosen to trust with the complete truth about his husband. "I was there when he needed to talk," she muttered.

"Ha," said Porthos. "Athos has been needing to talk as long as I've known him, but he doesn't let himself, not about things that matter. Telling you his secret, that's important, Dana. Hold on to that."

Athos' voice called harshly through the doorway. "D'Artagnan, Porthos, get in here now!" For a moment, Dana was embarrassed. Did he realise they had been gossiping about him?

As she entered the flight deck, all thoughts of Athos and his angsty past bled away. Aramis, closest to the doorway, reached out and caught Dana's hand, squeezing it gently between her own.

Everyone, even Bonnie who had slipped the *Hoyden* into autopilot, stood watching the enlarged media screen on the inside of the hatchway. It was the beginning of a press conference — the Regence stood behind a podium, speaking in her clear, confident voice. In the background, Dana could see Prince Alek and the Cardinal, standing much closer together than usual, grave and united.

"These recent attacks on citizens of the solar system make it clear that the alien race known to us as the Sun-kissed have no intention of meeting our overtures of peaceful negotiation with anything other than contempt," said the Regence, well aware that her words would be recorded and rebroadcast over and over in the years to come. She was speaking history, a kind of history they had hoped never to repeat.

"When all other options have failed, there is only one clear path remaining. As of today, our solar system is once again at war with the Sun-kissed. Let the God of All have mercy on their souls, for we have no mercy left for them. Not this time."

CHAPTER 31
MUSKETEERS AT WAR

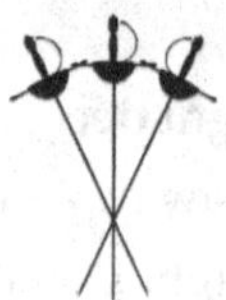

Dana stared at the viewscreen where the Regence's declaration of war still hung in the air. Her first thought was of Athos, of the terrible look in his eyes when he confessed to her that his husband had been a spy for the Sun-kissed. He had loved one of them, an alien, without even knowing it.

Right now, his jaw was tense. He muttered to Aramis, "Hell of a time to be without a ship."

"You'll have time to acquire a new helm and harness," Aramis said. "And a hull to wrap around it."

"Not a lot of time," Athos grated back. His eyes flicked to Dana, and the look on his face had nothing to do with that deep misery he had spilled out to her on the floor of the cellar of The Gilded Lily.

It was pity, she realised with a sinking feeling. It was — he was looking at her as if he expected her to be the one to fall apart. Why would he think that? Her three friends might be going off to war without her, but she was part of the Mecha Squad, it was hardly as if she would be left out altogether…

The screen shifted from the press conference to show the recent attacks that had inspired the Regence's declaration of war, and Dana's mouth went dry so fast that it stung the inside of her cheeks.

Gascon Station. That was Gascon Station.

She watched the broadcast in silence, taking in the details. Six incendiary bombs, planted in secret across the station, detonating at ten-minute intervals. Emergency response thrown into disarray. Life support disconnected across whole sectors of the station.

Ten thousand casualties. Even taking into account passing trade and miners on rec leave, that was a third of the population of Gascon. She couldn't even start thinking about specifics, about which areas had hit and which people she knew were most likely to have been where at that time of day. All she could hear was a faint buzzing sound in her ears.

Aramis squeezed Dana's hand.

Dana heard Athos and Porthos arguing about which of them were going to take over the helm from Bonnie. Athos insisted he was faster, but Porthos overruled him on the grounds that the *Hoyden* was her damned ship.

Dana wondered if Athos was even capable of flying right now. Had Grimaud given his last ampoule of nexus to Dana when they were busy crashing the *Parry-Riposte,* or did she have further supplies with her?

The broadcast flicked from the damage done to Gascon Station to a repeat of the Regence's declaration of war, then the edited highlights of the questions she had answered afterwards.

"I need to contact my family," Dana said aloud. No one heard her in all the arguing, so she repeated it again, louder.

Porthos turned to her. "I have subspace credit. Give Bonnie your residential codes and she'll try to get the call through. Athos, if your butt even touches my chair I am going to kick you in it."

Bonnie relinquished the helm to Porthos, and drew Dana back into the cabin to connect the call. It didn't work the first time they tried, or the second. None of Dana's family comms were working: not her Maman or Papa's personal studs, nor the home mainframe, nor any of their work codes. Neither of her sisters replied. The emergency contact line was running hot, and Dana was unlikely to make it to the front of the queue before they got back to Paris.

"I'll keep trying," Bonnie said finally, taking the tablet out of Dana's shaking hands. "I'll get Planchet on to it, the kid is a genius with communications. Give us a little while, we'll get you through."

And she did, but it took an hour, and an hour is far too long to be thinking that your family might not exist anymore.

By the time the call came through, tensions were running high in the *Hoyden*. Whoever's idea it had been to cram all three Musketeers and Dana in one musket-class dart had been a dumbass. Aramis and Athos sniped at each other about religious doctrine, of all things, equally frustrated at their inability to make the ship go faster by mind control.

The newsreels only stopped showing the endless clips of the destruction on Gascon Station and the Regence's speech in order to report that fifty alien ships had unfolded in Truth space, rendering the planet and its orbital cities (Artemisia, Valentine, Lucretia, Rochelle) under siege. No shots had yet been fired, but it was clearly a message, as much as the attack on Gascon Station and the planet Freedom had been: *one planet at a time, we are coming for you.*

Porthos, flying the *Hoyden* as fast as she could thanks to the wonders of spaceship design and long-lasting power globes, refused to speak to Athos or Aramis except to say, "shut up both of you, stop acting like children," and "I will make you walk the fucking plank, I swear to God."

"Chief," Planchet said suddenly, her voice coming through Dana's comm from the *Morningstar* as if she was right next to her on the bunk. "I've got your call, standby."

Dana caught her breath and then she heard her mother's voice, business-like and firm over the subspace comm line. "Dana, is that you?"

"Maman," Dana burst out. "Are you — is everyone —" But no, asking about everyone was too much. She had watched lists of known fatalities grow with every repetition on the smaller vid screen in the cabin. So many names that she knew, friends and extended family and acquaintances. People she had grown up with. "Are you all right? Is Papa?"

"It's bad, darling, but we're holding on," said Maman. That assurance was enough to make Dana sob out loud. She wanted desperately to beg forgiveness for leaving home, and to swear to kill all the Sun-kissed.

Instead she stayed calm, asked sensible questions, and

tried not to break too hard inside as her mother reported what had been destroyed, and who was dead, and what was happening in the wake of the disaster.

At one point, Maman stopped talking altogether, and after a scrabbling sound, Dana's elder sister Debo came on instead, sounding stiff and robotic. "Di and Pippa were missing for six hours," she said, referring to the middle D'Artagnan sister and her wife. "The kids are okay. They weren't in the school that was hit. Papa didn't want you to know, but he's been evacuated to a medibay ship – we can't do more than field treatment on station. He was caught in one of the explosions. His burns are extensive."

As Dana listened, burying herself in the sound of her older sister's familiar voice, Athos and Aramis came to sit near her on the bunk.

Athos patted her briefly on the shoulder, in an 'if only we had swords I might be willing to talk about your feelings but let's face it, probably not' kind of way. He sat close enough to Dana that she could feel the warmth of him. Aramis had no restraint – every time Dana's voice stumbled over the very basic task of exchanging words with her sister and then her mother again, Aramis reached out and rubbed small circles against her lower back.

They were here, and her family were alive, and there was more to think about.

War, and what it meant for all of them.

24 hours later, her feet solidly planted on the ground of Lunar Palais, Dana stared at the mecha-suit. She had been immersed in ships – and darts in particular – for so long

that she could barely remember knowing what to do with one of these.

She was going to have to catch up fast.

"Cadet D'Artagnan," said a voice behind her. "Good to have you back from leave."

Dana turned, to find her commanding officer behind her. Commandant Essart was a short, solid woman with greying hair. She had a motherly air about her but she could yell as loud as Amiral Treville.

"Ready for service, boss," Dana said, saluting.

"Good to hear. The rosters for the next two months will be posted in the mess later today. Two mecha units will remain here on Lunar Palais for city security, and other two will be shipping out with the Royal Fleet to Truth Space."

The thought of staying here when the Fleet were going to war was awful beyond words. Of course they couldn't leave Paris and Lunar Palais defenceless, but Dana could not bear the idea of being left behind. She nodded, without saying anything.

Truth was as close to Freedom and the remains of Gascon Station as she was going to get while still contracted to the military. Would it be worse to be so damned close and still not home?

"You, however, will not be with any of them, if you accept this," said Essart. She handed over an envelope with a familiar blue fleur-de-lis seal upon it. "Amiral Treville is short on pilots for supply transport. She wants to buy out your contract, if you allow it. Your crew would be printing and ferrying supplies for the troops, providing parts for repair and replacement weapons, and running a medibay for the wounded. No military action expected."

Dana opened her mouth and closed it again. Treville wanted her. She'd be with the Musketeers, even if she still wouldn't be one of them. She would have her own ship: a supplies venturer rather than the musket-class dart she longed for.

If anything happened to Aramis, Athos or Porthos, Dana would be *right there* in the midst of the action, she wouldn't be left out of the loop. She might even get a glimpse of home.

If she stayed with the Mecha Squad, she had a 50% chance of combat, might have an opportunity to take bloody revenge against the bastard Sun-kissed.

"Can I think about it?" she asked, not realising she was going to say those words until they were spilling out of her mouth.

Essart looked almost sympathetic. "Take three hours, kid," she said. "Get your head on straight. Then report to me with your decision."

"Yes, boss."

Dana climbed inside the mecha suit and opened her thoughts to it, flexing her limbs and trying to get used to the odd sensation of controlling the heavy metal armour. She had been a long time away, but she was more attuned to the machine than when she first started. The reflexes would come back.

She thought about taking a mecha into combat, of blasting the Sun-kissed ships out of the sky of Truth. She thought about her Papa, lying in a medibay ship and complaining about being made to stay immobile while they worked on replacing his skin. She thought about how being here, protecting the Regence herself, was a vital job, and someone had to do it.

Dana had done enough for the Crown lately. It was time to think about what she wanted – what she had to offer the solar system. She made her choice.

I'm going to war.

Milord Vaniel de Winter was not a loving man. Love was for fools. He had no particular attachment to his daughter Morgan, the de Winter heir, who had been neatly packed off to a nursery from birth, and had a series of boarding schools lined up for her future. Milord's late wife, Delia de Winter, had not inspired much in the way of love during their short marriage. He had a higher tolerance for her sister Bee who was at least amusing, and loyal, and played a mean game of cards.

Romance and sex were political tools like any other. Milord allowed himself the occasional attraction, like his current hunger for the fascinating Marquise de Wardes, but only after he had formed a strategy for how that romance would be useful to his schemes.

If he loved anything at all, it was his ship.

The *Matagot* was a masterpiece of hidden depths. He was a dagger-class raven scout, polished black and gleaming on the outside. If you weren't paying attention – and people rarely did pay sufficient attention – he looked like any other messenger ship.

If you knew what to look for, you might notice how well preserved the ship was, without the usual wear and tear of anything piloted by a Raven. The hull was glossy and smooth, and the engine purred like the cat of legend from which the ship had taken his name.

A lot of money had been spent on keeping this ship in the kind of prime condition that a Raven messenger could never afford.

Officially, Milord and his sister-in-law were staying at the Julien, a five-star hotel on Lunar Palais. Bee spent most of her time there, with her irritating friends as they indulged in their usual riot of gaming, carousing and competitive sports. She had a suite on Paris Satellite itself for easy access to the rec centres and TeamJoust tanks.

Bee's friends were not the only reason that Milord avoided both hotel suites. The *Matagot* provided all his needs – including a double office that allowed Milord and his assistant Kitty to work in separate spaces so that her cheerful chatter did not drive him up the wall.

Milord liked his office – it was less spacious than the one he used back on Valour, but it had a desk and a comfortable couch and access to every comm frequency in the solar system. There was even room to pace back and forth, when his nervous energy got the better of him.

The dagger-class scout was roomier than most variations of this kind of ship. There were several cabins, a basic kitchen and a gym. More than most hotels had to offer, even if you were prepared to pay top credit.

Kitty's office was – something that Milord suffered, because good assistants were hard to find and while Kitty was bossy, overly talkative and high-pitched, she would also work twenty hours non-stop if he needed her to, she never asked stupid questions, and she did a good line in sarcastic banter which was, he had to admit, a great weakness of his.

In exchange for Kitty's relentless work ethic, her ability to remind him to eat and sleep at regular intervals, and the fact that she had worked for him for five years without reporting any of his more illegal activities to the Crown, Milord paid her very well and allowed her to decorate her office to her own taste.

If he kept his eyes straight ahead and walked very quickly on his way to his own office, he did not have to look at the bright pastel wall decorations and the collection of flying glitter pony toys that littered her desk.

The whole thing had become more tolerable once he installed a second coffee printer in his office. No one should be faced with rainbows and sparkly plush space unicorns when they were in search of coffee.

Today he was in the gym, using the treadmill while answering correspondence from the office back on Valour when Kitty's bright, cheery voice broke in on the music in his headphones. "Your smoking hot 1500 appointment is here early, Milord. Shall I show her to your office, or can I flirt with her while you make yourself ready?"

"Whichever my guest prefers," he said, maintaining the usual affable charm that he used around his assistant. It was good practice for him, the illusion of an intense but kind-hearted politician. Kitty's perception of him influenced how others saw him, and the cover of Milord Vaniel de Winter was too useful to risk. Vaniel de Winter found Kitty amusing, and allowed her to push him around because it made her feel useful. Milord hoped he would not have to kill her someday, because how the hell did one discreetly dispose of that many glitter ponies?

"Any word from the Marquise de Wardes' people?" he asked.

"She has taken up the Regence's offer to stay in residence at the Palace for some time," said Kitty. "Still working on that personal appointment, though. Everyone wants a piece of her. Might take more than a bunch of flowers and a pair of designer heels in a gift box, if you know what I mean."

Milord felt his mouth press into a thin line. The Marquise de Wardes would be a fascinating political ally to add to his collection, but so far his overtures had been met with polite reserve.

If he couldn't win her with gifts and conversation, he might have to invest the time and energy into a seduction.

Milord took a brief sonic shower and dressed in business clothes for the appointment. As he straightened his tie in the mirror, he shifted his hair from comfortable silver-blond back to brown. This guest knew both sides of him, but it was a code to him as much as to her. Silver meant flirting, espionage and pretending to be equals. Brown meant Valour politics, New Aristocracy, and business all the way.

Kitty was alone in her glitter pony paradise when Milord strode past her desk. Slurping her way through a foaming green tea frappe the size of her forearm, she waggled her fingernails at him in greeting.

Special Agent Rosnay Cho waited in Milord's office, her boots propped up on his desk and a cup of black coffee balanced on the arm of her chair. "Not interrupting anything, am I?" she asked.

Milord was unsettled by her early appearance. Appointment times should be as sacrosanct as contracts. "What's so urgent that it couldn't wait an hour?"

Ro surveyed him from beneath her dark sweep of hair. Her flight suit today was a bright musk pink, frivolous as always. It was one of many techniques she employed to make people underestimate how dangerous she was; Milord appreciated that about her. There were times when he wondered if Kitty, with her purple hair and sugared drinks and pony obsession, was doing the same thing. Possibly she was an assassin in disguise.

"I was at a loose end, and there's a lot to do today," Ro said carelessly. "Don't you know there's a war on?"

Milord rolled his eyes at her. He allowed a certain amount of teasing, for the same reason that Ro wore candy-coloured flight suits. It didn't hurt to let other people think you were fair game. Intimacy was like anything else – a tool to be carefully distributed, and then exploited. "How can I be of use to the Cardinal today?"

Ro blinked steadily at him. "I'm not here on behalf of her Eminence. The Regence has given me a mission, and I thought you might have useful intelligence."

Interesting. It wasn't unlike Ro to roll where the weather took her, but it surprised him that the Cardinal allowed her loyalties to be shared. Milord let his voice drop into a low, amused drawl. "I'm honoured. How can I help the Regence?"

"I'm on the lookout for an asset that the Prince Consort is upset to have lost."

He laughed at that. "Not the little tailor?"

"He's been kidnapped."

"He makes a habit of that." Milord raised his eyebrows at her. "Usually it's you."

Ro scowled. "Not this time. Do you know where he is?"

"I couldn't begin to imagine. But I promise I'll keep an eye out on my travels. People often turn up in the strangest places."

"The reward is very generous."

"I'll keep that in mind. Anything else?"

The stare he got from her was intense and thorough, as if she was trying to pull the knowledge of Conrad Su's whereabouts directly from his mind. "D'Artagnan," she said, after a moment.

Milord batted his eyelashes at her. "Who?"

Ro was impatient. "She's a new favourite of Prince Alek, and by extension, the Regence. Hangs around with Musketeers. Gets into trouble like it's her superpower."

"I don't know anyone by that name," Milord replied with his sweetest smile. It was true, to a point. The woman he had met on that train back on Valour had used a different identity.

"The Cardinal doesn't want anything to happen to Dana D'Artagnan," Ro said in a firm voice. "Not in retaliation for recent events, or anything else. Her Eminence is all for a unified front with the Crown for the duration of the war. D'Artagnan is off limits."

Neither of them mentioned diamonds, as the reason someone might wish to retaliate against the young pilot who had made herself so very difficult lately.

"D'Artagnan is off limits," Milord agreed. "Got it." He continued to smile, his gaze fixed on Ro's beautiful, scarred face until she took her leave of him.

"Always a pleasure, Milord," she said tiredly.

"You too, sweetness," he replied, and they kissed the corners of each other's mouths in polite pretence that they weren't now on opposing sides of a game that was getting interesting.

Milord waited until Ro was gone, and then chimed through the comm to Kitty. "Any more appointments this afternoon?"

"No, Milord de Winter," she said cheerfully.

"Let's take a joyride. File a flight plan for the Tower asteroid. I want to check on our guest."

"Whatever you say, boss. Will we be back by tomorrow evening? That's Karaoke night in the South quarter, and some very cute engies offered to buy me drinks."

"You know how I hate to interfere with your social life. This will be a short trip."

"Right you are, boss."

Milord stood at the door between their adjoining offices and examined himself in the mirrored surface. He straightened his tie and the collar of his shirt. Ro knew him too well. The only reason for her to arrive early was to rattle him.

He would not allow it. "Kitty, scratch that," he called through his comm. "We'll stay with the original plan. Our guest can wait a few more days." The last thing he wanted was to be tracked to the holding location of his prisoner. "Order a security sweep of the *Matagot*, from top to tail. Let's be sure Special Agent Cho didn't leave us any small, blinking gifts."

"Isn't she a friend of yours, Milord?" Kitty said in surprise.

"Oh, she is," he agreed, gazing at his reflection. He stretched his neck casually and let himself fall for a moment into his natural shape. Red blossomed across his skin, highlighting his cheekbones and the soft creases in the corners of his eyes. His eyes darkened to blown black pupils with tiny darts of golden light flecked through them. His skin flooded with the warmth that smelled like home.

In this moment, he was not Winter or Vaniel or Milord or Auden or Slate or Gray or any of the other names he had worn in service of his long career of pretending to be human. For a few precious seconds, he was gloriously himself.

Then he blinked back to Milord Vaniel de Winter, Secretary of the Interior on Valour: political obsessive, absent father, loyal brother-in-law and all-around good person to have in your corner. Tousled brown hair, pale skin, grey eyes.

"Rosnay Cho is a very good friend of mine," he assured Kitty, adjusting his cuffs and smoothing out the soft lines of his jacket. "That's what makes her so dangerous."

He would allow himself no more personal indulgences. There was a war on, after all.

A war against the human race, and the solar system they held so dear.

To be continued in

A Miracle of Spaceships (Musketeer Space 2)

A MIRACLE OF SPACESHIPS
MUSKETEER SPACE #2

THE STORY CONTINUES!

When aliens invade, the Royal Fleet rallies to defend the outer planets of the Solar System. Dana D'Artagnan digs deeper into a web of court politics and royal intrigue, desperate to unlock the secrets of a dangerously attractive spy who wears the face of a dead man.

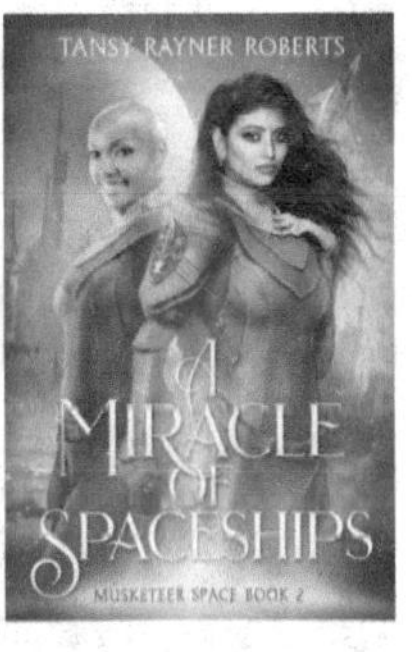

With Athos, Porthos and Aramis fighting on the front line of a space war, Dana will make any sacrifice she can to be at their side and protect the royal family — and the Solar System — from Milord's murderous machinations.

All Dana ever wanted was to be a Musketeer. Now all she wants is to save them.

JOYEUX

EXPLORE THE HIDDEN BACKSTORY OF OUR MUSKETEERS

There's mistletoe growing out of the walls, it's snowing inside the space station, and a scandal is brewing that could bring down the monarchy.

Merry Joyeux, Musketeers!

Joyeux on Paris Satellite is a seven-day festival of drunken bets, poor decision-making, religious contemplation and tinsel. Mostly, poor decision-making. Aramis is going through a breakup, Athos is haunted by the ghost of his ex-husband, and Porthos is fretting about both of her best friends.

Can they save the space station and the solar system?

A fast-paced, festive space opera novella, Joyeux is a prequel to the Musketeer Space series.

ABOUT THE AUTHOR

Tansy Rayner Roberts is an award-winning Australian science fiction and fantasy author who occasionally obsesses about musketeers. She lives with her family in Tasmania.

- Listen to Tansy on Sheep Might Fly, a podcast where she reads aloud her stories as audio serials.
- Read Tansy's stories before anyone else when you pledge to her Patreon: patreon.com/tansyrr
- What tea is Tansy drinking? Find out when you subscribe to her excellent newsletter.

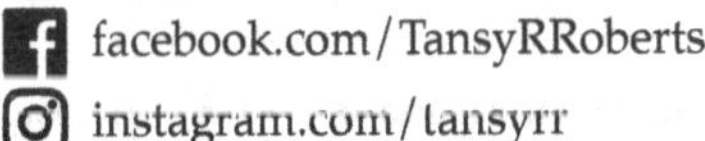

facebook.com/TansyRRoberts

instagram.com/tansyrr

ALSO BY TANSY RAYNER ROBERTS

TIME TRAVEL AND TALKING CATS

If you're looking for more chaotic science fiction with comedy, friendship and yearning, try *Time of the Cat*, a book about time travellers, lost media and talking cats.

Featuring far too many details about Cramberleigh, a TV series that never existed, including a full program guide.

WHEN YOU DON'T HAVE A DRAGON TO PROTECT YOU (AND YOUR ELIGIBLE BROTHER), YOUR ONLY OPTION IS TO BE THE DRAGON.

If you're looking for more classic literature retold with complex SFF worldbuilding, try *The Season of Dragons*, a witty retelling of *Pride and Prejudice* from the point of view of a character very similar to Caroline Bingley, who gets her own happy ending despite all the fortune-hunters and other threats that surround her family.

In which Lady Catherine de Bourgh is a literal dragon!